CLASSICS

Strange, haunting, bizarre, grotesque, rooted in reality, soaring with imagination, alive with people who never were and creations that one day might be. . . . Creatures and stories to set you shivering, gasping with terror, gaping with wonder . . .

. . . here are some of Ray Bradbury's very best stories of wonderfully improbable people, places and things. . . .

Bantam Spectra Books by Ray Bradbury
Ask your bookseller for the titles you have missed

THE MARTIAN CHRONICLES
SOMETHING WICKED THIS WAY COMES
DANDELION WINE
THE ILLUSTRATED MAN
THE HALLOWEEN TREE
THE TOYNBEE CONVECTOR
CLASSIC STORIES 1: THE GOLDEN APPLES OF THE SUN/R IS FOR
     ROCKET
CLASSIC STORIES 2: A MEDICINE FOR MELANCHOLY/S IS FOR SPACE
DEATH IS A LONELY BUSINESS
A GRAVEYARD FOR LUNATICS

Classic Stories 2

RAY BRADBURY

SELECTIONS FROM

A Medicine For Melancholy

AND

S Is For Space

BANTAM BOOKS

NEW YORK • TORONTO • LONDON • SYDNEY • AUCKLAND

*This edition contains the complete text
of the original hardcover edition.*
NOT ONE WORD HAS BEEN OMITTED.

CLASSIC STORIES 2: A MEDICINE FOR MELANCHOLY / S IS FOR SPACE

*A Bantam Book / published by arrangement with
Doubleday.
Bantam edition / May 1990*

A MEDICINE FOR MELANCHOLY *published by Bantam 1960.*
S IS FOR SPACE *published by Bantam 1970.*

ISBN 0-553-28638-2

Published simultaneously in the United States and Canada

PRINTED IN THE UNITED STATES OF AMERICA

RAD   0 9 8 7 6 5 4 3 2

ACKNOWLEDGMENTS

"In a Season of Calm Weather" and "The First Night of Lent" originally published in PLAYBOY. Copyright © 1956 by HMH Publishing Co., Inc.

"A Medicine for Melancholy" copyright © 1959 by Ray Bradbury.

"The Wonderful Ice Cream Suit" originally published in THE SATURDAY EVENING POST as "The Magic White Suit." Copyright © 1958 by The Curtis Publishing Company.

"Fever Dream" copyright © 1959 by Ray Bradbury.

"The Marriage Mender" copyright © 1959 by Ray Bradbury.

"The Town Where No One Got Off" originally published in ELLERY QUEEN'S MYSTERY MAGAZINE. Copyright © 1958 by Davis Publications, Inc.

"A Scent of Sarsaparilla" originally published in *Star Science Fiction Stories #1*, published by Ballantine Books, Inc.

"The Headpiece" originally published in LILLIPUT, London.

"The Time of Going Away" copyright © 1959 by Ray Bradbury.

"All Summer in a Day" and "Icarus Montgolfier Wright" originally published in FANTASY & SCIENCE FICTION MAGAZINE.

"Icarus Montgolfier Wright" copyright © 1956 by Ray Bradbury.

"The Gift" copyright © 1959 by Ray Bradbury.

"The Great Collision of Monday Last" originally published in ARGOSY, London, as "Collision of Monday."

"The Little Mice" originally published in ESCAPADE as "The Mice."

"The Shore Line at Sunset" copyright © 1959 by Ray Bradbury.

"The Day it Rained Forever" copyright © 1959 by Ray Bradbury.

"Chrysalis" originally published in AMAZING STORIES. Copyright 1946 by Ziff-Davis Publishing Company.

"Pillar of Fire" copyright 1948 by Love Romances Publishing Company, Inc.

"Zero Hour" copyright 1947 by Love Romances Publishing Company, Inc.

"The Man" originally published in THRILLING WONDER STORIES. Copyright 1948 by Standard Magazines. Inc.

"Time in Thy Flight" copyright 1953 by Ray Bradbury.

"The Pedestrian" copyright 1951 by Ray Bradbury.

"Hail and Farewell" copyright 1953 by Ray Bradbury.

"Invisible Boy" originally published in MADEMOISELLE. Copyright 1945 by Ray Bradbury.

"Come into My Cellar" copyright © 1962 by Ray Bradbury.

"The Million-Year Picnic" copyright 1946 by Ray Bradbury.

CONTENTS

A
MEDICINE
FOR
MELANCHOLY

For Dad,

whose love, very late in life, surprised his son.

And for Bernard Berenson *and* Nicky Mariano,

who gave me a new world.

IN A SEASON OF CALM WEATHER

George and Alice Smith detrained at Biarritz one summer noon and in an hour had run through their hotel onto the beach into the ocean and back out to bake upon the sand.

To see George Smith sprawled burning there, you'd think him only a tourist flown fresh as iced lettuce to Europe and soon to be transshipped home. But here was a man who loved art more than life itself.

"There . . ." George Smith sighed. Another ounce of perspiration trickled down his chest. Boil out the Ohio tap water, he thought, then drink down the best Bordeaux. Silt your blood with rich French sediment so you'll see with native eyes!

Why? Why eat, breathe, drink everything French? So that, given time, he might really begin to understand the genius of one man.

His mouth moved, forming a name.

"George?" His wife loomed over him. "I know what you've been thinking. I can read your lips."

He lay perfectly still, waiting.

"And?"

"Picasso," she said.

He winced. Someday she would learn to pronounce that name.

"Please," she said. "Relax. I know you heard the

rumor this morning, but you should see your eyes—your tic is back. All right, Picasso's here, down the coast a few miles away, visiting friends in some small fishing town. But you must forget it or our vacation's ruined."

"I wish I'd never heard the rumor," he said honestly.

"If only," she said, "you liked other painters."

Others? Yes, there were others. He could breakfast most congenially on Caravaggio still lifes of autumn pears and midnight plums. For lunch: those fire-squirting, thick-wormed Van Gogh sunflowers, those blooms a blind man might read with one rush of scorched fingers down fiery canvas. But the great feast? The paintings he saved his palate for? There, filling the horizon like Neptune risen, crowned with limeweed, alabaster, coral, paintbrushes clenched like tridents in horn-nailed fists, and with fishtail vast enough to fluke summer showers out over all Gibraltar—who else but the creator of *Girl Before a Mirror* and *Guernica?*

"Alice," he said patiently, "how can I explain? Coming down on the train, I thought, Good lord, it's *all* Picasso country!"

But was it really? he wondered. The sky, the land, the people, the flushed pink bricks here, scrolled electric-blue ironwork balconies there, a mandolin ripe as a fruit in some man's thousand fingerprinting hands, billboard tatters blowing like confetti in night winds—how much was Picasso, how much George Smith staring round the world with wild Picasso eyes? He despaired of answering. That old man had distilled turpentines and linseed oil so thoroughly through George Smith that they shaped his being, all Blue Period at twilight, all Rose Period at dawn.

"I keep thinking," he said aloud, "if we saved our money . . ."

"We'll never have five thousand dollars."

"I know," he said quietly. "But it's nice thinking we might bring it off someday. Wouldn't it be great to just step up to him, say 'Pablo, here's five thousand! Give us the sea, the sand, that sky, or any old thing you want, we'll be happy . . .'"

After a moment his wife touched his arm.

"I think you'd better go in the water now," she said.

"Yes," he said. "I'd better do just that."

White fire showered up when he cut the water.

During the afternoon George Smith came out and went into the ocean with the vast spilling motions of now warm, now cool people who at last, with the sun's decline, their bodies all lobster colors and colors of broiled squab and guinea hen, trudged for their wedding-cake hotels.

The beach lay deserted for endless mile on mile save for two people. One was George Smith, towel over shoulder, out for a last devotional.

Far along the shore another shorter, square-cut man walked alone in the tranquil weather. He was deeper-tanned, his close-shaven head dyed almost mahogany by the sun, and his eyes were clear and bright as water in his face.

So the shore-line stage was set, and in a few minutes the two men would meet. And once again Fate fixed the scales for shocks and surprises, arrivals and departures. And all the while these two solitary strollers did not for a moment think on coincidence, that unswum stream which lingers at man's elbow with every crowd in every town. Nor did they ponder the fact that if man dares dip into that stream he grabs a wonder in each hand. Like most, they shrugged at such folly and stayed well up the bank lest Fate should shove them in.

The stranger stood alone. Glancing about, he saw his aloneness, saw the waters of the lovely bay, saw the sun sliding down the late colors of the day, and then, half turning, spied a small wooden object on the sand. It was no more than the slender stick from a lime ice cream delicacy long since melted away. Smiling, he picked the stick up. With another glance around to reinsure his solitude, the man stooped again and, holding the stick gently, with light sweeps of his hand began to do the one thing in all the world he knew best how to do.

He began to draw incredible figures along the sand.

He sketched one figure and then moved over and, still looking down, completely focused on his work now, drew a second and a third figure, and after that a fourth and a fifth and a sixth.

George Smith, printing the shore line with his feet,

gazed here, gazed there, and then saw the man ahead.
George Smith, drawing nearer, saw that the man,
deeply tanned, was bending down. Nearer yet, and it
was obvious what the man was up to. George Smith
chuckled. Of course, of course . . . Alone on the beach
this man—how old? Sixty-five? Seventy?—was scrib-
bling and doodling away. How the sand flew! How the
wild portraits flung themselves out there on the shore!
How . . .

George Smith took one more step and stopped, very
still.

The stranger was drawing and drawing and did not
seem to sense that anyone stood immediately behind
him and the world of his drawings in the sand. By now
he was so deeply enchanted with his solitudinous cre-
ation that depth bombs set off in the bay might not have
stopped his flying hand nor turned him round.

George Smith looked down at the sand. And after a
long while, looking, he began to tremble.

For there on the flat shore were pictures of Grecian
lions and Mediterranean goats and maidens with flesh of
sand like powdered gold and satyrs piping on hand-
carved horns and children dancing, strewing flowers
along and along the beach with lambs gamboling after,
and musicians skipping to their harps and lyres and
unicorns racing youths toward distant meadows, wood-
lands, ruined temples, and volcanoes. Along the shore
in a never-broken line, the hand, the wooden stylus of
this man, bent down in fever and raining perspiration,
scribbled, ribboned, looped around over and up, across,
in, out, stitched, whispered, stayed, then hurried on as if
this traveling bacchanal must flourish to its end before
the sun was put out by the sea. Twenty, thirty yards or
more the nymphs and dryads and summer founts
sprang up in unraveled hieroglyphs. And the sand in the
dying light was the color of molten copper on which was
now slashed a message that any man in any time might
read and savor down the years. Everything whirled and
poised in its own wind and gravity. Now wine was being
crushed from under the grape-blooded feet of dancing
vintners' daughters, now steaming seas gave birth to
coin-sheathed monsters while flowered kites strewed

scent on blowing clouds . . . now . . . now . . . now . . .

The artist stopped.

George Smith drew back and stood away.

The artist glanced up, surprised to find someone so near. Then he simply stood there, looking from George Smith to his own creations flung like idle footprints down the way. He smiled at last and shrugged as if to say, Look what I've done; see what a child? You will forgive me, won't you? One day or another we are all fools . . . You too, perhaps? So allow an old fool this, eh? Good! Good!

But George Smith could only look at the little man with the sun-dark skin and the clear sharp eyes and say the man's name once, in a whisper, to himself.

They stood thus for perhaps another five seconds. George Smith staring at the sand-frieze, and the artist watching George Smith with amused curiosity. George Smith opened his mouth, closed it, put out his hand, took it back. He stepped toward the pictures, stepped away. Then he moved along the line of figures, like a man viewing a precious series of marbles cast up from some ancient ruin on the shore. His eyes did not blink, his hand wanted to touch but did not dare to touch. He wanted to run but did not run.

He looked suddenly at the hotel. Run, yes! Run! What? Grab a shovel, dig, excavate, save a chunk of this all-too-crumbling sand? Find a repairman, race him back here with plaster of Paris to cast a mold of some small fragile part of these? No, no. Silly, silly. Or . . . ? His eyes flicked to his hotel window. The camera! Run, get it, get back, and hurry along the shore, clicking, changing film, clicking, until . . .

George Smith whirled to face the sun. It burned faintly on his face; his eyes were two small fires from it. The sun was half underwater, and as he watched it sank the rest of the way in a matter of seconds.

The artist had drawn nearer and now was gazing into George Smith's face with great friendliness, as if he were guessing every thought. Now he was nodding his head in a little bow. Now the ice cream stick had fallen casually from his fingers. Now he was saying good night, good night. Now he was gone, walking back down the beach toward the south.

George Smith stood looking after him. After a full minute he did the only thing he could possibly do. He started at the beginning of the fantastic frieze of satyrs and fauns and wine-dipped maidens and prancing unicorns and piping youths and he walked slowly along the shore. He walked a long way, looking down at the free-running bacchanal. And when he came to the end of the animals and men he turned around and started back in the other direction, just staring down as if he had lost something and did not quite know where to find it. He kept on doing this until there was no more light in the sky or on the sand to see by.

He sat down at the supper table.

"You're late," said his wife. "I just had to come down alone. I'm ravenous."

"That's all right," he said.

"Anything interesting happen on your walk?" she asked.

"No," he said.

"You look funny; George, you didn't swim out too far, did you, and almost drown? I can tell by your face. You *did* swim out too far, didn't you?"

"Yes," he said.

"Well," she said, watching him closely. "Don't ever do that again. Now—what'll you have?"

He picked up the menu and started to read it and stopped suddenly.

"What's wrong?" asked his wife.

He turned his head and shut his eyes for a moment. "Listen."

She listened.

"I don't hear anything," she said.

"Don't you?"

"No. What is it?"

"Just the tide," he said after a while, sitting there, his eyes still shut. "Just the tide coming in."

A MEDICINE FOR MELANCHOLY
(or: THE SOVEREIGN REMEDY
REVEALED!)

"Send for some leeches; bleed her," said Doctor Gimp.

"She has no blood left!" cried Mrs. Wilkes. "Oh, Doctor, what ails our Camillia?"

"She's not right."

"Yes, yes?"

"She's poorly." The good doctor scowled.

"Go on, go on!"

"She's a fluttering candle flame, no doubt."

"Ah, Doctor Gimp," protested Mr. Wilkes. "You but tell us as you go out what we told you when you came in!"

"No, more! Give her these pills at dawn, high noon, and sunset. A sovereign remedy!"

"Damn, she's *stuffed* with sovereign remedies now!"

"Tut-tut! That's a shilling as I pass downstairs, sir."

"Go down and send the Devil up!" Mr. Wilkes shoved a coin in the good doctor's hand.

Whereupon the physician, wheezing, taking snuff, sneezing, stamped down into the swarming streets of London on a sloppy morn in the spring of 1762.

Mr. and Mrs. Wilkes turned to the bed where their sweet Camillia lay pale, thin, yes, but far from unlovely, with large wet lilac eyes, her hair a creek of gold upon her pillow.

"Oh," she almost wept. "What's to become of me? Since the start of spring, three weeks, I've been a ghost in my mirror; I frighten me. To think I'll die without seeing my twentieth birthday."

"Child," said the mother. "Where do you hurt?"

"My arms. My legs. My bosom. My head. How many doctors—six?—have turned me like a beef on a spit. No more. Please, let me pass away untouched."

"What a ghastly, what a mysterious illness," said the mother. "Oh, do something, Mr. Wilkes!"

"What?" asked Mr. Wilkes angrily. "She won't have the physician, the apothecary, or the priest!—and Amen to that!—they've wrung me dry! Shall I run in the street then and bring the Dustman up?"

"Yes," said a voice.

"What!" All three turned to stare.

They had quite forgotten her younger brother, Jamie, who stood picking his teeth at a far window, gazing serenely down into the drizzle and the loud rumbling of the town.

"Four hundred years ago," he said serenely, "it was tried, it worked. Don't bring the Dustman up, no, no. But let us hoist Camillia, cot and all, maneuver her downstairs, and set her up outside our door."

"Why? What for?"

"In a single hour"—Jamie's eyes jumped, counting—"a thousand folk rush by our gate. In one day, twenty thousand people run, hobble, or ride by. Each might eye my swooning sister, each count her teeth, pull her ear lobes, and all, all, mind you, would have a sovereign remedy to offer! One of them would just have to be right!"

"Ah," said Mr. Wilkes, stunned.

"Father!" said Jamie breathlessly. "Have you ever known one single man who didn't think he personally wrote *Materia Medica?* This green ointment for sour throat, that ox-salve for miasma or bloat? Right now, ten thousand self-appointed apothecaries sneak off down there, their wisdom lost to us!"

"Jamie boy, you're incredible!"

"Cease!" said Mrs. Wilkes. "No daughter of mine will be put on display in this or any street——"

"Fie, woman!" said Mr. Wilkes. "Camillia melts like snow and you hesitate to move her from this hot room? Come, Jamie, lift the bed!"

"Camillia?" Mrs. Wilkes turned to her daughter.

"I may as well die in the open," said Camillia, "where a cool breeze might stir my locks as I . . ."

"Bosh!" said the father. "You'll not die. Jamie, heave! Ha! There! Out of the way, wife! Up, boy, *higher!*"

"Oh," cried Camillia faintly. "I fly, I *fly* . . . !"

Quite suddenly a blue sky opened over London. The population, surprised by the weather, hurried out into the streets, panicking for something to see, to do, to buy. Blind men sang, dogs jigged, clowns shuffled and tumbled, children chalked games and threw balls as if it were carnival time.

Down into all this, tottering, their veins bursting from their brows, Jamie and Mr. Wilkes carried Camillia like a lady Pope sailing high in her sedan-chair cot, eyes clenched shut, praying.

"Careful!" screamed Mrs. Wilkes. "Ah, she's dead! No. There. Put her down. Easy . . ."

And at last the bed was tilted against the house front so that the River of Humanity surging by could see Camillia, a large pale Bartolemy Doll put out like a prize in the sun.

"Fetch a quill, ink, paper, lad," said the father. "I'll make notes as to symptoms spoken of and remedies offered this day. Tonight we'll average them out. Now——"

But already a man in the passing crowd had fixed Camillia with a sharp eye.

"She's sick!" he said.

"Ah," said Mr. Wilkes, gleefully. "It begins. The quill, boy. There. Go on, sir!"

"She's not well." The man scowled. "She does poorly."

"Does poorly——" Mr. Wilkes wrote, then froze. "Sir?" He looked up suspiciously. "Are you a physician?"

"I am, sir."

"I *thought* I knew the words! Jamie, take my cane, drive him off! Go, sir, be gone!"

But the man hastened off, cursing, mightily exasperated.

"She's not well, she does poorly . . . pah!" mimicked Mr. Wilkes, but stopped. For now a woman, tall and gaunt as a specter fresh risen from the tomb, was pointing a finger at Camillia Wilkes.

"Vapors," she intoned.

"Vapors," wrote Mr. Wilkes, pleased.

"Lung-flux," chanted the woman.

"Lung-flux!" Mr. Wilkes wrote, beaming. "Now, that's more *like* it!"

"A medicine for melancholy is needed," said the woman palely. "Be there mummy ground to medicine in your house? The best mummies are: Egyptian, Arabian, Hirasphatos, Libyan, all of great use in magnetic disorders. Ask for me, the Gypsy, at the Flodden Road. I sell stone parsley, male frankincense——"

"Flodden Road, stone parsley—slower, woman!"

"Opobalsam, pontic valerian——"

"Wait, woman! Opobalsam, yes! Jamie, stop her!"

But the woman, naming medicines, glided on.

A girl, no more than seventeen, walked up now and stared at Camillia Wilkes.

"She——"

"One moment!" Mr. Wilkes scribbled feverishly. "—magnetic disorders—pontic valerian—drat! Well, young girl, now. What do you see in my daughter's face? You fix her with your gaze, you hardly breathe. So?"

"She—" The strange girl searched deep into Camillia's eyes, flushed, and stammered. "She suffers from . . . from . . ."

"Spit it out!"

"She . . . she . . . oh!"

And the girl, with a last look of deepest sympathy, darted off through the crowd.

"Silly girl!"

"No, Papa," murmured Camillia, eyes wide. "Not silly. She *saw*. She *knew*. Oh, Jamie, run fetch her, make her tell!"

"No, she offered nothing! Whereas, the Gypsy, see her list!"

"I know it, Papa." Camillia, paler, shut her eyes.

Someone cleared his throat.

A butcher, his apron a scarlet battleground, stood bristling his fierce mustaches there.

"I have seen cows with this look," he said. "I have saved them with brandy and three new eggs. In winter I have saved myself with the same elixir——"

"My daughter is no cow, sir!" Mr. Wilkes threw down his quill. "Nor is she a butcher, nor is it January! Step back, sir, others wait!"

And indeed, now a vast crowd clamored, drawn by the others, aching to advise their favorite swig, recommend some country site where it rained less and shone more sun than in all England or your South of France. Old men and women, especial doctors as all the aged are, clashed by each other in bristles of canes, in phalanxes of crutches and hobble sticks.

"Back!" cried Mrs. Wilkes, alarmed. "They'll crush my daughter like a spring berry!"

"Stand off!" Jamie seized canes and crutches and threw them over the mob, which turned on itself to go seek their missing members.

"Father, I fail, I fail," gasped Camillia.

"Father!" cried Jamie. "There's but one way to stop this riot! Charge them! Make them pay to give us their mind on this ailment!"

"Jamie, you are my son! Quick, boy, paint a sign! Listen, people! Tuppence! Queue up please, a line! Tuppence to speak your piece! Get your money out, yes! That's it. You, sir. You, madame. And you, sir. Now, my quill! Begin!"

The mob boiled in like a dark sea.

Camillia opened one eye and swooned again.

Sundown, the streets almost empty, only a few strollers now. Camillia moth-fluttered her eyelids at a familiar clinking jingle.

"Three hundred and ninety-nine, four hundred pennies!" Mr. Wilkes counted the last money into a bag held by his grinning son. "There!"

"It will buy me a fine black funeral coach," said the pale girl.

"Hush! Did you imagine, family, so many people, two hundred, would pay to give us their opinion?"

"Yes," said Mrs. Wilkes. "Wives, husbands, children, are deaf to each other. So people gladly pay to have someone listen. Poor things, each today thought he and he alone knew quinsy, dropsy, glanders, could tell the slaver from the hives. So tonight we are rich and two hundred people are happy, having unloaded their full medical kit at our door."

"Gods, instead of quelling the riot, we had to drive them off snapping like pups."

"Read us the list, Father," said Jamie, "of two hundred remedies. Which one is true?"

"I care not," whispered Camillia, sighing. "It grows dark. My stomach is queasy from listening to the names! May I be taken upstairs?"

"Yes, dear. Jamie, lift!"

"Please," said a voice.

Half-bent, the men looked up.

There stood a Dustman of no particular size or shape, his face masked with soot from which shone water-blue eyes and a white slot of an ivory smile. Dust sifted from his sleeves and his pants as he moved, as he talked quietly, nodding.

"I couldn't get through the mob earlier," he said, holding his dirty cap in his hands. "Now, going home, here I am. Must I pay?"

"No, Dustman, you need not," said Camillia gently.

"Hold on——" protested Mr. Wilkes.

But Camillia gave him a soft look and he grew silent.

"Thank you, ma'am." The Dustman's smile flashed like warm sunlight in the growing dusk. "I have but one advice."

He gazed at Camillia. She gazed at him.

"Be this Saint Bosco's Eve, sir, ma'am?"

"Who knows? Not *me*, sir!" said Mr. Wilkes.

"I think it *is* Saint Bosco's Eve, sir. Also, it is the night of the Full Moon. So," said the Dustman humbly, unable to take his eyes from the lovely haunted girl, "you must leave your daughter out in the light of that rising moon."

"Out under the moon!" said Mrs. Wilkes.

"Doesn't that make the lunatic?" asked Jamie.

"Beg pardon, sir." The Dustman bowed. "But the full moon soothes all sick animal, be they human or plain field beast. There is a serenity of color, a quietude of touch, a sweet sculpturing of mind and body in full moonlight."

"It may rain——" said the mother uneasily.

"I swear," said the Dustman quickly. "My sister suffered this same swooning paleness. We set her like a potted lily out one spring night with the moon. She lives today in Sussex, the soul of reconstituted health!"

"Reconstituted! Moonlight! And will cost us not one penny of the four hundred we collected this day, Mother, Jamie, Camillia."

"No!" said Mrs. Wilkes. "I won't have it!"

"Mother," said Camillia.

She looked earnestly at the Dustman.

From his grimed face the Dustman gazed back, his smile like a little scimitar in the dark.

"Mother," said Camillia. "I feel it. The moon will cure me, it will, it will. . . ."

The mother sighed. "This is not my day, nor night. Let me kiss you for the last time, then. There."

And the mother went upstairs.

Now the Dustman backed off, bowing courteously to all.

"All night, now, remember, beneath the moon, not the slightest disturbance until dawn. Sleep well, young lady. Dream, and dream the best. Good night."

Soot was lost in soot; the man was gone.

Mr. Wilkes and Jamie kissed Camillia's brow.

"Father, Jamie," she said. "Don't worry."

And she was left alone to stare off where at a great distance she thought she saw a smile hung by itself in the dark blink off and on, then go round a corner, vanishing.

She waited for the rising of the moon.

* * *

Night in London, the voices growing drowsier in the
inns, the slamming of doors, drunken farewells, clocks
chiming. Camillia saw a cat like a woman stroll by in her
furs, saw a woman like a cat stroll by, both wise, both
Egyptian, both smelling of spice. Every quarter hour or
so a voice drifted down from above:

"You all right, child?"

"Yes, Father."

"Camillia?"

"Mother, Jamie, I'm fine."

And at last. "Good night."

"Good night."

The last lights out. London asleep.

The moon rose.

And the higher the moon, the larger grew Camillia's
eyes as she watched the alleys, the courts, the streets,
until at last, at midnight, the moon moved over her to
show her like a marble figure atop an ancient tomb.

A motion in darkness.

Camillia pricked her ears.

A faint melody sprang out on the air.

A man stood in the shadows of the court.

Camillia gasped.

The man stepped forth into moonlight, carrying a
lute which he strummed softly. He was a man well-
dressed, whose face was handsome and, now anyway,
solemn.

"A troubadour," said Camillia aloud.

The man, his finger on his lips, moved slowly forward and soon stood by her cot.

"What are you doing out so late?" asked the girl,
unafraid but not knowing why.

"A friend sent me to make you well." He touched
the lute strings. They hummed sweetly. He was indeed
handsome there in the silver light.

"That cannot be," she said, "for it was told me, the
moon is my cure."

"And so it will be, maiden."

"What songs do you sing?"

"Songs of spring nights, aches and ailments without
name. Shall I name your fever, maiden?"

"If you know it, yes."

"First, the symptoms: raging temperatures, sudden cold, heart fast then slow, storms of temper, then sweet calms, drunkenness from having sipped only well water, dizziness from being touched only *thus*——"

He touched her wrist, saw her melt toward delicious oblivion, drew back.

"Depressions, elations," he went on. "Dreams——"

"Stop!" she cried, enthralled. "You know me to the letter. Now, name my ailment!"

"I will." He pressed his lips to the palm of her hand so she quaked suddenly. "The name of the ailment is Camillia Wilkes."

"How strange." She shivered, her eyes glinting lilac fires. "Am I then my own affliction? How sick I make myself! Even now, feel my heart!"

"I feel it, so."

"My limbs, they burn with summer heat!"

"Yes. They scorch my fingers."

"But now, the night wind, see how I shudder, cold! I die, I swear it, I die!"

"I will not let you," he said quietly.

"Are you a doctor, then?"

"No, just your plain, your ordinary physician, like another who guessed your trouble this day. The girl who would have named it but ran off in the crowd."

"Yes, I saw in her eyes she knew what had seized me. But, now, my teeth chatter. And no extra blanket!"

"Give room, please. There. Let me see: two arms, two legs, head and body. I'm all here!"

"What, sir!"

"To warm you from the night, of course."

"How like a hearth! Oh, sir, sir, do I *know* you? Your name?"

Swiftly above her, his head shadowed hers. From it his merry clear-water eyes glowed as did his white ivory slot of a smile.

"Why, Bosco, of course," he said.

"Is there not a saint by that name?"

"Given an hour, you will call me so, yes."

His head bent closer. Thus sooted in shadow, she cried with joyous recognition to welcome her Dustman back.

"The world spins! I pass away! The cure, sweet Doctor, or all is lost!"

"The cure," he said. "And the cure is *this* . . ."

Somewhere, cats sang. A shoe, shot from a window, tipped them off a fence. Then all was silence and the moon . . .

"Shh . . ."

Dawn. Tiptoeing downstairs, Mr. and Mrs. Wilkes peered into their courtyard.

"Frozen stone dead from the terrible night, I *know* it!"

"No, wife, look! Alive! Roses in her cheeks! No, more! Peaches, persimmons! She glows all rosy-milky! Sweet Camillia, alive and well, made whole again!"

They bent by the slumbering girl.

"She smiles, she dreams; what's that she says?"

"The sovereign," sighed the girl, "remedy."

"What, what?"

The girl smiled again, a white smile, in her sleep.

"A medicine," she murmured, "for melancholy."

She opened her eyes.

"Oh, Mother, Father!"

"Daughter! Child! Come upstairs!"

"No." She took their hands, tenderly. "Mother? Father?"

"Yes?"

"No one will see. The sun but rises. Please. Dance with me."

They did not want to dance.

But, celebrating they knew not what, they did.

THE WONDERFUL ICE CREAM SUIT

It was summer twilight in the city, and out front of the quiet-clicking pool hall three young Mexican-American men breathed the warm air and looked around at the world. Sometimes they talked and sometimes they said nothing at all but watched the cars glide by like black panthers on the hot asphalt or saw trolleys loom up like thunderstorms, scatter lightning, and rumble away into silence.

"Hey," sighed Martínez at last. He was the youngest, the most sweetly sad of the three. "It's a swell night, huh? Swell."

As he observed the world it moved very close and then drifted away and then came close again. People, brushing by, were suddenly across the street. Buildings five miles away suddenly leaned over him. But most of the time everything—people, cars, and buildings—stayed way out on the edge of the world and could not be touched. On this quiet warm summer evening Martínez's face was cold.

"Nights like this you wish . . . lots of things."

"Wishing," said the second man, Villanazul, a man who shouted books out loud in his room but spoke only in whispers on the street. "Wishing is the useless pastime of the unemployed."

"Unemployed?" cried Vamenos, the unshaven. "Listen to him! We got no jobs, no money!"

"So," said Martínez, "we got no friends."

"True." Villanazul gazed off toward the green plaza where the palm trees swayed in the soft night wind. "Do you know what I wish? I wish to go into that plaza and speak among the businessmen who gather there nights to talk big talk. But dressed as I am, poor as I am, who would listen? So, Martínez, we have each other. The friendship of the poor is real friendship. We——"

But now a handsome young Mexican with a fine thin mustache strolled by. And on each of his careless arms hung a laughing woman.

"Madre mía!" Martínez slapped his own brow. "How does that one rate *two* friends?"

"It's his nice new white summer suit." Vamenos chewed a black thumbnail. "He looks sharp."

Martínez leaned out to watch the three people moving away, and then at the tenement across the street, in one fourth-floor window of which, far above, a beautiful girl leaned out, her dark hair faintly stirred by the wind. She had been there forever, which was to say for six weeks. He had nodded, he had raised a hand, he had smiled, he had blinked rapidly, he had even bowed to her, on the street, in the hall when visiting friends, in the park, downtown. Even now, he put his hand up from his waist and moved his fingers. But all the lovely girl did was let the summer wind stir her dark hair. He did not exist. He was nothing.

"Madre mía!" He looked away and down the street where the man walked his two friends around a corner. "Oh, if just I had one suit, one! I wouldn't need money if I *looked* okay."

"I hesitate to suggest," said Villanazul, "that you see Gómez. But he's been talking some crazy talk for a month now about clothes. I keep on saying I'll be in on it to make him go away. That Gómez."

"Friend," said a quiet voice.

"Gómez!" Everyone turned to stare.

Smiling strangely, Gómez pulled forth an endless thin yellow ribbon which fluttered and swirled on the summer air.

"Gómez," said Martínez, "what you doing with that tape measure?"

Gómez beamed. "Measuring people's skeletons."

"Skeletons!"

"Hold on." Gómez squinted at Martínez. *"Caramba!* Where you *been* all my life! Let's try *you!"*

Martínez saw his arm seized and taped, his leg measured, his chest encircled.

"Hold still!" cried Gómez. "Arm—perfect. Leg—chest—*perfecto!* Now quick, the height! There! Yes! Five foot five! You're in! Shake!" Pumping Martínez's hand, he stopped suddenly. "Wait. You got . . . ten bucks?"

"I have!" Vamenos waved some grimy bills. "Gómez, measure me!"

"All I got left in the world is nine dollars and ninety-two cents." Martínez searched his pockets. "That's enough for a new suit? Why?"

"Why? Because you got the right skeleton, that's why!"

"Señor Gómez, I don't hardly know you——"

"Know me? You're going to live with me! Come on!"

Gómez vanished into the poolroom. Martínez, escorted by the polite Villanazul, pushed by an eager Vamenos, found himself inside.

"Domínguez!" said Gómez.

Domínguez, at a wall telephone, winked at them. A woman's voice squeaked on the receiver.

"Manulo!" said Gómez.

Manulo, a wine bottle tilted bubbling to his mouth, turned.

Gómez pointed at Martínez.

"At last we found our fifth volunteer!"

Domínguez said, "I got a date, don't bother me——" and stopped. The receiver slipped from his fingers. His little black telephone book full of fine names and numbers went quickly back into his pocket. "Gómez, you——?"

"Yes, yes! Your money, now! *Ándale!"*

The woman's voice sizzled on the dangling phone.

Domínguez glanced at it uneasily.

Manulo considered the empty wine bottle in his hand and the liquor-store sign across the street.

Then very reluctantly both men laid ten dollars each on the green velvet pool table.

Villanazul, amazed, did likewise, as did Gómez, nudging Martínez. Martínez counted out his wrinkled bills and change. Gómez flourished the money like a royal flush.

"Fifty bucks! The suit costs sixty! All we need is ten bucks!"

"Wait," said Martínez. "Gómez, are we talking about *one* suit? *Uno?*"

"*Uno!*" Gómez raised a finger. "One wonderful white ice cream summer suit! White, white as the August moon!"

"But who will own this one suit?"

"Me!" said Manulo.

"Me!" said Domínguez.

"Me!" said Villanazul.

"Me!" cried Gómez. "*And* you, Martínez. Men, let's show him. Line up!"

Villanazul, Manulo, Domínguez, and Gómez rushed to plant their backs against the poolroom wall.

"Martínez, you too, the other end, line up! Now, Vamenos, lay that billiard cue across our heads!"

"Sure, Gómez, sure!"

Martínez, in line, felt the cue tap his head and leaned out to see what was happening. "Ah!" he gasped.

The cue lay flat on all their heads, with no rise or fall, as Vamenos slid it along, grinning.

"We're all the same height!" said Martínez.

"The same!" Everyone laughed.

Gómez ran down the line, rustling the yellow tape measure here and there on the men so they laughed even more wildly.

"Sure!" he said. "It took a month, four weeks, mind you, to find four guys the same size and shape as me, a month of running around measuring. Sometimes I found guys with five-foot-five skeletons, sure, but all the meat on their bones was too much or not enough. Sometimes their bones were too long in the legs or too short in the arms. Boy, all the bones! I tell you! But now, five of us, same shoulders, chests, waists, arms, and as for weight? Men!"

Manulo, Domínguez, Villanazul, Gómez, and at last Martínez stepped onto the scales which flipped ink-stamped cards at them as Vamenos, still smiling wildly, fed pennies. Heart pounding, Martínez read the cards.

"One hundred thirty-five pounds . . . one thirty-six . . . one thirty-three . . . one thirty-four . . . one thirty-seven . . . a miracle!"

"No," said Villanazul simply, "Gómez."

They all smiled upon that genius who now circled them with his arms.

"Are we not fine?" he wondered. "All the same size, all the same dream—the suit. So each of us will look beautiful at least one night each week, eh?"

"I haven't looked beautiful in years," said Martínez. "The girls run away."

"They will run no more, they will freeze," said Gómez, "when they see you in the cool white summer ice cream suit."

"Gómez," said Villanazul, "just let me ask one thing."

"Of course, *compadre.*"

"When we get this nice new white ice cream summer suit, some night you're not going to put it on and walk down to the Greyhound bus in it and go live in El Paso for a year in it, are you?"

"Villanazul, Villanazul, how can you say that?"

"My eye sees and my tongue moves," said Villanazul. "How about the *Everybody Wins!* Punchboard Lotteries you ran and you kept running when nobody won? How about the United Chili Con Carne and Frijole Company you were going to organize and all that ever happened was the rent ran out on a two-by-four office?"

"The errors of a child now grown," said Gómez. "Enough! In this hot weather someone may buy the special suit that is made just for us that stands waiting in the window of SHUMWAY'S SUNSHINE SUITS! We have fifty dollars. Now we need just one more skeleton!"

Martínez saw the men peer around the pool hall. He looked where they looked. He felt his eyes hurry past Vamenos, then come reluctantly back to examine his dirty shirt, his huge nicotined fingers.

"Me!" Vamenos burst out at last. "My skeleton, measure it, it's great! Sure, my hands are big, and my arms, from digging ditches! But——"

Just then Martínez heard passing on the sidewalk outside that same terrible man with his two girls, all laughing together.

He saw anguish move like the shadow of a summer cloud on the faces of the other men in this poolroom.

Slowly Vamenos stepped onto the scales and dropped his penny. Eyes closed, he breathed a prayer.

"Madre mía, please . . ."

The machinery whirred; the card fell out. Vamenos opened his eyes.

"Look! One thirty-five pounds! Another miracle!"

The men stared at his right hand and the card, at his left hand and a soiled ten-dollar bill.

Gómez swayed. Sweating, he licked his lips. Then his hand shot out, seized the money.

"The clothing store! The suit! *Vamos!"*

Yelling, everyone ran from the poolroom.

The woman's voice was still squeaking on the abandoned telephone. Martínez, left behind, reached out and hung the voice up. In the silence he shook his head. *"Santos,* what a dream! Six men," he said, "one suit. What will come of this? Madness? Debauchery? Murder? But I go with God. Gómez, wait for me!"

Martínez was young. He ran fast.

Mr. Shumway, of SHUMWAY'S SUNSHINE SUITS, paused while adjusting a tie rack, aware of some subtle atmospheric change outside his establishment.

"Leo," he whispered to his assistant. "Look . . ."

Outside, one man, Gómez, strolled by, looking in. Two men, Manulo and Domínguez, hurried by, staring in. Three men, Villanazul, Martínez, and Vamenos, jostling shoulders, did the same.

"Leo." Mr. Shumway swallowed. "Call the police!"

Suddenly six men filled the doorway.

Martínez, crushed among them, his stomach slightly upset, his face feeling feverish, smiled so wildly at Leo that Leo let go the telephone.

"Hey," breathed Martínez, eyes wide. "There's a great suit over there!"

"No." Manulo touched a lapel. *"This* one!"

"There is only one suit in all the world!" said Gómez coldly. "Mr. Shumway, the ice cream white, size thirty-four, was in your window just an hour ago! It's gone! You didn't——"

"Sell it?" Mr. Shumway exhaled. "No, no. In the dressing room. It's still on the dummy."

Martínez did not know if he moved and moved the crowd or if the crowd moved and moved him. Suddenly they were all in motion. Mr. Shumway, running, tried to keep ahead of them.

"This way, gents. Now which of you . . . ?"

"All for one, one for all!" Martínez heard himself say, and laughed. "We'll all try it on!"

"All?" Mr. Shumway clutched at the booth curtain as if his shop were a steamship that had suddenly tilted in a great swell. He stared.

That's it, thought Martínez, look at our smiles. Now, look at the skeletons behind our smiles! Measure here, there, up, down, yes, do you *see?*

Mr. Shumway saw. He nodded. He shrugged.

"All!" He jerked the curtain. "There! Buy it, and I'll throw in the dummy free!"

Martínez peered quietly into the booth, his motion drawing the others to peer too.

The suit was there.

And it was white.

Martínez could not breathe. He did not want to. He did not need to. He was afraid his breath would melt the suit. It was enough, just looking.

But at last he took a great trembling breath and exhaled, whispering, *"Ay. Ay, caramba!"*

"It puts out my eyes," murmured Gómez.

"Mr. Shumway," Martínez heard Leo hissing. "Ain't it dangerous precedent, to sell it? I mean, what if everybody bought *one* suit for *six* people?"

"Leo," said Mr. Shumway, "you ever hear one single fifty-nine-dollar suit make so many people happy at the same time before?"

"Angels' wings," murmured Martínez. "The wings of white angels."

Martínez felt Mr. Shumway peering over his shoulder into the booth. The pale glow filled his eyes.

"You know something, Leo?" he said in awe. "That's a *suit!*"

Gómez, shouting, whistling, ran up to the third-floor landing and turned to wave to the others, who staggered, laughed, stopped, and had to sit down on the steps below.

"Tonight!" cried Gómez. "Tonight you move in with me, eh? Save rent as well as clothes, eh? Sure! Martínez, you got the suit?"

"Have I?" Martínez lifted the white gift-wrapped box high. "From us to us! *Ay-hah!*"

"Vamenos, you got the dummy?"

"Here!"

Vamenos, chewing an old cigar, scattering sparks, slipped. The dummy, falling, toppled, turned over twice, and banged down the stairs.

"Vamenos! Dumb! Clumsy!"

They seized the dummy from him. Stricken, Vamenos looked about as if he'd lost something.

Manulo snapped his fingers. "Hey, Vamenos, we got to celebrate! Go borrow some wine!"

Vamenos plunged downstairs in a whirl of sparks.

The others moved into the room with the suit, leaving Martínez in the hall to study Gómez's face.

"Gómez, you look sick."

"I am," said Gómez. "For what have I done?" He nodded to the shadows in the room working about the dummy. "I pick Domínguez, a devil with the women. All right. I pick Manulo, who drinks, yes, but who sings as sweet as a girl, eh? Okay. Villanazul reads books. You, you wash behind your ears. But then what do I do? Can I wait? No! I got to buy that suit! So the last guy I pick is a clumsy slob who has the right to wear *my* suit——" He stopped, confused. "Who gets to wear *our* suit one night a week, fall down in it, or not come in out of the rain in it! Why, why, why did I do it!"

"Gómez," whispered Villanazul from the room. "The suit is ready. Come see if it looks as good using *your* light bulb."

Gómez and Martínez entered.

And there on the dummy in the center of the room was the phosphorescent, the miraculously white-fired ghost with the incredible lapels, the precise stitching, the neat buttonholes. Standing with the white illumination of the suit upon his cheeks, Martínez suddenly felt he was in church. White! White! It was white as the whitest vanilla ice cream, as the bottled milk in tenement halls at dawn. White as a winter cloud all alone in the moonlit sky late at night. Seeing it here in the warm summer-night room made their breath almost show on the air. Shutting his eyes, he could see it printed on his lids. He knew what color his dreams would be this night.

"White . . ." murmured Villanazul. "White as the snow on that mountain near our town in Mexico, which is called the Sleeping Woman."

"Say that again," said Gómez.

Villanazul, proud yet humble, was glad to repeat his tribute.

". . . white　as　the　snow　on　the　mountain called——"

"I'm back!"

Shocked, the men whirled to see Vamenos in the door, wine bottles in each hand.

"A party! Here! Now tell us, who wears the suit first tonight? Me?"

"It's too late!" said Gómez.

"Late! It's only nine-fifteen!"

"Late?" said everyone, bristling. "Late?"

Gómez edged away from these men who glared from him to the suit to the open window.

Outside and below it was, after all, thought Martínez, a fine Saturday night in a summer month and through the calm warm darkness the women drifted like flowers on a quiet stream. The men made a mournful sound.

"Gómez, a suggestion." Villanazul licked his pencil and drew a chart on a pad. "You wear the suit from nine-thirty to ten, Manulo till ten-thirty, Domínguez till eleven, myself till eleven-thirty, Martínez till midnight, and——"

"Why me *last?*" demanded Vamenos, scowling.

Martínez thought quickly and smiled. "After midnight is the *best* time, friend."

"Hey," said Vamenos, "that's right. I never thought of that. Okay."

Gómez sighed. "All right. A half hour each. But from now on, remember, we each wear the suit just one night a week. Sundays we draw straws for who wears the suit the extra night."

"Me!" laughed Vamenos. "I'm lucky!"

Gómez held onto Martínez, tight.

"Gómez," urged Martínez, "you first. Dress."

Gómez could not tear his eyes from that disreputable Vamenos. At last, impulsively, he yanked his shirt off over his head. "Ay-yeah!" he howled. *"Ay-yeee!"*

Whisper rustle . . . the clean shirt.

"Ah . . . !"

How clean the new clothes feel, thought Martínez, holding the coat ready. How clean they sound, how clean they smell!

Whisper . . . the pants . . . the tie, rustle . . . the suspenders. Whisper . . . now Martínez let loose the coat, which fell in place on flexing shoulders.

"Ole!"

Gómez turned like a matador in his wondrous suit-of-lights.

"Ole, Gómez, *ole!"*

Gómez bowed and went out the door.

Martínez fixed his eyes to his watch. At ten sharp he heard someone wandering about in the hall as if they had forgotten where to go. Martínez pulled the door open and looked out.

Gómez was there, heading for nowhere.

He looks sick, thought Martínez. No, stunned, shook up, surprised, many things.

"Gómez! This is the place!"

Gómez turned around and found his way through the door.

"Oh, friends, friends," he said. "Friends, what an experience! This suit! This suit!"

"Tell us, Gómez!" said Martínez.

"I can't, how can I say it!" He gazed at the heavens, arms spread, palms up.

"*Tell* us, Gómez!"

"I have no words, no words. You must see, yourself! Yes, you must see——" And here he lapsed into silence, shaking his head until at last he remembered they all stood watching him. "Who's next? Manulo?"

Manulo, stripped to his shorts, leapt forward.

"Ready!"

All laughed, shouted, whistled.

Manulo, ready, went out the door. He was gone twenty-nine minutes and thirty seconds. He came back holding to doorknobs, touching the wall, feeling his own elbows, putting the flat of his hand to his face.

"Oh, let me tell you," he said. "*Compadres,* I went to the bar, eh, to have a drink? But no, I did not go in the bar, do you hear? I did not drink. For as I walked I began to laugh and sing. Why, why? I listened to myself and asked this. Because. The suit made me feel better than wine ever did. The suit made me drunk, drunk! So I went to the *Guadalajara Refritería* instead and played the guitar and sang four songs, very high! The suit, ah, the suit!"

Domínguez, next to be dressed, moved out through the world, came back from the world.

The black telephone book! thought Martínez. He had it in his hands when he left! Now, he returns, hands empty! What? What?

"On the street," said Domínguez, seeing it all again, eyes wide, "on the street I walked, a woman cried, 'Domínguez, is that *you?*' Another said, 'Domínguez? No, Quetzalcoatl, the Great White God come from the East,' do you hear? And suddenly I didn't want to go with six women or eight, no. One, I thought. One! And to this one, who knows *what* I would say? 'Be mine!' Or 'Marry me!' *Caramba!* This suit is dangerous! But I did not care! I live, I live! Gómez, did it happen this way with you?"

Gómez, still dazed by the events of the evening, shook his head. "No, no talk. It's too much. Later, Villanazul . . . ?"

Villanazul moved shyly forward.

Villanazul went shyly out.

Villanazul came shyly home.

"Picture it," he said, not looking at them, looking at the floor, talking to the floor. "The Green Plaza, a group of elderly businessmen gathered under the stars and they are talking, nodding, talking. Now one of them whispers. All turn to stare. They move aside, they make a channel through which a white-hot light burns its way as through ice. At the center of the great light is this person. I take a deep breath. My stomach is jelly. My voice is very small, but it grows louder. And what do I say? I say, 'Friends. Do you know Carlyle's *Sartor Resartus*? In that book we find *his* Philosophy of Suits. . . .'"

And at last it was time for Martínez to let the suit float him out to haunt the darkness.

Four times he walked around the block. Four times he paused beneath the tenement porches, looking up at the window where the light was lit; a shadow moved, the beautiful girl was there, not there, away and gone, and on the fifth time there she was on the porch above, driven out by the summer heat, taking the cooler air. She glanced down. She made a gesture.

At first he thought she was waving to him. He felt like a white explosion that had riveted her attention. But she was not waving. Her hand gestured and the next moment a pair of dark-framed glasses sat upon her nose. She gazed at him.

Ah, ah, he thought, so that's it. So! Even the blind may see this suit! He smiled up at her. He did not have to wave. And at last she smiled back. She did not have to wave either. Then, because he did not know what else to do and he could not get rid of this smile that had fastened itself to his cheeks, he hurried, almost ran, around the corner, feeling her stare after him. When he looked back she had taken off her glasses and gazed now with the look of the nearsighted at what, at most, must be a moving blob of light in the great darkness here. Then for good measure he went around the block again, through a city so suddenly beautiful he wanted to yell, then laugh, then yell again.

Returning, he drifted, oblivious, eyes half closed, and seeing him in the door, the others saw not Martínez but themselves come home. In that moment, they sensed that something had happened to them all.

"You're late!" cried Vamenos, but stopped. The spell could not be broken.

"Somebody tell me," said Martínez. "Who am I?"

He moved in a slow circle through the room.

Yes, he thought, yes, it's the suit, yes, it had to do with the suit and them all together in that store on this fine Saturday night and then here, laughing and feeling more drunk without drinking as Manulo said himself, as the night ran and each slipped on the pants and held, toppling, to the others and, balanced, let the feeling get bigger and warmer and finer as each man departed and the next took his place in the suit until now here stood Martínez all splendid and white as one who gives orders and the world grows quiet and moves aside.

"Martínez, we borrowed three mirrors while you were gone. Look!"

The mirrors, set up as in the store, angled to reflect three Martínezes and the echoes and memories of those who had occupied this suit with him and known the bright world inside this thread and cloth. Now, in the shimmering mirror, Martínez saw the enormity of this thing they were living together and his eyes grew wet. The others blinked. Martínez touched the mirrors. They shifted. He saw a thousand, a million white-armored Martínezes march off into eternity, reflected, re-reflected, forever, indomitable, and unending.

He held the white coat out on the air. In a trance, the others did not at first recognize the dirty hand that reached to take the coat. Then:

"Vamenos!"

"Pig!"

"You didn't wash!" cried Gómez. "Or even shave, while you waited! *Compadres,* the bath!"

"The bath!" said everyone.

"No!" Vamenos flailed. "The night air! I'm dead!"

They hustled him yelling out and down the hall.

Now here stood Vamenos, unbelievable in white suit, beard shaved, hair combed, nails scrubbed.

His friends scowled darkly at him.

For was it not true, thought Martínez, that when Vamenos passed by, avalanches itched on mountaintops? If he walked under windows, people spat, dumped garbage, or worse. Tonight now, this night, he would stroll beneath ten thousand wide-opened windows, near balconies, past alleys. Suddenly the world absolutely sizzled with flies. And here was Vamenos, a fresh-frosted cake.

"You sure look keen in that suit, Vamenos," said Manulo sadly.

"Thanks." Vamenos twitched, trying to make his skeleton comfortable where all their skeletons had so recently been. In a small voice Vamenos said, "Can I go now?"

"Villanazul!" said Gómez. "Copy down these rules."

Villanazul licked his pencil.

"First," said Gómez, "don't fall down in that suit, Vamenos!"

"I won't."

"Don't lean against buildings in that suit."

"No buildings."

"Don't walk under trees with birds in them in that suit. Don't smoke. Don't drink——"

"Please," said Vamenos, "can I *sit down* in this suit?"

"When in doubt, take the pants off, fold them over a chair."

"Wish me luck," said Vamenos.

"Go with God, Vamenos."

He went out. He shut the door.

There was a ripping sound.

"Vamenos!" cried Martínez.

He whipped the door open.

Vamenos stood with two halves of a handkerchief torn in his hands, laughing.

"Rrrip! Look at your faces! Rrrip!" He tore the cloth again. "Oh, oh, your faces, your faces! Ha!"

Roaring, Vamenos slammed the door, leaving them stunned and alone.

Gómez put both hands on top of his head and turned away. "Stone me. Kill me. I have sold our souls to a demon!"

Villanazul dug in his pockets, took out a silver coin, and studied it for a long while.

"Here is my last fifty cents. Who else will help me buy back Vamenos' share of the suit?"

"It's no use." Manulo showed them ten cents. "We got only enough to buy the lapels and the buttonholes."

Gómez, at the open window, suddenly leaned out and yelled. "Vamenos! No!"

Below on the street, Vamenos, shocked, blew out a match and threw away an old cigar butt he had found somewhere. He made a strange gesture to all the men in the window above, then waved airily and sauntered on.

Somehow, the five men could not move away from the window. They were crushed together there.

"I bet he eats a hamburger in that suit," mused Villanazul. "I'm thinking of the mustard."

"Don't!" cried Gómez. "No, no!"

Manulo was suddenly at the door.

"I need a drink, bad."

"Manulo, there's wine here, that bottle on the floor——"

Manulo went out and shut the door.

A moment later Villanazul stretched with great exaggeration and strolled about the room.

"I think I'll walk down to the plaza, friends."

He was not gone a minute when Domínguez, waving his black book at the others, winked and turned the doorknob.

"Domínguez," said Gómez.

"Yes?"

"If you see Vamenos, by accident," said Gómez, "warn him away from Mickey Murrillo's Red Rooster Café. They got fights not only *on* TV but *out front* of the TV too."

"He wouldn't go into Murrillo's," said Domínguez. "That suit means too much to Vamenos. He wouldn't do anything to hurt it."

"He'd shoot his mother first," said Martínez.

"Sure he would."

Martínez and Gómez, alone, listened to Domínguez's footsteps hurry away down the stairs. They circled the undressed window dummy.

For a long while, biting his lips, Gómez stood at the window, looking out. He touched his shirt pocket twice, pulled his hand away, and then at last pulled something from the pocket. Without looking at it, he handed it to Martínez.

"Martínez, take this."

"What is it?"

Martínez looked at the piece of folded pink paper with print on it, with names and numbers. His eyes widened.

"A ticket on the bus to El Paso three weeks from now!"

Gómez nodded. He couldn't look at Martínez. He stared out into the summer night.

"Turn it in. Get the money," he said. "Buy us a nice white panama hat and a pale blue tie to go with the white ice cream suit, Martínez. Do that."

"Gómez——"

"Shut up. Boy, is it hot in here! I need air."

"Gómez. I am touched. Gómez——"

But the door stood open. Gómez was gone.

Mickey Murrillo's Red Rooster Café and Cocktail Lounge was squashed between two big brick buildings and, being narrow, had to be deep. Outside, serpents of red and sulphur-green neon fizzed and snapped. Inside, dim shapes loomed and swam away to lose themselves in a swarming night sea.

Martínez, on tiptoe, peeked through a flaked place on the red-painted front window.

He felt a presence on his left, heard breathing on his right. He glanced in both directions.

"Manulo! Villanazul!"

"I decided I wasn't thirsty," said Manulo. "So I took a walk."

"I was just on my way to the plaza," said Villanazul, "and decided to go the long way around."

As if by agreement, the three men shut up now and turned together to peer on tiptoe through various flaked spots on the window.

A moment later, all three felt a new very warm presence behind them and heard still faster breathing.

"Is our white suit in there?" asked Gómez's voice.

"Gómez!" said everybody, surprised. "Hi!"

"Yes!" cried Domínguez, having just arrived to find his own peephole. "There's the suit! And, praise God, Vamenos is still *in* it!"

"I can't see!" Gómez squinted, shielding his eyes. "What's he *doing?*"

Martínez peered. Yes! There, way back in the shadows, was a big chunk of snow and the idiot smile of Vamenos winking above it, wreathed in smoke.

"He's smoking!" said Martínez.

"He's drinking!" said Domínguez.

"He's eating a taco!" reported Villanazul.

"A *juicy* taco," added Manulo.

"No," said Gómez. "No, no, no . . ."

"Ruby Escuadrillo's with him!"

"Let me see that!" Gómez pushed Martínez aside.

Yes, there was Ruby! Two hundred pounds of glittering sequins and tight black satin on the hoof, her scarlet fingernails clutching Vamenos' shoulder. Her cowlike face, floured with powder, greasy with lipstick, hung over him!

"That hippo!" said Domínguez. "She's crushing the shoulder pads. Look, she's going to sit on his lap!"

"No, no, not with all that powder and lipstick!" said Gómez. "Manulo, inside! Grab that drink! Villanazul, the cigar, the taco! Domínguez, date Ruby Escuadrillo, get her away. *Ándale*, men!"

The three vanished, leaving Gómez and Martínez to stare, gasping, through the peephole.

"Manulo, he's got the drink, he's *drinking* it!"

"*Ay!* There's Villanazul, he's got the cigar, he's eating the taco!"

"Hey, Domínguez, he's got Ruby! What a *brave* one!"

A shadow bulked through Murrillo's front door, traveling fast.

"Gómez!" Martínez clutched Gómez's arm. "That was Ruby Escuadrillo's boy friend, Toro Ruíz. If he finds

her with Vamenos, the ice cream suit will be covered
with blood, *covered* with blood——"

"Don't make me nervous," said Gómez. "Quickly!"

Both ran. Inside they reached Vamenos just as Toro
Ruíz grabbed about two feet of the lapels of that wonderful ice cream suit.

"Let go of Vamenos!" said Martínez.

"Let go that *suit!*" corrected Gómez.

Toro Ruíz, tap-dancing Vamenos, leered at these in-
truders.

Villanazul stepped up shyly.

Villanazul smiled. "Don't hit him. Hit me."

Toro Ruíz hit Villanazul smack on the nose.

Villanazul, holding his nose, tears stinging his eyes,
wandered off.

Gómez grabbed one of Toro Ruíz's arms, Martínez
the other.

"Drop him, let go, *cabrón, coyote, vaca!*"

Toro Ruíz twisted the ice cream suit material until
all six men screamed in mortal agony. Grunting, sweating, Toro Ruíz dislodged as many as climbed on. He was
winding up to hit Vamenos when Villanazul wandered
back, eyes streaming.

"Don't hit him. Hit me!"

As Toro Ruíz hit Villanazul on the nose, a chair
crashed on Toro's head.

"Ai!" said Gómez.

Toro Ruíz swayed, blinking, debating whether to
fall. He began to drag Vamenos with him.

"Let go!" cried Gómez. "Let go!"

One by one, with great care, Toro Ruíz's banana-like
fingers let loose of the suit. A moment later he was ruins
at their feet.

"Compadres, this way!"

They ran Vamenos outside and set him down where
he freed himself of their hands with injured dignity.

"Okay, okay. My time ain't up. I still got two minutes
and, let's see—ten seconds."

"What!" said everybody.

"Vamenos," said Gómez, "you let a Guadalajara cow
climb on you, you pick fights, you smoke, you drink, you

eat tacos, and *now* you have the nerve to say your time ain't up?"

"I got two minutes and one second left!"

"Hey, Vamenos, you sure look sharp!" Distantly, a woman's voice called from across the street.

Vamenos smiled and buttoned the coat.

"It's Ramona Álvarez! Ramona, wait!" Vamenos stepped off the curb.

"Vamenos," pleaded Gómez. "What can you do in one minute and"—he checked his watch—"forty seconds!"

"Watch! Hey, Ramona!"

Vamenos loped.

"Vamenos, look out!"

Vamenos, surprised, whirled, saw a car, heard the shriek of brakes.

"No," said all five men on the sidewalk.

Martínez heard the impact and flinched. His head moved up. It looks like white laundry, he thought, flying through the air. His head came down.

Now he heard himself and each of the men make a different sound. Some swallowed too much air. Some let it out. Some choked. Some groaned. Some cried aloud for justice. Some covered their faces. Martínez felt his own fist pounding his heart in agony. He could not move his feet.

"I don't want to live," said Gómez quietly. "Kill me, someone."

Then, shuffling, Martínez looked down and told his feet to walk, stagger, follow one after the other. He collided with other men. Now they were trying to run. They ran at last and somehow crossed a street like a deep river through which they could only wade, to look down at Vamenos.

"Vamenos!" said Martínez. "You're alive!"

Strewn on his back, mouth open, eyes squeezed tight, tight, Vamenos motioned his head back and forth, back and forth, moaning.

"Tell me, tell me, oh, tell me, tell me."

"Tell you what, Vamenos?"

Vamenos clenched his fists, ground his teeth.

"The suit, what have I done to the suit, the suit, the suit!"

The men crouched lower.

"Vamenos, it's . . . why, it's *okay!*"

"You lie!" said Vamenos. "It's torn, it must be, it must be, it's torn, all around, *underneath?*"

"No." Martínez knelt and touched here and there. "Vamenos, all around, underneath even, it's okay!"

Vamenos opened his eyes to let the tears run free at last. "A miracle," he sobbed. "Praise the saints!" He quieted at last. "The car?"

"Hit and run." Gómez suddenly remembered and glared at the empty street. "It's good he didn't stop. We'd have——"

Everyone listened.

Distantly a siren wailed.

"Someone phoned for an ambulance."

"Quick!" said Vamenos, eyes rolling. "Set me up! Take off our coat!"

"Vamenos——"

"Shut up, idiots!" cried Vamenos. "The coat, that's it! Now, the pants, the pants, quick, quick, *peónes!* Those doctors! You seen movies? They rip the pants with razors to get them off! They don't *care!* They're maniacs! Ah, God, quick, quick!"

The siren screamed.

The men, panicking, all handled Vamenos at once.

"Right leg, *easy,* hurry, cows! Good! Left leg, now, left, you hear, there, easy, *easy!* Ow, God! Quick! Martínez, your pants, take them off!"

"What?" Martínez froze.

The siren shrieked.

"Fool!" wailed Vamenos. "All is lost! Your pants! Give me!"

Martínez jerked at his belt buckle.

"Close in, make a circle!"

Dark pants, light pants flourished on the air.

"Quick, here come the maniacs with the razors! Right leg on, left leg, *there!*"

"The zipper, cows, zip my zipper!" babbled Vamenos.

The siren died.

"Madre mía, yes, just in time! They arrive." Vamenos lay back down and shut his eyes. *"Gracias."*

Martínez turned, nonchalantly buckling on the white pants as the interns brushed past.

"Broken leg," said one intern as they moved Vamenos onto a stretcher.

"Compadres," said Vamenos, "don't be mad with me."

Gómez snorted. "Who's mad?"

In the ambulance, head tilted back, looking out at them upside down, Vamenos faltered.

"Compadres, when . . . when I come from the hospital . . . am I still in the bunch? You won't kick me out? Look, I'll give up smoking, keep away from Murrillo's, swear off women——"

"Vamenos," said Martínez gently, "don't promise nothing."

Vamenos, upside down, eyes brimming wet, saw Martínez there, all white now against the stars.

"Oh, Martínez, you sure look great in that suit. *Compadres,* don't he look *beautiful?"*

Villanazul climbed in beside Vamenos. The door slammed. The four remaining men watched the ambulance drive away.

Then, surrounded by his friends, inside the white suit, Martínez was carefully escorted back to the curb.

In the tenement, Martínez got out the cleaning fluid and the others stood around, telling him how to clean the suit and, later, how not to have the iron too hot and how to work the lapels and the crease and all. When the suit was cleaned and pressed so it looked like a fresh gardenia just opened, they fitted it to the dummy.

"Two o'clock," murmured Villanazul. "I hope Vamenos sleeps well. When I left him at the hospital, he looked good."

Manulo cleared his throat. "Nobody else is going out with that suit tonight, huh?"

The others glared at him.

Manulo flushed. "I mean . . . it's late. We're tired. Maybe no one will use the suit for forty-eight hours, huh? Give it a rest. Sure. Well. Where do we sleep?"

The night being still hot and the room unbearable,

they carried the suit on its dummy out and down the hall. They brought with them also some pillows and blankets. They climbed the stairs toward the roof of the tenement. There, thought Martínez, is the cooler wind, and sleep.

On the way, they passed a dozen doors that stood open, people still perspiring and awake, playing cards, drinking pop, fanning themselves with movie magazines.

I wonder, thought Martínez. I wonder if—— Yes!

On the fourth floor, a certain door stood open.

The beautiful girl looked up as the men passed. She wore glasses and when she saw Martínez she snatched them off and hid them under her book.

The others went on, not knowing they had lost Martínez, who seemed stuck fast in the open door.

For a long moment he could say nothing. Then he said:

"José Martínez."

And she said:

"Celia Obregón."

And then both said nothing.

He heard the men moving up on the tenement roof. He moved to follow.

She said quickly, "I saw you tonight!"

He came back.

"The suit," he said.

"The suit," she said, and paused. "But not the suit."

"Eh?" he said.

She lifted the book to show the glasses lying in her lap. She touched the glasses.

"I do not see well. You would think I would wear my glasses, but no. I walk around for years now, hiding them, seeing nothing. But tonight, even without the glasses, I see. A great whiteness passes below in the dark. So white! And I put on my glasses quickly!"

"The suit, as I said," said Martínez.

"The suit for a little moment, yes, but there is another whiteness above the suit."

"Another?"

"Your teeth! Oh, such white teeth, and so many!"

Martínez put his hand over his mouth.

"So happy, Mr. Martínez," she said. "I have not often seen such a happy face and such a smile."

"Ah," he said, not able to look at her, his face flushing now.

"So, you see," she said quietly, "the suit caught my eye, yes, the whiteness filled the night below. But the teeth were much whiter. Now, I have forgotten the suit."

Martínez flushed again. She, too, was overcome with what she had said. She put her glasses on her nose, and then took them off, nervously, and hid them again. She looked at her hands and at the door above his head.

"May I——" he said, at last.

"May you——"

"May I call for you," he asked, "when next the suit is mine to wear?"

"Why must you wait for the suit?" she said.

"I thought——"

"You do not need the suit," she said.

"But——"

"If it were just the suit," she said, "anyone would be fine in it. But no, I watched. I saw many men in that suit, all different, this night. So again I say, you do not need to wait for the suit."

"*Madre mía, madre mía!*" he cried happily. And then, quieter, "I will need the suit for a little while. A month, six months, a year. I am uncertain. I am fearful of many things. I am young."

"That is as it should be," she said.

"Good night, Miss——"

"Celia Obregón."

"Celia Obregón," he said, and was gone from the door.

The others were waiting on the roof of the tenement. Coming up through the trapdoor, Martínez saw they had placed the dummy and the suit in the center of the roof and put their blankets and pillows in a circle around it. Now they were lying down. Now a cooler night wind was blowing here, up in the sky.

Martínez stood alone by the white suit, smoothing the lapels, talking half to himself.

"Ay, *caramba*, what a night! Seems ten years since

seven o'clock, when it all started and I had no friends. Two in the morning, I got all *kinds* of friends. . . ." He paused and thought, Celia Obregón, Celia Obregón. ". . . all kinds of friends," he went on. "I got a room, I got clothes. You tell *me*. You know what?" He looked around at the men lying on the rooftop, surrounding the dummy and himself. "It's funny. When I wear this suit, I know I will win at pool, like Gómez. A woman will look at me like Domínguez. I will be able to sing like Manulo, sweetly. I will talk fine politics like Villanazul. I'm strong as Vamenos. So? So, tonight I am more than Martínez. I am Gómez, Manulo, Domínguez, Villanazul, Vamenos. I am everyone. Ay . . . ay . . ." He stood a moment longer by this suit which could save all the ways they sat or stood or walked. This suit which could move fast and nervous like Gómez or slow and thoughtfully like Villanazul or drift like Domínguez, who never touched ground, who always found a wind to take him somewhere. This suit which belonged to them but which also owned them all. This suit that was—what? A parade.

"Martínez," said Gómez. "You going to sleep?"

"Sure. I'm just thinking."

"What?"

"If we ever get rich," said Martínez softly, "it'll be kind of sad. Then we'll all have suits. And there won't be no more nights like tonight. It'll break up the old gang. It'll never be the same after that."

The men lay thinking of what had just been said.

Gómez nodded gently.

"Yeah . . . it'll never be the same . . . after that."

Martínez lay down on his blanket. In darkness, with the others, he faced the middle of the roof and the dummy, which was the center of their lives.

And their eyes were bright, shining, and good to see in the dark as the neon lights from nearby buildings flicked on, flicked off, flicked on, flicked off, revealing and then vanishing, revealing and then vanishing, their wonderful white vanilla ice cream summer suit.

FEVER DREAM

They put him between fresh, clean, laundered sheets and there was always a newly squeezed glass of thick orange juice on the table under the dim pink lamp. All Charles had to do was call and Mom or Dad would stick their heads into his room to see how sick he was. The acoustics of the room were fine; you could hear the toilet gargling its porcelain throat of mornings, you could hear rain tap the roof or sly mice run in the secret walls or the canary singing in its cage downstairs. If you were very alert, sickness wasn't too bad.

He was thirteen, Charles was. It was mid-September, with the land beginning to burn with autumn. He lay in the bed for three days before the terror overcame him.

His hand began to change. His right hand. He looked at it and it was hot and sweating there on the counterpane alone. It fluttered, it moved a bit. Then it lay there, changing color.

That afternoon the doctor came again and tapped his thin chest like a little drum. "How are you?" asked the doctor, smiling. "I know, don't tell me: 'My *cold* is fine, Doctor, but *I* feel awful!' Ha!" He laughed at his own oft-repeated joke.

Charles lay there and for him that terrible and ancient jest was becoming a reality. The joke fixed itself in his mind. His mind touched and drew away from it in a pale terror. The doctor did not know how cruel he was with his jokes! "Doctor," whispered Charles, lying flat and colorless. "My *hand*, it doesn't *belong* to me any more. This morning it *changed* into something else. I want you to change it back, Doctor, Doctor!"

The doctor showed his teeth and patted his hand. "It looks fine to me, son. You just had a little fever dream."

"But it changed, Doctor, oh, Doctor," cried Charles, pitifully holding up his pale wild hand. "It *did!*"

The doctor winked. "I'll give you a pink pill for that." He popped a tablet onto Charles' tongue. "Swallow!"

"Will it make my hand change back and become *me*, again?"

"Yes, yes."

The house was silent when the doctor drove off down the road in his car under the quiet, blue September sky. A clock ticked far below in the kitchen world. Charles lay looking at his hand.

It did not change back. It was still something else.

The wind blew outside. Leaves fell against the cool window.

At four o'clock his other hand changed. It seemed almost to become a fever. It pulsed and shifted, cell by cell. It beat like a warm heart. The fingernails turned blue and then red. It took about an hour for it to change and when it was finished, it looked just like any ordinary hand. But it was not ordinary. It no longer was him any more. He lay in a fascinated horror and then fell into an exhausted sleep.

Mother brought the soup up at six. He wouldn't touch it. "I haven't any hands," he said, eyes shut.

"Your hands are perfectly good," said Mother.

"No," he wailed. "My hands are gone. I feel like I have stumps. Oh, Mama, Mama, hold me, hold me, I'm scared!"

She had to feed him herself.

"Mama," he said, "get the doctor, please, again. I'm so sick."

"The doctor'll be here tonight at eight," she said, and went out.

At seven, with night dark and close around the house, Charles was sitting up in bed when he felt the thing happening to first one leg and then the other. "Mama! Come quick!" he screamed.

But when Mama came the thing was no longer happening.

When she went downstairs, he simply lay without fighting as his legs beat and beat, grew warm, red-hot, and the room filled with the warmth of his feverish change. The glow crept up from his toes to his ankles and then to his knees.

"May I come in?" The doctor smiled in the doorway.

"Doctor!" cried Charles. "Hurry, take off my blankets!"

The doctor lifted the blankets tolerantly. "There you are. Whole and healthy. Sweating, though. A little fever. I told you not to move around, bad boy." He pinched the moist pink cheek. "Did the pills help? Did your hand change back?"

"No, no, now it's my other hand and my legs!"

"Well, well, I'll have to give you three more pills, one for each limb, eh, my little peach?" laughed the doctor.

"Will they help me? Please, please. What've I *got?*"

"A mild case of scarlet fever, complicated by a slight cold."

"Is it a germ that lives and has more little germs in me?"

"Yes."

"Are you *sure* it's scarlet fever? You haven't taken any tests!"

"I guess I know a certain fever when I see one," said the doctor, checking the boy's pulse with cool authority.

Charles lay there, not speaking until the doctor was crisply packing his black kit. Then in the silent room, the boy's voice made a small, weak pattern, his eyes alight with remembrance. "I read a book once. About petrified trees, wood turning to stone. About how trees fell and rotted and minerals got in and built up and they look just like trees, but they're not, they're stone." He stopped. In the quiet warm room his breathing sounded.

"Well?" asked the doctor.

"I've been thinking," said Charles after a time. "Do germs ever get big? I mean, in biology class they told us about one-celled animals, amoebas and things, and how millions of years ago they got together until there was a bunch and they made the first body. And more and more cells got together and got bigger and then finally maybe there was a fish and finally here *we* are, and all we are is a bunch of cells that decided to get together, to help each other out. Isn't that right?" Charles wet his feverish lips.

"What's all this about?" The doctor bent over him.

"I've got to tell you this. Doctor, oh, I've got to!" he cried. "What would happen, oh just pretend, please pretend, that just like in the old days, a lot of microbes got together and wanted to make a bunch, and reproduced and made *more*——"

His white hands were on his chest now, crawling toward his throat.

"And they decided to *take over* a person!" cried Charles.

"Take over a person?"

"Yes, *become* a person. *Me*, my hands, my feet! What if a disease somehow knew how to kill a person and yet live after him?"

He screamed.

The hands were on his neck.

The doctor moved forward, shouting.

At nine o'clock the doctor was escorted out to his car by the mother and father, who handed him his bag. They conversed in the cool night wind for a few minutes. "Just be sure his hands are kept strapped to his legs," said the doctor. "I don't want him hurting himself."

"Will he be all right, Doctor?" The mother held to his arm a moment.

He patted her shoulder. "Haven't I been your family physician for thirty years? It's the fever. He imagines things."

"But those bruises on his throat, he almost choked himself."

"Just you keep him strapped; he'll be all right in the morning."

The car moved off down the dark September road.

At three in the morning, Charles was still awake in his small black room. The bed was damp under his head and his back. He was very warm. Now he no longer had any arms or legs, and his body was beginning to change. He did not move on the bed, but looked at the vast blank ceiling space with insane concentration. For a while he had screamed and thrashed, but now he was weak and hoarse from it, and his mother had gotten up a number of times to soothe his brow with a wet towel. Now he was silent, his hands strapped to his legs.

He felt the walls of his body change, the organs shift, the lungs catch fire like burning bellows of pink alcohol. The room was lighted up as with the flickerings of a hearth.

Now he had no body. It was all gone. It was under him, but it was filled with a vast pulse of some burning, lethargic drug. It was as if a guillotine had neatly lopped off his head, and his head lay shining on a midnight pillow while the body, below, still alive, belonged to somebody else. The disease had eaten his body and from the eating had reproduced itself in feverish duplicate.

There were the little hand hairs and the fingernails and the scars and the toenails and the tiny mole on his right hip, all done again in perfect fashion.

I am dead, he thought. I've been killed, and yet I live. My body is dead, it is all disease and nobody will know. I will walk around and it will not be me, it will be something else. It will be something all bad, all evil, so big and so evil it's hard to understand or think about. Something that will buy shoes and drink water and get married some day maybe and do more evil in the world than has ever been done.

Now the warmth was stealing up his neck, into his cheeks, like a hot wine. His lips burned, his eyelids, like leaves, caught fire. His nostrils breathed out blue flame, faintly, faintly.

This will be all, he thought. It'll take my head and my brain and fix each eye and every tooth and all the marks in my brain, and every hair and every wrinkle in my ears, and there'll be nothing left of me.

He felt his brain fill with a boiling mercury. He felt his left eye clench in upon itself and, like a snail, withdraw, shift. He was blind in his left eye. It no longer belonged to him. It was enemy territory. His tongue was gone, cut out. His left cheek was numbed, lost. His left ear stopped hearing. It belonged to someone else now. This thing that was being born, this mineral thing replacing the wooden log, this disease replacing healthy animal cell.

He tried to scream and he was able to scream loud and high and sharply in the room, just as his brain flooded down, his right eye and right ear were cut out, he was blind and deaf, all fire, all terror, all panic, all death.

His scream stopped before his mother ran through the door to his side.

It was a good, clear morning, with a brisk wind that helped carry the doctor up the path before the house. In the window above, the boy stood, fully dressed. He did not wave when the doctor waved and called, "What's this? Up? My God!"

The doctor almost ran upstairs. He came gasping into the bedroom.

"What are you doing out of bed?" he demanded of the boy. He tapped his thin chest, took his pulse and temperature. "Absolutely amazing! Normal. Normal, by God!"

"I shall never be sick again in my life," declared the boy, quietly, standing there, looking out the wide window. "Never."

"I hope not. Why, you're looking fine, Charles."

"Doctor?"

"Yes, Charles?"

"Can I go to school *now?*" asked Charles.

"Tomorrow will be time enough. You sound positively eager."

"I am. I like school. All the kids. I want to play with

them and wrestle with them, and spit on them and play with the girls' pigtails and shake the teacher's hand, and rub my hands on all the cloaks in the cloakroom, and I want to grow up and travel and shake hands with people all over the world, and be married and have lots of children, and go to libraries and handle books and—*all* of that I want to!" said the boy, looking off into the September morning. "What's the name you called me?"

"What?" The doctor puzzled. "I called you nothing but Charles."

"It's better than no name at all, I guess." The boy shrugged.

"I'm glad you want to go back to school," said the doctor.

"I really anticipate it," smiled the boy. "Thank you for your help, Doctor. Shake hands."

"Glad to."

They shook hands gravely, and the clear wind blew through the open window. They shook hands for almost a minute, the boy smiling up at the old man and thanking him.

Then, laughing, the boy raced the doctor downstairs and out to his car. His mother and father followed for the happy farewell.

"Fit as a fiddle!" said the doctor. "Incredible!"

"And strong," said the father. "He got out of his straps himself during the night. Didn't you, Charles?"

"Did I?" said the boy.

"You did! How?"

"Oh," the boy said, "that was a long time ago."

"A long time ago!"

They all laughed, and while they were laughing, the quiet boy moved his bare foot on the sidewalk and merely touched, brushed against a number of red ants that was scurrying about on the sidewalk. Secretly, his eyes shining, while his parents chatted with the old man, he saw the ants hesitate, quiver, and lie still on the cement. He sensed they were cold now.

"Good-by!"

The doctor drove away, waving.

The boy walked ahead of his parents. As he walked

he looked away toward the town and began to hum "School Days" under his breath.

"It's good to have him well again," said the father.

"Listen to him. He's so looking forward to school!"

The boy turned quietly. He gave each of his parents a crushing hug. He kissed them both several times.

Then without a word he bounded up the steps into the house.

In the parlor, before the others entered, he quickly opened the bird cage, thrust his hand in, and petted the yellow canary, *once*.

Then he shut the cage door, stood back, and waited.

THE MARRIAGE MENDER

In the sun the headboard was like a fountain, tossing up plumes of clear light. It was carved with lions and gargoyles and bearded goats. It was an awe-inspiring object even at midnight, as Antonio sat on the bed and unlaced his shoes and put his large calloused hand out to touch its shimmering harp. Then he rolled over into this fabulous machine for dreaming, and he lay breathing heavily, his eyes beginning to close.

"Every night," his wife's voice said, "we sleep in the mouth of a calliope."

Her complaint shocked him. He lay a long while before daring to reach up his hard-tipped fingers to stroke the cold metal of the intricate headboard, the threads of this lyre that had sung many wild and beautiful songs down the years.

"This is no calliope," he said.

"It cries like one," Maria said. "A billion people on this world tonight have beds. Why, I ask the saints, not us?"

"This," said Antonio gently, "is a bed." He plucked a little tune on the imitation brass harp behind his head. To his ears it was "Santa Lucia."

"This bed has humps like a herd of camels was under it."

"Now, Mama," Antonio said. He called her Mama

when she was mad, though they had no children. "You were never this way," he went on, "until five months ago when Mrs. Brancozzi downstairs bought her new bed."

Maria said wistfully, "Mrs. Brancozzi's bed. It's like snow. It's all flat and white and smooth."

"I don't want any damn snow, all flat and white and smooth! These springs—feel them!" he cried angrily. "They know me. They recognize that this hour of night I lie *thus*, at two o'clock, *so!* Three o'clock *this* way, four o'clock *that*. We are like a tumbling act, we've worked together for years and know all the holds and falls."

Maria sighed, and said, "Sometimes I dream we're in the taffy machine at Bartole's candy store."

"This bed," he announced to the darkness, "served our family before Garibaldi! From this wellspring alone came precincts of honest voters, a squad of clean-saluting Army men, two confectioners, a barber, four second leads for *Il Trovatore* and *Rigoletto*, and two geniuses so complex they never *could* decide what to do in their lifetime! Not to forget enough beautiful women to provide ballrooms with their finest decoration. A cornucopia of plenty, this bed! A veritable harvesting machine!"

"We have been married two years," she said with dreadful control over her voice. "Where are *our* second leads for *Rigoletto*, our geniuses, our ballroom decorations?"

"Patience, Mama."

"Don't call me Mama! While this bed is busy favoring you all night, never once has it done for me. Not even so much as a baby *girl!*"

He sat up. "You've let these women in this tenement ruin you with their dollar-down, dollar-a-week talk. Has Mrs. Brancozzi children? Her and her new bed that she's had for five months?"

"No! But *soon!* Mrs. Brancozzi says . . . and her bed, so beautiful."

He slammed himself down and yanked the covers over him. The bed screamed like all the Furies rushing through the night sky, fading away toward the dawn.

The moon changed the shape of the window pattern on the floor. Antonio awoke. Maria was not beside him.

He got up and went to peer through the half-open door of the bathroom. His wife stood at the mirror looking at her tired face.

"I don't feel well," she said.

"We argued." He put out his hand to pat her. "I'm sorry. We'll think it over. About the bed, I mean. We'll see how the money goes. And if you're not well tomorrow, see the doctor, eh? Now, come back to bed."

At noon the next day, Antonio walked from the lumberyard to a window where stood fine new beds with their covers invitingly turned back.

"I," he whispered to himself, "am a beast."

He checked his watch. Maria, at this time, would be going to the doctor's. She had been like cold milk this morning; he had told her to go. He walked on to the candy-store window and watched the taffy machine folding and threading and pulling. Does taffy scream? he wondered. Perhaps, but so high we cannot hear it. He laughed. Then, in the stretched taffy, he saw Maria. Frowning, he turned and walked back to the furniture store. No. Yes. No. Yes! He pressed his nose to the icy window. Bed, he thought, you in there, new bed, do you *know* me? Will you be kind to my back, nights?"

He took out his wallet slowly, and peered at the money. He sighed, gazed for a long time at that flat marbletop, that unfamiliar enemy, that new bed. Then, shoulders sagging, he walked into the store, his money held loosely in his hand.

"Maria!" He ran up the steps two at a time. It was nine o'clock at night and he had managed to beg off in the middle of his overtime at the lumberyard to rush home. He rushed through the open doorway, smiling.

The apartment was empty.

"Ah," he said disappointedly. He laid the receipt for the new bed on top of the bureau where Maria might see it when she entered. On those few evenings when he worked late she visited with any one of several neighbors downstairs.

I'll go find her, he thought, and stopped. No. I want to tell her alone. I'll wait. He sat on the bed. "Old bed," he said, "good-by to you. I am very sorry." He patted the brass lions nervously. He paced the floor. *Come on, Maria.* He imagined her smile.

He listened for her quick running on the stair, but he heard only a slow, measured tread. He thought: That's not my Maria, slow like that, no.

The doorknob turned.

"Maria!"

"You're early!" She smiled happily at him. Did she guess? Was it written on his face? "I've been downstairs," she cried, "telling everyone!"

"Telling everyone?"

"The doctor! I saw the doctor!"

"The doctor?" He looked bewildered. "And?"

"And, Papa, *and*——"

"Do you mean—Papa?"

"Papa, Papa, Papa, Papa!"

"Oh," he said, gently, "you walked so carefully on the stairs."

He took hold of her, but not too tight, and he kissed her cheeks, and he shut his eyes, and he yelled. Then he had to wake a few neighbors and tell them, shake them, tell them again. There had to be a little wine and a careful waltz around, an embracing, a trembling, a kissing of brow, eyelids, nose, lips, temples, ears, hair, chin —and then it was past midnight.

"A miracle," he sighed.

They were alone in their room again, the air warm from the people who had been here a minute before, laughing, talking. But now they were alone again.

Turning out the light, he saw the receipt on the bureau. Stunned, he tried to decide in what subtle and delicious way to break this additional news to her.

Maria sat upon her side of the bed in the dark, hypnotized with wonder. She moved her hands as if her body was a strange doll, taken apart, and now to be put back together again, limb by limb, her motions as slow as if she lived beneath a warm sea at midnight. Now, at last, careful not to break herself, she lay back upon the pillow.

"Maria, I have something to tell you."

"Yes?" she said faintly.

"Now that you are as you are." He squeezed her hand. "You deserve the comfort, the rest, the beauty of a new bed."

She did not cry out happily or turn to him or seize him. Her silence was a thinking silence.

He was forced to continue. "This bed is nothing but a pipe organ, a calliope."

"It is a bed," she said.

"A herd of camels sleep under it."

"No," she said quietly, "from it will come precincts of honest voters, captains enough for *three* armies, two ballerinas, a famous lawyer, a very tall policeman, and seven basso profundos, altos, and sopranos."

He squinted across the dimly lighted room at the receipt upon the bureau. He touched the worn mattress under him. The springs moved softly to recognize each limb, each tired muscle, each aching bone.

He sighed. "I never argue with you, little one."

"Mama," she said.

"Mama," he said.

And then as he closed his eyes and drew the covers to his chest and lay in the darkness by the great fountain, in the sight of a jury of fierce metal lions and amber goat and smiling gargoyles, he listened. And he heard it. It was very far away at first, very tentative, but it came clearer as he listened.

Softly, her arm back over her head. Maria's finger tips began to tap a little dance on the gleaming harp strings, on the shimmering brass pipes of the ancient bed. The music was—yes, of course: "Santa Lucia!" His lips moved to it in a warm whisper. Santa Lucia! Santa Lucia.

It was very beautiful.

THE TOWN WHERE NO ONE GOT OFF

Crossing the continental United States by night, by day, on the train, you flash past town after wilderness town where nobody ever gets off. Or rather, no person who doesn't *belong*, no person who hasn't roots in these country graveyards ever bothers to visit their lonely stations or attend their lonely views.

I spoke of this to a fellow passenger, another salesman like myself, on the Chicago–Los Angeles train as we crossed Iowa.

"True," he said. "People get off in Chicago; everyone gets off there. People get off in New York, get off in Boston, get off in L.A. People who don't live there go there to see and come back to tell. But what tourist ever just got off at Fox Hill, Nebraska, to *look* at it? You? Me? No! I don't know anyone, got no business there, it's no health resort, so why bother?"

"Wouldn't it be a fascinating change," I said, "some year to plan a really different vacation? Pick some village lost on the plains where you don't know a soul and go there for the hell of it?"

"You'd be bored stiff."

"I'm not bored thinking of it!" I peered out the window. "What's the next town coming up on this line?"

"Rampart Junction."

I smiled. "Sounds good. I might get off there."

"You're a liar and a fool. What you want? Adventure? Romance? Go ahead, jump off the train. Ten seconds later you'll call yourself an idiot, grab a taxi, and race us to the next town."

"Maybe."

I watched telephone poles flick by, flick by, flick by. Far ahead I could see the first faint outlines of a town.

"But I don't think so," I heard myself say.

The salesman across from me looked faintly surprised.

For slowly, very slowly, I was rising to stand. I reached for my hat. I saw my hand fumble for my own suitcase. I was surprised myself.

"Hold on!" said the salesman. "What're you doing?"

The train rounded a curve suddenly. I swayed. Far ahead I saw one church spire, a deep forest, a field of summer wheat.

"It looks like I'm getting off the train," I said.

"Sit down," he said.

"No," I said. "There's something about that town up ahead. I've got to go see. I've got the time. I don't have to be in L.A., really, until next Monday. If I don't get off the train now, I'll always wonder what I missed, what I let slip by when I had the chance to see it."

"We were just talking. There's nothing there."

"You're wrong," I said. "There is."

I put my hat on my head and lifted the suitcase in my hand.

"By God," said the salesman, "I think you're really going to do it."

My heart beat quickly. My face was flushed.

The train whistled. The train rushed down the track. The town was near!

"Wish me luck," I said.

"Luck!" he cried.

I ran for the porter, yelling.

There was an ancient flake-painted chair tilted back against the station-platform wall. In this chair, completely relaxed so he sank into his clothes, was a man of some seventy years whose timbers looked as if he'd been nailed there since the station was built. The sun had burned his face dark and tracked his cheek with lizard folds and stitches that held his eyes in a perpetual squint. His hair smoked ash-white in the summer wind. His blue shirt, open at the neck to show white clock springs, was bleached like the staring late afternoon sky. His shoes were blistered as if he had held them, uncaring, in the mouth of a stove, motionless, forever. His shadow under him was stenciled a permanent black.

As I stepped down the old man's eyes flicked every door on the train and stopped, surprised, at me.

I thought he might wave.

But there was only a sudden coloring of his secret eyes; a chemical change that was recognition. Yet he had not twitched so much as his mouth, an eyelid, a finger. An invisible bulk had shifted inside him.

The moving train gave me an excuse to follow it with my eyes. There was no one else on the platform. No autos waited by the cobwebbed, nailed-shut office. I alone had departed the iron thunder to set foot on the choppy waves of platform lumber.

The train whistled over the hill.

Fool! I thought. My fellow passenger had been right. I would panic at the boredom I already sensed in this place. All right, I thought, fool, yes, but run, no!

I walked my suitcase down the platform, not looking at the old man. As I passed, I heard his thin bulk shift again, this time so I could hear it. His feet were coming down to touch and tap the mushy boards.

I kept walking.

"Afternoon," a voice said faintly.

I knew he did not look at me but only at that great cloudless spread of shimmering sky.

"Afternoon," I said.

I started up the dirt road toward the town. One hundred yards away, I glanced back.

The old man, still seated there, stared at the sun, as if posing a question.

I hurried on.

I moved through the dreaming late afternoon town, utterly anonymous and alone, a trout going upstream, not touching the banks of a clear-running river of life that drifted all about me.

My suspicions were confirmed: it was a town where nothing happened, where occurred only the following events:

At four o'clock sharp, the Honneger Hardware door slammed as a dog came out to dust himself in the road. Four-thirty, a straw sucked emptily at the bottom of a soda glass, making a sound like a great cataract in the drugstore silence. Five o'clock, boys and pebbles plunged in the town river. Five-fifteen, ants paraded in the slanting light under some elm trees.

And yet—I turned in a slow circle—somewhere in this town there must be something worth seeing. I knew it was there. I knew I had to keep walking and looking. I knew I would find it.

I walked. I looked.

All through the afternoon there was only one constant and unchanging factor: the old man in the bleached blue pants and shirt was never far away. When I sat in the drugstore he was out front spitting tobacco that rolled itself into tumblebugs in the dust. When I stood by the river he was crouched downstream making a great thing of washing his hands.

Along about seven-thirty in the evening, I was walking for the seventh or eighth time through the quiet streets when I heard footsteps beside me.

I looked over, and the old man was pacing me, looking straight ahead, a piece of dried grass in his stained teeth.

"It's been a long time," he said quietly.

We walked along in the twilight.

"A long time," he said, "waitin' on that station platform."

"You?" I said.

"Me." He nodded in the tree shadows.

"Were you waiting for someone at the station?"

"Yes," he said. "You."

"Me?" The surprise must have shown in my voice. "But why . . . ? You never saw me before in your life."

"Did I say I did? I just said I was waitin'."

We were on the edge of town now. He had turned and I had turned with him along the darkening riverbank toward the trestle where the night trains ran over going east, going west, but stopping rare few times.

"You want to know anything about me?" I asked, suddenly. "You the sheriff?"

"No, not the sheriff. And no, I don't want to know nothing about you." He put his hands in his pockets. The sun was set now. The air was suddenly cool. "I'm just surprised you're here at last, is all."

"Surprised?"

"Surprised," he said, "and . . . pleased."

I stopped abruptly and looked straight at him.

"How long have you been sitting on that station platform?"

"Twenty years, give or take a few."

I knew he was telling the truth; his voice was as easy and quiet as the river.

"Waiting for me?" I said.

"Or someone like you," he said.

We walked on in the growing dark.

"How you like our town?"

"Nice, quiet," I said.

"Nice, quiet." He nodded. "Like the people?"

"People look nice and quiet."

"They are," he said. "Nice, quiet."

I was ready to turn back but the old man kept talking and in order to listen and be polite I had to walk with him in the vaster darkness, the tides of field and meadow beyond town.

"Yes," said the old man, "the day I retired, twenty years ago, I sat down on that station platform and there I been, sittin', doin' nothin', waitin' for something to happen, I didn't know what, I didn't know, I couldn't say. But when it finally happened, I'd know it, I'd look at it and say, yes, sir, that's what I was waitin' for. Train wreck? No. Old woman friend come back to town after fifty years? No. No. It's hard to say. Someone. Something. And it seems to have something to do with you. I wish I could say——"

"Why don't you try?" I said.

The stars were coming out. We walked on.

"Well," he said slowly, "you know much about your own insides?"

"You mean my stomach or you mean psychologically?"

"That's the word. I mean your head, your brain, you know much about *that?*"

The grass whispered under my feet. "A little."

"You hate many people in your time?"

"Some."

"We all do. It's normal enough to hate, ain't it, and not only hate but, while we don't talk about it, don't we sometimes want to hit people who hurt us, even *kill* them?"

"Hardly a week passes we don't get that feeling," I said, "and put it away."

"We put away all our lives," he said. "The town says thus and so, Mom and Dad say this and that, the law says such and such. So you put away one killing and another and two more after that. By the time you're my age, you got lots of that kind of stuff between your ears. And unless you went to war, nothin' ever happened to get rid of it."

"Some men trapshoot or hunt ducks," I said. "Some men box or wrestle."

"And some don't. I'm talkin' about them that don't. Me. All my life I've been saltin' down those bodies, puttin' 'em away on ice in my head. Sometimes you get mad at a town and the people in it for makin' you put things aside like that. You like the old cave men who just gave a hell of a yell and whanged someone on the head with a club."

"Which all leads up to . . . ?"

"Which all leads up to: everybody'd like to do one killin' in his life, to sort of work off that big load of stuff, all those killin's in his mind he never did have the guts to do. And once in a while a man has a chance. Someone runs in front of his car and he forgets the brakes and keeps goin'. Nobody can prove nothin' with that sort of thing. The man don't even tell himself he did it. He just didn't get his foot on the brake in time. But you know and I know what really happened, don't we?"

"Yes," I said.

The town was far away now. We moved over a small

stream on a wooden bridge, just near the railway embankment.

"Now," said the old man, looking at the water, "the only kind of killin' worth doin' is the one where nobody can guess who did it or why they did it or who they did it to, right? Well, I got this idea maybe twenty years ago. I don't think about it every day or every week. Sometimes months go by, but the idea's this: only one train stops here each day, sometimes not even that. Now, if you wanted to kill someone you'd have to wait, wouldn't you, for years and years, until a complete and actual stranger came to your town, a stranger who got off the train for no reason, a man nobody knows and who don't know nobody in the town. Then, and only then, I thought, sittin' there on the station chair, you could just go up and when nobody's around, kill him and throw him in the river. He'd be found miles downstream. Maybe he'd never be found. Nobody would ever think to come to Rampart Junction to find him. He wasn't goin' there. He was on his way someplace else. There, that's my whole idea. And I'd know that man the minute he got off the train. Know him, just as clear . . ."

I had stopped walking. It was dark. The moon would not be up for an hour.

"Would you?" I said.

"Yes," he said. I saw the motion of his head looking at the stars. "Well, I've talked enough." He sidled close and touched my elbow. His hand was feverish, as if he had held it to a stove before touching me. His other hand, his right hand, was hidden, tight and bunched, in his pocket. "I've talked enough."

Something screamed.

I jerked my head.

Above, a fast flying night express razored along the unseen tracks, flourished light on hill, forest, farm, town dwellings, field, ditch, meadow, plowed earth and water, then, raving high, cut off away, shrieking, gone. The rails trembled for a little while after that. Then, silence.

The old man and I stood looking at each other in the dark. His left hand was still holding my elbow. His other hand was still hidden.

"May I say something?" I said at last.

The old man nodded.

"About myself," I said. I had to stop. I could hardly breathe. I forced myself to go on. "It's funny. I've often thought the same way as you. Sure, just today, going cross-country, I thought, How perfect, how perfect, how really perfect it could be. Business has been bad for me, lately. Wife sick. Good friend died last week. War in the world. Full of boils, myself. It would do me a world of good——"

"What?" the old man said, his hand on my arm.

"To get off this train in a small town," I said, "where nobody knows me, with this gun under my arm, and find someone and kill them and bury them and go back down to the station and get on and go home and nobody the wiser and nobody ever to know who did it, ever. Perfect, I thought, a perfect crime. And I got off the train."

We stood there in the dark for another minute, staring at each other. Perhaps we were listening to each other's hearts beating very fast, very fast indeed.

The world turned under me. I clenched my fists. I wanted to fall. I wanted to scream like the train.

For suddenly I saw that all the things I had just said were not lies put forth to save my life.

All the things I had just said to this man were true.

And now I knew why I had stepped from the train and walked up through this town. I knew what I had been looking for.

I heard the old man breathing hard and fast. His hand was tight on my arm as if he might fall. His teeth were clenched. He leaned toward me as I leaned toward him. There was a terrible silent moment of immense strain as before an explosion.

He forced himself to speak at last. It was the voice of a man crushed by a monstrous burden.

"How do I know you got a gun under your arm?"

"You don't know." My voice was blurred. "You can't be sure."

He waited. I thought he was going to faint.

"That's how it is?" he said.

"That's how it is," I said.

He shut his eyes tight. He shut his mouth tight.

After another five seconds, very slowly, heavily, he managed to take his hand away from my own immensely heavy arm. He looked down at his right hand then, and took it, empty, out of his pocket.

Slowly, with great weight, we turned away from each other and started walking blind, completely blind, in the dark.

The midnight Passenger-to-be-picked-up flare sputtered on the tracks. Only when the train was pulling out of the station did I lean from the open Pullman door and look back.

The old man was seated there with his chair tilted against the station wall, with his faded blue pants and shirt and his sun-baked face and his sun-bleached eyes. He did not glance at me as the train slid past. He was gazing east along the empty rails where tomorrow or the next day or the day after the day after that, a train, some train, any train, might fly by here, might slow, might stop. His face was fixed, his eyes were blindly frozen, toward the east. He looked a hundred years old.

The train wailed.

Suddenly old myself, I leaned out, squinting.

Now the darkness that had brought us together stood between. The old man, the station, the town, the forest, were lost in the night.

For an hour I stood in the roaring blast staring back at all that darkness.

A SCENT OF SARSAPARILLA

Mr. William Finch stood quietly in the dark and blowing attic all morning and afternoon for three days. For three days in late November, he stood alone, feeling the soft white flakes of Time falling out of the infinite cold steel sky, silently, softly, feathering the roof and powdering the eaves. He stood, eyes shut. The attic, wallowed in seas of wind in the long sunless days, creaked every bone and shook down ancient dusts from its beams and warped timbers and lathings. It was a mass of sighs and torments that ached all about him where he stood sniffing its elegant dry perfumes and feeling of its ancient heritages. Ah. Ah.

Listening, downstairs, his wife, Cora, could not hear him walk or shift or twitch. She imagined she could only hear him breathe, slowly out and in, like a dusty bellows, alone up there in the attic, high in the windy house.

"Ridiculous," she muttered.

When he hurried down for lunch the third afternoon, he smiled at the bleak walls, the chipped plates, the scratched silverware, and even at his wife!

"What's all the excitement?" she demanded.

"Good spirits is all. Wonderful spirits!" he laughed. He seemed almost hysterical with joy. He was seething in a great warm ferment which, obviously, he had trouble concealing. His wife frowned.

"What's that *smell?*"

"Smell, smell, smell?"

"Sarsaparilla." She sniffed suspiciously. "That's what it is!"

"Oh, it couldn't be!" His hysterical happiness stopped as quickly as if she'd switched him off. He seemed stunned, ill at ease, and suddenly very careful.

"Where did you go this morning?" she asked.

"You *know* I was cleaning the attic."

"Mooning over a lot of trash. I didn't hear a sound. Thought maybe you weren't in the attic at all. What's that?" She pointed.

"Well, now how did *those* get there?" he asked the world.

He peered down at the pair of black spring-metal bicycle clips that bound his thin pants cuffs to his bony ankles.

"Found them in the attic," he answered himself. "Remember when we got out on the gravel road in the early morning on our tandem bike, Cora, forty years ago, everything fresh and new?"

"If you don't finish that attic today, I'll come up and toss everything out myself."

"Oh, no," he cried. "I have everything the way I want it!"

She looked at him coldly.

"Cora," he said, eating his lunch, relaxing, beginning to enthuse again, "you know what attics are? They're Time Machines, in which old, dim-witted men like me can travel back forty years to a time when it was summer all year round and children raided ice wagons. Remember how it tasted? You held the ice in your handkerchief. It was like sucking the flavor of linen and snow at the same time."

Cora fidgeted.

It's not impossible, he thought, half closing his eyes, trying to see it and build it. Consider an attic. Its very atmosphere is Time. It deals in other years, the cocoons and chrysalises of another age. All the bureau drawers are little coffins where a thousand yesterdays lie in state.

Oh, the attic's a dark, friendly place, full of Time, and if you stand in the very center of it, straight and tall, squinting your eyes, and thinking and thinking, and smelling the Past, and putting out your hands to feel of Long Ago, why, it . . .

He stopped, realizing he had spoken some of this aloud. Cora was eating rapidly.

"Well, wouldn't it be interesting," he asked the part in her hair, "if Time Travel *could* occur? And what more logical, proper place for it to happen than in an attic like *ours*, eh?"

"It's not always summer back in the old days," she said. "It's just your crazy memory. You remember all the good things and forget the bad. It wasn't always summer."

"Figuratively speaking, Cora, it was."

"Wasn't."

"What I mean is this," he said, whispering excitedly, bending forward to see the image he was tracing on the blank dining-room wall. "If you rode your unicycle carefully between the years, balancing, hands out, careful, careful, if you rode from year to year, spent a week in 1909, a day in 1900, a month or a fortnight somewhere else, 1905, 1898, you could stay with summer the rest of your life."

"Unicycle?"

"You know, one of those tall chromium one-wheeled bikes, single-seater, the performers ride in vaudeville shows, juggling. Balance, true balance, it takes, not to fall off, to keep the bright objects flying in the air, beautiful, up and up, a light, a flash, a sparkle, a bomb of brilliant colors, red, yellow, blue, green, white, gold; all the Junes and Julys and Augusts that ever were, in the air, about you, at once, hardly touching your hands, flying, suspended, and you, smiling, among them. Balance, Cora, *balance*."

"Blah," she said, "blah, blah." And added, "blah!"

He climbed the long cold stairs to the attic, shivering.

There were nights in winter when he woke with porcelain in his bones, with cool chimes blowing in his ears, with frost piercing his nerves in a raw illumination like white-cold fireworks exploding and showering down in flaming snows upon a silent land deep in his subconscious. He was cold, cold, cold, and it would take a score of endless summers, with their green torches and bronze suns to thaw him free of his wintry sheath. He was a great tasteless chunk of brittle ice, a snowman put to bed each night, full of confetti dreams, tumbles of crystal and flurry. And there lay winter outside forever, a great leaden wine press smashing down its colorless lid of sky, squashing them all like so many grapes, mashing color and sense and being from everyone, save the children who fled on skis and toboggans down mirrored hills which reflected the crushing iron shield that hung lower above town each day and every eternal night.

Mr. Finch lifted the attic trap door. But here, *here.* A dust of summer sprang up about him. The attic dust simmered with heat left over from other seasons. Quietly, he shut the trap door down.

He began to smile.

The attic was quiet as a thundercloud before a storm. On occasion, Cora Finch heard her husband murmuring, murmuring, high up there.

At five in the afternoon, singing *My Isle of Golden Dreams,* Mr. Finch flipped a crisp new straw hat in the kitchen door. "Boo!"

"Did you sleep all afternoon?" snapped his wife. "I called up at you four times and no answer."

"Sleep?" He considered this and laughed, then put his hand quickly over his mouth. "Well, I guess I did."

Suddenly she saw him. "My God!" she cried, "where'd you get that coat?"

He wore a red candy-striped coat, a high white, choking collar and ice cream pants. You could smell the straw hat like a handful of fresh hay fanned in the air.

"Found 'em in an old trunk."

She sniffed. "Don't smell of moth balls. Looks brand-new."

"Oh, no!" he said hastily. He looked stiff and uncomfortable as she eyed his costume.

"This isn't a summer-stock company," she said.

"Can't a fellow have a little fun?"

"That's all you've ever had," she slammed the oven door. "While I've stayed home and knitted, lord knows, you've been down at the store helping ladies' elbows in and out doors."

He refused to be bothered. "Cora." He looked deep into the crackling straw hat. "Wouldn't it be nice to take a Sunday walk the way we used to do, with your silk parasol and your long dress whishing along, and sit on those wire-legged chairs at the soda parlor and smell the drugstore the way they used to smell? Why don't drugstores smell that way any more? And order two sarsaparillas for us, Cora, and then ride out in our 1910 Ford to Hannahan's Pier for a box supper and listen to the brass band. How about it?"

"Supper's ready. Take that dreadful uniform off."

"If you could make a wish and take a ride on those oak-laned country roads like they had before cars started rushing, would you *do* it?" he insisted, watching her.

"Those old roads were dirty. We came home looking like Africans. Anyway," she picked up a sugar jar and shook it, "this morning I had forty dollars here. Now it's gone! Don't tell me you ordered those clothes from a costume house. They're brand-new; they didn't come from any trunk!"

"I'm——" he said.

She raved for half an hour, but he could not bring himself to say anything. The November wind shook the house and as she talked, the snows of winter began to fall again in the cold steel sky.

"Answer me!" she cried. "Are you crazy, spending our money that way, on clothes you can't wear?"

"The attic," he started to say.

She walked off and sat in the living room.

The snow was falling fast now and it was a cold dark November evening. She heard him climb up the stepladder, slowly, into the attic, into that dusty place of other years, into that black place of costumes and props and Time, into a world separate from this world below.

* * *

He closed the trap door down. The flashlight, snapped on, was company enough. Yes, here was all of Time compressed in a Japanese paper flower. At the touch of memory, everything would unfold into the clear water of the mind, in beautiful blooms, in spring breezes, larger than life. Each of the bureau drawers slid forth, might contain aunts and cousins and grandmamas, ermined in dust. Yes, Time was here. You could feel it breathing, an atmospheric instead of a mechanical clock.

Now the house below was as remote as another day in the past. He half shut his eyes and looked and looked on every side of the waiting attic.

Here, in prismed chandelier, were rainbows and mornings and noons as bright as new rivers flowing endlessly back through time. His flashlight caught and flickered them alive, the rainbows leapt up to curve the shadows back with colors, with colors like plums and strawberries and Concord grapes, with colors like cut lemons and the sky where the clouds drew off after storming and the blue was there. And the dust of the attic was incense burning and all of time burning, and all you need do was peer into the flames. It was indeed a great machine of Time, this attic, he knew, he felt, he was sure, and if you touched prisms here, doorknobs there, plucked tassels, chimed crystals, swirled dust, punched trunk hasps and gusted the vox humana of the old hearth bellows until it puffed the soot of a thousand ancient fires into your eyes, if, indeed, you played this instrument, this warm machine of parts, if you fondled all of its bits and pieces, its levers and changers and movers, then, then, *then!*

He thrust out his hands to orchestrate, to conduct, to flourish. There was music in his head, in his mouth shut tight, and he played the great machine, the thunderously silent organ, bass, tenor, soprano, low, high, and at last, at last, a chord that shuddered him so that he had to shut his eyes.

About nine o'clock that night she heard him calling, "Cora!" She went upstairs. His head peered down at her from above, smiling at her. He waved his hat. "Good-by, Cora."

"What do you mean?" she cried.

"I've thought it over for three days and I'm saying good-by."

"Come down out of there, you fool!"

"I drew five hundred dollars from the bank yesterday. I've been thinking about this. And then when *it* happened, well . . . Cora . . ." He shoved his eager hand down. "For the last time, will you come along with me?"

"In the attic? Hand down that stepladder, William Finch. I'll climb up there and run you out of that filthy place!"

"I'm going to Hannahan's Pier for a bowl of clam chowder," he said. "And I'm requesting the brass band to play 'Moonlight Bay.' Oh, come on, Cora . . ." He motioned his extended hand.

She simply stared at his gentle, questioning face.

"Good-by," he said.

He waved gently, gently. Then his face was gone, the straw hat was gone.

"William!" she screamed.

The attic was dark and silent.

Shrieking, she ran and got a chair and used it to groan her way up into the musty darkness. She flourished a flashlight. "William! William!"

The dark spaces were empty. A winter wind shook the house.

Then she saw the far west attic window, ajar.

She fumbled over to it. She hesitated, held her breath. Then, slowly, she opened it. The ladder was placed outside the window, leading down onto a porch roof.

She pulled back from the window.

Outside the opened frame the apple trees shone bright green, it was twilight of a summer day in July. Faintly, she heard explosions, firecrackers going off. She heard laughter and distant voices. Rockets burst in the warm air, softly, red, white, and blue, fading.

She slammed the window and stood reeling. "William!"

Wintry November light glowed up through the trap in the attic floor behind her. Bent to it, she saw the snow whispering against the cold clear panes down in that November world where she would spend the next thirty years.

She did not go near the window again. She sat alone in the black attic, smelling the one smell that did not seem to fade. It lingered like a sigh of satisfaction, on the air. She took a deep, long breath.

The old, the familiar, the unforgettable scent of drugstore sarsaparilla.

THE HEADPIECE

The parcel arrived in the late afternoon mail. Mr. Andrew Lemon knew what was inside by shaking it. It whispered in there like a large hairy tarantula.

It took him some time to get up his courage, tremble the wrappings open, and remove the lid from the white cardboard box.

There the bristly thing lay on its snowy tissue bed, as impersonal as the black horsehair clock springs stuffed in an old sofa. Andrew Lemon chuckled.

"Indians come and gone, left this piece of a massacre behind as a sign, a warning. Well. *There!*"

And he fitted the new patent-leather black shining toupee to his naked scalp. He tugged at it like someone touching his cap to passers-by.

The toupee fit perfectly, covering the neat coin-round hole which marred the top of his brow. Andrew Lemon gazed at the strange man in the mirror and yelled with delight.

"Hey there, who're you? Face's familiar, but, by gosh now, pass you on the street without looking twice! Why? Because, *it's* gone! Darn hole's covered, nobody'd guess it was ever there. Happy New Year, man, that's what it is, Happy New Year!"

He walked around and around his little apartment, smiling, needing to do something, but not yet ready to open the door and surprise the world. He walked by the mirror, glancing sidewise at someone going past there and each time laughed and shook his head. Then he sat down in the rocker and rocked, grinning, and tried to look at a couple of copies of *Wild West Weekly* and then *Thrilling Movie Magazine*. But he couldn't keep his right hand from crawling up along his face, tremulously, to feel at the rim of that crisp new sedge above his ears.

"Let me buy you a drink, young fellow!"

He opened the fly-specked medicine cabinet and took three gulps from a bottle. Eyes watering, he was on the verge of cutting himself a chew of tobacco when he stopped, listening.

Outside in the dark hallway there was a sound like a field mouse moving softly, daintily on the threadbare carpeting.

"Miss Fremwell!" he said to the mirror.

Suddenly the toupee was off his head and into the box as if, frightened, it had scuttled back there of itself. He clapped the lid down, sweating cold, afraid of even the sound that woman made moving by like a summer breeze.

He tiptoed to a door that was nailed shut in one wall and bent his raw and now furiously blushing head. He heard Miss Fremwell unlock her door and shut it and move delicately about her room with little tinkles of chinaware and chimes of cutlery, turning in a merry-go-round to make her dinner. He backed away from that door that was bolted, locked, latched, and driven shut with its four-inch hard steel nails. He thought of the nights he had flinched in bed, thinking he heard her quietly pulling out the nails, pulling out the nails, touching at the bolts and slithering the latch . . . And how it always took him an hour to turn away toward sleep after that.

Now she would rustle about her room for an hour or so. It would grow dark. The stars would be out and shining when he tapped on her door and asked if she'd sit on the porch or walk in the park. Then the only way she could possibly know of this third blind and staring eye in his head would be to run her hand in a Braille-like motion there. But her small white fingers had never moved within a thousand miles of that scar which was no more to her than, well, one of those pockmarks off on the full moon tonight. His toe brushed a copy of *Wonder Science Tales.* He snorted. Perhaps if she thought at all of his damaged head—she wrote songs and poems, didn't she, once in a while?—she figured that a long time back a meteor had run and hit him and vanished up there where there were no shrubs or trees, where it was just white, above his eyes. He snorted again and shook his head. Perhaps, perhaps. But however she thought, he would see her only when the sun had set.

He waited another hour, from time to time spitting out the window into the warm summer night.

"Eight-thirty. Here goes."

He opened the hall door and stood for a moment looking back at that nice new toupee hidden in its box. No, he still could not bring himself to wear it.

He stepped along the hall to Miss Naomi Fremwell's door, a door so thinly made it seemed to beat with the sound of her small heart there behind it.

"Miss Fremwell," he whispered.

He wanted to cup her like a small white bird in his great bowled hands, speak soft to her quietness. But then, in wiping the sudden perspiration from his brow, he found again the pit and only at the last quick moment saved himself from falling over, in, and screaming, down! He clapped his hand to that place to cover that emptiness. After he had held his hand tight to the hole for a long moment he was then afraid to pull his hand away. It had changed. Instead of being afraid he might fall in there, he was afraid something terrible, something secret, something private, might gush out and drown him.

He brushed his free hand across her door, disturbing little more than dust.

"Miss Fremwell?"

He looked to see if there were too many lamps lit under her doorsill, the light of which might strike out at him when she swung the door wide. The very thrust of lamplight alone might knock his hand away, and reveal that sunken wound. Then mightn't she peer through it, like a keyhole, into his life?

The light was dim under the doorsill.

He made a fist of one hand and brought it down gently, three times, on Miss Fremwell's door.

The door opened and moved slowly back.

Later, on the front porch, feverishly adjusting and readjusting his senseless legs, perspiring, he tried to work around to asking her to marry him. When the moon rose high, the hole in his brow looked like a leaf shadow fallen there. If he kept one profile to her, the crater did not show; it was hidden away over on the other side of his world. It seemed that when he did this, though, he only had half as many words and felt only half a man.

"Miss Fremwell," he managed to say at last.

"Yes?" She looked at him as if she didn't quite see him.

"Miss Naomi, I don't suppose you ever really noticed me lately."

She waited. He went on.

"I've been noticing you. Fact is, well, I might as well put it right out on the line and get it over with. We been sitting out here on the porch for quite a few months. I mean we've known each other a long time. Sure, you're a good fifteen years younger than me, but would there be anything wrong with our getting engaged, do you think?"

"Thank you very much, Mr. Lemon," she said quickly. She was very polite. "But I——"

"Oh, I know," he said, edging forward with the words. "I know! It's my head, it's always this darn thing up here on my head!"

She looked at his turned-away profile in the uncertain light.

"Why, no, Mr. Lemon, I don't think I would say that, I don't think that's it at all. I have wondered a bit about it, certainly, but I don't think it's an interference in any way. A friend of mine, a very dear friend, married a man once, I recall, who had a wooden leg. She told me she didn't even know he had it after a while."

"It's always this darn hole," cried Mr. Lemon bitterly. He took out his plug of tobacco, looked at it as if he might bite it, decided not to, and put it away. He formed a couple of fists and stared at them bleakly as if they were big rocks. "Well, I'll tell you all about it, Miss Naomi. I'll tell you how it happened."

"You don't have to if you don't want."

"I was married once, Miss Naomi. Yes, I was, darn it. And one day my wife she just took hold of a hammer and hit me right on the head!"

Miss Fremwell gasped. It was as if she had been struck herself.

Mr. Lemon brought one clenching fist down through the warm air.

"Yes, ma'am, she hit me straight on with that hammer, she did. I tell you, the world blew up on me. Everything fell down on me. It was like the house coming down in one heap. That one little hammer buried me, *buried* me! The pain? I can't tell you!"

Miss Fremwell turned in on herself. She shut her eyes and thought, biting her lips. Then she said, "Oh, poor Mr. Lemon."

"She did it so calm," said Mr. Lemon, puzzled. "She just stood over me where I lay on the couch and it was a Tuesday afternoon about two o'clock and she said, 'Andrew, wake up!' and I opened my eyes and looked at her is all and then she hit me with that hammer. Oh, Lord."

"But why?" asked Miss Fremwell.

"For no reason, no reason at all. Oh, what an ornery woman."

"But why should she do a thing like that?" said Miss Fremwell.

"I told you: for no reason."

"Was she crazy?"

"Must of been. Oh, yes, she *must* of been."

"Did you prosecute her?"

"Well, no, I didn't. After all, she didn't know what she was doing."

"Did it knock you out?"

Mr. Lemon paused and there it was again, so clear, so tall, in his mind, the old thought of it. Seeing it there, he put it in words.

"No, I remember just standing up. I stood up and I said to her, 'What'd you do?' and I stumbled toward her. There was a mirror. I saw the hole in my head, deep, and blood coming out. It made an Indian of me. She just stood there, my wife did. And at last she screamed three kinds of horror and dropped that hammer on the floor and ran out the door."

"Did you faint then?"

"No. I didn't faint. I got out on the street some way and I mumbled to somebody I needed a doctor. I got on a bus, mind you, a bus! And paid my fare! And said to leave me by some doctor's house downtown. Everybody screamed, I tell you. I got sort of weak then, and next thing I knew the doctor was working on my head, had it cleaned out like a new thimble, like a bunghole in a barrel . . ."

He reached up and touched that spot now, fingers hovering over it as a delicate tongue hovers over the vacated area where once grew a fine tooth.

"A neat job. The doctor kept staring at me too, as if he expected me to fall down dead any minute."

"How long did you stay in the hospital?"

"Two days. Then I was up and around, feeling no better, no worse. By that time my wife had picked up and skedaddled."

"Oh, my goodness, my goodness," said Miss Fremwell, recovering her breath. "My heart's going like an egg beater. I can hear and feel and see it all, Mr. Lemon. Why, why, oh, *why* did she do it?"

"I already told you, for no reason I could see. She was just took with a notion, I guess."

"But there must have been an argument——?"

Blood drummed in Mr. Lemon's cheeks. He felt that place up there on his head glow like a fiery crater. "There wasn't no argument. I was just sitting, peaceful as you please. I like to sit, my shoes off, my shirt unbuttoned, afternoons."

"Did you—did you know any other women?"

"No, never none!"

"You didn't—drink?"

"Just a nip once in a while, you know how it is."

"Did you gamble?"

"No, no, no!"

"But a hole punched in your head like that, Mr. Lemon, my land, my land! All over nothing?"

"You women are all alike. You see something and right off you expect the worst. I tell you there was no reason. She just fancied hammers."

"What did she say before she hit you?"

"Just 'Wake up, Andrew.' "

"No, before that."

"Nothing. Not for half an hour or an hour, anyway. Oh, she said something about wanting to go shopping for something or other, but I said it was too hot. I'd better lie down, I didn't feel so good. She didn't appreciate how I felt. She must have got mad and thought about it for an hour and grabbed that hammer and come in and gone kersmash. I think the weather got her too."

Miss Fremwell sat back thoughtfully in the lattice shadow, her brows moving slowly up and then slowly down.

"How long were you married to her?"

"A year. I remember we got married in July and in July it was I got sick."

"Sick?"

"I wasn't a well man. I worked in a garage. Then I got these backaches so I couldn't work and had to lie down afternoons. Ellie, she worked in the First National Bank."

"I see," said Miss Fremwell.

"What?"

"Nothing," she said.

"I'm an easy man to get on with. I don't talk too much. I'm easygoing and relaxed. I don't waste money. I'm economical. Even Ellie had to admit that. I don't argue. Why, sometimes Ellie would jaw at me and jaw at me, like bouncing a ball hard on a house, but me not bouncing back. I just sat. I took it easy. What's the use of always stirring around and talking, right?"

Miss Fremwell looked over at Mr. Lemon's brow in the moonlight. Her lips moved, but he could not hear what she said.

Suddenly she straightened up and took a deep breath and blinked around surprised to see the world out beyond the porch lattice. The sounds of traffic came in to the porch now, as if they had been tuned up; they had been so quiet for a time. Miss Fremwell took a deep breath and let it out.

"As you yourself say, Mr. Lemon, nobody ever got anywhere arguing."

"Right!" he said. "I'm easygoing, I tell you——"

But Miss Fremwell's eyes were lidded now and her mouth was strange. He sensed this and tapered off.

A night wind blew fluttering her light summer dress and the sleeves of his shirt.

"It's late," said Miss Fremwell.

"Only nine o'clock!"

"I have to get up early tomorrow."

"But you haven't answered my question yet, Miss Fremwell."

"Question?" She blinked. "Oh, the question. Yes." She rose from the wicker seat. She hunted around in the dark for the screen-door knob. "Oh now, Mr. Lemon, let me think it over."

"That's fair enough," he said. "No use arguing, is there?"

The screen door closed. He heard her find her way down the dark warm hall. He breathed shallowly, feeling of the third eye in his head, the eye that saw nothing.

He felt a vague unhappiness shift around inside his chest like an illness brought on by too much talking. And then he thought of the fresh white gift box waiting with its lid on in his room. He quickened. Opening the screen door, he walked down the silent hall and went into his room. Inside he slipped and almost fell on a slick copy of *True Romance Tales*. He switched on the light excitedly, smiling, fumbled the box open, and lifted the toupee from the tissues. He stood before the bright mirror and followed directions with the spirit gum and tapes and tucked it here and stuck it there and shifted it again and combed it neat. Then he opened the door and walked along the hall to knock for Miss Fremwell.

"Miss Naomi?" he called, smiling.

The light under her door clicked out at the sound of his voice.

He stared at the dark keyhole with disbelief.

"Oh, Miss Naomi?" he said again, quickly.

Nothing happened in the room. It was dark. After a moment he tried the knob experimentally. The knob rattled. He heard Miss Fremwell sigh. He heard her say something.

Again the words were lost. Her small feet tapped to the door. The light came on.

"Yes?" she said, behind the panel.

"Look, Miss Naomi," he entreated. "Open the door. Look."

The bolt of the door snapped back. She jerked the door open about an inch. One of her eyes looked at him sharply.

"Look," he announced proudly, adjusting the toupee so it very definitely covered the sunken crater. He imagined he saw himself in her bureau mirror and was pleased. "Look here, Miss Fremwell!"

She opened the door a bit wider and looked. Then she slammed the door and locked it. From behind the thin paneling her voice was toneless.

"I can still see the hole, Mr. Lemon," she said.

THE FIRST NIGHT OF LENT

So you want to know all the whys and wherefores of the Irish? What shapes them to their Dooms and runs them on their way? you ask. Well, listen, then. For though I've known but a single Irishman in all my life, I knew him, without pause, for one hundred and forty-four consecutive nights. Stand close; perhaps in him you'll see that entire race which marches out of the rains but to vanish through the mists; hold on, here they come! Look out, there they go!

This Irishman, his name was Nick.

During the autumn of 1953, I began a screenplay in Dublin, and each afternoon a hired cab drove me thirty miles out from the River Liffey to the huge grey Georgian country house where my producer-director rode to hounds. There, we discussed my eight pages of daily script through the long fall, winter, and early spring evenings. Then, each midnight, ready to turn back to the Irish Sea and the Royal Hibernian Hotel, I'd wake the operator in the Kilcock village exchange and have her put me through to the warmest, if totally unheated, spot in town.

"Heber Finn's pub?" I'd shout, once connected. "Is Nick there? Could you send him along here, please?"

My mind's eye saw them, the local boys, lined up, peering over the barricade at that freckled mirror so like a frozen winter pond and themselves discovered all drowned and deep under that lovely ice. Amid all their jostlings and their now-here's-a-secret-in-a-stage-whisper-commotion stood Nick, my village driver, his quietness abounding. I heard Heber Finn sing out from the phone. I heard Nick start up and reply:

"Just look at me, headin' for the door!"

Early on, I learned that "headin' for the door" was no nerve-shattering process that might affront dignity or destroy the fine filigree of any argument being woven with great and breathless beauty at Heber Finn's. It was, rather, a gradual disengagement, a leaning of the bulk so one's gravity was diplomatically shifted toward that far empty side of the public room where the door, shunned by all, stood neglected. Meantime, a dozen conversational warps and woofs must be ticked, tied, and labeled so next morn, with hoarse cries of recognition, patterns might be seized and the shuttle thrown with no pause for breath or thought.

Timing it, I figured the long part of Nick's midnight journey—the length of Heber Finn's—took half an hour. The short part—from Finn's to the house where I waited—took but five minutes.

So it was on the night before the first night of Lent. I called. I waited.

And at last, down through the night forest, thrashed the 1931 Chevrolet, peat-turf colored on top like Nick. Car and driver gasped, sighed, wheezed softly, easily, gently as they nudged into the courtyard and I groped down the front steps under a moonless but brightly starred sky.

I peered through the car window at unstirred dark; the dashboard had been dead these many years.

"Nick . . . ?"

"None other," he whispered secretly. "And ain't it a fine warm evenin'?"

The temperature was fifty. But, Nick'd been no nearer Rome than the Tipperary shore line; so weather was relative.

"A fine warm evening." I climbed up front and gave the squealing door its absolutely compulsory, rust-splintering slam. "Nick, how've you been since?"

"Ah." He let the car bulk and grind itself down the forest path. "I got me health. Ain't that all-and-everything with Lent comin' on tomorra?"

"Lent," I mused. "What will you give up for Lent, Nick?"

"I been turnin' it over." Nick sucked his cigarette suddenly; the pink, lined mask of his face blinked off the smoke. "And why not these terrible things ya see in me mouth? Dear as gold-fillin's, and a dread congestor of the lungs they be. Put it all down, add 'em up, and ya got a sick loss by the year's turnin', ya know. So ya'll not find these filthy creatures in me face again the whole time of Lent, and, who knows, after!"

"Bravo!" said I, a non-smoker.

"Bravo, says I to meself," wheezed Nick, one eye flinched with smoke.

"Good luck," I said.

"I'll need it," whispered Nick, "with the Sin's own habit to be broke."

And we moved with firm control, with thoughtful shift of weight, down and around a turfy hollow and through a mist and into Dublin at thirty-one easy miles an hour.

Bear with me while I stress it: Nick was the most careful driver in all God's world, including any sane, small, quiet, butter-and-milk producing country you name.

Above all, Nick stands innocent and sainted when compared to those motorists who key that small switch marked paranoia each time they fuse themselves to their bucket seats in Los Angeles, Mexico City, or Paris. Also, to those blind men who, forsaking tin cups and canes, but still wearing their Hollywood dark-glasses, laugh insanely down the Via Veneto, shaking brake-drum lining like carnival serpentine out their race-car windows. Consider the Roman ruins; surely they are the wreckage strewn and left by those motor-biking otters who, all night beneath your hotel window, shriek down dark Roman alleys, Christians hell-bent for the Colosseum lion pits.

Nick, now. See his easy hands loving the wheel in a

slow clock-like turning as soft and silent as winter con-
stellations snow down the sky. Listen to his mist-breath-
ing voice all night-quiet as he charms the road, his foot a
tenderly benevolent pat on the whispering accelerator,
never a mile under thirty, never two miles over. Nick,
Nick, and his steady boat gentling a mild sweet lake
where all Time slumbers. Look, compare. And bind
such a man to you with summer grasses, gift him with
silver, shake his hand warmly at each journey's end.

"Good night, Nick," I said at the hotel. "See you
tomorrow."

"God willing," whispered Nick.

And he drove softly away.

Let twenty-three hours of sleep, breakfast, lunch,
supper, late night-cap pass. Let hours of writing bad
script into fair script fade to peat mist and rain, and
there I come again, another midnight, out of that Georgian mansion, its door throwing a warm hearth of color
before me as I tread down the steps to feel Braille-wise
in fog for the car I know hulks there; I hear its enlarged
and asthmatic heart gasping in the blind air, and Nick
coughing his "gold by the ounce is not more precious"
cough.

"Ah, there you are, sir!" said Nick.

And I climbed in the sociable front seat and gave the
door its slam. "Nick," I said, smiling.

And then the impossible happened. The car jerked
as if shot from the blazing mouth of a cannon, roared,
took off, bounced, skidded, then cast itself in full, ston-
ing ricochet down the path among shattered bushes and
writhing shadows. I snatched my knees as my head hit
the car top four times.

Nick! I almost shouted. Nick!

Visions of Los Angeles, Mexico City, Paris, jumped
through my mind. I gazed in frank dismay at the speed-
ometer. Eighty, ninety, one hundred kilometers; we
shot out a great blast of gravel behind and hit the main
road, rocked over a bridge and slid down in the midnight streets of Kilcock. No sooner in than out of town at
one hundred ten kilometers, I felt all Ireland's grass put
down its ears when we, with a yell, jumped over a rise.

Nick! I thought, and turned, and there he sat, only one thing the same. On his lips a cigarette burned, blinding first one eye, then the other.

But the rest of Nick, behind the cigarette, was changed as if the Adversary himself had squeezed and molded and fired him with a dark hand. There he was, whirling the wheel round-about, over-around; here we frenzied under trestles, out of tunnels, here knocked crossroad signs spinning like weathercocks in whirlwinds.

Nick's face; the wisdom was drained from it, the eyes neither gentle nor philosophical, the mouth neither tolerant, nor at peace. It was a face washed raw, a scalded, peeled potato, a face more like a blinding searchlight raking its steady and meaningless glare ahead while his quick hands snaked and bit and bit the wheel again to lean us round curves and jump us off cliff after cliff of night.

It's not Nick, I thought, it's his brother. Or a dire thing's come in his life, some destroying affliction or blow, a family sorrow or sickness, yes, that's the answer.

And then Nick spoke, and his voice, it was changed too. Gone was the mellow peat bog, the moist sod, the warm fire in out of the cold rain, gone the gentle grass. Now the voice fairly cracked at me, a clarion, a trumpet, all iron and tin.

"Well, how ya been since!" Nick shouted. "How is it with ya!" he cried.

And the car, it too had suffered violence. It protested the change, yes, for it was an old and much-beaten thing that had done its time and now only wished to stroll along, like a crusty beggar toward sea and sky, careful of its breath and bones. But Nick would have none of that, and cadged the wreck on as if thundering toward Hell, there to warm his cold hands at some special blaze. Nick leaned, the car leaned; great livid gases blew out in fireworks from the exhaust. Nick's frame, my frame, the car's frame, all together, were wracked and shuddered and ticked wildly.

My sanity was saved from being torn clean off the bone by a simple act. My eyes, seeking the cause of our plaguing flight, ran over the man blazing here like a sheet of ignited vapor from the Abyss, and laid hands to the answering clue.

"Nick," I gasped, "it's the first night of Lent!"

"So?" Nick said, surprised.

"So," I said, "remembering your Lenten promise, why's that cigarette in your mouth?"

Nick did not know what I meant for a moment. Then he cast his eyes down, saw the jiggling smoke, and shrugged.

"Ah," he said, "I give up the *other.*"

And suddenly it all came clear.

The other one hundred forty odd nights, at the door of the old Georgian house I had accepted from my employer a fiery douse of scotch or bourbon or some-such drink "against the chill." Then, breathing summer wheat or barley or oats or whatever from my scorched and charcoaled mouth, I had walked out to a cab where sat a man who, during all the long evenings' wait for me to phone for his services, had *lived* in Heber Finn's pub.

Fool! I thought, how could you have forgotten this!

And there in Heber Finn's, during the long hours of lacy talk that was like planting and bringing to crop a garden among busy men, each contributing his seed or flower, and wielding the implements, their tongues, and the raised, foam-hived glasses, their own hands softly curled about the dear drinks, there Nick had taken into himself a mellowness.

And that mellowness had distilled itself down in a slow rain that damped his smoldering nerves and put the wilderness fires in every limb of him out. Those same showers laved his face to leave the tidal marks of wisdom, the lines of Plato and Aeschylus there. The harvest mellowness colored his cheeks, warmed his eyes soft, lowered his voice to a husking mist, and spread in his chest to slow his heart to a gentle jog trot. It rained out his arms to loosen his hard-mouthed hands on the shuddering wheel and sit him with grace and ease in his horse-hair saddle as he gentled us through the fogs that kept us and Dublin apart.

And with the malt on my own tongue, fluming up my sinus with burning vapors, I had never detected the scent of any spirits on my old friend here.

"Ah," said Nick again. "Yes; I give up the *other*."

The last bit of jigsaw fell in place.

Tonight, the first night of Lent.

Tonight, for the first time in all the nights I had driven with him, Nick was sober.

All those other one hundred and forty-odd nights, Nick hadn't been driving careful and easy just for my safety, no, but because of the gentle weight of mellowness sloping now on this side, now on that side of him as we took the long, scything curves.

Oh, who really knows the Irish, say I, and which half of them is which? Nick?—who is Nick?—and what in the world is he? Which Nick's the real Nick, the one that everyone knows?

I will not think on it!

There is only *one* Nick for me. The one that Ireland shaped herself with her weathers and waters, her seedings and harvestings, her brans and mashes, her brews, bottlings, and ladlings-out, her summer-grain-colored pubs astir and advance with the wind in the wheat and barley by night, you may hear the good whisper way out in forest, on bog, as you roll by. That's Nick to the teeth, eye, and heart, to his easygoing hands. If you ask what makes the Irish what they are, I'd point on down the road and tell where you turn to Heber Finn's.

The first night of Lent, and before you count nine, we're in Dublin! I'm out of the cab and it's puttering there at the curb and I lean in to put my money in the hands of my driver. Earnestly, pleadingly, warmly, with all the friendly urging in the world, I look into that fine man's raw, strange, torchlike face.

"Nick," I said.

"Sir!" he shouted.

"Do me a favor," I said.

"Anything!" he shouted.

"Take this extra money," I said, "and buy the biggest bottle of Irish moss you can find. And just before you pick me up tomorrow night, Nick, drink it down, drink it all. Will you do that, Nick? Will you promise me, cross your heart and hope to die, to do that?"

He thought on it, and the very thought damped down the ruinous blaze in his face.

"Ya make it terrible hard on me," he said.

I forced his fingers shut on the money. At last he put it in his pocket and faced silently ahead.

"Good night, Nick," I said. "See you tomorrow."

"God willing," said Nick.

And he drove away.

THE TIME OF GOING AWAY

The thought was three days and three nights growing. During the days he carried it like a ripening peach in his head. During the nights he let it take flesh and sustenance, hung out on the silent air, colored by country moon and country stars. He walked around and around the thought in the silence before dawn. On the fourth morning he reached up an invisible hand, picked it, and swallowed it whole.

He arose as swiftly as possible and burned all his old letters, packed a few clothes in a very small case, and put on his midnight suit and a tie the shiny color of ravens' feathers, as if he were in mourning. He sensed his wife in the door behind him watching his little play with the eyes of a critic who may leap on stage any moment and stop the show. When he brushed past her, he murmured, "Excuse me."

"Excuse me!" she cried. "Is that all you say? Creeping around here, planning a trip!"

"I didn't plan it; it happened," he said. "Three days ago I got this premonition. I knew I was going to die."

"Stop that kind of talk," she said. "It makes me nervous."

The horizon was mirrored softly in his eyes. "I hear my blood running slow. Listening to my bones is like standing in an attic hearing the beams shift and the dust settle."

"You're only seventy-five," said his wife. "You stand on your own two legs, see, hear, eat, and sleep good, don't you? What's all this talk?"

"It's the natural tongue of existence speaking to me," said the old man. "Civilization's got us too far away from our natural selves. Now you take the pagan island-ers——"

"I won't!"

"Everyone knows the pagan islanders got a feel for when it's time to die. They walk around shaking hands with friends and give away all their earthly goods——"

"Don't their wives have a say?"

"They give some of their earthly goods to their wives."

"I should think so!"

"And some to their friends——"

"I'll argue that!"

"And some to their friends. Then they paddle their canoes off into the sunset and never return."

His wife looked high up along him as if he were timber ripe for cutting. "Desertion!" she said.

"No, no, Mildred; death, pure and simple. The Time of Going Away, they call it."

"Did anyone ever charter a canoe and follow to see what those fools were up to?"

"Of course not," said the old man, mildly irritated. "That would spoil everything."

"You mean they had other wives and pretty friends off on another island?"

"No, no, it's just a man needs aloneness, serenity, when his juices turn cold."

"If you could prove those fools really died, I'd shut up." His wife squinted one eye. "Anyone ever *find* their bones on those far islands?"

"The fact is that they just sail on into the sunset, like animals who sense the Great Time at hand. Beyond that, I don't wish to know."

"Well, *I* know," said the old woman. "You been read-ing more articles in the *National Geographic* about the Elephants' Boneyard."

"Graveyard, not Boneyard!" he shouted.

"Graveyard, Boneyard. I thought I burned those magazines; you got some hid?"

"Look here, Mildred," he said severely, seizing the suitcase again. "My mind points north; nothing you say can head me south. I'm tuned to the infinite secret well springs of the primitive soul."

"You're tuned to whatever you read last in that bog trotters' gazette!" She pointed a finger at him. "You think I got no memory?"

His shoulders fell. "Let's not go through the list again, please."

"What about the hairy mammoth episode?" she asked. "When they found that frozen elephant in the Russian tundra thirty years back? You and Sam Hertz, that old fool, with your fine idea of running off to Siberia to corner the world market in canned edible hairy mammoth. You think I don't still hear you saying, 'Imagine the prices members of the National Geographic Society will pay to have the tender meat of the Siberian hairy mammoth, ten thousand years old, ten thousand years extinct right in their homes!' You think my scars have healed from that?"

"I see them clearly," he said.

"You think I've forgotten the time you went out to find the Lost Tribe of the Osseos, or whatever, in Wisconsin some place where you could dogtrot to town Saturday nights and tank up, and fell in that quarry and broke your leg and laid there three nights?"

"Your recall," he said, "is total."

"Then what's this about pagan natives and the Time of Going Away? I'll tell you what it is—it's the Time of Staying at Home! It's the time when fruit don't fall off the trees into your hand, you got to walk to the store for it. And why do we *walk* to the store for it? Someone in this house, I'll name no names, took the car apart like a clock some years back and left it strewn all down the yard. I've raised auto parts in my garden ten years come Thursday. Ten more years and all that's left of our car is little heaps of rust. Look out that window! It's leaf-raking-and-burning time. It's chopping-trees-and-sawing-wood-for-the-fire time. It's clean-out-stoves-

and-hang-storm-doors-and-windows time. It's shingle-the-roof-time, *that's* what it is, and if you think you're out to escape it, think again!"

He placed his hand to his chest. "It pains me you have so little trust in my natural sensitivity to oncoming Doom."

"It pains *me* that *National Geographics* fall in the hands of crazy old men. I see you read those pages then fall into those dreams I always have to sweep up after. Those *Geographic* and *Popular Mechanics* publishers should be forced to see all the half-finished rowboats, helicopters, and one-man batwing gliders in our attic, garage, and cellar. Not only *see,* but cart them home!"

"Chatter on," he said. "I stand before you, a white stone sinking in the tides of Oblivion. For God's sake, woman, can't I drag myself off to die in peace?"

"Plenty of time for Oblivion when I find you stone cold across the kindling pile."

"Jesting Pilate!" he said. "Is recognition of one's own mortality nothing but vanity?"

"You're chewing it like a plug of tobacco."

"Enough!" he said. "My earthly goods are stacked on the back porch. Give them to the Salvation Army."

"The *Geographics* too?"

"Yes, damn it, the *Geographics!* Now stand aside!"

"If you're going to die, you won't need that suitcase full of clothing," she said.

"Hands off, woman! It may take some few hours. Am I to be stripped of my last creature comforts? This should be a tender scene of parting. Instead—bitter recriminations, sarcasm, doubt strewn to every wind."

"All right," she said. "Go spend a cold night in the woods."

"I'm not necessarily going to the woods."

"Where else is there for a man in Illinois to go to die?"

"Well," he said and paused. "Well, there's always the open highway."

"And be run down, of course; I'd forgotten that."

"No, no!" He squeezed his eyes shut, then opened them again. "The empty side roads leading nowhere, everywhere, through night forests, wilderness, to distant lakes. . . ."

"Now, you're not going to go rent a canoe, are you, and paddle off? Remember the time you tipped over and almost drowned at Fireman's Pier?"

"Who said anything about canoes?"

"You did! Pagan islanders, you said, paddling off into the great unknown."

"That's the South Seas! Here a man has to strike off on foot to find his natural source, seek his natural end. I might walk north along the Lake Michigan shore, the dunes, the wind, the big breakers there."

"Willie, Willie," she said softly, shaking her head. "Oh, Willie, Willie, what will I do with you?"

He lowered his voice. "Just let me have my head," he said.

"Yes," she said, quietly. "Yes." And tears came to her eyes.

"Now, now," he said.

"Oh, Willie . . ." She looked a long while at him. "Do you really think with all your heart you're not going to live?"

He saw himself reflected, small but perfect, in her eye, and looked away uneasily. "I thought all night about the universal tide that brings man in and takes him out. Now it's morning and good-by."

"Good-by?" She looked as if she'd never heard the word before.

His voice was unsteady. "Of course, if you absolutely insist I stay, Mildred——"

"No!" She braced herself and blew her nose. "You feel what you feel; I can't fight that!"

"You *sure?*" he said.

"You're the one that's sure, Willie," she said. "Get on along now. Take your heavy coat; the nights are cold."

"But——" he said.

She ran and brought his coat and kissed his cheek and drew back quickly before he could enclose her in his bear hug. He stood there working his mouth, gazing at the big armchair by the fire. She threw open the front door. "You got food?"

"I won't need . . ." He paused. "I got a boiled ham

sandwich and some pickles in my case. Just one. That's all I figured I'd . . ."

And then he was out the door and down the steps and along the path toward the woods. He turned and was going to say something but thought better of it, waved, and went on.

"Now, Will," she called. "Don't overdo. Don't make too much distance the first hour! You get tired, sit down! You get hungry, eat! And . . ."

But here she had to stop and turn away and get out her handkerchief.

A moment later she looked up the path and it looked as though nobody had passed there in the last ten thousand years. It was so empty she had to go in and shut the door.

Nighttime, nine o'clock, nine-fifteen, stars out, moon round, house lights strawberry-colored through the curtains, the chimney blowing long comet tails of fireworks, sighing warm. Down the chimney, sounds of pots and pans and cutlery, fire on the hearth, like a great orange cat. In the kitchen, the big iron cookstove full of jumping flames, pans boiling, bubbling, frying, vapors and steams in the air. From time to time the old woman turned and her eyes listened and her mouth listened, wide, to the world outside this house, this fire, and this food.

Nine-thirty and, from a great distance away from the house, a solid whacking, chunking sound.

The old woman straightened up and laid down a spoon.

Outside, the dull solid blows came again and again in the moonlight. The sound went on for three or four minutes, during which she hardly moved except to tighten her mouth or her fists with each solid chunking blow. When the sounds stopped, she threw herself at the stove, the table, stirring, pouring, lifting, carrying, setting down.

She finished just as new sounds came from the dark land outside the windows. Footsteps came slowly up the path, heavy shoes weighed the front porch.

She went to the door and waited for a knock.

None came.

She waited a full minute.

Outside on the porch a great bulk stirred and shifted from side to side uneasily.

Finally she sighed and called sharply at the door. "Will, is that you breathing out there?"

No answer. Only a kind of sheepish silence behind the door.

She snatched the door wide.

The old man stood there, an incredible stack of cordwood in his arm. His voice came from behind the stack.

"Saw smoke in the chimney; figured you might need wood," he said.

She stood aside. He came in and placed the wood carefully by the hearth, not looking at her.

She looked out on the porch and picked up the suitcase and brought it in and shut the door.

She saw him sitting at the dinner table.

She stirred the soup on the stove to a great boiling whirl.

"Roast beef in the oven?" he asked quietly.

She opened the oven door. The steam breathed across the room to wrap him up. He closed his eyes, seated there, bathed.

"What's that other smell, the burning?" he asked a moment later.

She waited, back turned, and finally said, *"National Geographics."*

He nodded slowly, saying nothing.

Then the food was on the table, warm and tremulous, and there was a moment of silence after she sat down and looked at him. She shook her head. She looked at him. Then she shook her head again silently.

"Do you want to ask the blessing?" she said.

"You," he said.

They sat there in the warm room by the bright fire and bowed their heads and closed their eyes. She smiled and began.

"Thank you, Lord . . ."

ALL SUMMER IN A DAY

"Ready?"

"Ready."

"Now?"

"Soon."

"Do the scientists really know? Will it happen today, will it?"

"Look, look; see for yourself!"

The children pressed to each other like so many roses, so many weeds, intermixed, peering out for a look at the hidden sun.

It rained.

It had been raining for seven years; thousands upon thousands of days compounded and filled from one end to the other with rain, with the drum and gush of water, with the sweet crystal fall of showers and the concussion of storms so heavy they were tidal waves come over the islands. A thousand forests had been crushed under the rain and grown up a thousand times to be crushed again. And this was the way life was forever on the planet Venus, and this was the schoolroom of the children of the rocket men and women who had come to a raining world to set up civilization and live out their lives.

"It's stopping, it's stopping!"

"Yes, yes!"

Margot stood apart from them, from these children who could never remember a time when there wasn't rain and rain and rain. They were all nine years old, and if there had been a day, seven years ago, when the sun came out for an hour and showed its face to the stunned world, they could not recall. Sometimes, at night, she heard them stir, in remembrance, and she knew they were dreaming and remembering gold or a yellow crayon or a coin large enough to buy the world with. She knew they thought they remembered a warmness, like a blushing in the face, in the body, in the arms and legs and trembling hands. But then they always awoke to the tatting drum, the endless shaking down of clear bead necklaces upon the roof, the walk, the gardens, the forests, and their dreams were gone.

All day yesterday they had read in class about the sun. About how like a lemon it was, and how hot. And they had written small stories or essays or poems about it:

> *I think the sun is a flower,*
> *That blooms for just one hour.*

That was Margot's poem, read in a quiet voice in the still classroom while the rain was falling outside.

"Aw, you didn't write that!" protested one of the boys.

"I did," said Margot. "I did."

"William!" said the teacher.

But that was yesterday. Now the rain was slackening, and the children were crushed in the great thick windows.

"Where's teacher?"

"She'll be back."

"She'd better hurry, we'll miss it!"

They turned on themselves, like a feverish wheel, all tumbling spokes.

Margot stood alone. She was a very frail girl who looked as if she had been lost in the rain for years and the rain had washed out the blue from her eyes and the red from her mouth and the yellow from her hair. She was an old photograph dusted from an album, whitened away, and if she spoke at all her voice would be a ghost. Now she stood, separate, staring at the rain and the loud wet world beyond the huge glass.

"What're *you* looking at?" said William.

Margot said nothing.

"Speak when you're spoken to." He gave her a shove. But she did not move; rather she let herself be moved only by him and nothing else.

They edged away from her, they would not look at her. She felt them go away. And this was because she would play no games with them in the echoing tunnels of the underground city. If they tagged her and ran, she stood blinking after them and did not follow. When the class sang songs about happiness and life and games her lips barely moved. Only when they sang about the sun and the summer did her lips move as she watched the drenched windows.

And then, of course, the biggest crime of all was that she had come here only five years ago from Earth, and she remembered the sun and the way the sun was and the sky was when she was four in Ohio. And they, they had been on Venus all their lives, and they had been only two years old when last the sun came out and had long since forgotten the color and heat of it and the way it really was. But Margot remembered.

"It's like a penny," she said once, eyes closed.

"No it's not!" the children cried.

"It's like a fire," she said, "in the stove."

"You're lying, you don't remember!" cried the children.

But she remembered and stood quietly apart from all of them and watched the patterning windows. And once, a month ago, she had refused to shower in the school shower rooms, had clutched her hands to her ears and over her head, screaming the water mustn't touch her head. So after that, dimly, dimly, she sensed it, she was different and they knew her difference and kept away.

There was talk that her father and mother were taking her back to Earth next year; it seemed vital to her that they do so, though it would mean the loss of thousands of dollars to her family. And so, the children hated her for all these reasons of big and little consequence. They hated her pale snow face, her waiting silence, her thinness, and her possible future.

"Get away!" The boy gave her another push. "What're you waiting for?"

Then, for the first time, she turned and looked at him. And what she was waiting for was in her eyes.

"Well, don't wait around here!" cried the boy savagely. "You won't see nothing!"

Her lips moved.

"Nothing!" he cried. "It was all a joke, wasn't it?" He turned to the other children. "Nothing's happening today. *Is* it?"

They all blinked at him and then, understanding, laughed and shook their heads. "Nothing, nothing!"

"Oh, but," Margot whispered, her eyes helpless. "But this is the day, the scientists predict, they say, they *know*, the sun . . ."

"All a joke!" said the boy, and seized her roughly. "Hey, everyone, let's put her in a closet before teacher comes!"

"No," said Margot, falling back.

They surged about her, caught her up and bore her, protesting, and then pleading, and then crying, back into a tunnel, a room, a closet, where they slammed and locked the door. They stood looking at the door and saw it tremble from her beating and throwing herself against it. They heard her muffled cries. Then, smiling, they turned and went out and back down the tunnel, just as the teacher arrived.

"Ready, children?" She glanced at her watch.

"Yes!" said everyone.

"Are we all here?"

"Yes!"

The rain slackened still more.

They crowded to the huge door.

The rain stopped.

It was as if, in the midst of a film concerning an avalanche, a tornado, a hurricane, a volcanic eruption, something had, first, gone wrong with the sound apparatus, thus muffling and finally cutting off all noise, all of the blasts and repercussions and thunders, and then, second, ripped the film from the projector and inserted in its place a peaceful tropical slide which did not move or tremor. The world ground to a standstill. The silence was so immense and unbelievable that you felt your ears had been stuffed or you had lost your hearing altogether. The children put their hands to their ears. They stood apart. The door slid back and the smell of the silent, waiting world came in to them.

The sun came out.

It was the color of flaming bronze and it was very large. And the sky around it was a blazing blue tile color. And the jungle burned with sunlight as the children, released from their spell, rushed out, yelling, into the springtime.

"Now, don't go too far," called the teacher after them. "You've only two hours, you know. You wouldn't want to get caught out!"

But they were running and turning their faces up to the sky and feeling the sun on their cheeks like a warm iron; they were taking off their jackets and letting the sun burn their arms.

"Oh, it's better than the sun lamps, isn't it?"

"Much, much better!"

They stopped running and stood in the great jungle that covered Venus, that grew and never stopped growing, tumultuously, even as you watched it. It was a nest of octopi, clustering up great arms of fleshlike weed, wavering, flowering in this brief spring. It was the color of rubber and ash, this jungle, from the many years without sun. It was the color of stones and white cheeses and ink, and it was the color of the moon.

The children lay out, laughing, on the jungle mattress, and heard it sigh and squeak under them, resilient and alive. They ran among the trees, they slipped and fell, they pushed each other, they played hide-and-seek and tag, but most of all they squinted at the sun until tears ran down their faces, they put their hands up to that yellowness and that amazing blueness and they breathed of the fresh, fresh air and listened and listened to the silence which suspended them in a blessed sea of no sound and no motion. They looked at everything and savored everything. Then, wildly, like animals escaped

from their caves, they ran and ran in shouting circles.
They ran for an hour and did not stop running.

And then——

In the midst of their running one of the girls wailed.

Everyone stopped.

The girl, standing in the open, held out her hand.

"Oh, look, look," she said, trembling.

They came slowly to look at her opened palm.

In the center of it, cupped and huge, was a single
raindrop.

She began to cry, looking at it.

They glanced quietly at the sky.

"Oh. Oh."

A few cold drops fell on their noses and their cheeks
and their mouths. The sun faded behind a stir of mist. A
wind blew cool around them. They turned and started
to walk back toward the underground house, their
hands at their sides, their smiles vanishing away.

A boom of thunder startled them and like leaves
before a new hurricane, they tumbled upon each other
and ran. Lightning struck ten miles away, five miles
away, a mile, a half mile. The sky darkened into midnight in a flash.

They stood in the doorway of the underground for a
moment until it was raining hard. Then they closed the
door and heard the gigantic sound of the rain falling in
tons and avalanches, everywhere and forever.

"Will it be seven more years?"

"Yes. Seven."

Then one of them gave a little cry.

"Margot!"

"What?"

"She's still in the closet where we locked her."

"Margot."

They stood as if someone had driven them, like so
many stakes, into the floor. They looked at each other
and then looked away. They glanced out at the world
that was raining now and raining and raining steadily.
They could not meet each other's glances. Their faces
were solemn and pale. They looked at their hands and
feet, their faces down.

"Margot."

.One of the girls said, "Well . . . ?"

No one moved.

"Go on," whispered the girl.

They walked slowly down the hall in the sound of cold rain. They turned through the doorway to the room in the sound of the storm and thunder, lightning on their faces, blue and terrible. They walked over to the closet door slowly and stood by it.

Behind the closet door was only silence.

They unlocked the door, even more slowly, and let Margot out.

THE GIFT

Tomorrow would be Christmas, and even while the three of them rode to the rocket port the mother and father were worried. It was the boy's first flight into space, his very first time in a rocket, and they wanted everything to be perfect. So when, at the custom's table, they were forced to leave behind his gift which exceeded the weight limit by no more than a few ounces and the little tree with the lovely white candles, they felt themselves deprived of the season and their love.

The boy was waiting for them in the Terminal room. Walking toward him, after their unsuccessful clash with the Interplanetary officials, the mother and father whispered to each other.

"What shall we do?"

"Nothing, nothing. What *can* we do?"

"Silly rules!"

"And he so wanted the tree!"

The siren gave a great howl and people pressed forward into the Mars Rocket. The mother and father walked at the very last, their small pale son between them, silent.

"I'll think of something," said the father.

"What . . . ?" asked the boy.

And the rocket took off and they were flung headlong into dark space.

The rocket moved and left fire behind and left Earth behind on which the date was December 24, 2052, heading out into a place where there was no time at all, no month, no year, no hour. They slept away the rest of the first "day." Near midnight, by their Earth-time New York watches, the boy awoke and said, "I want to go look out the porthole."

There was only one port, a "window" of immensely thick glass of some size, up on the next deck.

"Not quite yet," said the father. "I'll take you up later."

"I want to see where we are and where we're going."

"I want you to wait for a reason," said the father.

He had been lying awake, turning this way and that, thinking of the abandoned gift, the problem of the season, the lost tree and the white candles. And at last, sitting up, no more than five minutes ago, he believed he had found a plan. He need only carry it out and this journey would be fine and joyous indeed.

"Son," he said, "in exactly one half hour it will be Christmas."

"Oh," said the mother, dismayed that he had mentioned it. Somehow she had rather hoped that the boy would forget.

The boy's face grew feverish and his lips trembled. "I know, I know. Will I get a present, will I? Will I have a tree? You promised——"

"Yes, yes, all that, and more," said the father.

The mother started. "But——"

"I mean it," said the father. "I really mean it. All and more, much more. Excuse me, now. I'll be back."

He left them for about twenty minutes. When he came back he was smiling. "Almost time."

"Can I hold your watch?" asked the boy, and the watch was handed over and he held it ticking in his fingers as the rest of the hour drifted by in fire and silence and unfelt motion.

"It's Christmas *now!* Christmas! Where's my present?"

"Here we go," said the father and took his boy by the

shoulder and led him from the room, down the hall, up a rampway, his wife following.

"I don't understand," she kept saying.

"You will. Here we are," said the father.

They had stopped at the closed door of a large cabin. The father tapped three times and then twice in a code. The door opened and the light in the cabin went out and there was a whisper of voices.

"Go on in, son," said the father.

"It's dark."

"I'll hold your hand. Come on, Mama."

They stepped into the room and the door shut, and the room was very dark indeed. And before them loomed a great glass eye, the porthole, a window four feet high and six feet wide, from which they could look out into space.

The boy gasped.

Behind him the father and the mother gasped with him, and then in the dark room some people began to sing.

"Merry Christmas, son," said the father.

And the voices in the room sang the old, the familiar carols, and the boy moved forward slowly until his face was pressed against the cool glass of the port. And he stood there for a long long time, just looking and looking out into space and the deep night at the burning and the burning of ten billion billion white and lovely candles . . .

THE GREAT COLLISION
OF MONDAY LAST

The man staggered through the flung-wide doors of Heber Finn's pub as if struck by lightning. Reeling, blood on his face, coat, and torn pants, his moan froze every customer at the bar. For a time you heard only the soft foam popping in the lacy mugs, as the customers turned, some faces pale, some pink, some veined and wattle-red. Every eyelid down the line gave a blink.

The stranger swayed in his ruined clothes, eyes wide, lips trembling. The drinkers clenched their fist. Yes! they cried, silently—go on, man! what *happened?*

The stranger leaned far out on the air.

"Collision," he whispered. "Collision on the road." Then, chopped at the knees, he fell.

"Collision!" A dozen men rushed at the body.

"Kelly!" Heber Finn vaulted the bar. "Get to the road! Mind the victim; easy does it! Joe, run for the Doc!"

"Wait!" said a quiet voice.

From the private stall at the dark end of the pub, the cubby where a philosopher might brood, a dark man blinked out at the crowd.

"Doc!" cried Heber Finn. "It's you!"

Doctor and men hustled out into the night.

"Collision . . ." The man on the floor twitched his lips.

"Softly, boys." Heber Finn and two others gentled the victim atop the bar. He looked handsome as death on the fine inlaid wood with the prismed mirror making him two dread calamities for the price of one.

Outside on the steps, the crowd halted, shocked as if an ocean had sunk Ireland in the dusk and now bulked all about them. Fog in fifty-foot rollers and breakers put out the moon and stars. Blinking, cursing, the men leapt out to vanish in the deeps.

Behind, in the bright doorframe, a young man stood. He was neither red enough nor pale enough of face, nor dark enough or light enough in spirit to be Irish, and so must be American. He was. That established, it follows he dreaded interfering with what seemed village ritual. Since arriving in Ireland, he could not shake the feeling that at all times he was living stage center of the Abbey Theatre. Now, not knowing his lines, he could only stare after the rushing men.

"But," he protested weakly, "I didn't hear any cars on the road."

"You did not!" said an old man almost pridefully. Arthritis limited him to the top step where he teetered, shouting at the white tides where his friends had submerged. "Try the crossroad, boys! That's where it most often does!"

"The crossroad!" Far and near, footsteps rang.

"Nor," said the American, "did I hear a collision."

The old man snorted with contempt. "Ah, we don't be great ones for commotion, nor great crashing sounds. But collision you'll see if you step on out there. Walk, now, don't run! It's the devil's own night. Running blind you might hit into Kelly, beyond, who's a great one for running just to squash his lungs. Or you might head on with Feeney, too drunk to find any road, never mind what's *on* it! You got a torch, a flash? Blind you'll be, but use it. Walk now, you *hear?*"

The American groped through the fog to his car, found his flashlight, and, immersed in the night beyond Heber Finn's, made direction by the heavy clubbing of shoes and a rally of voices ahead. A hundred yards off in eternity the men approached, grunting whispers: "Easy now!" "Ah, the shameful blight!" "Hold on, don't jiggle him!"

The American was flung aside by a steaming lump of men who swept suddenly from the fog, bearing atop themselves a crumpled object. He glimpsed a blood-stained and livid face high up there, then someone cracked his flashlight down.

By instinct, sensing the far whiskey-colored light of Heber Finn's, the catafalque surged on toward that fixed and familiar harbor.

Behind came dim shapes and a chilling insect rattle.

"Who's that!" cried the American.

"Us, with the vehicles," someone husked. "You might say—we got the collision."

The flashlight fixed them. The American gasped. A moment later, the battery failed.

But not before he had seen two village lads jogging along with no trouble at all, easily, lightly, toting under their arms two ancient black bicycles minus front and tail lights.

"What . . . ?" said the American.

But the lads trotted off, the accident with them. The fog closed in. The American stood abandoned on an empty road, his flashlight dead in his hand.

By the time he opened the door at Heber Finn's, both "bodies" as they called them, had been stretched on the bar.

"We got the bodies on the bar," said the old man, turning as the American entered.

And there was the crowd lined up not for drinks, but blocking the way so the Doc had to shove sidewise from one to another of these relics of blind driving by night on the misty roads.

"One's Pat Nolan," whispered the old man. "Not working at the moment. The other's Mr. Peevey from Meynooth, in candy and cigarettes mostly." Raising his voice, "Are they dead now, Doc?"

"Ah, be still, won't you?" The Doc resembled a sculptor troubled at finding some way to finish up two full-length marble statues at once. "Here, let's put one victim on the floor!"

"The floor's a tomb," said Heber Finn. "He'll catch

his death down there. Best leave him up where the warm air gathers from our talk."

"But," said the American quietly, confused, "I've never heard of an accident like this in all my life. Are you sure there were absolutely no cars? Only these two men on their *bikes?*"

"Only!" The old man shouted. "Great God, man, a fellow working up a drizzling sweat can pump along at sixty kilometers. With a long downhill glide his bike hits ninety or ninety-five! So here they come, these two, no front or tail lights——"

"Isn't there a law against that?"

"To hell with government interference! So here the two come, no lights, flying home from one town to the next. Thrashing like Sin Himself's at their behinds! Both going opposite ways but both on the same side of the road. Always ride the wrong side of the road, it's safer, they say. But look on these lads, fair destroyed by all that official palaver. Why? Don't you see? One remembered it, but the other didn't! Better if the officials kept their mouths shut! For here the two be, dying."

"Dying?" The American stared.

"Well, think on it, man! What stands between two able-bodied hell-bent fellas jumping along the path from Kilcock to Meynooth? Fog! Fog is all! Only fog to keep their skulls from bashing together. Why, look when two chaps hit at a cross like that, it's like a strike in bowling alleys, tenpins flying! Bang! There go your friends, nine feet up, heads together like dear chums met, flailing the air, their bikes clenched like two tomcats. Then they all fall down and just lay there, feeling around for the Dark Angel."

"Surely these men won't——"

"Oh, won't they? Why, last year alone in all the Free State no night passed some soul did not meet in fatal collision with another!"

"You mean to say over three hundred Irish bicyclists die every year, hitting each other?"

"God's truth and a pity."

"I never ride my bike nights." Heber Finn eyed the bodies. "I walk."

"But still then the damn bikes run you down!" said

the old man. "Awheel or afoot, some idiot's always panting up Doom the other way. They'd sooner split you down the seam than wave hello. Oh, the brave men I've seen ruined or half-ruined or worse, and headaches their lifetimes after." The old man trembled his eyelids shut. "You might almost think, mightn't you, that human beings was not made to handle such delicate instruments of power."

"Three hundred dead each year." The American seemed dazed.

"And that don't count the 'walking wounded' by the thousands every fortnight who, cursing, throw their bikes in the bog forever and take government pensions to salve their all-but-murdered bodies."

"Should we stand here talking?" The American gestured helplessly toward the victims. "Is there a hospital?"

"On a night with no moon," Heber Finn continued, "best walk out through the middle of fields and be damned to the evil roads! That's how I have survived into this my fifth decade."

"Ah . . ." The men stirred restlessly.

The Doc, sensing he had withheld information too long, feeling his audience drift away, now snatched their attention back by straightening up briskly and exhaling.

"Well!"

The pub quickened into silence.

"This chap here——" The Doc pointed. "Bruises, lacerations, and agonizing backaches for two weeks running. As for the other lad, however——" And here the Doc let himself scowl for a long moment at the paler one there looking rouged, waxed, and ready for final rites. "Concussion."

"Concussion!"

The quiet wind rose and fell in the silence.

"He'll survive if we run him quick now to Meynooth Clinic. So whose car will volunteer?"

The crowd turned as a staring body toward the American. He felt the gentle shift as he was drawn from outside the ritual to its deep and innermost core. He flushed, remembering the front of Heber Finn's pub, where seventeen bicycles and one automobile were parked at this moment. Quickly, he nodded.

"There! A volunteer, lads! Quick now, hustle this boy —gently!—to our good friend's vehicle!"

The men reached out to lift the body, but froze when the American coughed. They saw him circle his hand to all, and tip his cupped fingers to his lips. They gasped in soft surprise. The gesture was not done when drinks foamed down the bar.

"For the road!"

And now even the luckier victim, suddenly revived, face like cheese, found a mug gentled to his hand with whispers.

"Here, lad, here . . . tell us . . ."

". . . what happened, eh? eh?"

Then the body was gone off the bar, the potential wake over, the room empty save for the American, the Doc, the revived lad, and two softly cudgeling friends. Outside you could hear the crowd putting the one serious result of the great collision into the volunteer's car.

The Doc said, "Finish your drink, Mr.——?"

"McGuire," said the American.

"By the saints, he's Irish!"

No, thought the American, far away, looking numbly around at the pub, at the recovered bicyclist seated, waiting for the crowd to come back and mill about him, seeing the blood-spotted floor, the two bicycles tilted near the door like props from a vaudeville turn, the dark night waiting outside with its improbable fog, listening to the roll and cadence and gentle equilibrium of these voices balanced each in its own throat and environment. No, thought the American named McGuire, I'm almost, but certainly not quite, Irish . . .

"Doctor," he heard himself say as he placed money on the bar, "do you often have auto wrecks, collisions, between people in *cars?*"

"Not in our town!" The Doc nodded scornfully east. "If you like that sort of thing, now, Dublin's the very place for it!"

Crossing the pub together, the Doc took his arm as if to impart some secret which would change his Fates. Thus steered, the American found the stout inside himself a shifting weight he must accommodate from side to side as the Doc breathed soft in his ear.

"Look here now, McGuire, admit it, you've driven but little in Ireland, right? Then, listen! Driving to Meynooth, fog and all, you'd best take it fast! Raise a din! Why? Scare the cyclists and cows off the path, both sides! If you drive slow, why you'll creep up on and do away with dozens before they know what took them off! And another thing: when a car approaches, douse your lights! Pass each other, lights out, in safety. Them devil's own lights have put out more eyes and demolished more innocents than all of seeing's worth. Is it clear, now? Two things: speed, and douse your lights when cars loom up!"

At the door, the American nodded. Behind him he heard the one victim, settled easy in his chair, working the stout around on his tongue, thinking, preparing, beginning his tale:

"Well, I'm on me way home, blithe as you please, asailing downhill near the cross when——"

Outside in the car with the other collision victim moaning softly in the back seat, the Doc offered final advice.

"Always wear a cap, lad. If you want to walk nights ever, on the roads, that is. A cap'll save you the frightful migraines should you meet Kelly or Moran or any other hurtling full-tilt the other way, full of fiery moss and hard-skulled from birth. Even on foot, these men are dangerous. So you see, there's rules for pedestrians too in Ireland, and wear a cap at night is Number One!"

Without thinking, the American fumbled under the seat, brought forth a brown tweed cap purchased in Dublin that day, and put it on. Adjusting it, he looked out at the dark mist boiling across the night. He listened to the empty highway waiting for him ahead, quiet, quiet, quiet, but not quiet somehow. For hundreds of long strange miles up and down all of Ireland he saw a thousand crossroads covered with a thousand fogs through which one thousand tweed-capped, grey-mufflered phantoms wheeled along in mid-air, singing, shouting, and smelling of Guinness Stout.

He blinked. The phantoms shadowed off. The road lay empty and dark and waiting.

Taking a deep breath, shutting his eyes, the American named McGuire turned the key in the switch and stepped on the starter.

THE LITTLE MICE

"They're very odd," I said. "The little Mexican couple."

"How do you mean?" asked my wife.

"Never a sound," I said. "Listen."

Ours was a house deep back in among tenements, to which another half house had been added. When my wife and I purchased the house, we rented the additional quarters which lay walled up against one side of our parlor. Now, listening at this particular wall, we heard our hearts beat.

"I know they're home," I whispered. "But in the three years they've lived here I've never heard a dropped pan, a spoken word, or the sound of a light switch. Good God, what are they *doing* in there?"

"I'd never thought," said my wife. "It *is* peculiar."

"Only one light on, that same dim little blue twenty-five-watt bulb they burn in their parlor. If you walk by and peer in their front door, there *he* is, sitting in his armchair, not saying a word, his hands in his lap. There she is, sitting in the other armchair, looking at him, saying nothing. They don't move."

"At first glance I always think they're not home," said my wife. "Their parlor's so dark. But if you stare long enough, your eyes get used to it and you can make them out, sitting there."

"Some day," I said, "I'm going to run in, turn on their lights, and yell! My God, if *I* can't stand their silence, how can they? They can talk, can't they?"

"When he pays the rent each month, he says hello."

"What else?"

"Good-by."

I shook my head. "When we meet in the alley he smiles and runs."

My wife and I sat down for an evening of reading, the radio, and talk. "Do they have a radio?"

"No radio, television, telephone. Not a book, magazine, or paper in their house."

"Ridiculous!"

"Don't get so excited."

"I know, but you can't sit in a dark room two or three years and not speak, not listen to a radio, not read or even eat, can you? I've never smelled a steak or an egg frying. Damn it, I don't believe I've ever heard them go to bed!"

"They're doing it to mystify us, dear."

"They're succeeding!"

I went for a walk around the block. It was a nice summer evening. Returning, I glanced idly in their front door. The dark silence was there, and the heavy shapes, sitting, and the little blue light burning. I stood a long time, finishing my cigarette. It was only in turning to go that I saw him in the doorway, looking out with his bland, plump face. He didn't move. He just stood there, watching me.

"Evening," I said.

Silence. After a moment, he turned, moving away into the dark room.

In the morning, the little Mexican left the house at seven o'clock, alone, hurrying down the alley, observing the same silence he kept in his rooms. She followed at eight o'clock, walking carefully, all lumpy under her dark coat, a black hat balanced on her frizzy, beauty-parlor hair. They had gone to work this way, remote and silent, for years.

"Where do they work?" I asked at breakfast.

"He's a blast-furnace man at U.S. Steel here. She sews in a dress loft somewhere."

"That's hard work."

I typed a few pages of my novel, read, idled; typed some more. At five in the afternoon I saw the little Mexican woman come home, unlock her door, hurry inside, hook the screen, and lock the door tight.

He arrived at six sharp in a rush. Once on their back porch, however, he became infinitely patient. Quietly, raking his hand over the screen, lightly, like a fat mouse scrabbling, he waited. At last she let him in. I did not see their mouths move.

Not a sound during suppertime. No frying. No rattle of dishes. Nothing.

I saw the small blue lamp go on.

"That's how he is," said my wife, "when he pays the rent. Raps so quietly I don't hear. I just happen to glance out the window and there he is. God knows how long he's waited, standing, sort of 'nibbling' at the door."

Two nights later, on a beautiful July evening, the little Mexican man came out on the back porch and looked at me, working in the garden and said, "You're crazy!" He turned to my wife. "You're crazy too!" He waved his plump hand quietly. "I don't like you. Too much *noise.* I don't like you. You're crazy."

He went back into his little house.

August, September, October, November. The "mice," as we now referred to them, lay quietly in their dark nest. Once my wife gave him some old magazines with his rent receipt. He accepted these politely, with a smile and a bow, but no word. An hour later she saw him put the magazines in the yard incinerator and strike a match.

The next day he paid the rent three months in advance, no doubt figuring that he would only have to see us up close once every twelve weeks. When I saw him on the street he crossed quickly to the other side to greet an imaginary friend. She, similarly, ran by me, smiling wildly, bewildered, nodding. I never got nearer than twenty yards to her. If there was plumbing to be fixed in their house, they went silently forth on their own, not telling us, and brought back a plumber who worked, it seemed, with a flashlight.

"God damnedest thing," he told me when I saw him in the alley. "Damn fool place there hasn't got any light bulbs in the sockets. When I asked where they all were, damn it, they just *smiled* at me!"

I lay at night thinking about the little mice. Where were they from? Mexico, yes. What part? A farm, a small village, somewhere by a river? Certainly no city or town. But a place where there were stars and the normal lights and darknesses, the goings and comings of the moon and the sun they had known the better part of their lives. Yet here they were, far, far away from home, in an impossible city, he sweating out the hell of blast furnaces all day, she bent to jittering needles in a sewing loft. They came home then to this block, through a loud city, avoided clanging streetcars and saloons that screamed like red parrots along their way. Through a million shriekings they ran back to their parlor, their blue light, their comfortable chairs, and their silence. I often thought of this. Late at night I felt if I put out my hand, in the dark of my own bedroom, I might feel adobe and hear a cricket and a river running by under the moon and someone singing softly to a faint guitar.

Late one December evening the next-door tenement burned. Flames roared at the sky, bricks fell in avalanches, and sparks littered the roof where the quiet mice lived.

I pounded their door.

"Fire!" I cried. "Fire!"

They sat motionless in their blue-lighted room.

I pounded violently. "You *hear?* Fire!"

The fire engines arrived. They gushed water into the tenement. More bricks fell. Four of them smashed holes in the little house. I climbed to the roof, extinguished the small fires there, and scrambled down, my face dirty and my hands cut. The door to the little house opened. The quiet little Mexican and his wife stood in the doorway, solid and unmoved.

"Let me in!" I cried. "There's a hole in your roof; some sparks may have fallen in your bedroom!"

I pulled the door wide, pushed past them.

"No!" the little man grunted.

"Ah!" the little woman ran in a circle like a broken toy.

I was inside with a flashlight. The little man seized my arm.

I smelled his breath.

And then my flashlight shot through the rooms of their house. Light sparkled on a hundred wine bottles standing in the hall, two hundred bottles shelved in the kitchen, six dozen along the parlor wallboards, more of the same on bedroom bureaus and in closets. I do not know if I was more impressed with the hole in the bedroom ceiling or the endless glitter of so many bottles. I lost count. It was like an invasion of gigantic shining beetles, struck dead, deposited, and left by some ancient disease.

In the bedroom I felt the little man and woman behind me in the doorway. I heard their loud breathing and I could feel their eyes. I raised the beam of my flashlight away from the glittering bottles, I focused it carefully, and for the rest of my visit, on the hole in the yellow ceiling.

The little woman began to cry. She cried softly. Nobody moved.

The next morning they left.

Before we even knew they were going, they were half down the alley at 6 A.M., carrying their luggage, which was light enough to be entirely empty. I tried to stop them. I talked to them. They were old friends, I said. Nothing had changed, I said. They had nothing to do with the fire, I said, or the roof. They were innocent bystanders, I *insisted!* I would fix the roof myself, no charge, no charge to them! But they did not look at me. They looked at the house and at the open end of the alley ahead of them while I talked. Then, when I stopped they nodded to the alley as if agreeing that it was time to go, and walked off, and then began to run, it seemed, away from me, toward the street where there were streetcars and buses and automobiles and many loud avenues stretching in a maze. They hurried proudly, though, heads up, not looking back.

* * *

It was only by accident I ever met them again. At Christmas time, one evening, I saw the little man running quietly along the twilight street ahead of me. On a personal whim I followed. When he turned, I turned. At last, five blocks away from our old neighborhood, he scratched quietly at the door of a little white house. I saw the door open, shut, and lock him in. As night settled over the tenement city, a small light burned like blue mist in the tiny living room as I passed. I thought I saw, but probably imagined, two silhouettes there, he on his side of the room in his own particular chair, and she on her side of the room, sitting, sitting in the dark, and one or two bottles beginning to collect on the floor behind the chairs, and not a sound, not a sound between them. Only the silence.

I did not go up and knock. I strolled by. I walked on along the avenue, listening to the parrot cafés scream. I bought a newspaper, a magazine, and a quarter-edition book. Then I went home to where all the lights were lit and there was warm food upon the table.

THE SHORE LINE AT SUNSET

Tom, knee-deep in the waves, a piece of driftwood in his hand, listened.

The house, up toward the Coast Highway in the late afternoon, was silent. The sounds of closets being rummaged, suitcase locks snapping, vases being smashed, and of a final door crashing shut, all had faded away.

Chico, standing on the pale sand, flourished his wire strainer to shake out a harvest of lost coins. After a moment, without glancing at Tom, he said, "Let her go."

So it was every year. For a week or a month, their house would have music swelling from the windows, there would be new geraniums potted on the porch rail, new paint on the doors and steps. The clothes on the wire line changed from harlequin pants to sheath dresses to handmade Mexican frocks like white waves breaking behind the house. Inside, the paintings on the walls shifted from imitation Matisse to pseudo-Italian Renaissance. Sometimes, looking up, he would see a woman drying her hair like a bright yellow flag on the wind. Sometimes the flag was black or red. Sometimes the woman was tall, sometimes short, against the sky. But there was never more than one woman at a time. And, at last, a day like today came . . .

Tom placed his driftwood on the growing pile near

where Chico sifted the billion footprints left by people long vanished from their holidays.

"Chico. What are we doing here?"

"Living the life of Reilly, boy!"

"I don't feel like Reilly, Chico."

"Work at it, boy!"

Tom saw the house a month from now, the flowerpots blowing dust, the walls hung with empty squares, only sand carpeting the floors. The rooms would echo like shells in the wind. And all night every night bedded in separate rooms he and Chico would hear a tide falling away and away down a long shore, leaving no trace.

Tom nodded, imperceptibly. Once a year he himself brought a nice girl here, knowing she was right at last and that in no time they would be married. But his women always stole silently away before dawn, feeling they had been mistaken for someone else, not being able to play the part. Chico's friends left like vacuum cleaners, with a terrific drag, roar, rush, leaving no lint unturned, no clam unprized of its pearl, taking their purses with them like toy dogs which Chico had petted as he opened their jaws to count their teeth.

"That's four women so far this year."

"Okay, referee." Chico grinned. "Show me the way to the showers."

"Chico——" Tom bit his lower lip, then went on. "I been thinking. Why don't we split up?"

Chico just looked at him.

"I mean," said Tom, quickly, "maybe we'd have better luck, alone."

"Well, I'll be goddamned," said Chico slowly, gripping the strainer in his big fists before him. "Look here, boy, don't you know the facts? You and me, we'll be here come the year 2000. A couple of crazy dumb old gooney-birds drying their bones in the sun. Nothing's ever going to happen to us now, Tom, it's too late. Get that through your head and shut up."

Tom swallowed and looked steadily at the other man. "I'm thinking of leaving—next week."

"Shut up, shut up, and get to work!"

Chico gave the sand an angry showering rake that tilled him forty-three cents in dimes, pennies, and nickels. He stared blindly at the coins shimmering down the wires like a pinball game all afire.

Tom did not move, holding his breath.

They both seemed to be waiting for something.

The something happened.

"Hey . . . hey . . . hey . . ."

From a long way off down the coast a voice called. The two men turned slowly.

"Hey . . . hey . . . oh, hey . . . !"

A boy was running, yelling, waving, along the shore two hundred yards away. There was something in his voice that made Tom feel suddenly cold. He held onto his own arms, waiting.

"Hey!"

The boy pulled up, gasping, pointing back along the shore.

"A woman, a funny woman, by the North Rock!"

"A woman!" The words exploded from Chico's mouth and he began to laugh. "Oh, no, no!"

"What you mean, a 'funny' woman?" asked Tom.

"I don't know," cried the boy, his eyes wide. "You got to come see! Awful funny!"

"You mean 'drowned'?"

"Maybe! She came out of the water, she's lying on the shore, you got to see, yourself . . . funny . . ." The boy's voice died. He gazed off north again. "She's got a fish's tail."

Chico laughed. "Not before supper, please."

"Please!" cried the boy, dancing now. "No lie! Oh, hurry!"

He ran off, sensed he was not followed, and looked back in dismay.

Tom felt his lips move. "Boy wouldn't run this far for a joke, would he, Chico?"

"People have run further for less."

Tom started walking. "All right, son."

"Thanks, mister, oh thanks!"

The boy ran. Twenty yards up the coast, Tom looked back. Behind him, Chico squinted, shrugged, dusted his hands wearily, and followed.

They moved north along the twilight beach, their skin weathered in tiny folds about their burnt pale eyes,

looking younger for their hair cut close to the skull so
you could not see the grey. There was a fair wind and
the ocean rose and fell with prolonged concussions.

"What," said Tom, "what if we get to North Rock
and it's true? The ocean *has* washed some *thing* up?"

But before Chico could answer, Tom was gone, his
mind racing down coasts littered with horseshoe crabs,
sand dollars, starfish, kelp, and stone. From all the times
he'd talked on what lives in the sea, the names returned
with the breathing fall of waves. Argonauts, they whispered, codlings, pollacks, houndfish, tautog, tench, sea
elephant, they whispered, gillings, flounders, and be-
luga, the white whale, and grampus, the sea dog . . .
always you thought how these must look from their
deep-sounding names. Perhaps you would never in
your life see them rise from the salt meadows beyond
the safe limits of the shore, but they were there, and
their names, with a thousand others, made pictures.
And you looked and wished you were a frigate-bird that
might fly nine thousand miles around to return some
year with the full size of the ocean in your head.

"Oh, quick!" The boy had run back to peer in Tom's
face. "It might be gone!"

"Keep your shirt on, boy," said Chico.

They came around the North Rock. A second boy
stood there, looking down.

Perhaps from the corner of his eye, Tom saw something on the sand that made him hesitate to look
straight at it, but fix instead on the face of the boy
standing there. The boy was pale and he seemed not to
breathe. On occasion he remembered to take a breath,
his eyes focused, but the more they saw there on the
sand the more they took time off from focusing and
turned blank and looked stunned. When the ocean
came in over his tennis shoes, he did not move or notice.

Tom glanced away from the boy to the sand.

And Tom's face, in the next moment, became the
face of the boy. His hands assumed the same curl at his
sides and his mouth moved to open and stay half open
and his eyes, which were light in color, seemed to
bleach still more with so much looking.

The setting sun was ten minutes above the sea.

"A big wave came in and went out," said the first boy, "and here she was."

They looked at the woman lying there.

Her hair was very long and it lay on the beach like the threads of an immense harp. The water stroked along the threads and floated them up and let them down, each time in a different fan and silhouette. The hair must have been five or six feet long and now it was strewn on the hard wet sand and it was the color of limes.

Her face . . .

The men bent half down in wonder.

Her face was white sand sculpture, with a few water drops shimmering on it like summer rain upon a cream-colored rose. Her face was that moon which when seen by day is pale and unbelievable in the blue sky. It was milk-marble veined with faint violet in the temples. The eyelids, closed down upon the eyes, were powdered with a faint water color, as if the eyes beneath gazed through the fragile tissue of the lids and saw them standing there above her, looking down and looking down. The mouth was a pale flushed sea-rose, full and closed upon itself. And her neck was slender and white and her breasts were small and white, now covered, uncovered, covered, uncovered in the flow of water, the ebb of water, the flow, the ebb, the flow. And the breasts were flushed at their tips, and her body was startlingly white, almost an illumination, a white-green lightning against the sand. And as the water shifted her, her skin glinted like the surface of a pearl.

The lower half of her body changed itself from white to very pale blue, from very pale blue to pale green, from pale green to emerald green, to moss and lime green, to scintillas and sequins all dark green, all flowing away in a fount, a curve, a rush of light and dark, to end in a lacy fan, a spread of foam and jewel on the sand. The two halves of this creature were so joined as to reveal no point of fusion where pearl woman, woman of a whiteness made of cream-water and clear sky merged with that half which belonged to the amphibious slide and rush of current that came up on the shore and shelved down the shore, tugging its half toward its proper home. The woman was the sea, and the sea was woman. There was no flaw or seam, no wrinkle or stitch; the illusion, if illusion it was, held perfectly together and the blood from one moved into and through and mingled with what must have been the ice waters of the other.

"I wanted to run get help." The first boy seemed not to want to raise his voice. "But Skip said she was dead and there's no help for that. Is she?"

"She was never alive," said Chico. "Sure," he went on, feeling their eyes on him suddenly. "It's something left over from a movie studio. Liquid rubber skinned over a steel frame. A prop, a dummy."

"Oh, no, it's real!"

"We'll find a label somewhere," said Chico. "Here."

"Don't!" cried the first boy.

"Hell." Chico touched the body to turn it, and stopped. He knelt there, his face changing.

"What's the matter?" asked Tom.

Chico took his hand away and looked at it. "I was wrong." His voice faded.

Tom took the woman's wrist. "There's a pulse."

"You're feeling your own heartbeat."

"I just don't know . . . maybe . . . maybe . . ."

The woman was there and her upper body was all moon pearl and tidal cream and her lower body all slithering ancient green-black coins that slid upon themselves in the shift of wind and water.

"There's a trick somewhere!" cried Chico, suddenly.

"No. No!" Just as suddenly Tom burst out in laughter. "No trick! My God, my God, I feel great! I haven't felt so great since I was a kid!"

They walked slowly around her. A wave touched her white hand so the fingers faintly softly waved. The gesture was that of someone asking for another and another wave to come in and lift the fingers and then the wrist and then the arm and then the head and finally the body and take all of them together back down out to sea.

"Tom." Chico's mouth opened and closed. "Why don't you go get our truck?"

Tom didn't move.

"You hear me?" said Chico.

"Yes, but——"

"But what? We could sell this somewhere, I don't know—the university, that aquarium at Seal Beach or . . . well, hell, why couldn't we just set up a place? Look." He shook Tom's arm. "Drive to the pier. Buy us three hundred pounds of chipped ice. When you take anything out of the water you *need* ice, don't you?"

"I never thought."

"Think about it! Get moving!"

"I don't know, Chico."

"What you mean? She's real, isn't she?" He turned to the boys. "*You* say she's real, don't you? Well, then, what are we waiting for?"

"Chico," said Tom. "You better go get the ice yourself."

"Someone's got to stay and make sure she don't go back out with the tide!"

"Chico," said Tom. "I don't know how to explain. I don't want to get that ice for you."

"I'll go myself, then. Look, boys, build the sand up here to keep the waves back. I'll give you five bucks apiece. Hop to it!"

The sides of the boys' faces were bronze-pink from the sun which was touching the horizon now. Their eyes were a bronze color looking at Chico.

"My God!" said Chico. "This is better than finding ambergris!" He ran to the top of the nearest dune, called, "Get to work!" and was gone.

Now Tom and the two boys were left with the lonely woman by the North Rock and the sun was one-fourth of the way below the western horizon. The sand and the woman were pink-gold.

"Just a little line," whispered the second boy. He drew his fingernail along under his own chin, gently. He nodded to the woman. Tom bent again to see the faint line under either side of her firm white chin, the small, almost invisible line where the gills were or had been and were now almost sealed shut, invisible.

He looked at the face and the great strands of hair spread out in a lyre on the shore.

"She's beautiful," he said.

The boys nodded without knowing it.

Behind them, a gull leaped up quickly from the dunes. The boys gasped and turned to stare.

Tom felt himself trembling. He saw the boys were trembling too. A car horn hooted. Their eyes blinked, suddenly afraid. They looked up toward the highway.

A wave poured about the body, framing it in a clear white pool of water.

Tom nodded the boys to one side.

The wave moved the body an inch in and two inches out toward the sea.

The next wave came and moved the body two inches in and six inches out toward the sea.

"But——" said the first boy.

Tom shook his head.

The third wave lifted the body two feet down toward the sea. The wave after that drifted the body another foot down the shingles and the next three moved it six feet down.

The first boy cried out and ran after it.

Tom reached him and held his arm. The boy looked helpless and afraid and sad.

For a moment there were no more waves. Tom looked at the woman, thinking, she's true, she's real, she's mine . . . but . . . she's dead. Or will be if she stays here.

"We can't let her go," said the first boy. "We can't, we just can't!"

The other boy stepped between the woman and the sea. "What would we do with her?" he wanted to know, looking at Tom, "if we kept her?"

The first boy tried to think. "We could—we could——" He stopped and shook his head. "Oh, my Gosh."

The second boy stepped out of the way and left a path from the woman to the sea.

The next wave was a big one. It came in and went out and the sand was empty. The whiteness was gone and the black diamonds and the great threads of the harp.

They stood by the edge of the sea, looking out, the

man and the two boys, until they heard the truck driving up on the dunes behind them.

The last of the sun was gone.

They heard footsteps running on the dunes and someone yelling.

They drove back down the darkening beach in the light truck with the big treaded tires in silence. The two boys sat in the rear on the bags of chipped ice. After a long while, Chico began to swear steadily, half to himself, spitting out the window.

"Three hundred pounds of ice. Three hundred *pounds* of ice! What do I do with it now? And I'm soaked to the skin, soaked! You didn't even move when I jumped in and swam out to look around! Idiot, idiot! You haven't changed! Like every other time, like always, you do nothing, nothing, just stand there, stand there, do nothing, just stare!"

"And what did you do, I ask, what?" said Tom, in a tired voice, looking ahead. "The same as you always did, just the same, no different, no different at all. You should've seen yourself."

They dropped the boys off at their beach house. The youngest spoke in a voice you could hardly hear against the wind. "Gosh, nobody'll ever believe . . ."

The two men drove down the coast and parked.

Chico sat for two or three minutes waiting for his fists to relax on his lap, and then he snorted.

"Hell. I guess things turn out for the best." He took a deep breath. "It just came to me. Funny. Twenty, thirty years from now, middle of the night, our phone'll ring. It'll be one of those two boys, grown-up, calling long-distance from a bar somewhere. Middle of the night, them calling to ask one question. It's *true*, isn't it? they'll say. It *did* happen, didn't it? Back in 1958, it really happened to *us*? And we'll sit there on the edge of the bed, middle of the night, saying, Sure, boy, sure, it really happened to us in 1958. And they'll say, Thanks, and we'll say, Don't mention it, any old time. And we'll all say good night. And maybe they won't call again for a couple of years."

The two men sat on their front-porch steps in the dark.

"Tom?"

"What?"

Chico waited a moment.

"Tom, next week—you're not going away."

It was not a question but a quiet statement.

Tom thought about it, his cigarette dead in his fingers. And he knew that now he could never go away. For tomorrow and the day after the day after that he would walk down and go swimming there in all the green and white fires and the dark caverns in the hollows under the strange waves. Tomorrow and tomorrow and tomorrow.

"Yes, Chico. I'm staying here."

Now the silver looking glasses advanced in a crumpling line all along the coast from a thousand miles north to a thousand miles south. The mirrors did not reflect so much as one building or one tree or one highway or one car or even one man himself. The mirrors reflected only the quiet moon and then shattered into a billion bits of glass that spread out in a glaze on the shore. Then the sea was dark awhile, preparing another line of mirrors to rear up and surprise the two men who sat there for a long time never once blinking their eyes, waiting.

THE DAY IT RAINED FOREVER

The hotel stood like a hollowed dry bone under the very center of the desert sky where the sun burned the roof all day. All night, the memory of the sun stirred in every room like the ghost of an old forest fire. Long after dusk, since light meant heat, the hotel lights stayed off. The inhabitants of the hotel preferred to feel their way blind through the halls in their never-ending search for cool air.

This one particular evening Mr. Terle, the proprietor, and his only boarders, Mr. Smith and Mr. Fremley, who looked and smelled like two ancient rags of cured tobacco, stayed late on the long veranda. In their creaking glockenspiel rockers they gasped back and forth in the dark, trying to rock up a wind.

"Mr. Terle . . . ? Wouldn't it be *really* nice . . . someday . . . if you could buy . . . air conditioning . . . ?"

Mr. Terle coasted awhile, eyes shut.

"Got no money for such things, Mr. Smith."

The two old boarders flushed; they hadn't paid a bill now in twenty-one years.

Much later Mr. Fremley sighed a grievous sigh. "Why, why don't we all just quit, pick up, get outa here, move to a decent city? Stop this swelterin' and fryin' and sweatin'."

"Who'd buy a dead hotel in a ghost town?" said Mr. Terle quietly. "No. No, we'll just set here and wait, wait for that great day, January 29."

Slowly, all three men stopped rocking.

January 29.

The one day in all the year when it really let go and rained.

"Won't wait long." Mr. Smith tilted his gold railroad watch like the warm summer moon in his palm. "Two hours and nine minutes from now it'll *be* January 29. But I don't see nary a cloud in ten thousand miles."

"It's rained every January 29 since I was born!" Mr. Terle stopped, surprised at his own loud voice. "If it's a day late this year, I won't pull God's shirttail."

Mr. Fremley swallowed hard and looked from east to west across the desert toward the hills. "I wonder . . . will there ever be a gold rush hereabouts again?"

"No gold," said Mr. Smith. "And what's more, I'll make you a bet—no rain. No rain tomorrow or the day after the day after tomorrow. No rain all the rest of this year."

The three old men sat staring at the big sun-yellowed moon that burned a hole in the high stillness.

After a long while, painfully, they began to rock again.

The first hot morning breezes curled the calendar pages like a dried snake skin against the flaking hotel front.

The three men, thumbing their suspenders up over their hat rack shoulders, came barefoot downstairs to blink out at that idiot sky.

"January 29 . . ."

"Not a drop of mercy there."

"Day's young."

"*I'm* not." Mr. Fremley turned and went away.

It took him five minutes to find his way up through the delirious hallways to his hot, freshly baked bed.

At noon, Mr. Terle peered in.

"Mr. Fremley . . . ?"

"Damn desert cactus, that's us!" gasped Mr. Fremley, lying there, his face looking as if at any moment it might fall away in a blazing dust on the raw plank floor. "But even the best damn cactus got to have just a sip of water before it goes back to another year of the same damn furnace. I tell you I won't move again, I'll lie here an' die if I don't hear more than birds pattin' around up on that roof!"

"Keep your prayers simple and your umbrella handy," said Mr. Terle and tiptoed away.

At dusk, on the hollow roof a faint pattering sounded.

Mr. Fremley's voice sang out mournfully from his bed.

"Mr. Terle, that ain't rain! That's you with the garden hose sprinklin' well water on the roof! Thanks for tryin', but cut it out, now."

The pattering sound stopped. There was a sigh from the yard below.

Coming around the side of the hotel a moment later, Mr. Terle saw the calendar fly out and down in the dust.

"Damn January 29!" cried a voice. "Twelve more months! Have to wait twelve more months, now!"

Mr. Smith was standing there in the doorway. He stepped inside and brought out two dilapidated suitcases and thumped them on the porch.

"Mr. Smith!" cried Mr. Terle. "You can't leave after thirty years!"

"They say it rains twenty days a month in Ireland," said Mr. Smith. "I'll get a job there and run around with my hat off and my mouth open."

"You can't go!" Mr. Terle tried frantically to think of something; he snapped his fingers. "You owe me nine thousand dollars rent!"

Mr. Smith recoiled; his eyes got a look of tender and unexpected hurt in them.

"I'm sorry." Mr. Terle looked away. "I didn't mean that. Look now—you just head for Seattle. Pours two inches a week there. Pay me when you can, or never. But do me a favor: wait till midnight. It's cooler then, anyhow. Get you a good night's walk toward the city."

"Nothin'll happen between now and midnight."

"You got to have faith. When everything else is gone, you got to believe a thing'll happen. Just stand here with

me, you don't have to sit, just stand here and think of
rain. That's the last thing I'll ever ask of you."

On the desert sudden little whirlwinds of dust
twisted up, sifted down. Mr. Smith's eyes scanned the
sunset horizon.

"What do I think? Rain, oh you rain, come along
here? Stuff like that?"

"Anything. Anything at all!"

Mr. Smith stood for a long time between his two
mangy suitcases and did not move. Five, six minutes
ticked by. There was no sound, save the two men's
breathing in the dusk.

Then at last, very firmly, Mr. Smith stooped to grasp
the luggage handles.

Just then, Mr. Terle blinked. He leaned forward,
cupping his hand to his ear.

Mr. Smith froze, his hands still on the luggage.

From away among the hills, a murmur, a soft and
tremulous rumble.

"Storm coming!" hissed Mr. Terle.

The sound grew louder; a kind of whitish cloud rose
up from the hills.

Mr. Smith stood tall on tiptoe.

Upstairs Mr. Fremley sat up like Lazarus.

Mr. Terle's eyes grew wider and yet wider to take
hold of what was coming. He held to the porch rail like
the captain of a calm-foundered vessel feeling the first
stir of some tropic breeze that smelled of lime and the
ice-cool white meat of coconut. The smallest wind
stroked over his aching nostrils as over the flues of a
white-hot chimney.

"There!" cried Mr. Terle. "There!"

And over the last hill, shaking out feathers of fiery
dust, came the cloud, the thunder, the racketing storm.

Over the hill the first car to pass in twenty days flung
itself down the valley with a shriek, a thud, and a wail.

Mr. Terle did not dare to look at Mr. Smith.

Mr. Smith looked up, thinking of Mr. Fremley in his
room.

Mr. Fremley, at the window, looked down and saw
the car expire and die in front of the hotel.

For the sound that the car made was curiously final.

It had come a very long way on blazing sulphur roads, across salt flats abandoned ten million years ago by the shingling off of waters. Now, with wire-ravelings like cannibal hair sprung up from seams, with a great eyelid of canvas top thrown back and melted to spearmint gum over the rear seat, the auto, a Kissel car, vintage 1924, gave a final shuddering as if to expel its ghost upon the air.

The old woman in the front seat of the car waited patiently, looking in at the three men and the hotel as if to say, Forgive me, my friend is ill; I've known him a long while, and now I must see him through his final hour. So she just sat in the car waiting for the faint convulsions to cease and for the great relaxation of all the bones which signifies that the final process is over. She must have sat a full half minute longer listening to her car, and there was something so peaceful about her that Mr. Terle and Mr. Smith leaned slowly toward her. At last she looked at them with a grave smile and raised her hand.

Mr. Fremley was surprised to see his hand go out the window, above and wave back to her.

On the porch Mr. Smith murmured, "Strange. It's not a storm. And I'm not disappointed. How come?"

But Mr. Terle was down the path and to the car.

"We thought you were . . . that is . . ." He trailed off. "Terle's my name, Joe Terle."

She took his hand and looked at him with absolutely clear and unclouded light blue eyes like water that has melted from snow a thousand miles off and come a long way, purified by wind and sun.

"Miss Blanche Hillgood," she said, quietly. "Graduate of the Grinnell College, unmarried teacher of music, thirty years high-school glee club and student orchestra conductor, Green City, Iowa, twenty years private teacher of piano, harp, and voice, one month retired and living on a pension and now, taking my roots with me, on my way to California."

"Miss Hillgood, you don't look to be going anywhere from here."

"I had a feeling about that." She watched the two men circle the car cautiously. She sat like a child on the lap of a rheumatic grandfather, undecided. "Is there nothing we can do?"

"Make a fence of the wheels, dinner gong of the brake drums, the rest'll make a fine rock garden."

Mr. Fremley shouted from the sky. "Dead? I say, is the car dead? I can *feel* it from here! Well—it's way past time for supper!"

Mr. Terle put out his hand. "Miss Hillgood, that there is Joe Terle's Desert Hotel, open twenty-six hours a day. Gila monsters and road runners please register before going upstairs. Get you a night's sleep, free, we'll knock our Ford off its blocks and drive you to the city come morning."

She let herself be helped from the car. The machine groaned as if in protest at her going. She shut the door carefully with a soft click.

"One friend gone, but the other still with me. Mr. Terle, could you please bring her in out of the weather?"

"Her, ma'am?"

"Forgive me, I never think of things but what they're people. The car was a man, I suppose, because it took me places. But a harp, now, don't you agree, is female?"

She nodded to the rear seat of the car. There, tilted against the sky like an ancient scrolled leather ship prow cleaving the wind, stood a case which towered above any driver who might sit up in front and sail the desert calms or the city traffics.

"Mr. Smith," said Mr. Terle, "lend a hand."

They untied the huge case and hoisted it gingerly out between them.

"What you got there?" cried Mr. Fremley from above.

Mr. Smith stumbled. Miss Hillgood gasped. The case shifted in the two men's arms.

From within the case came a faint musical humming.

Mr. Fremley, above, heard. It was all the answer he needed. Mouth open, he watched the lady and the two men and their boxed friend sway and vanish in the cavernous porch below.

"Watch out!" said Mr. Smith. "Some damn fool left his luggage here——" He stopped. "Some damn fool? *Me!*"

The two men looked at each other. They were not perspiring any more. A wind had come up from some-where, a gentle wind that fanned their shirt collars and flapped the strewn calendar gently in the dust.

"*My* luggage . . ." said Mr. Smith.

Then they all went inside.

"More wine, Miss Hillgood? Ain't had wine on the table in years."

"Just a touch, if you please."

They sat by the light of a single candle which made the room an oven and struck fire from the good silver-ware and the uncracked plates as they talked and drank warm wine and ate.

"Miss Hillgood, get on with your life."

"All my life," she said, "I've been so busy running from Beethoven to Bach to Brahms, I never noticed I was twenty-nine. Next time I looked up I was forty. Yesterday, seventy-one. Oh, there were men; but they'd given up singing at ten and given up flying when they were twelve. I always figured we were born to fly, one way or other, so I couldn't stand most men shuffling along with all the iron of the earth in their blood. I never met a man who weighed less than nine hundred pounds. In their black business suits, you could hear them roll by like funeral wagons."

"So you flew away?"

"Just in my mind, Mr. Terle. It's taken sixty years to make the final break. All that time I grabbed onto picco-los and flutes and violins because they make streams in the air, you know, like streams and rivers on the ground. I rode every tributary and tried every freshwater wind from Handel on down to a whole slew of Strausses. It's been the far way around that's brought me here."

"How'd you finally make up your mind to leave?" asked Mr. Smith.

"I looked around last week and said, 'Why, look, you've been flying *alone!* No one in all Green City really cares *if* you fly or how high you go. It's always, 'Fine, Blanche,' or 'thanks for the recital at the PTA tea, Miss

H.' But no one really listening. And when I talked a long time ago about Chicago or New York, folks swatted me and laughed. 'Why be a little frog in a big pond when you can be the biggest frog in all Green City!' So I stayed on, while the folks who gave me advice moved away or died or both. The rest had wax in their ears. Just last week I shook myself and said, 'Hold on! Since when do *frogs* have wings?' "

"So now you're headin' west?" said Mr. Terle.

"Maybe to play in pictures or in that orchestra under the stars. But somewhere I just must play at last for someone who'll hear and really listen. . . ."

They sat there in the warm dark. She was finished, she had said it all now, foolish or not—and she moved back quietly in her chair.

Upstairs someone coughed.

Miss Hillgood heard, and rose.

It took Mr. Fremley a moment to ungum his eyelids and make out the shape of the woman bending down to place the tray by his rumpled bed.

"What you all talking about down there just now?"

"I'll come back later and tell you word for word," said Miss Hillgood. "Eat now. The salad's fine." She moved to leave the room.

He said, quickly, "You goin' to stay?"

She stopped half out the door and tried to trace the expression on his sweating face in the dark. He, in turn, could not see her mouth or eyes. She stood a moment longer, silently, then went on down the stairs.

"She must not've heard me," said Mr. Fremley.

But he knew she had heard.

Miss Hillgood crossed the downstairs lobby to fumble with the locks on the upright leather case.

"I must pay you for my supper."

"On the house," said Mr. Terle.

"I must pay," she said, and opened the case.

There was a sudden flash of gold.

The two men quickened in their chairs. They squinted at the little old woman standing beside the tremendous heart-shaped object which towered above her with its shining columbined pedestal atop which a calm Grecian face with antelope eyes looked serenely at them even as Miss Hillgood looked now.

The two men shot each other the quickest and most startled of glances, as if each had guessed what might happen next. They hurried across the lobby, breathing hard, to sit on the very edge of the hot velvet lounge, wiping their faces with damp handkerchiefs.

Miss Hillgood drew a chair under her, rested the golden harp gently back on her shoulder, and put her hands to the strings.

Mr. Terle took a breath of fiery air and waited.

A desert wind came suddenly along the porch outside, tilting the chairs so they rocked this way and that like boats on a pond at night.

Mr. Fremley's voice protested from above. "What's goin' on down there?"

And then Miss Hillgood moved her hands.

Starting at the arch near her shoulder, she played her fingers out along the simple tapestry of wires toward the blind and beautiful stare of the Greek goddess on her column, and then back. Then for a moment she paused and let the sounds drift up through the baked lobby air and into all the empty rooms.

If Mr. Fremley shouted, above, no one heard. For Mr. Terle and Mr. Smith were so busy jumping up to stand riven in the shadows, they heard nothing save the storming of their own hearts and the shocked rush of all the air in their lungs. Eyes wide, mouths dropped, in a kind of pure insanity, they stared at the two women there, the blind Muse proud on her golden pillar, and the seated one, gentle eyes closed, her small hands stretched forth on the air.

Like a girl, they both thought wildly, like a little girl putting her hands out a window to feel what? Why, of course, of course!

To feel the rain.

The echo of the first shower vanished down remote causeways and roof drains, away.

Mr. Fremley, above, rose from his bed as if pulled round by his ears.

Miss Hillgood played.

She played and it wasn't a tune they knew at all, but

it was a tune they had heard a thousand times in their long lives, words or not, melody or not. She played and each time her fingers moved, the rain fell pattering through the dark hotel. The rain fell cool at the open windows and the rain rinsed down the baked floor boards of the porch. The rain fell on the roof top and fell on hissing sand, it fell on rusted car and empty stable and dead cactus in the yard. It washed the windows and laid the dust and filled the rain barrels and curtained the doors with beaded threads that might part and whisper as you walked through. But more than anything the soft touch and coolness of it fell on Mr. Smith and Mr. Terle. Its gentle weight and pressure moved them down and down until it had seated them again. By its continuous budding and prickling on their faces it made them shut up their eyes and mouths and raise their hands to shield it away. Seated there, they felt their heads tilt slowly back to let the rain fall where it would.

The flash flood lasted a minute, then faded away as the fingers trailed down the loom, let drop a few last bursts and squalls and then stopped.

The last chord hung in the air like a picture taken when lightning strikes and freezes a billion drops of water on their downward flight. Then the lightning went out. The last drops fell through darkness in silence.

Miss Hillgood took her hands from the strings, her eyes still shut.

Mr. Terle and Mr. Smith opened their eyes to see those two miraculous women way over there across the lobby somehow come through the storm untouched and dry.

They trembled. They leaned forward as if they wished to speak. They looked helpless, not knowing what to do.

And then a single sound from high above in the hotel corridors drew their attention and told them what to do.

The sound came floating down feebly, fluttering like a tired bird beating its ancient wings.

The two men looked up and listened.

It was the sound of Mr. Fremley.

Mr. Fremley, in his room, applauding.

It took five seconds for Mr. Terle to figure out what it was. then he nudged Mr. Smith and began, himself, to beat his palms together. Then two men struck their hands in mighty explosions. The echoes ricocheted around about in the hotel caverns above and below, striking walls, mirrors, windows, trying to fight free of the rooms.

Miss Hillgood opened her eyes now, as if this new storm had come on her in the open, unprepared.

The men gave their own recital. They smashed their hands together so fervently it seemed they had fistfuls of firecrackers to set off, one on another. Mr. Fremley shouted. Nobody heard. Hands winged out, banged shut again and again until fingers puffed up and the old men's breath came short and they put their hands at last on their knees, a heart pounding inside each one.

Then, very slowly, Mr. Smith got up and still looking at the harp, went outside and carried in the suitcases. He stood at the foot of the lobby stairs looking for a long while at Miss Hillgood. He glanced down at her single piece of luggage resting there by the first tread. He looked from her suitcase to her and raised his eyebrows questioningly.

Miss Hillgood looked at her harp, at her suitcase, at Mr. Terle, and at last back to Mr. Smith.

She nodded once.

Mr. Smith bent down and with his own luggage under one arm and her suitcase in the other, he started the long slow climb up the stairs in the gentle dark. As he moved, Miss Hillgood put the harp back on her shoulder and either played in time to his moving or he moved in time to her playing, neither of them knew which.

Half up the flight, Mr. Smith met Mr. Fremley who, in a faded robe, was testing his slow way down.

Both stood there, looking deep into the lobby at the one man on the far side in the shadows, and the two women further over, no more than a motion and a gleam. Both thought the same thoughts.

The sound of the harp playing, the sound of the cool water falling every night and every night of their lives, after this. No spraying the roof with the garden hose now any more. Only sit on the porch or lie in your night bed and hear the falling . . . the falling . . . the falling . . .

Mr. Smith moved on up the stair; Mr. Fremley moved down.

The harp, the harp. Listen, listen!

The fifty years of drought were over.

The time of the long rains had come.

S
IS
FOR
SPACE

For Charles Beaumont
who lived in that little house
halfway up in the next block
most of my life.

And for Bill Nolan
and Bill Idelson, friend of Rush Gook,
and for Paul Condylis . . .

Because . . .

INTRODUCTION

Jules Verne was my father.

H. G. Wells was my wise uncle.

Edgar Allan Poe was the batwinged cousin we kept high in the back attic room.

Flash Gordon and Buck Rogers were my brothers and friends.

There you have my ancestry.

Adding, of course, the fact that in all probability Mary Wollstonecraft Shelley, author of *Frankenstein,* was my mother.

With a family like that, how else could I have turned out than as I did: a writer of fantasy and most curious tales of science fiction.

I lived up in the trees with Tarzan a good part of my life with my hero Edgar Rice Burroughs. When I swung down out of the foliage I asked for a toy typewriter during my twelfth year, at Christmas. On this rattletrap machine I wrote my first John Carter, Warlord of Mars, imitation sequels, and from memory tapped out whole episodes of *Chandu the Magician.*

I sent away boxtops and think I joined every secret radio society that existed. I saved comic strips, most of which I still have in great boxes down in my California basement. I went to movie matinees. I devoured the works of H. Rider Haggard and Robert Louis Stevenson.

In the midst of my young summers I leapt high and dove deep down into the vast ocean of Space, long long before the Space Age itself was more than a fly speck on the two-hundred-inch Mount Palomar telescope.

In other words, I was in love with everything I did. My heart did not beat, it exploded. I did not warm toward a subject, I boiled over. I have always run fast and yelled loud about a list of great and magical things I knew I simply could not live without.

I was a beardless boy-magician who pulled irritable rabbits out of papier-mâché hats. I became a bearded man-magician who pulled rockets out of his typewriter and out of a Star Wilderness that stretched as far as eye and mind could see and imagine.

My enthusiasm stood me well over the years. I have never tired of the rockets and the stars. I never cease enjoying the good fun of scaring heck out of myself with some of my weirder, darker tales.

So here in this new collection of stories you will find not only *S is for Space,* but a series of subtitles that might well read: *D is for Dark,* or *T is for Terrifying,* or *D is for Delight.* Here you will find just about every side of my nature and my life that you might wish to discover. My ability to laugh out loud with the sheer discovery that I am alive in a strange, wild, and exhilarating world. My equally great ability to jump and raise up a crop of goosepimples when I smell strange mushrooms growing in my cellar at midnight, or hear a spider fiddling away at his tapestry-web in the closet just before sunrise.

You who read, and I who write, are very much the same. The young person locked away in me has dared to write these stories for your pleasure. We meet on the common ground of an uncommon Age, and share out our gifts of dark and light, good dream and bad, simple joy and not so simple sorrow.

The boy-magician speaks from another year. I stand aside and let him say what he most needs to say. I listen and enjoy.

I hope you will, too.

RAY BRADBURY
Los Angeles, California
December 1, 1965

CHRYSALIS

Rockwell didn't like the room's smell. Not so much McGuire's odor of beer, or Hartley's unwashed, tired smell—but the sharp insect tang rising from Smith's cold green-skinned body lying stiffly naked on the table. There was also a smell of oil and grease from the nameless machinery gleaming in one corner of the small room.

The man Smith was a corpse. Irritated, Rockwell rose from his chair and packed his stethoscope. "I must get back to the hospital. War rush. You understand, Hartley. Smith's been dead eight hours. If you want further information call a post-mortem—"

He stopped as Hartley raised a trembling, bony hand. Hartley gestured at the corpse—this corpse with brittle hard green shell grown solid over every inch of flesh. "Use your stethoscope again, Rockwell. Just once more. Please."

Rockwell wanted to complain, but instead he sighed, sat down, and used the stethoscope. You have to treat fellow doctors politely. You press your stethoscope into cold green flesh, pretending to listen—

The small, dimly lit room exploded around him. Exploded in one green cold pulsing. It hit Rockwell's ears like fists. It hit him. He saw his own fingers jerk over the recumbent corpse.

He heard a pulse.

Deep in the dark body the heart beat once. It sounded like an echo in fathoms of sea water.

Smith was dead, unbreathing, mummified. But at the core of that deadness—his heart lived. Lived, stirring like a small unborn baby!

Rockwell's crisp surgeon's fingers darted rapidly. He bent his head. In the light it was dark-haired, with flecks of gray in it. He had an even, level, nice-looking face. About thirty-five. He listened again and again, with sweat coming cold on his smooth cheeks. The pulse was not to be believed.

One heartbeat every thirty-five seconds.

Smith's respiration—how could you believe that, too, one breath of air every four minutes. Lungcase movement imperceptible. Body temperature?

Sixty degrees.

Hartley laughed. It was not a pleasant laugh. More like an echo that had gotten lost. "He's alive," he said tiredly. "Yes, he is. He almost fooled me many times. I injected adrenaline to speed that pulse, but it was no use. He's been this way for twelve weeks. And I couldn't stand keeping him a secret any longer. That's why I phoned you, Rockwell. He's—unnatural."

The impossibility of it overwhelmed Rockwell with an inexplicable excitement. He tried to lift Smiths' eyelids. He couldn't. They were webbed with epidermis. So were the lips. So were the nostrils. There was no way for Smith to breathe—

"Yet, he's breathing." Rockwell's voice was numb. He dropped his stethoscope blankly, picked it up, and saw his fingers shaking.

Hartley grew tall, emaciated, nervous over the table. "Smith didn't like my calling you. I called anyway. Smith warned me not to. Just an hour ago."

Rockell's eyes dilated into hot black circles. "How could he warn you? He can't move."

Hartley's face, all razor-sharp bone, hard jaw, tight squinting gray eyes, twitched nervously. Smith— *thinks*. I know his thoughts. He's afraid you'll expose him to the world. He hates me. Why? I want to kill him, that's why. Here." Hartley fumbled blindly for a blue-steel revolver in his rumpled, stained coat. "Murphy. Take this. Take it before I use it on Smith's foul body!"

Murphy pulled back, his thick red face afraid. "Don't like guns. You take it, Rockwell."

Like a scalpel, Rockwell made his voice slash. "Put the gun away, Hartley. After three months tending one patient you've got a psychological blemish. Sleep'll help that." He licked his lips. "What sort of disease has Smith got?"

Hartley swayed. His mouth moved words out slowly. Falling asleep on his feet, Rockwell realized. "Not diseased," Hartley managed to say. "Don't know what. But I resent him, like a kid resents the birth of a new brother or sister. He's wrong. Help me. Help me, will you?"

"Of course." Rockwell smiled. "My desert sanitarium's the place to check him over, good. Why—why Smith's the most incredible medical phenomenon in history. Bodies just don't act this way!"

He got no further. Hartley had his gun pointed right at Rockwell's stomach. "Wait. Wait. You—you're not going to *bury* Smith! I thought you'd help me. Smith's not healthy. I want him killed! He's dangerous! I know he is!"

Rockwell blinked. Hartley was obviously psychoneurotic. Didn't know what he was saying. Rockwell straightened his shoulders, feeling cool and calm inside. "Shoot Smith and I'll turn you in for murder. You're overworked mentally and physically. Put the gun away."

They stared at one another.

Rockwell walked forward quietly and took the gun, patted Hartley understandingly on the shoulder, and gave the weapon to Murphy, who looked at it as if it would bite him. "Call the hospital, Murphy. I'm taking a week off. Maybe longer. Tell them I'm doing research at the sanitarium."

A scowl formed in the red fat flesh of Murphy's face. "What do I do with this gun?"

Hartley shut his teeth together, hard. "Keep it. You'll want to use it—later."

Rockwell wanted to shout it to the world that he was

sole possessor of the most incredible human in history. The sun was bright in the desert sanitarium room where Smith lay, not saying a word, on his table; his handsome face frozen into a green, passionless expression.

Rockwell walked into the room quietly. He used the stethoscope on the green chest. It scraped, making the noise of metal tapping a beetle's carapace.

McGuire stood by, eyeing the body dubiously, smelling of several recently acquired beers.

Rockwell listened intently. "The ambulance ride may have jolted him. No use taking a chance—"

Rockwell cried out.

Heavily, McGuire lumbered to his side. "What's wrong?"

"Wrong?" Rockwell stared about in desperation. He made one hand into a fist. "Smith's dying!"

"How do you know? Hartley said Smith plays possum. He's fooled you again—"

"No!" Rockwell worked furiously over the body, injecting drugs. Any drugs. Swearing at the top of his voice. After all this trouble, he *couldn't* lose Smith. No, not now.

Shaking, jarring, twisting deep down inside, going completely liquidly mad, Smith's body sounded like dim volcanic tides bursting.

Rockwell fought to remain calm. Smith was a case unto himself. Normal treatment did nothing for him. What then? What?

Rockwell stared. Sunlight gleamed on Smith's hard flesh. Hot sunlight. It flashed, glinting off the stethoscope tip. The sun. As he watched, clouds shifted across the sky outside, taking the sun away. The room darkened. Smith's body shook into silence. The volcanic tides died.

"McGuire! Pull the blinds! Before the sun comes back!"

McGuire obeyed.

Smith's heart slowed down to its sluggish, infrequent breathing.

"Sunlight's bad for Smith. It counteracts something. I don't know what or why, but it's not good—" Rockwell relaxed. "Lord, I wouldn't want to lose Smith. Not for anything. He's different, making his own standards, doing things men have never done. Know something, Murphy?"

"What?"

"Smith's not in agony. He's not dying either. He wouldn't be better off dead, no matter what Hartley says. Last night as I arranged Smith on the stretcher, readying him for his trip to this sanitarium, I realized, suddenly, that Smith *likes* me."

"Gah. First Hartley. Now you. Did Smith *tell* you that?"

"He didn't tell me. But he's not unconscious under all that hard skin. He's aware. Yes, that's it. He's aware."

"Pure and simply—he's petrifying. He'll die. It's been weeks since he was fed. Hartley said so. Hartley fed him intravenously until the skin toughened so a needle couldn't poke through it."

Whining, the cubicle door swung slowly open. Rockwell started. Hartley, his sharp face relaxed after hours of sleep, his eyes still a bitter gray, hostile, stood tall in the door. "If you'll leave the room," he said, quietly, "I'll destroy Smith in a very few seconds. Well?"

"Don't come a step closer." Rockwell walked, feeling irritation, to Hartley's side. "Every time you visit, you'll have to be searched. Frankly, I don't trust you." There were no weapons. "Why didn't you tell me about the sunlight?"

"Eh?" Soft and slow Hartley said it. "Oh—yes. I forgot. I tried shifting Smith weeks ago. Sunlight struck him and he began *really* dying. Naturally, I stopped trying to move him. Smith seemed to know what was coming, vaguely. Perhaps he planned it; I'm not sure. While he was still able to talk and eat ravenously, before his body stiffened completely, he warned me not to move him for a twelve-week period. Said he didn't like the sun. Said it would spoil things. I thought he was joking. He wasn't. He ate like an animal, a hungry, wild animal, fell into a coma, and here he is—" Hartley swore under his breath. "I'd rather hoped you'd leave him in the sun long enough to kill him inadvertently."

McGuire shifted his two hundred fifty pounds. "Look here, now. What if we catch Smith's disease?"

Hartley looked at the body, his pupils shrinking. "Smith's not diseased. Don't you recognize degeneration when you see it? It's like cancer. You don't catch it, you inherit a tendency. I didn't begin to fear and hate Smith until a week ago when I discovered he was breathing and existing and thriving with his nostrils and mouth sealed. It can't happen. It mustn't happen."

McGuire's voice trembled. "What if you and I and Rockwell all turn green and a plague sweeps the country—what then?"

"Then," replied Rockwell, "if I'm wrong, perhaps I am, I'll die. But it doesn't worry me in the least."

He turned back to Smith and went on with his work.

A bell. A bell. Two bells, two bells. A dozen bells, a hundred bells. Ten thousand and a million clangorous, hammering metal dinning bells. All born at once in the silence, squalling, screaming, hurting echoes, bruising ears!

Ringing, chanting with loud and soft, tenor and bass, low and high voices. Great-armed clappers knocking the shells and ripping air with the thrusting din of sound!

With all those bells ringing, Smith could not immediately know where he was. He knew that he could not see, because his eyelids were sealed tight, knew he could not speak because his lips had grown together. His ears were clamped shut, but the bells hammered nevertheless.

He could not see. But yes, yes, he could, and it was like inside a small dark red cavern, as if his eyes were turned inward upon his skull. And Smith tried to twist his tongue, and suddenly, trying to scream, he knew his tongue was gone, that the place where it used to be was vacant, an itching spot that wanted a tongue but couldn't have it just *now*.

No tongue. Strange. Why? Smith tried to stop the bells. They ceased, blessing him with a silence that wrapped him up in a cold blanket. Things were happening. Happening.

Smith tried to twitch a finger, but he had no control. A foot, a leg, a toe, his head, everything. Nothing moved. Torso, limbs—immovable, frozen in a concrete coffin.

A moment later came the dread discovery that he was no longer breathing. Not with his lungs, anyway.

"BECAUSE I HAVE NO LUNGS!" he screamed. Inwardly he screamed and that mental scream was drowned, webbed, clotted, and journeyed drowsily down in a red, dark tide. A red drowsy tide that sleepily swathed the scream, garroted it, took it all away, making Smith rest easier.

I am not afraid, he thought. I understand that which I do not understand. I understand that I do not fear, yet know not the reason.

No tongue, no nose, no lungs.

But they would come later. Yes, they would. Things were—happening.

Through the pores of his shelled body air slid, like rain needling each portion of him, giving life. Breathing through a billion gills, breathing oxygen and nitrogen and hydrogen and carbon dioxide, and using it all. Wondering. Was his heart still beating?

But yes, it was beating. Slow, slow, slow. A red dim susurrance, a flood, a river surging around him, slow, slower, slower. So nice.

So restful.

The jigsaw pieces fitted together faster as the days drifted into weeks. McGuire helped. A retired surgeon-medico, he'd been Rockwell's secretary for a number of years. Not much help, but good company.

Rockwell noted that McGuire joked gruffly about Smith, nervously; and a lot. Trying to be calm. But one day McGuire stopped, thought it over, and drawled, "Hey, it just came to me! Smith's alive. He should be dead. But he's alive. Good God!"

Rockwell laughed. "What in blazes do you think I'm working on? I'm bringing an X-ray machine out next week so I can find out what's going on inside Smith's shell." Rockwell jabbed with a hypo needle. It broke on the hard shell.

Rockwell tried another needle, and another, until

finally he punctured, drew blood, and placed the slides under the microscope for study. Hours later he calmly shoved a serum test under McGuire's red nose, and spoke quickly.

"Lord, I can't believe it. His blood's germicidal. I dropped a streptococci colony into it and the strep was annihilated in eight seconds! You could inject every known disease into Smith and he'd destroy them all, thrive on them!"

It was only a matter of hours until other discoveries. It kept Rockwell sleepless, tossing at night, wondering, theorizing the titanic ideas over and over. For instance—

Hartley'd fed Smith so many cc's of blood-food every day of his illness until recently. NONE OF THAT FOOD HAD EVER BEEN ELIMINATED. All of it had been stored, not in bulk-fats, but in a perfectly abnormal solution, an x-liquid contained in high concentrate form in Smith's blood. An ounce of it would keep a man well fed for three days. This x-liquid circulated through the body until it was actually needed, when it was seized upon and used. More serviceable than fat. Much more!

Rockwell glowed with his discovery. Smith had enough x-liquid stored in him to last months and months more. Self-sustaining.

McGuire, when told, contemplated his paunch sadly.

"I wish I stored my food that way."

That wasn't all. Smith needed little air. What air he had he seemed to acquire by an osmotic process through his skin. And he used every molecule of it. No waste.

"And," finished Rockwell, "eventually Smith's heart might even take vacations from beating, entirely!"

"Then he'd be dead," said McGuire.

"To you and I, yes. To Smith—maybe. Just maybe. Think of it, McGuire. Collectively, in Smith, we have a self-purifying blood stream demanding no replenishment but an interior one for months, having little breakdown and no elimination of wastes whatsoever because every molecule is utilized, self-evolving, and fatal to any and all microbic life. All this, and Hartley speaks of degeneration!"

Hartley was irritated when he heard of the discoveries. But he still insisted that Smith was degenerating. Dangerous.

McGuire tossed his two cents in. "How do we know that this isn't some super microscopic disease that annihilates all other bacteria while it works on its victim. After all—malarial fever is sometimes used surgically to cure syphilis; why not a new bacillus that conquers all?"

"Good point," said Rockwell. "But we're not sick, are we?"

"It may have to incubate in our bodies."

"A typical old-fashioned doctor's response. No matter what happens to a man, he's 'sick'—if he varies from the norm. That's your idea, Hartley," declared Rockwell, "not mine. Doctors aren't satisfied unless they diagnose and label each case. Well, I think that Smith's healthy; so healthy you're afraid of him."

"You're crazy," said McGuire.

"Maybe. But I don't think Smith needs medical interference. He's working out his own salvation. You believe he's degenerating. I say he's growing."

"Look at Smith's skin," complained McGuire.

"Sheep in wolf's clothing. Outside, the hard, brittle epidermis. Inside, ordered regrowth, change. Why? I'm on the verge of knowing. These changes inside Smith are so violent that they need a shell to protect their action. And as for you, Hartley, answer me truthfully, when you were young, were you afraid of insects, spiders, things like that?"

"Yes."

"There you are. A phobia. A phobia you use against Smith. That explains your distaste for Smith's change."

In the following weeks, Rockwell went back over Smith's life carefully. He visited the electronics lab where Smith had been employed and fallen ill. He probed the room where Smith had spent the first weeks of his "illness" with Hartley in attendance. He examined the machinery there. Something about radiations . . .

While he was away from the sanitarium, Rockwell locked Smith tightly, and had McGuire guard the door in case Hartley got any unusual ideas.

The details of Smith's twenty-three years were simple. He had worked for five years in the electronics lab, experimenting. He had never been seriously sick in his life.

And as the days went by Rockwell took long walks in the dry-wash near the sanitarium, alone. It gave him time to think and solidify the incredible theory that was becoming a unit in his brain.

And one afternoon he paused by a night-blooming jasmine outside the sanitarium, reached up, smiling, and plucked a dark shining object off of a high branch. He looked at the object and tucked it in his pocket. Then he walked into the sanitarium.

He summoned McGuire in off the veranda. McGuire came. Hartley trailed behind, threatening, complaining. The three of them sat in the living quarters of the building.

Rockwell told them.

"Smith's not diseased. Germs can't live in him. He's *not* inhabited by banshees or weird monsters who've 'taken over' his body. I mention this to show I've left no stone untouched. I reject all normal diagnoses of Smith. I offer the most important, the most easily accepted possibility of—delayed hereditary mutation."

"Mutation?" McGuire's voice was funny.

Rockwell held up the shiny dark object in the light.

"I found this on a bush in the garden. It'll illustrate my theory to perfection. After studying Smith's symptoms, examining his laboratory, and considering several of these"—he twirled the dark object in his fingers— "I'm certain. It's metamorphosis. It's regeneration, change, mutation *after* birth. Here. Catch. This is Smith."

He tossed the object to Hartley. Hartley caught it.

"This is the chrysalis of a caterpillar," said Hartley. Rockwell nodded. "Yes, it is."

"You don't mean to infer that Smith's a—*chrysalis?*"

"I'm positive of it," replied Rockwell.

Rockwell stood over Smith's body in the darkness of

evening. Hartley and McGuire sat across the patient's room, quiet, listening. Rockwell touched Smith softly. "Suppose that there's more to life than just being born, living seventy years, and dying. Suppose there's one more great step up in man's existence, and Smith has been the first of us to make that step.

"Looking at a caterpillar, we see what we consider a static object. But it changes to a butterfly. Why? There are no final theories explaining it. It's progress, mainly. The pertinent thing is that a supposedly unchangeable object weaves itself into an intermediary object, wholly unrecognizable, a chrysalis, and emerges a butterfly. Outwardly the chrysalis looks dead. This is misdirection. Smith has misdirected us, you see. Outwardly, dead. Inwardly, fluids whirlpool, reconstruct, rush about with wild purpose. From grub to mosquito, from caterpillar to butterfly, from Smith to—?"

"Smith a chrysalis?" McGuire laughed heavily.

"Yes."

"Humans don't work that way."

"Stop it, McGuire. This evolutionary step's too great for your comprehension. Examine this body and tell me anything else. Skin, eyes, breathing, blood flow. Weeks of assimilating food for his brittle hibernation. Why did he eat all that food, why did he need that x-liquid in his body except for his metamorphosis? And the cause of it all was—radiations. Hard radiations from Smith's laboratory equipment. Planned or accidental I don't know. It touched some part of his essential gene-structure, some part of the evolutionary structure of man that wasn't scheduled for working for thousands of years yet, perhaps."

"Do you think that some day all men—?"

"The maggot doesn't stay in the stagnant pond, the grub in the soil, or the caterpillar on a cabbage leaf. They change, spreading across space in waves.

"Smith's the answer to the problem 'What happens next for man, where do we go from here?' We're faced with the blank wall of the universe and the fatality of living in that universe, and man as he is today is not prepared to go against the universe. The least exertion tires man, overwork kills his heart, disease his body.

Maybe Smith will be prepared to answer the philosophers' problem of life's purpose. Maybe he can give it new purpose.

"Why, we're just petty insects, all of us, fighting on a pinhead planet. Man isn't meant to remain here and be sick and small and weak, but he hasn't discovered the secret of the greater knowledge yet.

"But—change man. Build your perfect man. Your—your superman, if you like. Eliminate petty mentality, give him complete physiological, neurological, psychological control of himself: give him clear, incisive channels of thought, give him an indefatigable blood stream, a body that can go months without outside food, that can adjust to any climate anywhere and kill any disease. Release man from the shackles of flesh and flesh misery and then he's no longer a poor, petty little man afraid to dream because he knows his frail body stands between him and the fulfillment of dreams, then he's ready to wage war, the only war worth waging—the conflict of man reborn and the whole confounded universe!"

Breathless, voice hoarse, heart pounding, Rockwell tensed over Smith, placed his hands admiringly, firmly on the cold length of the chrysalis and shut his eyes. The power and drive and belief in Smith surged through him. He was right. He was right. He knew he was right. He opened his eyes and looked at McGuire and Hartley who were mere shadows in the dim shielded light of the room.

After a silence of several seconds, Hartley snuffed out his cigarette. "I don't believe that theory."

McGuire said, "How do you know Smith's not just a mess of jelly inside? Did you X-ray him?"

"I couldn't risk it, it might interfere with his change, like the sunlight did."

"So he's going to be a superman? What will he look like?"

"We'll wait and see."

"Do you think he can hear us talking about him now?"

"Whether or not he can, there's one thing certain—, we're sharing a secret we weren't intended to know.

Smith didn't plan on myself and McGuire entering the case. He had to make the most of it. But a superman doesn't like people to know about him. Humans have a nasty way of being envious, jealous, and hateful. Smith knew he wouldn't be safe if found out. Maybe that explains your hatred, too, Hartley."

They all remained silent, listening. Nothing sounded. Rockwell's blood whispered in his temples, that was all. There was Smith, no longer Smith, a container labeled SMITH, its contents unknown.

"If what you say *is* true," said Hartley, "then indeed we should destroy him. Think of the power over the world he would have. And if it affects his brain as I think it will affect it—he'll try to kill us when he escapes because we are the only ones who know about him. He'll hate us for prying."

Rockwell said it easily. "I'm not afraid."

Hartley remained silent. His breathing was harsh and loud in the room.

Rockwell came around the table, gesturing.

"I think we'd better say good-night now, don't you?"

The thin rain swallowed Hartley's car. Rockwell closed the door, instructed McGuire to sleep downstairs tonight on a cot fronting Smith's room, and then he walked upstairs to bed.

Undressing, he had time to conjure over all the unbelievable events of the passing weeks. A superman. Why not? Efficiency, strength—

He slipped into bed.

When. When does Smith emerge from his chrysalis? When?

The rain drizzled quietly on the roof of the sanitarium.

McGuire lay in the middle of the sound of rain and the earthquaking of thunder, slumbering on the cot, breathing heavy breaths. Somewhere, a door creaked, but McGuire breathed on. Wind gusted down the hall. McGuire grunted and rolled over. A door closed softly and the wind ceased.

Footsteps tread softly on the deep carpeting. Slow

footsteps, aware and alert and ready. Footsteps. Mc-Guire blinked his eyes and opened them.

In the dim light a figure stood over him.

Upstairs, a single light in the hall thrust down a yellow shaft near McGuire's cot.

An odor of crushed insect filled the air. A hand moved. A voice started to speak.

McGuire screamed.

Because the hand that moved into the light was green.

Green.

"Smith!"

McGuire flung himself ponderously down the hall, yelling.

"He's walking! He can't walk, but he's walking!"

The door rammed open under McGuire's bulk. Wind and rain shrieked in around him and he was gone into the storm, babbling.

In the hall, the figure was motionless. Upstairs a door opened swiftly and Rockwell ran down the steps. The green hand moved back out of the light behind the figure's back.

"Who is it?" Rockwell paused halfway.

The figure stepped into the light.

Rockwell's eyes narrowed.

"Hartley! What are you doing back here?"

"Something happened," said Hartley. "You'd better get McGuire. He ran out in the rain babbling like a fool."

Rockwell kept his thoughts to himself. He searched Hartley swiftly with one glance and then ran down the hall and out into the cold wind.

"McGuire! McGuire, come back you idiot!"

The rain fell on Rockwell's body as he ran. He found McGuire about a hundred yards from the sanitarium, blubbering.

"Smith—Smith's walking . . ."

"Nonsense. Hartley came back, that's all."

"I saw a green hand. It moved."

"You dreamed."

"No. No." McGuire's face was flabby pale, with water on it. "I saw a green hand, believe me. Why did Hartley come back? He—"

At the mention of Hartley's name, full comprehension came smashing to Rockwell. Fear leaped through his mind, a mad blur of warning, a jagged edge of silent screaming for help.

"Hartley!"

Shoving McGuire abruptly aside, Rockwell twisted and leaped back toward the sanitarium, shouting. Into the hall, down the hall—

Smith's door was broken open.

Gun in hand, Hartley was in the center of the room. He turned at the noise of Rockwell's running. They both moved simultaneously. Hartley fired his gun and Rockwell pulled the light switch.

Darkness. Flame blew across the room, profiling Smith's rigid body like a flash photo. Rockwell jumped at the flame. Even as he jumped, shocked deep, realizing why Hartley had returned. In that instant before the lights blinked out Rockwell had a glimpse of Hartley's fingers.

They were a brittle mottled green.

Fists then. And Hartley collapsing as the lights came on, and McGuire, dripping wet at the door, shook out the words, "Is—is Smith killed?"

Smith wasn't harmed. The shot had passed over him.

"This fool, this fool," cried Rockwell, standing over Hartley's numbed shape. "Greatest case in history and he tries to destroy it!"

Hartley came around, slowly. "I should've known. Smith warned you."

"Nonsense, he—" Rockwell stopped, amazed. Yes. That sudden premonition crashing into his mind. Yes. Then he glared at Hartley. "Upstairs with you. You're being locked in for the night. McGuire, you, too. So you can watch him."

McGuire croaked. "Hartley's hand. Look at it. It's green. It was Hartley in the hall—not Smith!"

Hartley stared at his fingers. "Pretty, isn't it?" he said, bitterly. "I was in range of those radiations for a long time at the start of Smith's illness. I'm going to be a —creature—like Smith. It's been this way for several days. I kept it hidden. I tried not to say anything. To-night, I couldn't stand it any longer, and I came back to destroy Smith for what he's done to me . . ."

A dry noise racked, dryly, splitting the air. The three of them froze.

Three tiny flakes of Smith's chrysalis flicked up and then spiraled down to the floor.

Instantly, Rockwell was to the table, and gaping.

"It's starting to crack. From the collar-bone V to the navel, a microscopic fissure! He'll be out of his chrysalis soon!"

McGuire's jowls trembled. "And then what?"

Hartley's words were bitter sharp. "We'll have a su-perman. Question: what does a superman look like? Answer: nobody knows."

Another crust of flakes crackled open.

McGuire shivered. "Will you try to talk to him?"

"Certainly."

"Since when do—butterflies—speak?"

"Oh, Good God, McGuire!"

With the two others securely imprisoned upstairs, Rockwell locked himself into Smith's room and bedded down on a cot, prepared to wait through the long wet night, watching, listening, thinking.

Watching the tiny flakes flicking off the crumbling skin of chrysalis as the Unknown within struggled qui-etly outward.

Just a few more hours to wait. The rain slid over the house, pattering. What *would* Smith look like? A change in the earcups perhaps for greater hearing; extra eyes, maybe; a change in the skull structure, the facial setup, the bones of the body, the placement of organs, the texture of skin, a million and one changes.

Rockwell grew tired and yet was afraid to sleep. Eyelids heavy, heavy. What if he was wrong? What if his theory was entirely disjointed? What if Smith was only so much moving jelly inside? What if Smith was mad, insane—so different that he'd be a world menace? No. No. Rockwell shook his head groggily. Smith was per-fect. Perfect. There'd be no room for evil thought in Smith. Perfect.

The sanitarium was death quiet. The only noise was the faint crackle of chrysalis flakes skimming to the hard floor . . .

Rockwell slept. Sinking into the darkness that blotted out the room as dreams moved in upon him. Dreams in which Smith arose, walked in stiff, parched gesticulations and Hartley, screaming, wielded an ax, shining, again and again into the green armor of the creature and hacked it into liquid horror. Dreams in which McGuire ran babbling through a rain of blood. Dreams in which—

Hot sunlight. Hot sunlight all over the room. It was morning. Rockwell rubbed his eyes, vaguely troubled by the fact that someone had raised the blinds. Someone had—he leaped! Sunlight! There was no way for the blinds to be up. They'd been down for weeks! He cried out.

The door was open. The sanitarium was silent. Hardly daring to turn his head, Rockwell glanced at the table. Smith should have been lying there.

He wasn't.

There was nothing but sunlight on the table. That— and a few remnants of shattered chrysalis. Remnants.

Brittle shards, a discarded profile cleft in two pieces, a shell segment that had been a thigh, a trace of arm, a splint of chest—these were the fractured remains of Smith!

Smith was gone. Rockwell staggered to the table, crushed. Scrabbling like a child among the rattling papyrus of skin. Then he swung about, as if drunk, and swayed out of the room and pounded up the stairs, shouting:

"Hartley! What did you do with him? Hartley! Did you think you could kill him, dispose of his body, and leave a few bits of shell behind to throw me off trail?"

The door to the room where McGuire and Hartley had slept was locked. Fumbling, Rockwell unlocked it. Both McGuire and Hartley were there.

"You're here," said Rockwell, dazed. "You weren't downstairs, then. Or did you unlock the door, come down, break in, kill Smith and—no, no."

"What's wrong?"

"Smith's gone! McGuire, did Hartley move out of this room?"

"Not all night."

"Then—there's only one explanation—Smith emerged from his chrysalis and escaped during the night! I'll never see him, I'll never get to see him, damn it! What a fool I was to sleep!"

"That settles it!" declared Hartley. "The man's dangerous or he would have stayed and let us see him! God only knows what he is."

"We've got to search, then. He can't be far off. We've got to search then! Quick now, Hartley. McGuire!"

McGuire sat heavily down. "I won't budge. Let him find himself. I've had enough."

Rockwell didn't wait to hear more. He went downstairs with Hartley close after him. McGuire puffed down a few moments later.

Rockwell moved wildly down the hall, halted at the wide windows that overlooked the desert and the mountains with morning shining over them. He squinted out, and wondered if there was any chance at all of finding Smith. The first superbeing. The first perhaps in a new long line. Rockwell sweated. Smith wouldn't leave without revealing himself to at least Rockwell. He couldn't leave. Or could he?

The kitchen door swung open, slowly.

A foot stepped through the door, followed by another. A hand lifted against the wall. Cigarette smoke moved from pursed lips.

"Somebody looking for me?"

Stunned, Rockwell turned. He saw the expression on Hartley's face, heard McGuire choke with surprise. The three of them spoke one word together, as if given their cue:

"Smith."

Smith exhaled cigarette smoke. His face was red-pink as he had been sunburnt, his eyes were glittering blue. He was barefoot and his nude body was attired in one of Rockwell's old robes.

"Would you mind telling me where I am? What have

I been doing for the last three or four months? Is this a—hospital or isn't it?"

Dismay slammed Rockwell's mind, hard. He swallowed.

"Hello. I. That is—Don't you remember—anything?"

Smith displayed his fingertips. "I recall turning green, if that's what you mean. Beyond that—nothing." He raked his pink hand through his nut-brown hair with the vigor of a creature newborn and glad to breathe again.

Rockwell slumped back against the wall. He raised his hands, with shock, to his eyes, and shook his head. Not believing what he saw he said, "What time did you come out of the chrysalis?"

"What time did I come out of—what?"

Rockwell took him down the hall to the next room and pointed to the table.

"I don't see what you mean," said Smith, frankly sincere. "I found myself standing in this room half an hour ago, stark naked."

"That's all?" said McGuire, hopefully. He seemed relieved.

Rockwell explained the origin of the chrysalis on the table.

Smith frowned. "That's ridiculous. Who *are* you?"

Rockwell introduced the others.

Smith scowled at Hartley. "When I first was sick you came, didn't you. I remember. At the radiations plant. But this is silly. What disease was it?"

Hartley's cheek muscles were taut wire. "No disease. Don't *you* know anything about it?"

"I find myself with strange people in a strange sanitarium. I find myself naked in a room with a man sleeping on a cot. I walk around the sanitarium, hungry. I go to the kitchen, find food, eat, hear excited voices, and then am accused of emerging from a chrysalis. What am I supposed to think? Thanks, by the way, for this robe, for food, and the cigarette I borrowed. I didn't want to wake you at first, Mr. Rockwell. I didn't know who you were and you looked dead tired."

"Oh, that's all right." Rockwell wouldn't let himself

believe it. Everything was crumbling. With every word Smith spoke, his hopes were pulled apart like the crumpled chrysalis. "How do you feel?"

"Fine. Strong. Remarkable, when you consider how long I was under."

"Very remarkable," said Hartley.

"You can imagine how I felt when I saw the calendar. All those months—crack—gone. I wondered what I'd been doing all that time."

"So have we."

McGuire laughed. "Oh, leave him alone, Hartley. Just because you hated him—"

"Hated?" Smith's brows went up. "Me? Why?"

"Here. This is why!" Hartley thrust his fingers out. "Your damned radiations. Night after night sitting by you in your laboratory. What can I do about it?"

"Hartley," warned Rockwell. "Sit down. Be quiet."

"I won't sit down and I won't be quiet! Are you both fooled by this imitation of a man, this pink fellow who's carrying on the greatest hoax in history? If you had any sense you'd destroy Smith before he escapes!"

Rockwell apologized for Hartley's outburst.

Smith shook his head. "No, let him talk. What's this about?"

"You know already!" shouted Hartley, angrily. "You've lain there for months, listening, planning. You can't fool me. You've got Rockwell bluffed, disappointed. He expected you to be a superman. Maybe you are. But whatever you are, you're not Smith any more. Not any more. It's just another of your misdirections. We weren't supposed to know all about you, and the world shouldn't know about you. You could kill us, easily, but you'd prefer to stay and convince us that you're normal. That's the best way. You could have escaped a few minutes ago, but that would have left the seeds of suspicion behind. Instead, you waited, to convince us that you're normal."

"He *is* normal," complained McGuire.

"No he's not. His mind's different. He's clever."

"Give him word association tests then," said McGuire.

"He's too clever for that, too."

"It's very simple, then. We take blood tests, listen to his heart, and inject serums into him."

Smith looked dubious. "I feel like an experiment, but if you really want to. This is silly."

That shocked Hartley. He looked at Rockwell. "Get the hypos," he said.

Rockwell got the hypos, thinking. Now, maybe after all, Smith was a superman. His blood. That superblood. Its ability to kill germs. His heartbeat. His breathing. Maybe Smith was a superman and didn't know it. Yes. Yes, maybe—

Rockwell drew blood from Smith and slid it under a microscope. His shoulders sagged. It was normal blood. When you dropped germs into it the germs took a normal length of time to die. The blood was no longer super germicidal. The x-liquid, too, was gone. Rockwell sighed miserably. Smith's temperature was normal. So was his pulse. His sensory and nervous system responded according to rule.

"Well, that takes care of that," said Rockwell, softly.

Hartley sank into a chair, eyes widened, holding his head between bony fingers. He exhaled. "I'm sorry. I guess my—mind—it just imagined things. The months were so long. Night after night. I got obsessed, and afraid. I've made a fool out of myself. I'm sorry. I'm sorry." He stared at his green fingers. "But what about myself?"

Smith said, "I recovered. You'll recover, too, I guess. I can sympathize with you. But it wasn't bad . . . I don't really recall anything."

Hartley relaxed. "But—yes I guess you're right. I don't like the idea of my body getting hard, but it can't be helped. I'll be all right."

Rockwell was sick. The tremendous letdown was too much for him. The intense drive, the eagerness, the hunger and curiosity, the fire, had all sunk within him. So *this* was the man from the chrysalis? The same man who had gone in. All this waiting and wondering for nothing.

He gulped a breath of air, tried to steady his innermost, racing thoughts. Turmoil. This pink-cheeked, fresh-voiced man who sat before him smoking calmly, was no more than a man who had suffered some partial skin petrification, and whose glands had gone wild from radiation, but, nevertheless, just a man now and nothing more. Rockwell's mind, his overimaginative, fantastic mind had seized upon each facet of the illness and built it into a perfect organism of wishful thinking. Rockwell was deeply shocked, deeply stirred and disappointed.

The question of Smith's living without food, his pure blood, low temperature, and the other evidences of superiority were now fragments of a strange illness. An illness and nothing more. Something that was over, done and gone, and left nothing behind but brittle scraps on a sunlit tabletop. There'd be a chance to watch Hartley now, if his illness progressed, and report the new sickness to the medical world.

But Rockwell didn't care about illness. He cared about perfection. And that perfection had been split and ripped and torn and it was gone. His dream was gone. His supercreature was gone. He didn't care if the whole world went hard, green, brittle-mad now.

Smith was shaking hands all around. "I'd better get back to Los Angeles. Important work for me to do at the plant. I have my old job waiting for me. Sorry I can't stay on. You understand."

"You should stay on and rest a few days, at least," said Rockwell. He hated to see the last wisp of his dream vanish.

"No thanks. I'll drop by your office in a week or so for another checkup, though, Doctor, if you like? I'll drop in every few weeks for the next year or so so you can check me, yes?"

"Yes. Yes, Smith. Do that, will you please? I'd like to talk your illness over with you. You're lucky to be alive."

McGuire said, happily. "I'll drive you to L.A."

"Don't bother. I'll walk to Tujunga and get a cab. I want to walk. It's been so long, I want to see what it feels like."

Rockwell lent him an old pair of shoes and an old suit of clothes.

"Thanks, Doctor. I'll pay you what I owe you as soon as possible."

"You don't owe me a penny. It was interesting."

"Well, good-bye, Doctor. Mr. McGuire. Hartley."

"Good-bye, Smith."

"Good-bye."

Smith walked down the path to the dry wash, which was already baked dry by the late afternoon sun. He walked easily and happily and whistled. I wish I could whistle now, thought Rockwell tiredly.

Smith turned once, waved to them, and then he strode up the hillside and went on over it toward the distant city.

Rockwell watched him go as a small child watches his favorite sand castle eroded and annihilated by the waves of the sea. "I can't believe it," he said, over and over again. "I can't believe it. The whole thing's ending so soon, so abruptly for me. I'm dull and empty inside."

"Everything looks *rosy* to me!" chuckled McGuire happily.

Hartley stood in the sun. His green hands hung softly at his side and his white face was really relaxed for the first time in months, Rockwell realized. Hartley said, softly,

"I'll come out all right. I'll come out all right. Oh, thank God for that. Thank God for that. I won't be a monster. I won't be anything but myself." He turned to Rockwell. "Just remember, remember, don't let them bury me by mistake. Don't let them bury me by mistake, thinking I'm dead. Remember that."

Smith took the path across the dry wash and up the hill. It was late afternoon already and the sun had started to vanish behind blue hills. A few stars were visible. The odor of water, dust, and distant orange blossoms hung in the warm air.

Wind stirred. Smith took deep breaths of air. He walked.

Out of sight, away from the sanitarium, he paused and stood very still. He looked up at the sky.

Tossing away the cigarette he'd been smoking, he mashed it precisely under one heel. Then he straightened his well-shaped body, tossed his brown hair back, closed his eyes, swallowed, and relaxed his fingers at his sides.

With nothing of effort, just a little murmur of sound, Smith lifted his body gently from the ground into the warm air.

He soared up quickly, quietly—and very soon he was lost among the stars as Smith headed for outer space . . .

PILLAR OF FIRE

He came out of the earth, hating. Hate was his father; hate was his mother.

It was good to walk again. It was good to leap up out of the earth, off of your back, and stretch your cramped arms violently and try to take a deep breath!

He *tried*. He cried out.

He couldn't breathe. He flung his arms over his face and tried to breathe. It was impossible. He walked on the earth, he came out of the earth. But he was dead. He couldn't breathe. He could take air into his mouth and force it half down his throat, with withered moves of long-dormant muscles, wildly, wildly! And with this little air he could shout and cry! He wanted to have tears, but he couldn't make them come, either. All he knew was that he was standing upright, he was dead, he shouldn't be walking! He couldn't breathe and yet he stood.

The smells of the world were all about him. Frustratedly, he tried to smell the smells of autumn. Autumn was burning the land down into ruin. All across the country the ruins of summer lay; vast forests bloomed with flame, tumbled down timber on empty, unleafed timber. The smoke of the burning was rich, blue, and invisible.

He stood in the graveyard, hating. He walked

through the world and yet could not taste nor smell of it. He heard, yes. The wind roared on his newly opened ears. But he was dead. Even though he walked he knew he was dead and should expect not too much of himself or this hateful living world.

He touched the tombstone over his own empty grave. He knew his own name again. It was a good job of carving.

WILLIAM LANTRY

That's what the gravestone said.
His fingers trembled on the cool stone surface.

BORN 1898——DIED 1933

Born *again* . . . ?
What year? He glared at the sky and the midnight autumnal stars moving in slow illuminations across the windy black. He read the tiltings of centuries in those stars. Orion thus and so, Aurega here! and where Taurus? *There!*

His eyes narrowed. His lips spelled out the year: "2349."

An odd number. Like a school sum. They used to say a man couldn't encompass any number over a hundred. After that it was all so damned abstract there was no use counting. This was the year 2349! A numeral, a sum. And here he was, a man who had lain in his hateful dark coffin, hating to be buried, hating the living people above who lived and lived and lived, hating them for all the centuries, until today, now, born out of hatred, he stood by his own freshly excavated grave, the smell of raw earth in the air, perhaps, but he could not smell it!

"I," he said, addressing a poplar tree that was shaken by the wind, "am an anachronism." He smiled faintly.

He looked at the graveyard. It was cold and empty. All of the stones had been ripped up and piled like so many flat bricks, one atop another, in the far corner by the wrought iron fence. This had been going on for two endless weeks. In his deep secret coffin he had heard the heartless, wild stirring as the men jabbed the earth with cold spades and tore out the coffins and carried away the withered ancient bodies to be burned. Twisting with fear in his coffin, he had waited for them to come to him.

Today they had arrived at his coffin. But—late. They had dug down to within an inch of the lid. Five o'clock bell, time for quitting. Home to supper. The workers had gone off. Tomorrow they would finish the job, they said, shrugging into their coats.

Silence had come to the emptied tombyard.

Carefully, quietly, with a soft rattling of sod, the coffin lid had lifted.

William Lantry stood trembling now, in the last cemetery on Earth.

"Remember?" he asked himself, looking at the raw earth. "Remember those stories of that last man on Earth? Those stories of men wandering in ruins, alone? Well, you, William Lantry, are a switch on the old story. Do you *know* that? You are the last *dead* man in the whole world!"

There were no more dead people. Nowhere in any land was there a dead person. Impossible! Lantry did not smile at this. No, not impossible at all in this foolish, sterile, unimaginative, antiseptic age of cleansings and scientific methods! People died, oh my God, yes. But—*dead* people? Corpses? They didn't exist!

What *happened* to dead people?

The graveyard was on a hill. William Lantry walked through the dark burning night until he reached the edge of the graveyard and looked down upon the new town of Salem. It was all illumination, all color. Rocket ships cut fire above it, crossing the sky to all the far ports of Earth.

In his grave the new violence of this future world had driven down and seeped into William Lantry. He had been bathed in it for years. He knew all about it, with a hating dead man's knowledge of such things.

Most important of all, he knew what these fools did with dead men.

He lifted his eyes. In the center of the town a massive stone finger pointed at the stars. It was three hundred feet high and fifty feet across. There was a wide entrance and a drive in front of it.

In the town, theoretically, thought William Lantry, say you have a dying man. In a moment he will be dead. What happens? No sooner is his pulse cold when a certificate is flourished, made out, his relatives pack him into a car-beetle and drive him swiftly to—

The Incinerator!

That functional finger, that Pillar of Fire pointing at the stars. Incinerator. A functional, terrible name. But truth is truth in this future world.

Like a stick of kindling your Mr. Dead Man is shot into the furnace.

Flume!

William Lantry looked at the top of the gigantic pistol shoving at the stars. A small pennant of smoke issued from the top.

There's where your dead people go.

"Take care of yourself, William Lantry," he murmured. "You're the last one, the rare item, the last dead man. All the other graveyards of Earth have been blasted up. This is the last graveyard and you're the last dead man from the centuries. These people don't believe in having dead people about, much less walking dead people. Everything that can't be used goes up like a matchstick. Superstitions right along with it!"

He looked at the town. All right, he thought, quietly, I hate you. You hate me, or you *would* if you knew I existed. You don't believe in such things as vampires or ghosts. Labels without referents, you cry! You snort. All right, snort! Frankly, I don't believe in *you*, either! I don't *like* you! You and your Incinerators.

He trembled. How very close it had been. Day after day they had hauled out the other dead ones, burned them like so much kindling. An edict had been broadcast around the world. He had heard the digging men talk as they worked!

"I guess it's a good idea, this cleaning up the graveyards," said one of the men.

"Guess so," said another. "Grisly custom. Can you imagine? Being buried, I mean! Unhealthy! All them germs!"

"Sort of a shame. Romantic, kind of. I mean, leaving just this one graveyard untouched all these centuries. The other graveyards were cleaned out, what year was it, Jim?"

"About 2260, I think. Yeah, that was it, 2260, almost a hundred years ago. But some Salem Committee, they got on their high horse and they said, 'Look here, let's have just *one* graveyard left, to remind us of the customs of the barbarians.' And the government scratched its head, thunk it over, and said, 'Okay. Salem it is. But all other graveyards go, you understand, all!' "

"And away they went," said Jim.

"Sure, they sucked out 'em with fire and steam shovels and rocket-cleaners. If they knew a man was buried in a cow pasture, they fixed him! Evacuated them, they did. Sort of cruel, I say."

"I hate to sound old-fashioned, but still there were a lot of tourists came here every year, just to see what a real graveyard was like."

"Right. We had nearly a million people in the last three years visiting. A good revenue. But—a government order is an order. The government says no more morbidity, so flush her out we do! Here we go. Hand me that spade, Bill."

William Lantry stood in the autumn wind, on the hill. It was good to walk again, to feel the wind and to hear the leaves scuttling like mice on the road ahead of him. It was good to see the bitter cold stars almost blown away by the wind.

It was even good to know fear again.

For fear rose in him now, and he could not put it away. The very fact that he was walking made him an enemy. And there was not another friend, another dead man, in all of the world, to whom one could turn for help or consolation. It was the whole melodramatic living world against one. William Lantry. It was the whole vampire-disbelieving, body-burning, graveyard-annihilating world against a man in a dark suit on a dark autumn hill. He put out his pale cold hands into the city illumination. You have pulled the tombstones, like teeth, from the yard, he thought. Now I will find some way to push your Incinerators down into rubble. I will make dead people again, and I will make friends in so doing. I cannot be alone and lonely. I must start manufacturing friends very soon. Tonight.

"War is declared," he said, and laughed. It was pretty silly, one man declaring war on an entire world.

The world did not answer back. A rocket crossed the sky on a rush of flame, like an Incinerator taking wing.

Footsteps. Lantry hastened to the edge of the cemetery. The diggers, coming back to finish up their work? No. Just someone, a man, walking by.

As the man came abreast the cemetery gate, Lantry stepped swiftly out. "Good evening," said the man, smiling.

Lantry struck the man in the face. The man fell. Lantry bent quietly down and hit the man a killing blow across the neck with the side of his hand.

Dragging the body back into shadow, he stripped it and changed clothes with it. It wouldn't do for a fellow to go wandering about this future world with ancient clothing on. He found a small pocket knife in the man's coat; not much of a knife, but enough if you knew how to handle it properly. He knew how.

He rolled the body down into one of the already opened and exhumed graves. In a minute he had shoveled dirt down upon it, just enough to hide it. There was little chance of it being found. They wouldn't dig the same grave twice.

He adjusted himself in his new loose-fitting metallic suit. Fine, fine.

Hating. William Lantry walked down into town, to do battle with the Earth.

II

The Incinerator was open. It never closed. There was a wide entrance, all lighted up with hidden illumination, there was a helicopter landing table and a beetle drive. The town itself was dying down after another day of the dynamo. The lights were going dim, and the only quiet, lighted spot in the town now was the Incinerator. God, what a practical name, what an unromantic name.

William Lantry entered the wide, well-lighted door. It was an entrance, really; there were no doors to open or shut. People could go in and out, summer or winter, the inside was always warm. Warm from the fire that rushed whispering up the high round flue to where the whirlers, the propellors, the air jets pushed the leafy gray ashes on away for a ten-mile ride down the sky.

There was the warmth of the bakery here. The halls were floored with rubber parquet. You couldn't make a noise if you wanted to. Music played in hidden throats somewhere. Not music of death at all, but music of life and the way the sun lived inside the Incinerator; or the sun's brother, anyway. You could hear the flame floating inside the heavy brick wall.

William Lantry descended a ramp. Behind him he heard a whisper and turned in time to see a beetle stop before the entranceway. A bell rang. The music, as if at a signal, rose to ecstatic heights. There was joy in it.

From the beetle, which opened from the rear, some attendants stepped carrying a golden box. It was six feet long and there were sun symbols on it. From another beetle the relatives of the man in the box stepped and followed as the attendants took the golden box down a ramp to a kind of altar. On the side of the altar were the words, "WE THAT WERE BORN OF THE SUN RETURN TO THE SUN." The golden box was deposited upon the altar, the music leaped upward, the Guardian of this place spoke only a few words, then the attendants picked up the golden box, walked to a transparent wall, a safety lock, also transparent, and opened it. The box was shoved into the glass slot. A moment later an inner lock opened, the box was injected into the interior of the flue, and vanished instantly in quick flame.

The attendants walked away. The relatives without a word turned and walked out. The music played.

William Lantry approached the glass fire lock. He peered through the wall at the vast, glowing never-ceasing heart of the Incinerator. It burned steadily, without a flicker, singing to itself peacefully, It was so solid it was like a golden river flowing up out of the earth toward the sky. Anything you put into the river was borne upward, vanished.

Lantry felt again his unreasoning hatred of this thing, this monster, cleansing fire.

A man stood at his elbow. "May I help you, sir?"

"What?" Lantry turned abruptly. "What did you say?"

"May I be of service?"

"I—that is—" Lantry looked quickly at the ramp and the door. His hands trembled at his sides. "I've never been in here before."

"Never?" The Attendant was surprised.

That had been the wrong thing to say, Lantry realized. But it was said, nevertheless. "I mean," he said. "Not really. I mean, when you're a child, somehow, you don't pay attention. I suddenly realized tonight that I didn't really *know* the Incinerator."

The Attendant smiled. "We never know anything, do we, really? I'll be glad to show you around."

"Oh, no. Never mind. It—it's a wonderful place."

"Yes, it is." The Attendant took pride in it. "One of the finest in the world, I think."

"I—" Lantry felt he must explain further. "I haven't had many relatives die on me since I was a child. In fact, none. So, you see I haven't been here for many years."

"I see." The Attendant's face seemed to darken somewhat.

What've I said now, thought Lantry. What in God's name is wrong? What've I done? If I'm not careful I'll get myself shoved right into that monstrous firetrap. What's wrong with this fellow's face? He seems to be giving me more than the usual going-over.

"You wouldn't be one of the men who've just returned from Mars, would you?" asked the Attendant.

"No. Why do you ask?"

"No matter." The Attendant began to walk off. "If you want to know anything, just ask me."

"Just one thing," said Lantry.

"What's that?"

"This."

Lantry dealt him a stunning blow across the neck.

He had watched the fire-trap operator with expert eyes. Now, with the sagging body in his arms, he touched the button that opened the warm outer lock, placed the body in, heard the music rise, and saw the inner lock open. The body shot out into the river of fire. The music softened.

"Well done, Lantry, well done."

Barely an instant later another Attendant entered the room. Lantry was caught with an expression of pleased excitement on his face. The Attendant looked around as if expecting to find someone, then he walked toward Lantry. "May I help you?"

"Just looking," said Lantry.

"Rather late at night," said the Attendant.

"I couldn't sleep."

That was the wrong answer, too. Everybody slept in this world. Nobody had insomnia. If you did you simply turned on a hypno-ray, and, sixty seconds later, you were snoring. Oh, he was just *full* of wrong answers. First he had made the fatal error of saying he had never been in the Incinerator before, when he knew that all children were brought here on tours, every year, from the time they were four, to instill the idea of the clean fire death and the Incinerator in their minds. Death was a bright fire, death was warmth and the sun. It was not a dark, shadowed thing. That was important in their education. And he, pale, thoughtless fool, had immediately gabbled out his ignorance.

And another thing, this paleness of his. He looked at his hands and realized with growing terror that a pale man also was nonexistent in this world. They would suspect his paleness. That was why the first attendant had asked, "Are you one of those men newly returned from Mars?" Here, now, this new Attendant was clean and bright as a copper penny, his cheeks red with health and energy. Lantry hid his pale hands in his pockets. But he was finally aware of the searching the Attendant did on his face.

"I mean to say," said Lantry, "I didn't *want* to sleep. I wanted to think."

"Was there a service held here a moment ago?" asked the Attendant, looking about.

"I don't know, I just came in."

"I thought I heard the fire lock open and shut."

"I don't know," said Lantry.

The man pressed a wall button. "Anderson?"

A voice replied. "Yes."

"Locate Saul for me, will you?"

"I'll ring the corridors." A pause. "Can't find him."

"Thanks." The Attendant was puzzled. He was beginning to make little sniffing motions with his nose. "Do you—*smell* anything?"

Lantry sniffed. "No. Why?"

"I *smell* something."

Lantry took hold of the knife in his pocket. He waited.

"I remember once when I was a kid," said the man. "And we found a cow lying dead in the field. It had been there two days in the hot sun. That's what this smell is. I wonder what it's from?"

"Oh, I know what it is," said Lantry quietly. He held out his hand. "Here."

"What?"

"Me, of course."

"You?"

"Dead several hundred years."

"You're an odd joker." The Attendant was puzzled.

"Very." Lantry took out the knife. "Do you know what this is?"

"A knife."

"Do you ever use knives on people any more?"

"How do you mean?"

"I mean—killing them, with knives or guns or poison?"

"You *are* an odd joker!" The man giggled awkwardly.

"I'm going to kill you," said Lantry.

"Nobody kills anybody," said the man.

"Not any more they don't. But they used to, in the old days."

"I know they did."

"This will be the first murder in three hundred years. I just killed your friend. I just shoved him into the fire lock."

That remark had the desired effect. It numbed the man so completely, it shocked him so thoroughly with its illogical aspects that Lantry had time to walk forward. He put the knife against the man's chest. "I'm going to kill you."

"That's silly," said the man, numbly. "People don't do that."

"Like this," said Lantry. "You see?"

The knife slid into the chest. The man stared at it for a moment. Lantry caught the falling body.

III

The Salem flue exploded at six that morning. The great fire chimney shattered into ten thousand parts and flung itself into the earth and into the sky and into the houses of the sleeping people. There was fire and sound, more fire than autumn made burning in the hills.

William Lantry was five miles away at the time of the explosion. He saw the town ignited by the great spreading cremation of it. And he shook his head and laughed a little bit and clapped his hands smartly together.

Relatively simple. You walked around killing people who didn't believe in murder, had only heard of it indirectly as some dim gone custom of the old barbarian races. You walked into the control room of the Incinerator and said, "How do you work this Incinerator?" and the control man told you, because everybody told the truth in this world of the future, nobody lied, there was no reason to lie, there was no danger to lie *against*. There was only one criminal in the world, and nobody knew HE existed yet.

Oh, it was an incredibly beautiful setup. The Control Man had told him just how the Incinerator worked, what pressure gauges controlled the flood of fire gases going up the flue, what levers were adjusted or readjusted. He and Lantry had had quite a talk. It was an easy, free world. People trusted people. A moment later Lantry had shoved a knife in the Control Man also and set the pressure gauges for an overload to occur half an hour later, and walked out of the Incinerator halls, whistling.

Now even the sky was palled with the vast black cloud of the explosion.

"This is only the first," said Lantry, looking at the sky. "I'll tear all the others down before they even suspect there's an unethical man loose in their society. They can't account for a variable like me. I'm beyond their understanding. I'm incomprehensible, impossible, therefore I do not exist. My God, I can kill hundreds of thousands of them before they even realize murder is out in the world again. I can make it look like an accident each time. Why, the idea is so huge, it's unbelievable!"

The fire burned the town. He sat under a tree for a long time, until morning. Then, he found a cave in the hills, and went in, to sleep.

He awoke at sunset with a sudden dream of fire. He saw himself pushed into the flue, cut into sections by flame, burned away to nothing. He sat up on the cave floor, laughing at himself. He had an idea.

He walked down into the town and stepped into an audio booth. He dialed OPERATOR. "Give me the Police Department," he said.

"I beg your pardon?" said the operator.

He tried again. "The Law Force," he said.

"I will connect you with the Peace Control," she said, at last.

A little fear began ticking inside him like a tiny watch. Suppose the operator recognized the term Police Department as an anachronism, took his audio number, and sent someone out to investigate? No, she wouldn't do that. Why should she suspect? Paranoids were nonexistent in this civilization.

"Yes, the Peace Control," he said.

A buzz. A man's voice answered. "Peace Control. Stephens speaking."

"Give me the Homicide Detail," said Lantry, smiling.

"The *what?*"

"Who investigates murders?"

"I beg your pardon, what are you talking about?"

"Wrong number." Lantry hung up, chuckling. Ye gods, there was no such a thing as a Homicide Detail.

There were no murders, therefore they needed no detectives. Perfect, perfect!

The audio rang back. Lantry hesitated, then answered.

"Say," said the voice on the phone. "Who *are* you?"

"The man just left who called," said Lantry, and hung up again.

He ran. They would recognize his voice and perhaps send someone out to check. People didn't lie. *He* had just lied. They knew his voice. He had lied. Anybody who lied needed a psychiatrist. They would come to pick him up to see why he was lying. For no *other* reason. They suspected him of nothing else. Therefore —he must run.

Oh, how very carefully he must act from now on. He knew nothing of this world, this odd straight truthful ethical world. Simply by looking pale you were suspect. Simply by not sleeping nights you were suspect. Simply by not bathing, by smelling like a—dead cow?—you were suspect. Anything.

He must go to a library. But that was dangerous, too. What were libraries like today? Did they have books or did they have film spools which projected books on a screen? Or did people have libraries at home, thus eliminating the necessity of keeping large main libraries?

He decided to chance it. His use of archaic terms might well make him suspect again, but now it was very important he learn all that could be learned of this foul world into which he had come again. He stopped a man on the street. "Which way to the library?"

The man was not surprised. "Two blocks east, one block north."

"Thank you."

Simple as that.

He walked into the library a few minutes later.

"May I help you?"

He looked at the librarian. May I help you, may I help you. What a world of helpful people! "I'd like to 'have' Edgar Allan Poe." His verb was carefully chosen. He didn't say 'read.' He was too afraid that books were passé, that printing itself was a lost art. Maybe all 'books' today were in the form of fully delineated three-dimensional motion pictures. How in blazes could you make a motion picture out of Socrates, Schopenhauer, Nietzsche, and Freud?

"What was that name again?"

"Edgar Allan Poe."

"There is no such author listed in our files."

"Will you please check?"

She checked. "Oh, yes. There's a red mark on the file card. He was one of the authors in the Great Burning of 2265."

"How ignorant of me."

"That's all right," she said. "Have you heard much of him?"

"He had some interesting barbarian ideas on death," said Lantry.

"Horrible ones," she said, wrinkling her nose. "Ghastly."

"Yes. Ghastly. Abominable, in fact. Good thing he was burned. Unclean. By the way, do you have any of Lovecraft?"

"Is that a sex book?"

Lantry exploded with laughter. "No, no. It's a man."

She riffled the file. "He was burned, too. Along with Poe."

"I suppose that applies to Machen and a man named Derleth and one named Ambrose Bierce, also?"

"Yes." She shut the file cabinet. "All burned. And good riddance." She gave him an odd warm look of interest. "I bet you've just come back from Mars."

"Why do you say that?"

"There was another explorer in here yesterday. He'd just made the Mars hop and return. He was interested in supernatural literature, also. It seems there are actually 'tombs' on Mars."

"What are 'tombs'?" Lantry was learning to keep his mouth closed.

"You know, those things they once buried people in."

"Barbarian custom. Ghastly!"

"*Isn't* it? Well, seeing the Martian tombs made this young explorer curious. He came and asked if we had any of those authors you mentioned. Of course we haven't even a smitch of their stuff." She looked at his pale face. "You *are* one of the Martian rocket men, aren't you?"

"Yes," he said. "Got back on the ship the other day."

"The other young man's name was Burke."

"Of course. Burke! Good friend of mine!"

"Sorry I can't help you. You'd best get yourself some vitamin shots and some sun lamps. You look terrible, Mr.——?"

"Lantry. I'll be good. Thanks ever so much. See you next Hallows' Eve!"

"Aren't you the clever one." She laughed. "If there *were* a Hallows' Eve, I'd make it a date."

"But they burned *that*, too," he said.

"Oh, they burned everything," she said. "Good night."

"Good night." And he went on out.

Oh, how carefully he was balanced in this world! Like some kind of dark gyroscope, whirling with never a murmur, a very silent man. As he walked along the eight o'clock evening street he noticed with particular interest that there was not an unusual amount of lights about. There were the usual street lights at each corner, but the blocks themselves were only faintly illuminated. Could it be that these remarkable people were not *afraid of the dark?* Incredible nonsense! *Every one* was afraid of the dark. *Even he* himself had been afraid, as a child. It was as natural as eating.

A little boy ran by on pelting feet, followed by six others. They yelled and shouted and rolled on the dark cool October lawn, in the leaves. Lantry looked on for several minutes before addressing himself to one of the small boys who was for a moment taking a respite, gathering his breath into his small lungs, as a boy might blow to refill a punctured paper bag.

"Here, now," said Lantry. "You'll wear yourself out."

"Sure," said the boy.

"Could you tell me," said the man, "why there are no street lights in the middle of the blocks?"

"Why?" asked the boy.

"I'm a teacher, I thought I'd test your knowledge," said Lantry.

"Well," said the boy, "you don't need lights in the middle of the block, that's why."

"But it gets rather dark," said Lantry.

"So?" said the boy.

"Aren't you afraid?" asked Lantry.

"Of what?" asked the boy.

"The dark," said Lantry.

"Ho ho," said the boy. "Why should I be?"

"Well," said Lantry. "It's black, it's dark. And after all, street lights were invented to take away the dark and take away fear."

"That's silly. Street lights were made so you could see where you were walking. Outside of that there's nothing."

"You miss the whole point—" said Lantry. "Do you mean to say you would sit in the middle of an empty lot all night and not be afraid?"

"Of what?"

"Of what, of what, of what, you little ninny! Of the dark!"

"Ho ho."

"Would you go out in the hills and stay all night in the dark?"

"Sure."

"Would you stay in a deserted house alone?"

"Sure."

"And not be afraid?"

"Sure."

"You're a liar!"

"Don't you call me nasty names!" shouted the boy. Liar was the improper noun, indeed. It seemed to be the worst thing you could call a person.

Lantry was completely furious with the little monster. "Look," he insisted. "Look into my eyes . . ."

The boy looked.

Lantry bared his teeth slightly. He put out his hands, making a clawlike gesture. He leered and gesticulated and wrinkled his face into a terrible mask of horror.

"Ho ho," said the boy. "You're funny."

"*What* did you say?"

"You're funny. Do it again. Hey, gang, c'mere! This man does funny things!"

"Never mind."

"Do it again, sir."

"Never mind, never mind. Good night!" Lantry ran off.

"Good night, sir. And mind the dark, sir!" called the little boy.

Of all the stupidity, of all the rank, gross, crawling, jelly-mouthed stupidity! He had never seen the like of it in his life! Bringing the children up without so much as an *ounce* of imagination! Where was the fun in being children if you didn't imagine things?

He stopped running. He slowed and for the first time began to appraise himself. He ran his hand over his face and bit his fingers and found that he himself was standing midway in the block and he felt uncomfortable. He moved up to the street corner where there was a glowing lantern. "That's better," he said, holding his hands out like a man to an open warm fire.

He listened. There was not a sound except the night breathing of the crickets. Finally there was a fire-hush as a rocket swept the sky. It was the sound a torch might make brandished gently on the dark air.

He listened to himself and for the first time he realized what there was so peculiar to himself. There was not a sound in him. The little nostril and lung noises were absent. His lungs did not take nor give oxygen or carbon dioxide; they did not move. The hairs in his nostrils did not quiver with warm combing air. That faint purling whisper of breathing did not sound in his nose. Strange. Funny. A noise you never heard when you were alive, the breath that fed your body, and yet, once dead, oh how you missed it!

The only other time you ever heard it was on deep dreamless awake nights when you wakened and listened and heard first your nose taking and gently poking out the air, and then the dull deep dim red thunder of the blood in your temples, in your eardrums, in your throat, in your aching wrists, in your warm loins, in your chest. All of those little rhythms, gone. The wrist beat gone, the throat pulse gone, the chest vibration gone. The sound of the blood coming up down around and through, up down around and through. Now it was like listening to a statue.

And yet he *lived.* Or, rather, moved about. And how was this done, over and above scientific explanations, theories, doubts?

By one thing, and one thing alone.

Hatred.

Hatred was a blood in him, it went up down around and through, up down around and through. It was a heart in him, not beating, true, but warm. He was— what? Resentment. Envy. They said he could not lie any longer in his coffin in the cemetery. He had *wanted* to. He had never had any particular desire to get up and walk around. It had been enough, all these centuries, to lie in the deep box and feel but *not feel* the ticking of the million insect watches in the earth around, the moves of worms like so many deep thoughts in the soil.

But then they had come and said, "Out you go and into the furnace!" And that is the worst thing you can say to any man. You cannot tell him what to do. If you say you are dead, he will want not to be dead. If you say there are no such things as vampires, by God, that man will try to *be* one just for spite. If you say a dead man cannot walk, he will test his limbs. If you say murder is no longer occurring, he will make it occur. He was, *in toto,* all the impossible things. They had given birth to him with their practices and ignorances. Oh, how wrong they were. They needed to be shown. He would *show* them! Sun is *good,* so is *night,* there is nothing wrong with dark, *they* said.

Dark is horror, he shouted, silently, facing the little houses. It is *meant* for contrast. You must fear, you hear! That has always been the way of this world. You destroyers of Edgar Allan Poe and fine big-worded Lovecraft, you burner of Halloween masks and destroyer of pumpkin jack-o-lanterns! I will make night what it *once* was, the thing against which man built all his lanterned cities and his many children!

As if in answer to this, a rocket, flying low, trailing a

long rakish feather of flame. It made Lantry flinch and draw back.

IV

It was but ten miles to the little town of Science Port. He made it by dawn, walking. But even this was not good. At four in the morning a silver beetle pulled up on the road beside him.

"Hello," called the man inside.

"Hello," said Lantry, wearily.

"Why are you walking?" asked the man.

"I'm going to Science Port."

"Why don't you ride?"

"I *like* to walk."

"*Nobody* likes to walk. Are you sick? May I give you a ride?"

"Thanks, but I like to walk."

The man hesitated, then closed the beetle door. "Good night."

When the beetle was gone over the hill, Lantry retreated into a nearby forest. A world full of bungling, helping people. By God, you couldn't even *walk* without being accused of sickness. That meant only one thing. He must not walk any longer, he had to ride. He should have accepted that fellow's offer.

The rest of the night he walked far enough off the highway so that if a beetle rushed by he had time to vanish in the underbrush. At dawn he crept into an empty dry water drain and closed his eyes.

The dream was as perfect as a rimed snowflake.

He saw the graveyard where he had lain deep and ripe over the centuries. He heard the early morning footsteps of the laborers returning to finish their work.

"Would you mind passing me the shovel, Jim?"

"Here you go."

"Wait a minute, wait a minute!"

"What's up?"

"Look here. We didn't finish last night, did we?"

"No."

"There was one more coffin, wasn't there?"

"Yes."

"Well, here it is, and open!"

"You've got the wrong hole."

"What's the name say on the gravestone?"

"Lantry. William Lantry."

"That's him, that's the one! Gone!"

"What could have happened to it?"

"How do I know. The body was here last night."

"We can't be sure, we didn't look."

"God man, people don't bury empty coffins. He was in his box. Now he isn't."

"Maybe this box was empty."

"Nonsense. Smell that smell? He was here all right."

A pause.

"Nobody would have taken the body, would they?"

"What for?"

"A curiosity, perhaps."

"Don't be ridiculous. People just don't steal. Nobody steals."

"Well, then, there's only one solution."

"And?"

"He got up and walked away."

A pause. In the dark dream, Lantry expected to hear laughter. There was none. Instead, the voice of the grave-digger, after a thoughtful pause, said, "Yes. That's it, indeed. He got up and walked away."

"That's interesting to think about," said the other.

"Isn't it, though!"

Silence.

Lantry awoke. It had all been a dream, but, how realistic. How strangely the two men had carried on. But not unnaturally, oh, no. That was exactly how you expected men of the future to talk. Men of the future. Lantry grinned wryly. That was an anachronism for you. This *was* the future. This was happening *now*. It wasn't three hundred years from now, it was now, not then, or any other time. This wasn't the twentieth century. Oh, how calmly those two men in the dream had said, "He got up and walked away." "—interesting to think about." *"Isn't* it, though?" With never a quaver in their voices. With not so much as a glance over their shoulders or a tremble of spade in hand. But, of course, with their perfectly honest, logical minds, there was but one explanation; certainly nobody had *stolen* the corpse. *"Nobody* steals." The corpse had simply got up and walked off. The corpse was the only one who could have *possibly* moved the corpse. By the few casual slow words of the gravediggers Lantry knew what they were thinking. Here was a man that had lain in suspended animation, not really dead, for hundreds of years. The jarring about, the activity, had brought him back.

Everyone had heard of those little green toads that are sealed for centuries inside mud rocks or in ice patties, alive, alive oh! And how when scientists chipped them out and warmed them like marbles in their hands the little toads leapt about and frisked and blinked. Then it was only logical that the gravediggers think of William Lantry in like fashion.

But what if the various parts were fitted together in the next day or so? If the vanished body and the shattered, exploded incinerator were connected? What if this fellow named Burke, who had returned pale from Mars, went to the library again and said to the young woman he wanted some books and she said, "Oh, your friend Lantry was in the other day." And he'd say, 'Lantry who? Don't know anyone by that name.' And she'd say, "Oh, he *lied.*" And people in this time didn't lie. So it would all form and coalesce, item by item, bit by bit. A pale man who was pale and shouldn't be pale had lied and people don't lie, and a walking man on a lonely country road had walked and people don't walk any more, and a body was missing from a cemetery, and the Incinerator had blown up and and and—

They would come after him. They would find him. He would be easy to find. He walked. He lied. He was pale. They would find him and take him and stick him through the open fire lock of the nearest Burner and that would be your Mr. William Lantry, like a Fourth of July set-piece!

There was only one thing to be done efficiently and completely. He arose in violent moves. His lips were wide and his dark eyes were flared and there was a trembling and burning all through him. He must kill and kill and kill and kill and kill. He must make his enemies into friends, into people like himself who walked but shouldn't walk, who were pale in a land of pinks. He must kill and then kill and then kill again. He must make bodies and dead people and corpses. He must destroy Incinerator after Flue after Burner after Incinerator. Explosion on explosion. Death on death. Then, when the Incinerators were all in thrown ruin, and the hastily established morgues were jammed with the bodies of people shattered by the explosion, then he would begin his making of friends, his enrollment of the dead in his own cause.

Before they traced and found and killed him, they must be killed themselves. So far he was safe. He could kill and they would not kill back. People simply do not go around killing. That was his safety margin. He climbed out of the abandoned drain, stood in the road.

He took the knife from his pocket and hailed the next beetle.

It was like the Fourth of July! The biggest firecracker of them all. The Science Port Incinerator split down the middle and flew apart. It made a thousand small explosions that ended with a greater one. It fell upon the town and crushed houses and burned trees. It woke people from sleep and then put them to sleep again, forever, an instant later.

William Lantry, sitting in a beetle that was not his own, tuned idly to a station on the audio dial. The collapse of the Incinerator had killed some four hundred people. Many had been caught in flattened houses, others struck by flying metal. A temporary morgue was being set up at—

An address was given.

Lantry noted it with a pad and pencil.

He could go on this way, he thought, from town to town, from country to country, destroying the Burners, the Pillars of Fire, until the whole clean magnificent framework of flame and cauterization was tumbled. He made a fair estimate—each explosion averaged five hundred dead. You could work that up to a hundred thousand in no time.

He pressed the floor stud on the beetle. Smiling, he drove off through the dark streets of the city.

* * *

The city coroner had requisitioned an old warehouse. From midnight until four in the morning the gray beetles hissed down the rain-shiny streets, turned in, and the bodies were laid out on the cold concrete floors, with white sheets over them. It was a continuous flow until about four-thirty, then it stopped. There were about two hundred bodies there, white and cold.

The bodies were left alone; nobody stayed behind to tend them. There was no use tending the dead; it was a useless procedure; the dead could take care of themselves.

About five o'clock, with a touch of dawn in the east, the first trickle of relatives arrived to identify their sons or their fathers or their mothers or their uncles. The people moved quickly into the warehouse, made the identification, moved quickly out again. By six o'clock, with the sky still lighter in the east, this trickle had passed on, also.

William Lantry walked across the wide wet street and entered the warehouse.

He held a piece of blue chalk in one hand.

He walked by the coroner who stood in the entranceway talking to two others. ". . . drive the bodies to the Incinerator in Mellin Town, tomorrow . . ." The voices faded.

Lantry moved, his feet echoing faintly on the cool concrete. A wave of sourceless relief came to him as he walked among the shrouded figures. He was among his own. And—better than that! He had *created* these! He had made them dead! He had procured for himself a vast number of recumbent friends!

Was the coroner watching? Lantry turned his head. No. The warehouse was calm and quiet and shadowed in the dark morning. The coroner was walking away now; across the street, with his two attendants; a beetle had drawn up on the other side of the street, and the coroner was going over to talk with whoever was in the beetle.

William Lantry stood and made a blue chalk pentagram on the floor by each of the bodies. He moved swiftly, swiftly, without a sound, without blinking. In a few minutes, glancing up now and then to see if the coroner was still busy, he had chalked the floor by a hundred bodies. He straightened up and put the chalk in his pocket.

Now is the time for all good men to come to the aid of their party, now is the time for all good men to come to the aid of their party, now is the time for all good men to come to the aid of their party, now is the time . . .

Lying in the earth, over the centuries, the processes and thoughts of passing peoples and passing times had seeped down to him, slowly, as into a deep-buried sponge. From some death-memory in him now, ironically, repeatedly, a black typewriter clacked out black even lines of pertinent words:

Now is the time for all good men, for all good men, to come to the aid of—

William Lantry.

Other words—

Arise my love, and come away—

The quick brown fox jumped over . . . *Paraphrase it.* The quick risen body jumped over the tumbled Incinerator . . .

Lazarus, come forth from the tomb . . .

He knew the right words. He need only speak them as they had been spoken over the centuries. He need only gesture with his hands and speak the words, the dark words that would cause these bodies to quiver, rise and walk!

And when they had risen he would take them through the town, they would kill others, and the others would rise and walk. By the end of the day there would be thousands of good friends, walking with him. And what of the naïve, living people of this year, this day, this hour? They would be completely unprepared for it. They would go down to defeat because they would not be expecting war of any sort. They wouldn't believe it possible, it would all be over before they could convince themselves that such an illogical thing could happen.

He lifted his hands. His lips moved. He said the words. He began in a chanting whisper and then raised his voice, louder. He said the words again and again. His eyes were closed tightly. His body swayed. He spoke faster and faster. He began to move forward among the bodies. The dark words flowed from his mouth. He was enchanted with his own formulae. He stooped and made further blue symbols on the concrete, in the fashion of long-dead sorcerers, smiling, confident. Any moment now the first tremor of the still bodies, any moment now the rising, the leaping up of the cold ones!

His hands lifted in the air. His head nodded. He spoke, he spoke, he spoke. He gestured. He talked loudly over the bodies, his eyes flaring, his body tensed. "Now!" he cried, violently. "Rise, *all* of you!"

Nothing happened.

"Rise!" he screamed, with a terrible torment in his voice.

The sheets lay in white blue-shadow folds over the silent bodies.

"Hear me, and act!" he shouted.

Far away, on the street, a beetle hissed along.

Again, again, again he shouted, pleaded. He got down by each body and asked of it his particular violent favor. No reply. He strode wildly between the even white rows, flinging his arms up, stooping again and again to make blue symbols!

Lantry was very pale. He licked his lips. "Come on, get up," he said. "They have, they always have, for a thousand years. When you make a mark—so! and speak a word—so! they always rise! Why not now, why not you! Come on, come *on*, before *they* come back!"

The warehouse went up into shadow. There were steel beams across and down. In it, under the roof, there was not a sound, except the raving of a lonely man.

Lantry stopped.

Through the wide doors of the warehouse he caught a glimpse of the last cold stars of morning.

This was the year 2349.

His eyes grew cold and his hands fell to his sides. He did not move.

Once upon a time people shuddered when they heard the wind about the house, once people raised crucifixes and wolfbane, and believed in walking dead and bats and loping white wolves. And as long as they believed, then so long did the dead, the bats, the loping wolves exist. The mind gave birth and reality to them.

But . . .

He looked at the white sheeted bodies.

These people did not believe.

They had never believed. They would never believe. They had never imagined that the dead might walk. The dead went up flues in flame. They had never heard superstition, never trembled or shuddered or doubted in the dark. Walking dead people could not exist, they were illogical. This was the year 2349, man, after all!

Therefore, these people could not rise, could not walk again. They were dead and flat and cold. Nothing, chalk, imprecation, superstition, could wind them up and set them walking. They were dead and *knew* they were dead!

He was alone.

There were live people in the world who moved and drove beetles and drank quiet drinks in little dimly illumined bars by country roads, and kissed women and talked much good talk all day and every day.

But he was not alive.

Friction gave him what little warmth he possessed.

There were two hundred dead people here in this warehouse now, cold upon the floor. The first dead people in a hundred years who were allowed to be corpses for an extra hour or more. The first not to be immediately trundled to the Incinerator and lit like so much phosphorus.

He should be happy with them, among them.

He was not.

They were completely dead. They did not know nor believe in walking once the heart had paused and stilled itself. They were deader than dead ever was.

He was indeed alone, more alone than any man had ever been. He felt the chill of his aloneness moving up into his chest, strangling him quietly.

William Lantry turned suddenly and gasped.

While he had stood there, someone had entered the warehouse. A tall man with white hair, wearing a light weight tan overcoat and no hat. How long the man had been nearby there was no telling.

There was no reason to stay here. Lantry turned and started to walk slowly out. He looked hastily at the man as he passed and the man with the white hair looked back at him, curiously. Had he heard? The imprecations, the pleadings, the shoutings? Did he suspect? Lantry slowed his walk. Had this man seen him make the blue chalk marks? But then, would he interpret them as symbols of an ancient superstition? Probably not.

Reaching the door, Lantry paused. For a moment he did not want to do anything but lie down and be coldly, really dead again and be carried silently down the street to some distant burning flue and there dispatched in ash and whispering fire. If he was indeed alone and there was no chance to collect an army to his cause, what, then, existed as a reason for going on? Killing? Yes, he'd kill a few thousand more. But that wasn't enough. You can only do so much of that before they drag you down.

He looked at the cold sky.

A rocket went across the black heaven, trailing fire.

Mars burned red among a million stars.

Mars. The library. The librarian. Talk. Returning rocket men. Tombs.

Lantry almost gave a shout. He restrained his hand, which wanted so much to reach up into the sky and touch Mars. Lovely red star on the sky. Good star that gave him sudden new hope. If he had a living heart now it would be thrashing wildly, and sweat would be breaking out of him and his pulses would be stammering, and tears would be in his eyes!

He would go down to wherever the rockets sprang up into space. He would go to Mars, one way or another. He would go to the Martian tombs. There, there were bodies, he would bet his last hatred on it, that would rise and walk and work with him! Theirs was an ancient culture, much different from that of Earth, patterned on the Egyptian, if what the librarian had said was true. And the Egyptian—what a crucible of dark superstition and midnight terror that culture had been. Mars it *was*, then. Beautiful Mars!

But he must not attract attention to himself. He must move carefully. He wanted to run, yes, to get away, but that would be the worst possible move he could make. The man with the white hair was glancing at Lantry from time to time, in the entranceway. There were too many people about. If anything happened he would be outnumbered. So far he had taken on only *one* man at a time.

Lantry forced himself to stop and stand on the steps before the warehouse. The man with the white hair came on onto the steps also and stood, looking at the sky. He looked as if he was going to speak at any moment. He fumbled in his pockets and took out a packet of cigarettes.

V

They stood outside the morgue together, the tall, pink, white-haired man, and Lantry, hands in their pockets. It was a cool night with a white shell of a moon that washed a house here, a road there, and farther on, parts of a river.

"Cigarette?" The man offered Lantry one.

"Thanks."

They lit up together. The man glanced at Lantry's mouth. "Cool night."

"Cool."

They shifted their feet. "Terrible accident."

"Terrible."

"So many dead."

"So many."

Lantry felt himself some sort of delicate weight upon a scale. The other man did not seem to be looking at him, but rather listening and feeling toward him. There was a feathery balance here that made for vast discomfort. He wanted to move away and get out from under this balancing, weighing. The tall white-haired man said, "My name's McClure."

"Did you have any friends inside?" asked Lantry.

"No. A casual acquaintance. Awful accident."

"Awful."

They balanced each other. A beetle hissed by on the

road with its seventeen tires whirling quietly. The moon showed a little town farther over in the black hills.

"I say," said the man McClure.

"Yes."

"Could you answer me a question?"

"Be glad to." He loosened the knife in his coat pocket, ready.

"Is your name Lantry?" asked the man at last.

"Yes."

"*William* Lantry?"

"Yes."

"Then you're the man who came out of the Salem graveyard day before yesterday, aren't you?"

"Yes."

"Good Lord, I'm glad to meet you, Lantry! We've been trying to find you for the past twenty-four hours!"

The man seized his hand, pumped it, slapped him on the back.

"What, what?" said Lantry.

"Good Lord, man, why did you run off? Do you realize what an instance this is? We want to talk to you!"

McClure was smiling, glowing. Another handshake, another slap. "I *thought* it was you!"

The man is mad, thought Lantry. Absolutely mad. Here I've toppled his incinerators, killed people, and he's shaking my hand. Mad, mad!

"Will you come along to the Hall?" said the man, taking his elbow.

"Wh-what hall?" Lantry stepped back.

"The Science Hall, of course. It isn't every year we get a real case of suspended animation. In small animals, yes, but in a man, hardly! Will you come?"

"What's the act!" demanded Lantry, glaring. "What's all this talk."

"My dear fellow, what do you mean?" the man was stunned.

"Never mind. Is that the only reason you want to see me?"

"What other reason would there be, Mr. Lantry? You don't know how glad I am to see you!" He almost did a little dance. "I suspected. When we were in there together. You being so pale and all. And then the way you smoked your cigarette, something about it, and a lot of other things, all subliminal. But it is you, isn't it, it *is* you!"

"It is I. William Lantry." Dryly.

"Good fellow! Come along!"

The beetle moved swiftly through the dawn streets. McClure talked rapidly.

Lantry sat, listening, astounded. Here was this fool, McClure, playing his cards for him! Here was this stupid scientist, or whatever, accepting him not as a suspicious baggage, a murderous item. Oh no! Quite the contrary! Only as a suspended animation case was he considered! Not as a dangerous man at all. Far from it!

"Of course," cried McClure, grinning. "You didn't know where to go, whom to turn to. It was all quite incredible to you."

"Yes."

"I had a feeling you'd be there at the morgue tonight," said McClure, happily.

"Oh?" Lantry stiffened.

"Yes. Can't explain it. But you, how shall I put it? Ancient Americans? You had funny ideas on death. And you were among the dead so long, I felt you'd be drawn back by the accident, by the morgue and all. It's not very logical. Silly, in fact. It's just a feeling. I hate feelings but there it was. I came on a, I guess you'd call it a hunch, wouldn't you?"

"You might call it that."

"And there you were!"

"There I was," said Lantry.

"Are you hungry?"

"I've eaten."

"How did you get around?"

"I hitchhiked."

"You *what?*"

"People gave me rides on the road."

"Remarkable."

"I imagine it sounds that way." He looked at the passing houses. "So this is the era of space travel, is it?"

"Oh, we've been traveling to Mars for some forty years now."

"Amazing. And those big funnels, those towers in the middle of every town?"

"Those. Haven't you heard? The Incinerators. Oh, of course, they hadn't anything of that sort in your time. Had some bad luck with them. An explosion in Salem and one here, all in a forty-eight-hour period. You looked as if you were going to speak; what is it?"

"I was thinking," said Lantry. "How fortunate I got out of my coffin when I did. I might well have been thrown into one of your Incinerators and burned up."

"Quite."

Lantry toyed with the dials on the beetle dash. He wouldn't go to Mars. His plans were changed. If this fool simply refused to recognize an act of violence when he stumbled upon it, then let him be a fool. If they didn't connect the two explosions with a man from the tomb, all well and good. Let them go on deluding themselves. If they couldn't imagine someone being mean and nasty and murderous, heaven help them. He rubbed his hands with satisfaction. No, no Martian trip for you, as yet, Lantry lad. First, we'll see what can be done boring from the inside. Plenty of time. The Incinerators can wait an extra week or so. One has to be subtle, you know. Any more immediate explosions might cause quite a ripple of thought.

McClure was gabbling wildly on.

"Of course, you don't have to be examined immediately. You'll want a rest. I'll put you up at my place."

"Thanks. I don't feel up to being probed and pulled. Plenty of time in a week or so."

They drew up before a house and climbed out.

"You want to sleep, naturally."

"I've been asleep for centuries. Be glad to stay awake. I'm not a bit tired."

"Good." McClure let them into the house. He headed for the drink bar. "A drink will fix us up."

"You have one," said Lantry. "Later for me. I just want to sit down."

"By all means sit." McClure mixed himself a drink. He looked around the room, looked at Lantry, paused for a moment with the drink in his hand, tilted his head to one side, and put his tongue in his cheek. Then he shrugged and stirred the drink. He walked slowly to a chair and sat, sipping the drink quietly. He seemed to be listening for something. "There are cigarettes on the table," he said.

"Thanks." Lantry took one and lit it and smoked it. He did not speak for some time.

Lantry thought, I'm taking this all too easily. Maybe I should kill and run. He's the only one that has found me, yet. Perhaps this is all a trap. Perhaps we're simply sitting here waiting for the police. Or whatever in blazes they use for police these days. He looked at McClure. No. They weren't waiting for police. They were waiting for something else.

McClure didn't speak. He looked at Lantry's face and he looked at Lantry's hands. He looked at Lantry's chest a long time, with easy quietness. He sipped his drink. He looked at Lantry's feet.

Finally he said, "Where'd you get the clothing?"

"I asked someone for clothes and they gave these things to me. Darned nice of them."

"You'll find that's how we are in this world. All you have to do is ask."

McClure shut up again. His eyes moved. Only his eyes and nothing else. Once or twice he lifted his drink.

A little clock ticked somewhere in the distance.

"Tell me about yourself, Mr. Lantry."

"Nothing much to tell."

"You're modest."

"Hardly. You know about the past. I know nothing of the future, or I should say 'today' and day before yesterday. You don't learn much in a coffin."

McClure did not speak. He suddenly sat forward in his chair and then leaned back and shook his head.

They'll never suspect me, thought Lantry. They aren't superstitious, they simply *can't* believe in a dead man walking. Therefore, I'll be safe. I'll keep putting off the physical checkup. They're polite. They won't force me. Then, I'll work it so I can get to Mars. After that, the tombs, in my own good time, and the plan. God, how simple. How naïve these people are.

* * *

McClure sat across the room for five minutes. A coldness had come over him. The color was very slowly going from his face, as one sees the color of medicine vanishing as one presses the bulb at the top of a dropper. He leaned forward, saying nothing, and offered another cigarette to Lantry.

"Thanks." Lantry took it. McClure sat deeply back into his easy chair, his knees folded one over the other. He did not look at Lantry, and yet somehow did. The feeling of weighing and balancing returned. McClure was like a tall thin master of hounds listening for something that nobody else could hear. There are little silver whistles you can blow that only dogs can hear. McClure seemed to be listening acutely, sensitively for such an invisible whistle, listening with his eyes and with his half-opened, dry mouth, and with his aching, breathing nostrils.

Lantry sucked the cigarette, sucked the cigarette, sucked the cigarette, and, as many times, blew out, blew out, blew out. McClure was like some lean red-shagged hound listening and listening with a slick slide of eyes to one side, with an apprehension in that hand that was so precisely microscopic that one only sensed it, as one sensed the invisible whistle, with some part of the brain deeper than eyes or nostril or ear.

The room was so quiet the cigarette smoke made some kind of invisible noise rising to the ceiling. McClure was a thermometer, a chemist's scales, a listening hound, a litmus paper, an antennae; all these. Lantry did not move. Perhaps the feeling would pass. It had passed before. McClure did not move for a long while and then, without a word, he nodded at the sherry decanter, and Lantry refused as silently. They sat looking but not looking at each other, again and away, again and away.

McClure stiffened slowly. Lantry saw the color getting paler in those lean cheeks, and the hand tightening on the sherry glass, and a knowledge come at last to stay, never to go away, into the eyes.

Lantry did not move. He could not. All of this was of such a fascination that he wanted only to see, to hear what would happen next. It was McClure's show from here on in.

McClure said, "At first I thought it was the first psychosis I have ever seen. You, I mean. I thought, he's convinced himself, Lantry's convinced himself, he's quite insane, he's told himself to do all these little things." McClure talked as if in a dream, and continued talking and didn't stop.

"I said to myself, he purposely doesn't breathe through his nose. I watched your nostrils, Lantry. The little nostril hairs never once quivered in the last hour. That wasn't enough. It was a fact I filed. It wasn't enough. He breathes through his mouth, I said, on purpose. And then I gave you a cigarette and you sucked and blew, sucked and blew. None of it ever came out your nose. I told myself, well, that's all right. He doesn't inhale. Is that terrible, is that suspect? All in the mouth, all in the mouth. And then, I looked at your chest. I watched. It never moved up or down, it did nothing. He's convinced himself, I said to myself. He's convinced himself about all this. He doesn't move his chest, except slowly, when he thinks you're not looking. That's what I told myself."

The words went on in the silent room, not pausing, still in a dream. "And then I offered you a drink but you don't drink and I thought, he doesn't drink, I thought. Is *that* terrible? And I watched and watched you all this time. Lantry holds his breath, he's fooling himself. But now, yes, now, I understand it quite well. Now I know everything the way it is. Do you know how I know? I do not hear breathing in the room. I wait and I hear nothing. There is no beat of heart or intake of lung. The room is so silent. Nonsense, one might say, but I know. At the Incinerator I know. There is a difference. You enter a room where a man is on a bed and you know immediately whether he will look up and speak to you or whether he will not speak to you ever again. Laugh if you will, but one can tell. It is a subliminal thing. It is the whistle the dog hears when no human hears. It is the tick of a clock that has ticked so long one no longer notices. Something is in a room when a man lives in it. Something is not in the room when a man is dead in it."

* * *

McClure shut his eyes a moment. He put down his sherry glass. He waited a moment. He took up his cigarette and puffed it and then put it down in a black tray.

"I am alone in this room," he said.

Lantry did not move.

"You are dead," said McClure. "My mind does not know this. It is not a thinking thing. It is a thing of the senses and the subconscious. At first I thought, this man *thinks* he is dead, risen from the dead, a vampire. Is that not logical? Would not any man, buried as many centuries, raised in a superstitious, ignorant culture, think likewise of himself once risen from the tomb? Yes, that is logical. This man has hypnotized himself and fitted his bodily functions so that they would in no way interfere with his self-delusion, his great paranoia. He governs his breathing. He tells himself, I cannot hear my breathing, therefore I am dead. His inner mind censors the sound of breathing. He does not allow himself to eat or drink. These things he probably does in his sleep, with part of his mind, hiding the evidences of this humanity from his deluded mind at other times."

McClure finished it. "I was wrong. You are not insane. You are not deluding yourself. Nor me. This is all very illogical and—I must admit—almost frightening. Does that make you feel good, to think you frighten me? I have no label for you. You're a very odd man, Lantry. I'm glad to have met you. This will make an interesting report indeed."

"Is there anything wrong with me being dead?" said Lantry. "Is it a crime?"

"You must admit it's highly unusual."

"But, still now, is it a crime?" asked Lantry.

"We have no crime, no criminal court. We want to examine you, naturally, to find out how you have happened. It is like that chemical which, one minute is inert, the next is living cell. Who can say where what happened to what. You are that impossibility. It is enough to drive a man quite insane."

"Will I be released when you are done fingering me?"

"You will not be held. If you don't wish to be examined, you will not be. But I am hoping you will help by offering us your services."

"I might," said Lantry.

"But tell me," said McClure. "What were you doing at the morgue?"

"Nothing."

"I heard you talking when I came in."

"I was merely curious."

"You're lying. That is very bad, Mr. Lantry. The truth is far better. The truth is, is it not, that you are dead and, being the only one of your sort, were lonely. Therefore you killed people to have company."

"How does that follow?"

McClure laughed. "Logic, my dear fellow. Once I *knew* you were really dead, a moment ago, really a— what do you call it—a vampire (silly word!) I tied you immediately to the Incinerator blasts. Before that there was no reason to connect you. But once the one piece fell into place, the fact that you were dead, then it was simple to guess your loneliness, your hate, your envy, all of the tawdry motivations of a walking corpse. It took only an instant then to see the Incinerators blown to blazes, and then to think of you, among the bodies at the morgue, seeking help, seeking friends and people like yourself to work with—"

"Blast you!" Lantry was out of the chair. He was halfway to the other man when McClure rolled over and scuttled away, flinging the sherry decanter. With a great despair Lantry realized that, like an idiot, he had thrown away his one chance to kill McClure. He should have done it earlier. It had been Lantry's one weapon, his safety margin. If people in a society never *killed* each other, they never *suspected* one another. You could walk up to any one of them and kill him.

"Come back here!" Lantry threw the knife.

McClure got behind a chair. The idea of flight, of protection, of fighting, was still new to him. He had part of the idea, but there was still a bit of luck on Lantry's side if Lantry wanted to use it.

"Oh, no," said McClure, holding the chair between himself and the advancing man. "You want to kill me. It's odd, but true. I can't understand it. You want to cut me with that knife or something like that, and it's up to me to prevent you from doing such an odd thing."

"I *will* kill you!" Lantry let it slip out. He cursed himself. That was the worst possible thing to say.

Lantry lunged across the chair, clutching at McClure.

McClure was very logical. "It won't do you any good to kill me. You *know* that." They wrestled and held each other in a wild, toppling shuffle. Tables fell over, scattering articles. "You remember what happened in the morgue?"

"I don't care!" screamed Lantry.

"You didn't raise *those* dead, did you?"

"I don't care!" cried Lantry.

"Look here," said McClure, reasonably. "There will never be any more like you, ever, there's no use."

"Then I'll destroy all of you, all of you!" screamed Lantry.

"And then what? You'll still be alone, with no more like you about."

"I'll go to Mars. They have tombs there. I'll find more like myself!"

"No," said McClure. "The executive order went through yesterday. All of the tombs are being deprived of their bodies. They'll be burned in the next week."

They fell together to the floor. Lantry got his hands on McClure's throat.

"Please," said McClure. "Do you see, you'll *die*."

"What do you mean?" cried Lantry.

"Once you kill all of us, and you're alone, you'll die! The hate will die. That hate is what moved you, *nothing else!* That envy moves you. Nothing else! You'll die, inevitably. You're not immortal. You're not even alive, you're nothing but a moving hate."

"I don't care!" screamed Lantry, and began choking the man, beating his head with his fists, crouched on the defenseless body. McClure looked up at him with dying eyes.

The front door opened. Two men came in.

"I say," said one of them. "What's going on? A new game?"

Lantry jumped back and began to run.

"Yes, a new game!" said McClure, struggling up. "Catch him and you win!"

The two men caught Lantry. "We win," they said.

"Let me go!" Lantry thrashed, hitting them across their faces, bringing blood.

"Hold him tight!" cried McClure.

They held him.

"A rough game, what?" one of them said. "What do we do *now?*"

The beetle hissed along the shining road. Rain fell out of the sky and a wind ripped at the dark green wet trees. In the beetle, his hands on the half-wheel, McClure was talking. His voice was susurrant, a whispering, a hypnotic thing. The two other men sat in the back seat. Lantry sat, or rather lay, in the front seat, his head back, his eyes faintly open, the glowing green light of the dash dials showing on his cheeks. His mouth was relaxed. He did not speak.

McClure talked quietly and logically, about life and moving, about death and not moving, about the sun and the great sun Incinerator, about the emptied tombyard, about hatred and how hate lived and made a clay man live and move, and how illogical it all was, it all was, it all was. One was dead, was dead, was dead, that was all, all, all. One did not try to be otherwise. The car whispered on the moving road. The rain spattered gently on the windshield. The men in the back seat conversed quietly. Where were they going, going? To the Incinerator, of course. Cigarette smoke moved slowly up on the air, curling and tying into itself in gray loops and spirals. One was dead and must accept it.

Lantry did not move. He was a marionette, the strings cut. There was only a tiny hatred in his heart, in his eyes, like twin coals, feeble, glowing, fading.

I am Poe, he thought. I am all that is left of Edgar Allan Poe, and I am all that is left of Ambrose Bierce and all that is left of a man named Lovecraft. I am a gray night bat with sharp teeth, and I am a square black monolith monster. I am Osiris and Bal and Set. I am the Necronomicon, the Book of the Dead. I am the house of Usher, falling into flame. I am the Red Death. I am the man mortared into the catacomb with a cask of Amontillado . . . I am a dancing skeleton. I am a coffin, a shroud, a lightning bolt reflected in an old house window. I am an autumn-empty tree, I am a rapping, flinging shutter. I am a yellowed volume turned by a claw hand. I am an organ played in an attic at midnight. I am a mask, a skull mask behind an oak tree on the last day of October. I am a poison apple bobbling in a water tub for child noses to bump at, for child teeth to snap . . . I am a black candle lighted before an inverted cross. I am a coffin lid, a sheet with eyes, a foot-step on a black stairwell. I am Dunsany and Machen and I am the Legend of Sleepy Hollow. I am The Monkey's Paw and I am The Phantom Rickshaw. I am the Cat and the Canary, the Gorilla, the Bat. I am the ghost of Hamlet's father on the castle wall.

All of these things am I. And now these last things will be burned. While I lived *they* still lived. While I moved and hated and existed, *they* still existed. I am *all* that remembers them. I am all of them that *still* goes on, and will *not* go on after tonight. Tonight, all of us, Poe and Bierce and Hamlet's father, we burn together. They will make a big heap of us and burn us like a bonfire, like things of Guy Fawkes' day, gasoline, torches, cries, and all!

And what a wailing will we put up. The world will be clean of us, but in our going we shall say, oh what is the world like, clean of fear, where is the dark imagination from the dark time, the thrill and the anticipation, the suspense of old October, gone, never more to come again, flattened and smashed and burned by the rocket people, by the Incinerator people, destroyed and obliterated, to be replaced by doors that open and close and lights that go on and off without fear. If only you could remember how once *we* lived, what Halloween was to us, and what Poe was, and how we gloried in the dark morbidities. One more drink, dear friends, of Amontillado, before the burning. All of this, all, exists but in one last brain on earth. A whole world dying tonight. One more drink, pray.

"Here we are," said McClure.

* * *

The Incinerator was brightly lighted. There was quiet music nearby. McClure got out of the beetle, came around to the other side. He opened the door. Lantry simply lay there. The talking and the logical talking had slowly drained him of life. He was no more than wax now, with a small glow in his eyes. This future world, how the men *talked* to you, how logically they reasoned away your life. They wouldn't believe in him. The force of their disbelief froze him. He could not move his arms or his legs. He could only mumble senselessly, coldly, eyes flickering.

McClure and the two others helped him out of the car, put him in a golden box, and rolled him on a roller table into the warm glowing interior of the building.

I am Edgar Allan Poe, I am Ambrose Bierce, I am Halloween, I am a coffin, a shroud, a Monkey's Paw, a Phantom, a Vampire . . .

"Yes, yes," said McClure, quietly, over him. "I know. I know."

The table glided. The walls swung over him and by him, the music played. You are dead, you are logically dead.

I am Usher, I am the Maelstrom, I am the MS Found In A Bottle, I am the Pit and I am the Pendulum, I am the Telltale Heart, I am the Raven nevermore, nevermore.

"Yes," said McClure, as they walked softly. "I know."

"I am in the catacomb," cried Lantry.

"Yes, the catacomb," said the walking man over him.

"I am being chained to a wall, and there is no bottle of Amontillado here!" cried Lantry weakly, eyes closed.

"Yes," someone said.

There was movement. The flame door opened.

"Now someone is mortaring up the cell, closing me in!"

"Yes, I *know.*" A whisper.

The golden box slid into the flame lock.

"I'm being walled in! A very good joke indeed! Let us be gone!" A wild scream and much laughter.

"We know, we understand . . ."

The inner flame lock opened. The golden coffin shot forth into flame.

"For the love of God, Montresor! For the love of God!"

ZERO HOUR

Oh, it was to be so jolly! What a game! Such excitement they hadn't known in years. The children catapulted this way and that across the green lawns, shouting at each other, holding hands, flying in circles, climbing trees, laughing. Overhead the rockets flew, and beetle cars whispered by on the streets, but the children played on. Such fun, such tremulous joy, such tumbling and hearty screaming.

Mink ran into the house, all dirt and sweat. For her seven years she was loud and strong and definite. Her mother, Mrs. Morris, hardly saw her as she yanked out drawers and rattled pans and tools into a large sack.

"Heavens, Mink, what's going on?"

"The most exciting game ever!" gasped Mink, pink-faced.

"Stop and get your breath," said the mother.

"No, I'm all right," gasped Mink. "Okay I take these things, Mom?"

"But don't dent them," said Mrs. Morris.

"Thank you, thank you!" cried Mink, and boom! she was gone, like a rocket.

Mrs. Morris surveyed the fleeing tot. "What's the name of the game?"

"Invasion!" said Mink. The door slammed.

In every yard on the street children brought out

knives and forks and pokers and old stovepipes and can openers.

It was an interesting fact that this fury and bustle occurred only among the younger children. The older ones, those ten years and more, disdained the affair and marched scornfully off on hikes or played a more dignified version of hide-and-seek on their own.

Meanwhile, parents came and went in chromium beetles. Repairmen came to repair the vacuum elevators in houses, to fix fluttering television sets, or hammer upon stubborn food-delivery tubes. The adult civilization passed and repassed the busy youngsters, jealous of the fierce energy of the wild tots, tolerantly amused at their flourishings, longing to join in themselves.

"This and this and *this,*" said Mink, instructing the others with their assorted spoons and wrenches. "Do that, and bring *that* over here. No! *Here,* ninny! Right. Now get back while I fix this." Tongue in teeth, face wrinkled in thought. "Like that. See?"

"Yayyyy!" shouted the kids.

Twelve-year-old Joseph Connors ran up.

"Go away," said Mink straight at him.

"I wanna play," said Joseph.

"Can't!" said Mink.

"Why not?"

"You'd just make fun of us."

"Honest, I wouldn't."

"No. We know *you.* Go away or we'll kick you."

Another twelve-year-old boy whirred by on little motor skates. "Hey, Joe! Come on! Let them sissies play!"

Joseph showed reluctance and a certain wistfulness. "I *want* to play," he said.

"You're old," said Mink firmly.

"Not *that* old," said Joe sensibly.

"You'd only laugh and spoil the Invasion."

The boy on the motor skates made a rude lip noise. "Come on, Joe! Them and their fairies! Nuts!"

Joseph walked off slowly. He kept looking back, all down the block.

Mink was already busy again. She made a kind of apparatus with her gathered equipment. She had appointed another little girl with a pad and pencil to take down notes in painful slow scribbles. Their voices rose and fell in the warm sunlight.

All around them the city hummed. The streets were lined with good green and peaceful trees. Only the wind made a conflict across the city, across the country, across the continent. In a thousand other cities there were trees and children and avenues, businessmen in their quiet offices taping their voices, or watching televisors. Rockets hovered like darning needles in the blue sky. There was the universal, quiet conceit and easiness of men accustomed to peace, quite certain there would never be trouble again. Arm in arm, men all over earth were a united front. The perfect weapons were held in equal trust by all nations. A situation of incredibly beautiful balance had been brought about. There were no traitors among men, no unhappy ones, no disgruntled ones; therefore the world was based upon a stable ground. Sunlight illumined half the world and the trees drowsed in a tide of warm air.

Mink's mother, from her upstairs window, gazed down.

The children. She looked upon them and shook her head. Well, they'd eat well, sleep well, and be in school on Monday. Bless their vigorous little bodies. She listened.

Mink talked earnestly to someone near the rose bush —though there was no one there.

These odd children. And the little girl, what was her name? Anna? Anna took notes on a pad. First, Mink asked the rosebush a question, then called the answer to Anna.

"Triangle," said Mink.

"What's a tri," said Anna with difficulty, "angle?"

"Never mind," said Mink.

"How you spell it?" asked Anna.

"T-r-i——" spelled Mink slowly, then snapped, "Oh, spell it yourself!" She went on to other words. "Beam," she said.

"I haven't got tri," said Anna, "angle down yet!"

"Well, hurry, hurry!" cried Mink.

Mink's mother leaned out the upstairs window. "A-n-g-l-e," she spelled down at Anna.

"Oh, thanks, Mrs. Morris," said Anna.

"Certainly," said Mink's mother and withdrew, laughing, to dust the hall with an electro-duster magnet.

The voices wavered on the shimmery air. "Beam," said Anna. Fading.

"Four-nine-seven-A-and-B-and-X," said Mink, far away, seriously. "And a fork and a string and a—hex-hex-agony—hexagonal!"

At lunch Mink gulped milk at one toss and was at the door. Her mother slapped the table.

"You sit right back down," commanded Mrs. Morris. "Hot soup in a minute." She poked a red button on the kitchen butler, and ten seconds later something landed with a bump in the rubber receiver. Mrs. Morris opened it, took out a can with a pair of aluminum holders, unsealed it with a flick, and poured hot soup into a bowl.

During all this Mink fidgeted. "Hurry, Mom! This is a matter of life and death! Aw——"

"I was the same way at your age. Always life and death. I know."

Mink banged away at the soup.

"Slow down," said Mom.

"Can't," said Mink. "Drill's waiting for me."

"Who's Drill? What a peculiar name," said Mom.

"You don't know him," said Mink.

"A new boy in the neighborhood?" asked Mom.

"He's new all right," said Mink. She started on her second bowl.

"Which one is Drill?" asked Mom.

"He's around," said Mink evasively. "You'll make fun. Everybody pokes fun. Gee, darn."

"Is Drill shy?"

"Yes. No. In a way. Gosh, Mom, I got to run if we want to have the Invasion!"

"Who's invading what?"

"Martians invading Earth. Well, not exactly Martians. They're—I don't know. From up." She pointed her spoon.

"And *inside,*" said Mom, touching Mink's feverish brow.

Mink rebelled. "You're laughing! You'll kill Drill and everybody."

"I didn't mean to," said Mom. "Drill's a Martian?"

"No. He's—well—maybe from Jupiter or Saturn or Venus. Anyway, he's had a hard time."

"I imagine." Mrs. Morris hid her mouth behind her hand.

"They couldn't figure a way to attack Earth."

"We're impregnable," said Mom in mock seriousness.

"That's the word Drill used! Impreg—— That was the word, Mom."

"My, my, Drill's a brilliant little boy. Two-bit words."

"They couldn't figure a way to attack, Mom. Drill says—he says in order to make a good fight you got to have a new way of surprising people. That way you win. And he says also you got to have help from your enemy."

"A fifth column," said Mom.

"Yeah. That's what Drill said. And they couldn't figure a way to surprise Earth or get help."

"No wonder. We're pretty darn strong." Mom laughed, cleaning up. Mink sat there, staring at the table, seeing what she was talking about.

"Until, one day," whispered Mink melodramatically, "they thought of children!"

"Well!" said Mrs. Morris brightly.

"And they thought of how grown-ups are so busy they never look under rosebushes or on lawns!"

"Only for snails and fungus."

"And then there's something about dim-dims."

"Dim-dims?"

"Dimens-shuns."

"Dimensions?"

"Four of 'em! And there's something about kids under nine and imagination. It's real funny to hear Drill talk."

Mrs. Morris was tired. "Well, it must be funny. You're keeping Drill waiting now. It's getting late in the day

and, if you want to have your Invasion before your supper bath, you'd better jump."

"Do I have to take a bath?" growled Mink.

"You do. Why is it children hate water? No matter
what age you live in children hate water behind the
ears!"

"Drill says I won't have to take baths," said Mink.

"Oh, he does, does he?"

"He told all the kids that. No more baths. And we
can stay up till ten o'clock and go to two televisor shows
on Saturday 'stead of one!"

"Well, Mr. Drill better mind his p's and q's. I'll call
up his mother and——"

Mink went to the door. "We're having trouble with
guys like Pete Britz and Dale Jerrick. They're growing
up. They make fun. They're worse than parents. They
just won't believe in Drill. They're so snooty, 'cause
they're growing up. You'd think they'd know better.
They were little only a coupla years ago. I hate them
worst. We'll kill them *first.*"

"Your father and I last?"

"Drill says you're dangerous. Know why? 'Cause you
don't believe in Martians! They're going to let *us* run
the world. Well, not just us, but the kids over in the next
block, too. I might be queen." She opened the door.

"Mom?"

"Yes?"

"What's lodge-ick?"

"Logic? Why, dear, logic is knowing what things are
true and not true."

"He *mentioned* that," said Mink. "And what's im-
pres-sion-able?" It took her a minute to say it.

"Why, it means——" Her mother looked at the floor,
laughing gently. "It means—to be a child, dear."

"Thanks for lunch!" Mink ran out, then stuck her
head back in. "Mom, I'll be sure you won't be hurt
much, really!"

"Well, thanks," said Mom.

Slam went the door.

At four o'clock the audiovisor buzzed. Mrs. Morris
flipped the tab. "Hello, Helen!" she said in welcome.

"Hello, Mary. How are things in New York?"

"Fine. How are things in Scranton? You look tired."

"So do you. The children. Underfoot," said Helen.

Mrs. Morris sighed. "My Mink too. The super-Invasion."

Helen laughed. "Are your kids playing that game too?"

"Lord, yes. Tomorrow it'll be geometrical jacks and motorized hopscotch. Were we this bad when we were kids in '48?"

"Worse. Japs and Nazis. Don't know how my parents put up with me. Tomboy."

"Parents learn to shut their ears."

A silence.

"What's wrong, Mary?" asked Helen.

Mrs. Morris's eyes were half closed; her tongue slid slowly, thoughtfully, over her lower lip. "Eh?" She jerked. "Oh, nothing. Just thought about *that*. Shutting ears and such. Never mind. Where were we?"

"My boy Tim's got a crush on some guy named— *Drill*, I think it was."

"Must be a new password. Mink likes him too."

"Didn't know it had got as far as New York. Word of mouth, I imagine. Looks like a scrap drive. I talked to Josephine and she said her kids—that's in Boston—are wild on this new game. It's sweeping the country."

At that moment Mink trotted into the kitchen to gulp a glass of water. Mrs. Morris turned. "How're things going?"

"Almost finished," said Mink.

"Swell," said Mrs. Morris. "What's *that*?"

"A yo-yo," said Mink. "Watch."

She flung the yo-yo down its string. Reaching the end it—

It vanished.

"See?" said Mink. "Ope!" Dibbling her finger, she made the yo-yo reappear and zip up the string.

"Do that again," said her mother.

"Can't. Zero hour's five o'clock! 'By." Mink exited, zipping her yo-yo.

On the audiovisor, Helen laughed. "Tim brought one of those yo-yos in this morning, but when I got curious he said he wouldn't show it to me, and when I tried to work it, finally, it wouldn't work."

"You're not *impressionable,*" said Mrs. Morris.

"What?"

"Never mind. Something I thought of. Can I help you, Helen?"

"I wanted to get that black-and-white cake recipe——"

The hour drowsed by. The day waned. The sun lowered in the peaceful blue sky. Shadows lengthened on the green lawns. The laughter and excitement continued. One little girl ran away, crying. Mrs. Morris came out the front door.

"Mink, was that Peggy Ann crying?"

Mink was bent over in the yard, near the rosebush. "Yeah. She's a scarebaby. We won't let her play, now. She's getting too old to play. I guess she grew up all of a sudden."

"Is that why she cried? Nonsense. Give me a civil answer, young lady, or inside you come!"

Mink whirled in consternation, mixed with irritation. "I can't quit now. It's almost time. I'll be good. I'm sorry."

"Did you hit Peggy Ann?"

"No, honest. You ask her. It was something—well, she's just a scaredy pants."

The ring of children drew in around Mink where she scowled at her work with spoons and a kind of square-shaped arrangement of hammers and pipes. "There and there," murmured Mink.

"What's wrong?" said Mrs. Morris.

"Drill's stuck. Halfway. If we could only get him all the way through, it'd be easier. Then all the others could come through after him."

"Can I help?"

"No'm, thanks. I'll fix it."

"All right. I'll call you for your bath in half an hour. I'm tired of watching you."

She went in and sat in the electric relaxing chair, sipping a little beer from a half-empty glass. The chair massaged her back. Children, children. Children love and hate, side by side. Sometimes children loved you, hated you—all in half a second. Strange children, did they ever forget or forgive the whippings and the harsh, strict words of command? She wondered. How can you ever forget or forgive those over and above you, those tall and silly dictators?

Time passed. A curious, waiting silence came upon the street, deepening.

Five o'clock. A clock sang softly somewhere in the house in a quiet, musical voice: "Five o'clock—five o'clock. Time's a-wasting. Five o'clock," and purred away into silence.

Zero hour.

Mrs. Morris chuckled in her throat. Zero hour.

A beetle car hummed into the driveway. Mr. Morris. Mrs. Morris smiled. Mr. Morris got out of the beetle, locked it and called hello to Mink at her work. Mink ignored him. He laughed and stood for a moment watching the children. Then he walked up the front steps.

"Hello, darling."

"Hello, Henry."

She strained forward on the edge of the chair, listening. The children were silent. Too silent.

He emptied his pipe, refilled it. "Swell day. Makes you glad to be alive."

Buzz.

"What's that?" asked Henry.

"I don't know." She got up suddenly, her eyes widening. She was going to say something. She stopped it. Ridiculous. Her nerves jumped. "Those children haven't anything dangerous out there, have they?" she said.

"Nothing but pipes and hammers. Why?"

"Nothing electrical?"

"Heck, no," said Henry. "I looked."

She walked to the kitchen. The buzzing continued. "Just the same, you'd better go tell them to quit. It's after five. Tell them——" Her eyes widened and narrowed. "Tell them to put off their Invasion until tomorrow." She laughed, nervously.

The buzzing grew louder.

"What are they up to? I'd better go look, all right."
The explosion!

The house shook with dull sound. There were other explosions in other yards on other streets.

Involuntarily, Mrs. Morris screamed. "Up this way!" she cried senselessly, knowing no sense, no reason. Perhaps she saw something from the corners of her eyes; perhaps she smelled a new odor or heard a new noise. There was no time to argue with Henry to convince him. Let him think her insane. Yes, insane! Shrieking, she ran upstairs. He ran after her to see what she was up to. "In the attic!" she screamed. "That's where it is!" It was only a poor excuse to get him in the attic in time. Oh, God—in time!

Another explosion outside. The children screamed with delight, as if at a great fireworks display.

"It's not in the attic!" cried Henry. "It's outside!"

"No, no!" Wheezing, gasping, she fumbled at the attic door. "I'll show you. Hurry! I'll show you!"

They tumbled into the attic. She slammed the door, locked it, took the key, threw it into a far, cluttered corner.

She was babbling wild stuff now. It came out of her. All the subconscious suspicion and fear that had gathered secretly all afternoon and fermented like a wine in her. All the little revelations and knowledges and sense that had bothered her all day and which she had logically and carefully and sensibly rejected and censored. Now it exploded in her and shook her to bits.

"There, there," she said, sobbing against the door. "We're safe until tonight. Maybe we can sneak out. Maybe we can escape!"

Henry blew up too, but for another reason. "Are you crazy? Why'd you throw that key away? Blast it!"

"Yes, yes, I'm crazy, if it helps, but stay here with me!"

"I don't know how I can get out!"

"Quiet. They'll hear us. Oh, God, they'll find us soon enough——"

Below them, Mink's voice. The husband stopped. There was a great universal humming and sizzling, a screaming and giggling. Downstairs the audio-televisor buzzed and buzzed insistently, alarmingly, violently. *Is that Helen calling?* thought Mrs. Morris. *And is she calling about what I think she's calling about?*

Footsteps came into the house. Heavy footsteps.

"Who's coming in my house?" demanded Henry angrily. "Who's tramping around down there?"

Heavy feet. Twenty, thirty, forty, fifty of them. Fifty persons crowding into the house. The humming. The giggling of the children. "This way!" cried Mink, below.

"Who's downstairs?" roared Henry. "Who's there!"

"Hush. Oh, nonononono!" said his wife, weakly, holding him. "Please, be quiet. They might go away."

"Mom?" called Mink. "Dad?" A pause. "Where are you?"

Heavy footsteps, heavy, heavy, *very heavy* footsteps, came up the stairs. Mink leading them.

"Mom?" A hesitation. "Dad?" A waiting, a silence.

Humming. Footsteps toward the attic. Mink's first.

They trembled together in silence in the attic, Mr. and Mrs. Morris. For some reason the electric humming, the queer cold light suddenly visible under the door crack, the strange odor, and the alien sound of eagerness in Mink's voice finally got through to Henry Morris too. He stood, shivering, in the dark silence, his wife beside him.

"Mom! Dad!"

Footsteps. A little humming sound. The attic lock melted. The door opened. Mink peered inside, tall blue shadows behind her.

"Peekaboo," said Mink.

THE MAN

Captain Hart stood in the door of the rocket. "Why don't they come?" he said.

"Who knows?" said Martin, his lieutenant. "Do I know, Captain?"

"What kind of a place is this, anyway?" The captain lighted a cigar. He tossed the match out into the glittering meadow. The grass started to burn.

Martin moved to stamp it out with his boot.

"No," ordered Captain Hart, "let it burn. Maybe they'll come see what's happening then, the ignorant fools."

Martin shrugged and withdrew his foot from the spreading fire.

Captain Hart examined his watch. "An hour ago we landed here, and does the welcoming committee rush out with a brass band to shake our hands? No indeed! Here we ride millions of miles through space and the fine citizens of some silly town on some unknown planet ignore us!" He snorted, tapping his watch. "Well, I'll just give them five more minutes, and then——"

"And then what?" asked Martin, ever so politely, watching the captain's jowls shake.

"We'll fly over their blasted city again and scare blazes out of them." His voice grew quieter. "Do you think, Martin, maybe they didn't see us land?"

"They saw us. They looked up as we flew over."

"Then why aren't they running across the field? Are they hiding? Are they yellow?"

Martin shook his head. "No. Take these binoculars, sir. See for yourself. Everybody's walking around. They're not frightened. They—well, they don't seem to care."

Captain Hart placed the binoculars to his tired eyes. Martin looked up and had time to observe the lines and the grooves of irritation, tiredness, nervousness there. Hart looked a million years old; he never slept, he ate little, and drove himself on, on. Now his mouth moved, aged and drear, but sharp, under the held binoculars.

"Really, Martin, I don't know why we bother. We build rockets, we go to all the trouble of crossing space, searching for them, and this is what we get. Neglect. Look at those idiots wander about in there. Don't they realize how big this is? The first space flight to touch their provincial land. How many times does that happen? Are they that blasé?"

Martin didn't know.

Captain Hart gave him back the binoculars wearily. "Why do we do it, Martin? This space travel, I mean. Always on the go. Always searching. Our insides always tight, never any rest."

"Maybe we're looking for peace and quiet. Certainly there's none on Earth," said Martin.

"No, there's not, is there?" Captain Hart was thoughtful, the fire damped down. "Not since Darwin, eh? Not since everything went by the board, everything we used to believe in, eh? Divine power and all that. And so you think maybe that's why we're going out to the stars, eh, Martin? Looking for our lost souls, is that it? Trying to get away from our evil planet to a good one?"

"Perhaps, sir. Certainly we're looking for something."

Captain Hart cleared his throat and tightened back into sharpness. "Well, right now we're looking for the mayor of that city there. Run in, tell them who we are, the first rocket expedition to Planet Forty-three in Star

System Three. Captain Hart sends his salutations and desires to meet the mayor. On the double!"

"Yes, sir." Martin walked slowly across the meadow.

"Hurry!" snapped the captain.

"Yes, sir!" Martin trotted away. Then he walked again, smiling to himself.

The captain had smoked two cigars before Martin returned.

Martin stopped and looked up into the door of the rocket, swaying, seemingly unable to focus his eyes or think.

"Well?" snapped Hart. "What happened? Are they coming to welcome us?"

"No." Martin had to lean dizzily against the ship.

"Why not?"

"It's not important," said Martin. "Give me a cigarette, please, Captain." His fingers groped blindly at the rising pack, for he was looking at the golden city and blinking. He lighted one and smoked quietly for a long time.

"Say something!" cried the captain. "Aren't they interested in our rocket?"

Martin said, "What? Oh. The rocket?" He inspected his cigarette. "No, they're not interested. Seems we came at an inopportune time."

"Inopportune time!"

Martin was patient. "Captain, listen. Something big happened yesterday in that city. It's so big, so important that we're second-rate—second fiddle. I've got to sit down." He lost his balance and sat heavily, gasping for air.

The captain chewed his cigar angrily. "What happened?"

Martin lifted his head, smoke from the burning cigarette in his fingers, blowing in the wind. "Sir, yesterday, in that city, a remarkable man appeared—good, intelligent, compassionate, and infinitely wise!"

The captain glared at his lieutenant. "What's that to do with us?"

"It's hard to explain. But he was a man for whom they'd waited a long time—a million years maybe. And yesterday he walked into their city. That's why today, sir, our rocket landing means nothing."

The captain sat down violently. "Who was it? Not Ashley? He didn't arrive in his rocket before us and steal my glory, did he?" He seized Martin's arm. His face was pale and dismayed.

"Not Ashley, sir."

"Then it was Burton! I knew it. Burton stole in ahead of us and ruined my landing! You can't trust anyone any more."

"Not Burton, either, sir," said Martin quietly.

The captain was incredulous. "There were only three rockets. We were in the lead. This man who got here ahead of us? What was his name!"

"He didn't have a name. He doesn't need one. It would be different on every planet, sir."

The captain stared at his lieutenant with hard, cynical eyes.

"Well, what did he do that was so wonderful that nobody even looks at our ship?"

"For one thing," said Martin steadily, "he healed the sick and comforted the poor. He fought hypocrisy and dirty politics and sat among the people, talking, through the day."

"Is that so wonderful?"

"Yes, Captain."

"I don't get this." The captain confronted Martin, peered into his face and eyes. "You been drinking, eh?" He was suspicious. He backed away. "I don't understand."

Martin looked at the city. "Captain, if you don't understand, there's no way of telling you."

The captain followed his gaze. The city was quiet and beautiful and a great peace lay over it. The captain stepped forward, taking his cigar from his lips. He squinted first at Martin, then at the golden spires of the buildings.

"You don't mean—you *can't* mean—— That man you're talking about couldn't be——"

Martin nodded. "That's what I mean, sir."

The captain stood silently, not moving. He drew himself up.

"I don't believe it," he said at last.

At high noon Captain Hart walked briskly into the city, accompanied by Lieutenant Martin and an assistant who was carrying some electrical equipment. Every once in a while the captain laughed loudly, put his hands on his hips, and shook his head.

The mayor of the town confronted him. Martin set up a tripod, screwed a box onto it, and switched on the batteries.

"Are you the mayor?" The captain jabbed a finger out.

"I am," said the mayor.

The delicate apparatus stood between them, controlled and adjusted by Martin and the assistant. Instantaneous translations from any language were made by the box. The words sounded crisply on the mild air of the city.

"About this occurrence yesterday," said the captain. "It occurred?"

"It did."

"You have witnesses?"

"We have."

"May we talk to them?"

"Talk to any of us," said the mayor. "We are all witnesses."

In an aside to Martin the captain said, "Mass hallucination." To the mayor, "What did this man—this stranger—look like?"

"That would be hard to say," said the mayor, smiling a little.

"Why would it?"

"Opinions might differ slightly."

"I'd like your opinion, sir, anyway," said the captain. "Record this," he snapped to Martin over his shoulder. The lieutenant pressed the button of a hand recorder.

"Well," said the mayor of the city, "he was a very gentle and kind man. He was of a great and knowing intelligence."

"Yes—yes, I know, I know." The captain waved his fingers. "Generalizations. I want something specific. What did he look like?"

"I don't believe that is important," replied the mayor.

"It's very important," said the captain sternly. "I want a description of this fellow. If I can't get it from you, I'll get it from others." To Martin, "I'm sure it must have been Burton, pulling one of his practical jokes."

Martin would not look him in the face. Martin was coldly silent.

The captain snapped his fingers. "There was something or other—a healing?"

"Many healings," said the mayor.

"May I see one?"

"You may," said the mayor. "My son." He nodded at a small boy who stepped forward. "He was afflicted with a withered arm. Now, look upon it."

At this the captain laughed tolerantly. "Yes, yes. This isn't even circumstantial evidence, you know. I didn't see the boy's withered arm. I see only his arm whole and well. That's no proof. What proof have you that the boy's arm was withered yesterday and today is well?"

"My word is my proof," said the mayor simply.

"My dear man!" cried the captain. "You don't expect me to go on hearsay, do you? Oh no!"

"I'm sorry," said the mayor, looking upon the captain with what appeared to be curiosity and pity.

"Do you have any pictures of the boy before today?" asked the captain.

After a moment a large oil portrait was carried forth, showing the son with a withered arm.

"My dear fellow!" The captain waved it away. "Anybody can paint a picture. Paintings lie. I want a photograph of the boy."

There was no photograph. Photography was not a known art in their society.

"Well," sighed the captain, face twitching, "let me talk to a few other citizens. We're getting nowhere." He pointed at a woman. "You." She hesitated. "Yes, you; come here," ordered the captain. "Tell me about this *wonderful* man you saw yesterday."

The woman looked steadily at the captain. "He walked among us and was very fine and good."

"What color were his eyes?"

"The color of the sun, the color of the sea, the color of a flower, the color of the mountains, the color of the night."

"That'll do." The captain threw up his hands. "See, Martin? Absolutely nothing. Some charlatan wanders through whispering sweet nothings in their ears and——"

"Please, stop it," said Martin.

The captain stepped back. "What?"

"You heard what I said," said Martin. "I like these people. I believe what they say. You're entitled to your opinion, but keep it to yourself, sir."

"You can't talk to me this way," shouted the captain.

"I've had enough of your high-handedness," replied Martin. "Leave these people alone. They've got something good and decent, and you come and foul up the nest and sneer at it. Well, I've talked to them too. I've gone through the city and seen their faces, and they've got something you'll never have—a little simple faith, and they'll move mountains with it. You, you're boiled because someone stole your act, got here ahead and made you unimportant!"

"I'll give you five seconds to finish," remarked the captain. "I understand. You've been under a strain, Martin. Months of traveling in space, nostalgia, loneliness. And now, with this thing happening, I sympathize, Martin. I overlook your petty insubordination."

"I don't overlook your petty tyranny," replied Martin. "I'm stepping out. I'm staying here."

"You can't do that!"

"Can't I? Try and stop me. This is what I came looking for. I didn't know it, but this is it. This is for me. Take your filth somewhere else and foul up other nests with your doubt and your—scientific method!" He looked swiftly about. "These people have had an experience, and you can't seem to get it through your head that it's really happened and we were lucky enough to almost arrive in time to be in on it.

"People on Earth have talked about this man for

twenty centuries after he walked through the old
world. We've all wanted to see him and hear him, and
never had the chance. And now, today, we just missed
seeing him by a few hours."

Captain Hart looked at Martin's cheeks. "You're crying like a baby. Stop it."

"I don't care."

"Well, I do. In front of these natives we're to keep up
a front. You're overwrought. As I said, I forgive you."

"I don't want your forgiveness."

"You idiot. Can't you see this is one of Burton's tricks,
to fool these people, to bilk them, to establish his oil and
mineral concerns under a religious guise! You fool, Martin. You absolute fool! You should know Earthmen by
now. They'll do anything—blaspheme, lie, cheat, steal,
kill, to get their ends. Anything is fine if it works; the
true pragmatist, that's Burton. You know him!"

The captain scoffed heavily. "Come off it, Martin,
admit it; this is the sort of scaly thing Burton might carry
off, polish up these citizens and pluck them when
they're ripe."

"No," said Martin, thinking of it.

The captain put his hand up. "That's Burton. That's
him. That's his dirt, that's his criminal way. I have to
admire the old dragon. Flaming in here in a blaze and a
halo and a soft word and a loving touch, with a medi-
cated salve here and a healing ray there. That's Burton
all right!"

"No." Martin's voice was dazed. He covered his
eyes. "No, I won't believe it."

"You don't want to believe." Captain Hart kept at it.
"Admit it now. Admit it! It's just the thing Burton would
do. Stop daydreaming, Martin. Wake up! It's morning.
This is a real world and we're real, dirty people—Burton the dirtiest of us all!"

Martin turned away.

"There, there, Martin," said Hart, mechanically pat-
ting the man's back. "I understand. Quite a shock for
you. I know. A rotten shame, and all that. That Burton is
a rascal. You go take it easy. Let me handle this."

Martin walked off slowly toward the rocket.

Captain Hart watched him go. Then, taking a deep

breath, he turned to the woman he had been questioning. "Well. Tell me some more about this man. As you were saying, madam?"

Later the officers of the rocket ship ate supper on card tables outside. The captain correlated his data to a silent Martin who sat red-eyed and brooding over his meal.

"Interviewed three dozen people, all of them full of the same milk and hogwash," said the captain. "It's Burton's work all right, I'm positive. He'll be spilling back in here tomorrow or next week to consolidate his miracles and beat us out in our contracts. I think I'll stick on and spoil it for him."

Martin glanced up sullenly. "I'll kill him," he said.

"Now, now, Martin! There, there, boy."

"I'll kill him—so help me, I will."

"We'll put an anchor on his wagon. You have to admit he's clever. Unethical but clever."

"He's dirty."

"You must promise not to do anything violent." Captain Hart checked his figures. "According to this, there were thirty miracles of healing performed, a blind man restored to vision, a leper cured. Oh, Burton's efficient, give him that."

A gong sounded. A moment later a man ran up. "Captain, sir. A report! Burton's ship is coming down. Also the Ashley ship, sir!"

"See!" Captain Hart beat the table. "Here come the jackals to the harvest! They can't wait to feed. Wait till I confront them. I'll make them cut me in on this feast—I will!"

Martin looked sick. He stared at the captain.

"Business, my dear boy, business," said the captain.

Everybody looked up. Two rockets swung down out of the sky.

When the rockets landed they almost crashed.

"What's wrong with those fools?" cried the captain, jumping up. The men ran across the meadowlands to the steaming ships. The captain arrived. The airlock door popped open on Burton's ship.

A man fell out into their arms.

"What's wrong?" cried Captain Hart.

The man lay on the ground. They bent over him and he was burned, badly burned. His body was covered with wounds and scars and tissue that was inflamed and smoking. He looked up out of puffed eyes and his thick tongue moved in his split lips.

"What happened?" demanded the captain, kneeling down, shaking the man's arm.

"Sir, sir," whispered the dying man. "Forty-eight hours ago, back in Space Sector Seventy-nine DFS, off Planet One in this system, our ship, and Ashley's ship, ran into a cosmic storm, sir." Blood trickled from his mouth. "Wiped out. All crew. Burton dead. Ashley died an hour ago. Only three survivals."

"Listen to me!" shouted Hart, bending over the bleeding man. "You didn't come to this planet before this very hour?"

Silence.

"Answer me!" cried Hart.

The dying man said, "No. Storm. Burton dead two days ago. This first landing on any world in six months."

"Are you sure?" shouted Hart, shaking violently, gripping the man in his hands. "Are you sure?"

"Sure, sure," mouthed the dying man.

"Burton died two days ago? You're positive?"

"Yes, yes," whispered the man. His head fell forward. The man was dead.

The captain knelt beside the silent body. The captain's face twitched, the muscles jerking involuntarily. The other members of the crew stood back of him looking down. Martin waited. The captain asked to be helped to his feet, finally, and this was done. They stood looking at the city. "That means—"

"That means?" said Martin.

"We're the only ones who've been here," whispered Captain Hart. "And that man——"

"What about that man, Captain?" asked Martin.

The captain's face twitched senselessly. He looked very old indeed, and gray. His eyes were glazed. He moved forward in the dry grass.

"Come along, Martin. Come along. Hold me up; for

my sake, hold me. I'm afraid I'll fall. And hurry. We can't waste time—"

They moved, stumbling, toward the city, in the long dry grass, in the blowing wind.

Several hours later they were sitting in the mayor's auditorium. A thousand people had come and talked and gone. The captain had remained seated, his face haggard, listening, listening. There was so much light in the faces of those who came and testified and talked he could not bear to see them. And all the while his hands traveled, on his knees, together; on his belt, jerking and quivering.

When it was over, Captain Hart turned to the mayor and with strange eyes said:

"But you must know where he went?"

"He didn't say where he was going," replied the mayor.

"To one of the other nearby worlds?" demanded the captain.

"I don't know."

"You must know."

"Do you see him?" asked the mayor, indicating the crowd.

The captain looked. "No."

"Then he is probably gone," said the mayor.

"Probably, probably!" cried the captain weakly. "I've made a horrible mistake, and I want to see him now. Why, it just came to me, this is a most unusual thing in history. To be in on something like this. Why, the chances are one in billions we'd arrived at one certain planet among millions of planets the day after *he* came! You must know where he's gone!"

"Each finds him in his own way," replied the mayor gently.

"You're hiding him." The captain's face grew slowly ugly. Some of the old hardness returned in stages. He began to stand up.

"No," said the mayor.

"You know where he is then?" The captain's fingers twitched at the leather holster on his right side.

"I couldn't tell you where he is, exactly," said the mayor.

"I advise you to start talking," and the captain took out a small steel gun.

"There's no way," said the mayor, "to tell you anything."

"Liar!"

An expression of pity came into the mayor's face as he looked at Hart.

"You're very tired," he said. "You've traveled a long way and you belong to a tired people who've been without faith a long time, and you want to believe so much now that you're interfering with yourself. You'll only make it harder if you kill. You'll never find him that way."

"Where'd he go? He told you; you know. Come on, tell me!" The captain waved the gun.

The mayor shook his head.

"Tell me! Tell me!"

The gun cracked once, twice. The mayor fell, his arm wounded.

Martin leaped forward. "Captain!"

The gun flashed at Martin. "Don't interfere."

On the floor, holding his wounded arm, the mayor looked up. "Put down your gun. You're hurting yourself. You've never believed, and now that you think you believe, you hurt people because of it."

"I don't need you," said Hart, standing over him. "If I missed him by one day here, I'll go on to another world. And another and another. I'll miss him by half a day on the next planet, maybe, and a quarter of a day on the third planet, and two hours on the next, and an hour on the next, and half an hour on the next, and a minute on the next. But after that, one day I'll catch up with him! Do you hear that?" He was shouting now, leaning wearily over the man on the floor. He staggered with exhaustion. "Come along, Martin." He let the gun hang in his hand.

"No," said Martin. "I'm staying here."

"You're a fool. Stay if you like. But I'm going on, with the others, as far as I can go."

The mayor looked up at Martin. "I'll be all right. Leave me. Others will tend my wounds."

"I'll be back," said Martin. "I'll walk as far as the rocket."

They walked with vicious speed through the city. One could see with what effort the captain struggled to show all the old iron, to keep himself going. When he reached the rocket he slapped the side of it with a trembling hand. He holstered his gun. He looked at Martin.

"Well, Martin?"

Martin looked at him. "Well, Captain?"

The captain's eyes were on the sky. "Sure you won't —come with—with me, eh?"

"No, sir."

"It'll be a great adventure, by God. I know I'll find him."

"You are set on it now, aren't you, sir?" asked Martin.

The captain's face quivered and his eyes closed. "Yes."

"There's one thing I'd like to know."

"What?"

"Sir, when you find him—*if* you find him," asked Martin, "what will you ask of him?"

"Why——" The captain faltered, opening his eyes. His hands clenched and unclenched. He puzzled a moment and then broke into a strange smile. "Why, I'll ask him for a little—peace and quiet." He touched the rocket. "It's been a long time, a long, long time since—since I relaxed."

"Did you ever just try, Captain?"

"I don't understand," said Hart.

"Never mind. So long, Captain?"

"Good-bye, Mr. Martin."

The crew stood by the port. Out of their number only three were going on with Hart. Seven others were remaining behind, they said, with Martin.

Captain Hart surveyed them and uttered his verdict: "Fools!"

He, last of all, climbed into the airlock, gave a brisk salute, and laughed sharply. The door slammed.

The rocket lifted into the sky on a pillar of fire.

Martin watched it go far away and vanish.

At the meadow's edge the mayor, supported by several men, beckoned.

"He's gone," said Martin, walking up.

"Yes, poor man, he's gone," said the mayor. "And he'll go on, planet after planet, seeking and seeking, and always and always he will be an hour late, or a half hour late, or ten minutes late, or a minute late. And finally he will miss out by only a few seconds. And when he has visited three hundred worlds and is seventy or eighty years old he will miss out by only a fraction of a second, and then a smaller fraction of a second. And he will go on and on, thinking to find that very thing which he left behind here, on this planet, in this city——"

Martin looked steadily at the mayor.

The mayor put out his hand. "Was there ever any doubt of it?" He beckoned to the others and turned. "Come along now. We mustn't keep him waiting."

They walked into the city.

TIME IN THY FLIGHT

A wind blew the long years away past their hot faces. The Time Machine stopped.

"Nineteen hundred and twenty-eight," said Janet. The two boys looked past her.

Mr. Fields stirred. "Remember, you're here to observe the behavior of these ancient people. Be inquisitive, be intelligent, observe."

"Yes," said the girl and the two boys in crisp khaki uniforms. They wore identical haircuts, had identical wristwatches, sandals, and coloring of hair, eyes, teeth, and skin, though they were not related.

"Shh!" said Mr. Fields.

They looked out at a little Illinois town in the spring of the year. A cool mist lay on the early morning streets.

Far down the street a small boy came running in the last light of the marble-cream moon. Somewhere a great clock struck 5 A.M. far away. Leaving tennis-shoe prints softly in the quiet lawns, the boy stepped near the invisible Time Machine and cried up to a high dark house window.

The house window opened. Another boy crept down the roof to the ground. The two boys ran off with banana-filled mouths into the dark cold morning.

"Follow them," whispered Mr. Fields. "Study their life patterns. Quick!"

Janet and William and Robert ran on the cold pavements of spring, visible now, through the slumbering town, through a park. All about, lights flickered, doors clicked, and other children rushed alone or in gasping pairs down a hill to some gleaming blue tracks.

"Here it comes!" The children milled about before dawn. Far down the shining tracks a small light grew seconds later into steaming thunder.

"What is it?" screamed Janet.

"A train, silly, you've seen pictures of them!" shouted Robert.

And as the Time Children watched, from the train stepped gigantic gray elephants, steaming the pavements with their mighty waters, lifting question-mark nozzles to the cold morning sky. Cumbrous wagons rolled from the long freight flats, red and gold. Lions roared and paced in boxed darkness.

"Why—*this* must be a—circus!" Janet trembled.

"You think so? Whatever happened to them?"

"Like Christmas, I guess. Just vanished, long ago."
Janet looked around. "Oh, it's awful, isn't it."

The boys stood numbed. "It sure is."

Men shouted in the first faint gleam of dawn. Sleeping cars drew up, dazed faces blinked out at the children. Horses clattered like a great fall of stones on the pavement.

Mr. Fields was suddenly behind the children. "Disgusting, barbaric, keeping animals in cages. If I'd known this was here, I'd never let you come see. This is a terrible ritual."

"Oh, yes." But Janet's eyes were puzzled. "And yet, you know, it's like a nest of maggots. I want to study it."

"I don't know," said Robert, his eyes darting, his fingers trembling. "It's pretty crazy. We might try writing a thesis on it if Mr. Fields says it's all right . . ."

Mr. Fields nodded. "I'm glad you're digging in here, finding motives, studying this horror. All right—we'll see the circus this afternoon."

"I think I'm going to be sick," said Janet.

The Time Machine hummed.

"So that was a circus," said Janet, solemnly.

The trombone circus died in their ears. The last

thing they saw was candy-pink trapeze people whirling while baking powder clowns shrieked and bounded.

"You must admit psychovision's better," said Robert slowly.

"All those nasty animal smells, the excitement." Janet blinked. "That's bad for children, isn't it? And those older people seated with the children. Mothers, fathers, they called them. Oh, that *was* strange."

Mr. Fields put some marks in his class grading book.

Janet shook her head numbly. "I want to see it all again. I've missed the motives somewhere. I want to make that run across town again in the early morning. The cold air on my face—the sidewalk under my feet— the circus train coming in. Was it the air and the early hour that made the children get up and run to see the train come in? I want to retrace the entire pattern. Why should they be excited? I feel I've missed out on the answer."

"They all smiled so much," said William.

"Manic-depressives," said Robert.

"What are summer vacations? I heard them talk about it." Janet looked at Mr. Fields.

"They spent their summers racing about like idiots, beating each other up," replied Mr. Fields seriously.

"I'll take our State Engineered summers of work for children anytime," said Robert, looking at nothing, his voice faint.

The Time Machine stopped again.

"The Fourth of July," announced Mr. Fields. "Nineteen hundred and twenty-eight. An ancient holiday when people blew each other's fingers off."

They stood before the same house on the same street but on a soft summer evening. Fire wheels hissed, on front porches laughing children tossed things out that went bang!

"Don't run!" cried Mr. Fields. "It's not war, don't be afraid!"

But Janet's and Robert's and William's faces were pink, now blue, now white with fountains of soft fire.

"We're all right," said Janet, standing very still.

"Happily," announced Mr. Fields, "they prohibited

fireworks a century ago, did away with the whole messy explosion."

Children did fairy dances, weaving their names and destinies on the dark summer air with white sparklers.

"I'd like to do that," said Janet, softly. "Write my name on the air. See? I'd like that."

"What?" Mr. Fields hadn't been listening.

"Nothing," said Janet.

"Bang!" whispered William and Robert, standing under the soft summer trees, in shadow, watching, watching the red, white, and green fires on the beautiful summer night lawns. "Bang!"

October.

The Time Machine paused for the last time, an hour later in the month of burning leaves. People bustled into dim houses carrying pumpkins and corn shocks. Skeletons danced, bats flew, candles flamed, apples swung in empty doorways.

"Halloween," said Mr. Fields. "The acme of horror. This was the age of superstition, you know. Later they banned the Grimm Brothers, ghosts, skeletons, and all that claptrap. You children, thank God, were raised in an antiseptic world of no shadows or ghosts. You had decent holidays like William C. Chatterton's Birthday, Work Day, and Machine Day."

They walked by the same house in the empty October night, peering in at the triangle-eyed pumpkins, the masks leering in black attics and damp cellars. Now, inside the house, some party children squatted telling stories, laughing!

"I want to be inside with them," said Janet at last.

"Sociologically, of course," said the boys.

"No," she said.

"What?" asked Mr. Fields.

"No, I just want to be inside, I just want to stay here, I want to see it all and be here and never be anywhere else, I want firecrackers and pumpkins and circuses, I want Christmases and Valentines and Fourths, like we've seen."

"This is getting out of hand . . ." Mr. Fields started to say.

But suddenly Janet was gone. "Robert, William, come on!" She ran. The boys leaped after her.

"Hold on!" shouted Mr. Fields. "Robert! William, I've got you!" He seized the last boy, but the other escaped. "Janet, Robert—come back here! You'll never pass into the seventh grade! You'll fail, Janet, Bob— *Bob!*"

An October wind blew wildly down the street, vanishing with the children off among moaning trees.

William twisted and kicked.

"No, not you, too, William, you're coming home with me. We'll teach those other two a lesson they won't forget. So they want to stay in the past, do they?" Mr. Fields shouted so everyone could hear. "All right, Janet, Bob, stay in this horror, in this chaos! In a few weeks you'll come sniveling back here to me. But I'll be gone! I'm leaving you here to go mad in this world!"

He hurried William to the Time Machine. The boy was sobbing. "Don't make me come back here on any more Field Excursions ever again, please, Mr. Fields, please—"

"Shut up!"

Almost instantly the Time Machine whisked away toward the future, toward the underground hive cities, the metal buildings, the metal flowers, the metal lawns.

"Good-bye, Janet, Bob!"

A great cold October wind blew through the town like water. And when it had ceased blowing it had carried all the children, whether invited or uninvited, masked or unmasked, to the doors of houses which closed upon them. There was not a running child anywhere in the night. The wind whined away in the bare treetops.

And inside the big house, in the candlelight, someone was pouring cold apple cider all around, to everyone, no matter *who* they were.

THE PEDESTRIAN

To enter out into that silence that was the city at eight o'clock of a misty evening in November, to put your feet upon that buckling concrete walk, to step over grassy seams and make your way, hands in pockets, through the silences, that was what Mr. Leonard Mead most dearly loved to do. He would stand upon the corner of an intersection and peer down long moonlit avenues of sidewalk in four directions, deciding which way to go, but it really made no difference; he was alone in this world of A.D. 2053, or as good as alone, and with a final decision made, a path selected, he would stride off, sending patterns of frosty air before him like the smoke of a cigar.

Sometimes he would walk for hours and miles and return only at midnight to his house. And on his way he would see the cottages and homes with their dark windows, and it was not unequal to walking through a graveyard where only the faintest glimmers of firefly light appeared in flickers behind the windows. Sudden gray phantoms seemed to manifest upon inner room walls where a curtain was still undrawn against the night, or there were whisperings and murmurs where a window in a tomb-like building was still open.

Mr. Leonard Mead would pause, cock his head, listen, look, and march on, his feet making no noise on the lumpy walk. For long ago he had wisely changed to sneakers when strolling at night, because the dogs in intermittent squads would parallel his journey with barkings if he wore hard heels, and lights might click on and faces appear and an entire street be startled by the passing of a lone figure, himself, in the early November evening.

On this particular evening he began his journey in a westerly direction, toward the hidden sea. There was a good crystal frost in the air; it cut the nose and made the lungs blaze like a Christmas tree inside; you could feel the cold light going on and off, all the branches filled with invisible snow. He listened to the faint push of his soft shoes through autumn leaves with satisfaction, and whistled a cold quiet whistle between his teeth, occasionally picking up a leaf as he passed, examining its skeletal pattern in the infrequent lamplights as he went on, smelling its rusty smell.

"Hello, in there," he whispered to every house on every side as he moved. "What's up tonight on Channel 4, Channel 7, Channel 9? Where are the cowboys rushing, and do I see the United States Cavalry over the next hill to the rescue?"

The street was silent and long and empty, with only his shadow moving like the shadow of a hawk in midcountry. If he closed his eyes and stood very still, frozen, he could imagine himself upon the center of a plain, a wintry, windless American desert with no house in a thousand miles, and only dry river beds, the streets, for company.

"What is it now?" he asked the houses, noticing his wrist watch. "Eight-thirty P.M.? Time for a dozen assorted murders? A quiz? A revue? A comedian falling off the stage?"

Was that a murmur of laughter from within a moon-white house? He hesitated, but went on when nothing more happened. He stumbled over a particularly uneven section of sidewalk. The cement was vanishing under flowers and grass. In ten years of walking by night or day, for thousands of miles, he had never met another person walking, not once in all that time.

He came to a cloverleaf intersection which stood

silent where two main highways crossed the town. During the day it was a thunderous surge of cars, the gas stations open, a great insect rustling and a ceaseless jockeying for position as the scarab-beetles, a faint incense puttering from their exhausts, skimmed homeward to the far directions. But now these highways, too, were like streams in a dry season, all stone and bed and moon radiance.

He turned back on a side street, circling around toward his home. He was within a block of his destination when the lone car turned a corner quite suddenly and flashed a fierce white cone of light upon him. He stood entranced, not unlike a night moth, stunned by the illumination, and then drawn toward it.

A metallic voice called to him:

"Stand still. Stay where you are! Don't move!"

He halted.

"Put up your hands!"

"But—" he said.

"Your hands up! Or we'll shoot!"

The police, of course, but what a rare, incredible thing; in a city of three million, there was only *one* police car left, wasn't that correct? Ever since a year ago, 2052, the election year, the force had been cut down from three cars to one. Crime was ebbing; there was no need now for the police, save for this one lone car wandering and wandering the empty streets.

"Your name?" said the police car in a metallic whisper. He couldn't see the men in it for the bright light in his eyes.

"Leonard Mead," he said.

"Speak up!"

"Leonard Mead!"

"Business or profession?"

"I guess you'd call me a writer."

"No profession," said the police car, as if talking to itself. The light held him fixed, like a museum specimen, needle thrust through chest.

"You might say that," said Mr. Mead. He hadn't written in years. Magazines and books didn't sell any more. Everything went on in the tomblike houses at night now, he thought, continuing his fancy. The tombs, ill-lit by television light, where the people sat like the dead, the gray or multicolored lights touching their faces, but never really touching *them.*

"No profession," said the phonograph voice, hissing. "What are you doing out?"

"Walking," said Leonard Mead.

"Walking!"

"Just walking," he said simply, but his face felt cold.

"Walking, just walking, walking?"

"Yes, sir."

"Walking where? For what?"

"Walking for air. Walking to see."

"Your address!"

"Eleven South Saint James Street."

"And there is air *in* your house, you have an *air conditioner,* Mr. Mead?"

"Yes."

"And you have a viewing screen in your house to see with?"

"No."

"No?" There was a crackling quiet that in itself was an accusation.

"Are you married, Mr. Mead?"

"No."

"Not married," said the police voice behind the fiery beam. The moon was high and clear among the stars and the houses were gray and silent.

"Nobody wanted me," said Leonard Mead with a smile.

"Don't speak unless you're spoken to!"

Leonard Mead waited in the cold night.

"Just *walking,* Mr. Mead?"

"Yes."

"But you haven't explained for what purpose."

"I explained; for air, and to see, and just to walk."

"Have you done this often?"

"Every night for years."

The police car sat in the center of the street with its radio throat faintly humming.

"Well, Mr. Mead," it said.

"Is that all?" he asked politely.

"Yes," said the voice. "Here." There was a sigh, a

pop. The back door of the police car sprang wide. "Get in."

"Wait a minute, I haven't done anything!"

"Get in."

"I protest!"

"Mr. Mead."

He walked like a man suddenly drunk. As he passed the front window of the car he looked in. As he had expected there was no one in the front seat, no one in the car at all.

"Get in."

He put his hand to the door and peered into the back seat, which was a little cell, a little black jail with bars. It smelled of riveted steel. It smelled of harsh antiseptic; it smelled too clean and hard and metallic. There was nothing soft there.

"Now if you had a wife to give you an alibi," said the iron voice. "But——"

"Where are you taking me?"

The car hesitated, or rather gave a faint whirring click, as if information, somewhere, was dropping card by punch-slotted card under electric eyes. "To the Psychiatric Center for Research on Regressive Tendencies."

He got in. The door shut with a soft thud. The police car rolled through the night avenues, flashing its dim lights ahead.

They passed one house on one street a moment later, one house in an entire city of houses that were dark, but this one particular house had all of its electric lights brightly lit, every window a loud yellow illumination, square and warm in the cool darkness.

"That's *my* house," said Leonard Mead.

No one answered him.

The car moved down the empty river-bed streets and off away, leaving the empty streets with the empty sidewalks, and no sound and no motion all the rest of the chill November night.

HAIL AND FAREWELL

But of course he was going away, there was nothing else to do, the time was up, the clock had run out, and he was going very far away indeed. His suitcase was packed, his shoes were shined, his hair was brushed, he had expressly washed behind his ears, and it remained only for him to go down the stairs, out the front door, and up the street to the small-town station where the train would make a stop for him alone. Then Fox Hill, Illinois, would be left far off in his past. And he would go on, perhaps to Iowa, perhaps to Kansas, perhaps even to California; a small boy, twelve years old, with a birth certificate in his valise to show he had been born forty-three years ago.

"Willie!" called a voice belowstairs.

"Yes!" He hoisted his suitcase. In his bureau mirror he saw a face made of June dandelions and July apples and warm summer-morning milk. There, as always, was his look of the angel and the innocent, which might never, in the years of his life, change.

"Almost time," called the woman's voice.

"All right!" And he went down the stairs, grunting and smiling. In the living room sat Anna and Steve, their clothes painfully neat.

"Here I am!" cried Willie in the parlor door.

Anna looked like she was going to cry. "Oh, good Lord, you can't really be leaving us, can you, Willie?"

"People are beginning to talk," said Willie quietly. "I've been here three years now. But when people begin to talk, I know it's time to put on my shoes and buy a railway ticket."

"It's all so strange. I don't understand. It's so sudden," Anna said. "Willie, we'll miss you."

"I'll write you every Christmas, so help me. Don't you write me."

"It's been a great pleasure and satisfaction," said Steve, sitting there, his words the wrong size in his mouth. "It's a shame it had to stop. It's a shame you had to tell us about yourself. It's an awful shame you can't stay on."

"You're the nicest folks I ever had," said Willie, four feet high, in no need of a shave, the sunlight on his face.

And then Anna *did* cry. "Willie, Willie." And she sat down and looked as if she wanted to hold him but was afraid to hold him now; she looked at him with shock and amazement and her hands empty, not knowing what to do with him now.

"It's not easy to go," said Willie. "You get used to things. You want to stay. But it doesn't work. I tried to stay on once after people began to suspect. 'How horrible!' people said. 'All these years, playing with our innocent children,' they said, 'and us not guessing! Awful!' they said. And finally I had to just leave town one night. It's not easy. You know darned well how much I love both of you. Thanks for three swell years."

They all went to the front door. "Willie, where're you going?"

"I don't know. I just start traveling. When I see a town that looks green and nice, I settle in."

"Will you ever come back?"

"Yes," he said earnestly with his high voice. "In about twenty years it should begin to show in my face. When it does, I'm going to make a grand tour of all the mothers and fathers I've ever had."

They stood on the cool summer porch, reluctant to say the last words. Steve was looking steadily at an elm tree. "How many other folks've you stayed with, Willie? How many adoptions?"

Willie figured it, pleasantly enough. "I guess it's about five towns and five couples and over twenty years gone by since I started my tour."

"Well, we can't holler," said Steve. "Better to've had a son thirty-six months than none whatever."

"Well," said Willie, and kissed Anna quickly, seized at his luggage, and was gone up the street in the green noon light, under the trees, a very young boy indeed, not looking back, running steadily.

The boys were playing on the green park diamond when he came by. He stood a little while among the oak-tree shadows, watching them hurl the white, snowy baseball into the warm summer air, saw the baseball shadow fly like a dark bird over the grass, saw their hands open in mouths to catch this swift piece of summer that now seemed most especially important to hold onto. The boys' voices yelled. The ball lit on the grass near Willie.

Carrying the ball forward from under the shade trees, he thought of the last three years now spent to the penny, and the five years before that, and so on down the line to the year when he was really eleven and twelve and fourteen and the voices saying: "What's wrong with Willie, missus?" "Mrs. B., is Willie late a-growin'?" "Willie, you smokin' cigars lately?" The echoes died in summer light and color. His mother's voice: "Willie's twenty-one today!" And a thousand voices saying: "Come back, son, when you're fifteen; then maybe we'll give you a job."

He stared at the baseball in his trembling hand, as if it were his life, an interminable ball of years strung around and around and around, but always leading back to his twelfth birthday. He heard the kids walking toward him; he felt them blot out the sun, and they were older, standing around him.

"Willie! Where you goin'?" They kicked his suitcase.

How tall they stood to the sun. In the last few months it seemed the sun had passed a hand above their heads, beckoned, and they were warm metal drawn melting upwards; they were golden taffy pulled by an immense gravity to the sky, thirteen, fourteen years old, looking down upon Willie, smiling, but already beginning to neglect him. It had started four months ago:

"Choose up sides! Who wants Willie?"

"Aw, Willie's too little; we don't play with 'kids.' "

And they raced ahead of him, drawn by the moon and the sun and the turning seasons of leaf and wind, and he was twelve years old and not of them any more. And the other voices beginning again on the old, the dreadfully familiar, the cool refrain: "Better feed that boy vitamins, Steve." "Anna, does shortness *run* in your family?" And the cold fist kneading at your heart again and knowing that the roots would have to be pulled up again after so many good years with the "folks."

"Willie, where are you goin'?"

He jerked his head. He was back among the towering, shadowing boys who milled around him like giants at a drinking fountain bending down.

"Goin' a few days visitin' a cousin of mine."

"Oh." There was a day, a year ago, when they would have cared very much indeed. But now there was only curiosity for his luggage, their enchantment with trains and trips and far places.

"How about a coupla fast ones?" said Willie.

They looked doubtful, but, considering the circumstances, nodded. He dropped his bag and ran out; the white baseball was up in the sun, away to their burning white figures in the far meadow, up in the sun again, rushing, life coming and going in a pattern. Here, *there!* Mr. and Mrs. Robert Hanlon, Creek Bend, Wisconsin, 1932, the first couple, the first year! Here, there! Henry and Alice Boltz, Limeville, Iowa, 1935! The baseball flying. The Smiths, the Eatons, the Robinsons! 1939! 1945! Husband and wife, husband and wife, husband and wife, no children, no children, no children! A knock on this door, a knock on that.

"Pardon me. My name is William. I wonder if——"

"A sandwich? Come in, sit down. Where you *from*, son?"

The sandwich, a tall glass of cold milk, the smiling, the nodding, the comfortable, leisurely talking.

"Son, you look like you been traveling. You run *off* from somewhere?"

"No."

"Boy, are you an orphan?"

Another glass of milk.

"We always wanted kids. It never worked out. Never knew why. One of those things. Well, well. It's getting late, son. Don't you think you better hit for home?"

"Got no home."

"A boy like you? Not dry behind the ears? Your mother'll be worried."

"Got no home and no folks anywhere in the world. I wonder if—I wonder—could I sleep here tonight?"

"Well, now, son, I don't just know. We never considered taking in——" said the husband.

"We got chicken for supper tonight," said the wife, "enough for extras, enough for company. . . ."

And the years turning and flying away, the voices, and the faces, and the people, and always the same first conversations. The voice of Emily Robinson, in her rocking chair, in summer-night darkness, the last night he stayed with her, the night she discovered his secret, her voice saying:

"I look at all the little children's faces going by. And I sometimes think, What a shame, what a shame, that all these flowers have to be cut, all these bright fires have to put out. What a shame these, all of these you see in schools or running by, have to get tall and unsightly and wrinkle and turn gray or get bald and finally, all bone and wheeze, be dead and buried off away. When I hear them laugh I can't believe they'll ever go the road I'm going. Yet here they *come!* I still remember Wordsworth's poem: 'When all at once I saw a crowd, A host of golden daffodils; Beside the lake, beneath the trees, Fluttering and dancing in the breeze.' That's how I think of children, cruel as they sometimes are, mean as I know they can be, but not yet showing the meanness around their eyes or *in* their eyes, not yet full of tiredness. They're so eager for everything! I guess that's what I miss most in older folks, the eagerness gone nine times out of ten, the freshness gone, so much of the drive and life down the drain. I like to watch school let out each

day. It's like someone threw a bunch of flowers out the
school front doors. How does it feel, Willie? How does it
feel to be young forever? To look like a silver dime new
from the mint? Are you happy? Are you as fine as you
seem?"

The baseball whizzed from the blue sky, stung his
hand like a great pale insect. Nursing it, he heard his
memory say:

"I worked with what I had. After my folks died, after
I found I couldn't get man's work anywhere, I tried
carnivals, but they only laughed. 'Son,' they said, 'you're
not a midget, and even if you are, you look like a *boy!*
We want midgets with midgets' *faces!* Sorry, son, sorry.'
So I left home, started out, thinking: What was I? A boy.
I looked like a boy, sounded like a boy, so I might as well
go on being a boy. No use fighting it. No use screaming.
So what could I do? What job was handy? And then one
day I saw this man in a restaurant looking at another
man's pictures of his children. 'Sure wish I had kids,' he
said. 'Sure wish I had kids.' He kept shaking his head.
And me sitting a few seats away from him, a hamburger
in my hands. I sat there, *frozen!* At that very instant I
knew what my job would be for most of my life. There
was work for me, after all. Making lonely people happy.
Keeping myself busy. Playing forever. I knew I had to
play forever. Deliver a few papers, run a few errands,
mow a few lawns, maybe. But *hard* work? No. All I had
to do was be a mother's son and a father's pride: I turned
to the man down the counter from me. 'I beg your
pardon,' I said. I *smiled* at him. . . ."

"But, Willie," said Mrs. Emily long ago, "didn't you
ever get lonely? Didn't you ever want—*things*—that
grown-ups wanted?"

"I fought that out alone," said Willie. "I'm a boy, I
told myself, I'll have to live in a boy's world, read boys'
books, play boys' games, cut myself off from everything
else. I can't be both. I got to be only one thing—young.
And so I played that way. Oh, it wasn't easy. There were
times——" He lapsed into silence.

"And the family you lived with, they never knew?"

"No. Telling them would have spoiled everything. I

told them I was a runaway; I let them check through official channels, police. Then, when there was no re-cord, let them put in to adopt me. That was best of all; as long as they never guessed. But then, after three years, or five years, they guessed, or a traveling man came through, or a carnival man saw me, and it was over. It always had to end."

"And you're very happy and it's *nice* being a child for over forty years?"

"It's a living, as they say. And when you make other people happy, then you're almost happy too. I got my job to do and I do it. And anyway, in a few years now I'll be in my second childhood. All the fevers will be out of me and all the unfulfilled things and most of the dreams. Then I can relax, maybe, and play the role all the way."

He threw the baseball one last time and broke the reverie. Then he was running to seize his luggage. Tom, Bill, Jamie, Bob, Sam—their names moved on his lips. They were embarrassed at his shaking hands.

"After all, Willie, it ain't as if you're going to China or Timbuktu."

"That's right, isn't it?" Willie did not move.

"So long, Willie. See you next week!"

"So long, so long!"

And he was walking off with his suitcase again look-ing at the trees, going away from the boys and the street where he had lived, and as he turned the corner a train whistle screamed, and he began to run.

The last thing he saw and heard was a white ball tossed at a high roof, back and forth, back and forth, and two voices crying out as the ball pitched now up, down, and back through the sky, "Annie, annie, over! Annie, annie, over!" like the crying of birds flying off to the far south.

In the early morning, with the smell of the mist and the cold metal, with the iron smell of the train around him and a full night of traveling shaking his bones and his body, and a smell of the sun beyond the horizon, he awoke and looked out upon a small town just arising from sleep. Lights were coming on, soft voices mut-tered, a red signal bobbed back and forth, back and forth in the cold air. There was that sleeping hush in which echoes are dignified by clarity, in which echoes stand nakedly alone and sharp. A porter moved by, a shadow in shadows.

"Sir," said Willie.

The porter stopped.

"What town's this?" whispered the boy in the dark.

"Valleyville."

"How many people?"

"Ten thousand. Why? This your stop?"

"It looks green." Willie gazed out at the cold morning town for a long time. "It looks nice and quiet," said Willie.

"Son," said the porter, "you know where you *going?*"

"Here," said Willie, and got up quietly in the still, cool, iron-smelling morning, in the train dark, with a rustling and stir.

"I hope you know what you're doing, boy," said the porter.

"Yes, sir," said Willie. "I know what I'm doing." And he was down the dark aisle, luggage lifted after him by the porter, and out in the smoking, steaming-cold, beginning-to-lighten morning. He stood looking up at the porter and the black metal train against the few remaining stars. The train gave a great wailing blast of whistle, the porters cried out all along the line, the cars jolted, and his special porter waved and smiled down at the boy there, the small boy there with the big luggage who shouted up to him, even as the whistle screamed again.

"What?" shouted the porter, hand cupped to ear.

"Wish me luck!" cried Willie.

"Best of luck, son," called the porter, waving, smiling. "Best of luck, boy!"

"Thanks!" said Willie, in the great sound of the train, in the steam and roar.

He watched the black train until it was completely gone away and out of sight. He did not move all the time it was going. He stood quietly, a small boy twelve years old, on the worn wooden platform, and only after three entire minutes did he turn at last to face the empty streets below.

Then, as the sun was rising, he began to walk very fast, so as to keep warm, down into the new town.

INVISIBLE BOY

She took the great iron spoon and the mummified frog and gave it a bash and made dust of it, and talked to the dust while she ground it in her stony fists quickly. Her beady gray bird-eyes flickered at the cabin. Each time she looked, a head in the small thin window ducked as if she'd fired off a shotgun.

"Charlie!" cried Old Lady. "You come outa there! I'm fixing a lizard magic to unlock that rusty door! You come out now and I won't make the earth shake or the trees go up in fire or the sun set at high noon!"

The only sound was the warm mountain light on the high turpentine trees, a tufted squirrel chittering around and around on a green-furred log, the ants moving in a fine brown line at Old Lady's bare, blue-veined feet.

"You been starving in there two days, darn you!" she panted, chiming the spoon against a flat rock, causing the plump gray miracle bag to swing at her waist. Sweating sour, she rose and marched at the cabin, bearing the pulverized flesh. "Come out, now!" She flicked a pinch of powder inside the lock. "All right, I'll come get you!" she wheezed.

She spun the knob with one walnut-colored hand, first one way, then the other. "O Lord," she intoned "fling this door wide!"

When nothing flung, she added yet another philter and held her breath. Her long blue untidy skirt rustled as she peered into her bag of darkness to see if she had any scaly monsters there, any charm finer than the frog she'd killed months ago for such a crisis as this.

She heard Charlie breathing against the door. His folks had pranced off into some Ozark town early this week, leaving him, and he'd run almost six miles to Old Lady for company—she was by way of being an aunt or cousin or some such, and he didn't mind her fashions.

But then, two days ago, Old Lady, having gotten used to the boy around, decided to keep him for convenient company. She pricked her thin shoulder bone, drew out three blood pearls, spat wet over her right elbow, tromped on a crunch-cricket, and at the same instant clawed her left hand at Charlie, crying, "My son you are, you are my son, for all eternity!"

Charlie, bounding like a startled hare, had crashed off into the bush, heading for home.

But Old Lady, skittering quick as a gingham lizard, cornered him in a dead end, and Charlie holed up in this old hermit's cabin and wouldn't come out, no matter how she whammed door, window, or knothole with amber-colored fist or trounced her ritual fires, explaining to him that he was certainly her son *now*, all right.

"Charlie, you *there?*" she asked, cutting holes in the door planks with her bright little slippery eyes.

"I'm all of me here," he replied finally, very tired.

Maybe he would fall out on the ground any moment. She wrestled the knob hopefully. Perhaps a pinch too much frog powder had grated the lock wrong. She always overdid or underdid her miracles, she mused angrily, never doing them just *exact,* Devil take it!

"Charlie, I only wants someone to night-prattle to, someone to warm hands with at the fire. Someone to fetch kindling for me mornings, and fight off the spunks that come creeping of early fogs! I ain't got no fetchings on you for myself, son, just for your company." She smacked her lips. "Tell you what, Charles, you come out and I *teach* you things!"

"What things?" he suspicioned.

"Teach you how to buy cheap, sell high. Catch a

snow weasel, cut off its head, carry it warm in your hind pocket. There!"

"Aw," said Charlie.

She made haste. "Teach you to make yourself shot-proof. So if anyone bangs at you with a gun, nothing happens."

When Charlie stayed silent, she gave him the secret in a high, fluttering whisper. "Dig and stitch mouse-ear roots on Friday during full moon, and wear 'em around your neck in a white silk."

"You're *crazy,*" Charlie said.

"Teach you how to stop blood or make animals stand frozen or make blind horses see, all them things I'll teach you! Teach you to cure a swelled-up cow and unbewitch a goat. Show you how to make yourself invisible!"

"Oh," said Charlie.

Old Lady's heart beat like a Salvation tambourine. The knob turned from the other side.

"You," said Charlie, "are funning me."

"No, I'm not," exclaimed Old Lady. "Oh, Charlie, why, I'll make you like a window, see right through you. Why, child, you'll be surprised!"

"Real invisible?"

"Real invisible!"

"You won't fetch onto me if I walk out?"

"Won't touch a bristle of you, son."

"Well," he drawled reluctantly, "all right."

The door opened. Charlie stood in his bare feet, head down, chin against chest. "Make me invisible," he said.

"First we got to catch us a bat," said Old Lady. "Start lookin'!"

She gave him some jerky beef for his hunger and watched him climb a tree. He went high up and high up and it was nice seeing him there and it was nice having him here and all about after so many years alone with nothing to say good morning to but bird-droppings and silvery snail tracks.

Pretty soon a bat with a broken wing fluttered down out of the tree. Old Lady snatched it up, beating warm and shrieking between its porcelain white teeth, and

Charlie dropped down after it, hand upon clenched hand, yelling.

That night, with the moon nibbling at the spiced pine cones, Old Lady extracted a long silver needle from under her wide blue dress. Gumming her excitement and secret anticipation, she sighted up the dead bat and held the cold needle steady-steady.

She had long ago realized that her miracles, despite all perspirations and salts and sulphurs, failed. But she had always dreamt that one day the miracles might start functioning, might spring up in crimson flowers and silver stars to prove that God had forgiven her for her pink body and her pink thoughts and her warm body and her warm thoughts as a young miss. But so far God had made no sign and said no word, but nobody knew this except Old Lady.

"Ready?" she asked Charlie, who crouched cross-kneed, wrapping his pretty legs in long goose-pimpled arms, his mouth open, making teeth. "Ready," he whispered, shivering.

"There!" She plunged the needle deep in the bat's right eye. "So!"

"Oh!" screamed Charlie, wadding up his face.

"Now I wrap it in gingham, and here, put it in your pocket, keep it there, bat and all. Go on!"

He pocketed the charm.

"Charlie!" she shrieked fearfully. "Charlie, where *are* you? I can't *see* you, child!"

"Here!" he jumped so the light ran in red streaks up his body. "I'm here, Old Lady!" He stared wildly at his arms, legs, chest, and toes. "I'm here!"

Her eyes looked as if they were watching a thousand fireflies crisscrossing each other in the wild night air.

"Charlie, oh, you went *fast!* Quick as a humming-bird! Oh, Charlie, come *back* to me!"

"But I'm *here!*" he wailed.

"Where?"

"By the fire, the fire! And—and I can see myself. I'm not invisible at all!"

Old Lady rocked on her lean flanks. "Course *you* can see *you!* Every invisible person knows himself. Otherwise, how could you eat, walk, or get around places? Charlie, touch me. Touch me so I *know* you."

Uneasily he put out a hand.

She pretended to jerk, startled, at his touch. *"Ah!"*

"You mean to say you can't *find* me?" he asked. "Truly?"

"Not the least half rump of you!"

She found a tree to stare at, and stared at it with shining eyes, careful not to glance at him. "Why, I sure *did* a trick *that* time!" She sighed with wonder. "Whooeee. Quickest invisible I *ever* made! Charlie. Charlie, how you *feel?*"

"Like creek water—all stirred."

"You'll settle."

Then after a pause she added, "Well, what you going to do now, Charlie, since you're invisible?"

All sorts of things shot through his brain, she could tell. Adventures stood up and danced like fire in his eyes, and his mouth, just hanging, told what it meant to be a boy who imagined himself like the mountain winds. In a cold dream he said, "I'll run across wheat fields, climb snow mountains, steal white chickens off'n farms. I'll kick pink pigs when they ain't looking. I'll pinch pretty girls' legs when they sleep, snap their garters in schoolrooms." Charlie looked at Old Lady, and from the shiny tips of her eyes she saw something wicked shape his face. "And other things I'll do, I'll do, I will," he said.

"Don't try nothing on me," warned Old Lady. "I'm brittle as spring ice and I don't take handling." Then: "What about your folks?"

"My folks?"

"You can't fetch yourself home looking like that. Scare the inside ribbons out of them. Your mother'd faint straight back like timber falling. Think they want you about the house to stumble over and your ma have to call you every three minutes, even though you're in the room next her elbow?"

Charlie had not considered it. He sort of simmered down and whispered out a little "Gosh," and felt of his long bones carefully.

"You'll be mighty lonesome. People looking through

you like a water glass, people knocking you aside because they didn't reckon you to be underfoot. And women, Charlie, *women*—"

He swallowed. "What about women?"

"No woman will be giving you a second stare. And no woman wants to be kissed by a boy's mouth they can't even *find!*"

Charlie dug his bare toe in the soil contemplatively. He pouted. "Well, I'll stay invisible, anyway, for a spell. I'll have me some fun. I'll just be pretty careful, is all. I'll stay out from in front of wagons and horses and Pa. Pa shoots at the nariest sound." Charlie blinked. "Why, with me invisible, someday Pa might just up and fill me with buckshot, thinkin' I was a hill squirrel in the dooryard. Oh . . ."

Old Lady nodded at a tree. "That's likely."

"Well," he decided slowly, "I'll stay invisible for tonight, and tomorrow you can fix me back all whole again, Old Lady."

"Now if that ain't just like a critter, always wanting to be what he can't be," remarked Old Lady to a beetle on a log.

"What you mean?" said Charlie.

"Why," she explained, "it was real hard work, fixing you up. It'll take a little *time* for it to wear off. Like a coat of paint wears off, boy."

"You!" he cried. "You did this to me! Now you make me back, you make me seeable!"

"Hush," she said. "It'll wear off, a hand or a foot at a time."

"How'll it look, me around the hills with just one hand showing!"

"Like a five-winged bird hopping on the stones and bramble."

"Or a foot showing!"

"Like a small pink rabbit jumping thicket."

"Or my head floating!"

"Like a hairy balloon at the carnival!"

"How long before I'm *whole?*" he asked.

She deliberated that it might pretty well be an entire year.

He groaned. He began to sob and bite his lips and

make fists. "You magicked me, you did this, you did this thing to me. Now I won't be able to run home!"

She winked. "But you *can* stay here, child, stay on with me real comfort-like, and I'll keep you fat and saucy."

He flung it out: "You did this on purpose! You mean old hag, you want to keep me here!"

He ran off through the shrubs on the instant.

"Charlie, come back!"

No answer but the patter of his feet on the soft dark turf, and his wet choking cry which passed swiftly off and away.

She waited and then kindled herself a fire. "He'll be back," she whispered. And thinking inward on herself, she said, "And now I'll have me my company through spring and into late summer. Then, when I'm tired of him and want a silence, I'll send him home."

Charlie returned noiselessly with the first gray of dawn, gliding over the rimed turf to where Old Lady sprawled like a bleached stick before the scattered ashes.

He sat on some creek pebbles and stared at her.

She didn't dare look at him or beyond. He had made no sound, so how could she know he was anywhere about? She couldn't.

He sat there, tear marks on his cheeks.

Pretending to be just waking—but she had found no sleep from one end of the night to the other—Old Lady stood up, grunting and yawning, and turned in a circle to the dawn.

"Charlie?"

Her eyes passed from pines to soil, to sky, to the far hills. She called out his name, over and over again, and she felt like staring plumb straight at him, but she stopped herself. "Charlie? Oh, Charles!" she called, and heard the echoes say the very same.

He sat, beginning to grin a bit, suddenly, knowing he was close to her, yet she must feel alone. Perhaps he felt the growing of a secret power, perhaps he felt secure from the world, certainly he was *pleased* with his invisibility.

She said aloud, "Now where *can* that boy be? If he

only made a noise so I could tell just where he is, maybe I'd fry him a breakfast."

She prepared the morning victuals, irritated at his continuous quiet. She sizzled bacon on a hickory stick. "The smell of it will draw his nose," she muttered.

While her back was turned he swiped all the frying bacon and devoured it tastily.

She whirled, crying out, "Lord!"

She eyed the clearing suspiciously. "Charlie, that *you*?"

Charlie wiped his mouth clean on his wrists.

She trotted about the clearing, making like she was trying to locate him. Finally, with a clever thought, acting blind, she headed straight for him, groping. "Charlie, where *are* you?"

A lightning streak, he evaded her, bobbing, ducking.

It took all her will power not to give chase; but you can't chase invisible boys, so she sat down, scowling, sputtering, and tried to fry more bacon. But every fresh strip she cut he would steal bubbling off the fire and run away far. Finally, cheeks burning, she cried, "I know where you are! Right *there!* I hear you run!" She pointed to one side of him, not too accurate. He ran again. "Now you're there!" she shouted. "There, and there!" pointing to all the places he was in the next five minutes. "I hear you press a grass blade, knock a flower, snap a twig. I got fine shell ears, delicate as roses. They can hear the stars moving!"

Silently he galloped off among the pines, his voice trailing back, "Can't hear me when I'm set on a rock. I'll just *set!*"

All day he sat on an observatory rock in the clear wind, motionless and sucking his tongue.

Old Lady gathered wood in the deep forest, feeling his eyes weaseling on her spine. She wanted to babble: "Oh, I see you, I see you! I was only fooling about invisible boys! You're right there!" But she swallowed her gall and gummed it tight.

The following morning he did the spiteful things. He began leaping from behind trees. He made toad-faces, frog-faces, spider-faces at her, clenching down his lips

with his fingers, popping his raw eyes, pushing up his
nostrils so you could peer in and see his brain thinking.

Once she dropped her kindling. She pretended it
was a blue jay startled her.

He made a motion as if to strangle her.

She trembled a little.

He made another move as if to bang her shins and
spit on her cheek.

These motions she bore without a lid-flicker or a
mouth-twitch.

He stuck out his tongue, making strange bad noises.
He wiggled his loose ears so she wanted to laugh, and
finally she did laugh and explained it away quickly by
saying, "Sat on a salamander! Whew, how it poked!"

By high noon the whole madness boiled to a terrible
peak.

For it was at that exact hour that Charlie came racing down the valley stark boy-naked!

Old Lady nearly fell flat with shock!

"Charlie!" she almost cried.

Charlie raced naked up one side of a hill and naked
down the other—naked as day, naked as the moon, raw
as the sun and a newborn chick, his feet shimmering
and rushing like the wings of a low-skimming hum-
mingbird.

Old Lady's tongue locked in her mouth. What could
she say? Charlie, go dress? For *shame? Stop* that? *Could*
she? Oh, Charlie, Charlie, God! Could she say that now?
Well?

Upon the big rock, she witnessed him dancing up
and down, naked as the day of his birth, stomping bare
feet, smacking his hands on his knees and sucking in and
out his white stomach like blowing and deflating a circus balloon.

She shut her eyes tight and prayed.

After three hours of this she pleaded, "Charlie,
Charlie, come here! I got something to *tell* you!"

Like a fallen leaf he came, dressed again, praise the
Lord.

"Charlie," she said, looking at the pine trees, "I see
your right toe. *There* it is."

"You do?" he said.

"Yes," she said very sadly. "There it is like a horny toad on the grass. And there, up there's your left ear hanging on the air like a pink butterfly."

Charlie danced. "I'm forming in, I'm forming in!"

Old Lady nodded. "Here comes your ankle!"

"Gimme *both* my feet!" ordered Charlie.

"You got 'em."

"How about my hands?"

"I see one crawling on your knee like a daddy long-legs."

"How about the other one?"

"It's crawling too."

"I got a body?"

"Shaping up fine."

"I'll need my head to go home, Old Lady."

To go home, she thought wearily. "No!" she said, stubborn and angry. "No, you ain't got no head. No head at all," she cried. She'd leave that to the very last. "No head, no head," she insisted.

"No head?" he wailed.

"Yes, oh my God, yes, yes, you got your blamed head!" she snapped, giving up. "Now, fetch me back my bat with the needle in his eye!"

He flung it at her. "Haaaa-yoooo!" His yelling went all up the valley, and long after he had run toward home she heard his echoes, racing.

Then she plucked up her kindling with a great dry weariness and started back toward her shack, sighing, talking. And Charlie followed her all the way, *really* invisible now, so she couldn't see him, just hear him, like a pine cone dropping or a deep underground stream trickling, or a squirrel clambering a bough; and over the fire at twilight she and Charlie sat, him so invisible, and her feeding him bacon he wouldn't take, so she ate it herself, and then she fixed some magic and fell asleep with Charlie, made out of sticks and rags and pebbles, but still warm and her very own son, slumbering and nice in her shaking mother arms . . . and they talked about golden things in drowsy voices until dawn made the fire slowly, slowly wither out. . . .

COME INTO MY CELLAR

Hugh Fortnum woke to Saturday's commotions, and lay, eyes shut, savoring each in its turn.

Below, bacon in a skillet; Cynthia waking him with fine cookings instead of cries.

Across the hall, Tom *actually* taking a shower.

Far off in the bumble-bee dragon-fly light, whose voice was already cursing the weather, the time, and the tides? Mrs. Goodbody? Yes. That Christian giantess, six feet tall with her shoes off, the gardener extraordinary, the octogenarian-dietitian and town philosopher.

He rose, unhooked the screen, and leaned out to hear her cry:

"There! Take *that! This'll* fix you! Hah!"

"Happy Saturday, Mrs. Goodbody!"

The old woman froze in clouds of bug spray pumped from an immense gun.

"Nonsense!" she shouted. "With these fiends and pests to watch for?"

"What kind *this* time?" called Fortnum.

"I don't want to shout it to the jaybirds, but—" she glanced suspiciously around—"what would you say if I told you I was the first line of defense concerning Flying Saucers?"

"Fine," replied Fortnum. "There'll be rockets between the worlds any year now."

"There already *are!*" She pumped, aiming the spray under the hedge. "There! Take that!"

He pulled his head back in from the fresh day, somehow not as high-spirited as his first response had indicated. Poor soul, Mrs. Goodbody. Always the very essence of reason. And now what? Old age?

The doorbell rang.

He grabbed his robe and was half down the stairs when he heard a voice say, "Special Delivery. Fortnum?" and saw Cynthia turn from the front door, a small packet in her hand.

He put his hand out, but she shook her head.

"Special Delivery Air Mail for your son."

Tom was downstairs like a centipede.

"Wow! That must be from the Great Bayou Novelty Greenhouse!"

"I wish I were as excited about ordinary mail," observed Fortnum.

"Ordinary?!" Tom ripped the cord and paper wildly. "Don't you read the back pages of *Popular Mechanics?* Well, here *they* are!"

Everyone peered into the small open box.

"Here," said Fortnum, *"what* are?"

"The Sylvan Glade Jumbo-Giant Guaranteed Growth Raise-Them-in-Your-Cellar-for-Big-Profit Mushrooms!"

"Oh, of course," said Fortnum. "How silly of me."

Cynthia squinted. "Those little teeny bits—?"

"'Fabulous growth in twenty-four hours,'" Tom quoted from memory. "'Plant them in your own cellar—'"

Fortnum and wife exchanged glances.

"Well," she admitted, "it's better than frogs and green snakes."

"Sure is!" Tom ran.

"Oh, Tom," said Fortnum, lightly.

Tom paused at the cellar door.

"Tom," said his father. "Next time, fourth-class mail would do fine."

"Heck," said Tom. "They must've made a mistake,

thought I was some rich company. Air mail special, who can afford *that?*"

The cellar door slammed.

Fortnum, bemused, scanned the wrapper a moment, then dropped it into the wastebasket. On his way to the kitchen, he opened the cellar door.

Tom was already on his knees, digging with a hand-rake in the dirt of the back part of the cellar.

He felt his wife beside him, breathing softly, looking down into the cool dimness.

"Those *are* mushrooms, I hope. Not . . . toad-stools?"

Fortnum laughed. "Happy harvest, farmer!"

Tom glanced up and waved.

Fortnum shut the door, took his wife's arm, and walked her out to the kitchen, feeling fine.

Toward noon, Fortnum was driving toward the nearest market when he saw Roger Willis, a fellow Rotarian, and teacher of biology at the town high school, waving urgently from the sidewalk.

Fortnum pulled his car up and opened the door.

"Hi, Roger, give you a lift?"

Willis responded all too eagerly, jumping in and slamming the door.

"Just the man I want to see. I've put off calling for days. Could you play psychiatrist for five minutes, God help you?"

Fortnum examined his friend for a moment as he drove quietly on.

"God help you, yes. Shoot."

Willis sat back and studied his fingernails. "Let's just drive a moment. There. Okay. Here's what I want to say: something's wrong with the world."

Fortnum laughed easily. "Hasn't there always been?"

"No, no, I mean . . . something strange—something unseen—is happening."

"Mrs. Goodbody," said Fortnum, half to himself, and stopped.

"Mrs. Goodbody?"

"This morning. Gave me a talk on flying saucers."

"No." Willis bit the knuckle of his forefinger nervously. "Nothing like saucers. At least I don't think. Tell me, what is intuition?"

"The conscious recognition of something that's been subconscious for a long time. But don't quote this amateur psychologist!" He laughed again.

"Good, good!" Willis turned, his face lighting. He readjusted himself in the seat. "That's it! Over a long period, things gather, right? All of a sudden, you have to spit, but you don't remember saliva collecting. Your hands are dirty, but you don't know how they got that way. Dust falls on you every day and you don't feel it. But when you get enough dust collected up, there it is, you see and name it. That's intuition, as far as I'm concerned. Well, what kind of dust has been falling on *me?* A few meteors in the sky at night? Funny weather just before dawn? I don't know. Certain colors, smells, the way the house creaks at three in the morning? Hair prickling on my arms? All I know is, the dust *has* collected. Quite suddenly I *know.*"

"Yes," said Fortnum, disquieted. "But what *is* it you know?"

Willis looked at his hands in his lap.

"I'm afraid. I'm not afraid. Then I'm afraid again, in the middle of the day. Doctor's checked me. I'm A-1. No family problems. Joe's a fine boy, a good son. Dorothy? She's remarkable. With her, I'm not afraid of growing old or dying."

"Lucky man."

"But beyond my luck now. Scared stiff, really, for myself, my family; even, right now, for *you.*"

"Me?" said Fortnum.

They had stopped now by an empty lot near the market. There was a moment of great stillness, in which Fortnum turned to survey his friend. Willis's voice had suddenly made him cold.

"I'm afraid for everybody," said Willis. "Your friends, mine, and their friends, on out of sight. Pretty silly, eh?"

Willis opened the door, got out, and peered in at Fortnum. Fortnum felt he had to speak.

"Well—what do we *do* about it?"

Willis looked up at the sun burning blind in the great, remote sky.

"Be aware," he said, slowly. "Watch everything for a few days."

"Everything?"

"We don't use half what God gave us, 10 per cent of the time. We ought to hear more, feel more, smell more, taste more. Maybe there's something wrong with the way the wind blows these weeds there in the lot. Maybe it's the sun up on those telephone wires or the cicadas singing in the elm trees. If only we could stop, look, listen, a few days, a few nights, and compare notes. Tell me to shut up then, and I will."

"Good enough," said Fortnum, playing it lighter than he felt. "I'll look around. But how do I know the thing I'm looking for when I *see* it?"

Willis peered in at him sincerely. "You'll know. You've got to know. Or we're done for, all of us," he said quietly.

Fortnum shut the door, and didn't know what to say. He felt a flush of embarrassment creeping up his face. Willis sensed this.

"Hugh, do you think I'm—off my rocker?"

"Nonsense!" said Fortnum, too quickly. "You're just nervous, is all. You should take a couple of weeks off."

Willis nodded. "See you Monday night?"

"Any time. Drop around."

"I hope I will, Hugh. I really hope I will."

Then Willis was gone, hurrying across the dry weed-grown lot, toward the side entrance of the market.

Watching him go, Fortnum suddenly did not want to move. He discovered that very slowly he was taking deep breaths, weighing the silence. He licked his lips, tasting the salt. He looked at his arm on the doorsill, the sunlight burning the golden hairs. In the empty lot the wind moved all alone to itself. He leaned out to look at the sun, which stared back with one massive stunning blow of intense power that made him jerk his head in.

He exhaled. Then he laughed out loud. Then he drove away.

* * *

The lemonade glass was cool and deliciously sweaty. The ice made music inside the glass, and the lemonade was just sour enough, just sweet enough on his tongue. He sipped, he savored, he tilted back in the wicker rocking chair on the twilight front porch, his eyes closed. The crickets were chirping out on the lawn. Cynthia, knitting across from him on the porch, eyed him curiously. He could feel the pressure of her attention.

"What are you up to?" she said at last.

"Cynthia," he said, "is your intuition in running order? Is this earthquake weather? Is the land going to sink? Will war be declared? Or is it only that our delphinium will die of the blight?"

"Hold on. Let me feel my bones."

He opened his eyes and watched Cynthia in turn closing hers and sitting absolutely statue-still, her hands on her knees. Finally she shook her head and smiled.

"No. No war declared. No land sinking. Not even a blight. Why?"

"I've met a lot of Doom Talkers today. Well, two, anyway, and—"

The screen door burst wide. Fortnum's body jerked as if he had been struck. "What!"

Tom, a gardener's wooden flat in his arms, stepped out on the porch.

"Sorry," he said. "What's wrong, Dad?"

"Nothing," Fortnum stood up, glad to be moving. "Is that the crop?"

Tom moved forward, eagerly. "Part of it. Boy, they're doing great. In just seven hours, with lots of water, look how big the darn things are!" He set the flat on the table between his parents.

The crop was indeed plentiful. Hundreds of small grayish brown mushrooms were sprouting up in the damp soil.

"I'll be. . . ." said Fortnum, impressed.

Cynthia put out her hand to touch the flat, then took it away uneasily.

"I hate to be a spoilsport, but . . . there's no way for these to be anything else but mushrooms, is there?"

Tom looked as if he had been insulted. "What do you think I'm going to feed you? Poison fungoids?"

"That's just it," said Cynthia quickly. "How do you tell them apart?"

"Eat 'em," said Tom. "If you live, they're mushrooms. If you drop dead—*well!*"

He gave a great guffaw, which amused Fortnum, but only made his mother wince. She sat back in her chair.

"I—I don't like them," she said.

"Boy, oh, boy." Tom seized the flat angrily. "When are we going to have the next Wet Blanket Sale in *this* house!?"

He shuffled morosely away.

"Tom—" said Fortnum.

"Never mind," said Tom. "Everyone figures they'll be ruined by the boy entrepreneur. To heck with it!"

Fortnum got inside just as Tom heaved the mushrooms, flat and all, down the cellar stairs. He slammed the cellar door and ran angrily out the back door.

Fortnum turned back to his wife, who, stricken, glanced away.

"I'm sorry," she said. "I don't know why, I just *had* to say that to Tom."

The phone rang. Fortnum brought the phone outside on its extension cord.

"Hugh?" It was Dorothy Willis's voice. She sounded suddenly very old and very frightened. "Hugh . . . Roger isn't there, is he?"

"Dorothy? No."

"He's gone!" said Dorothy. "All his clothes were taken from the closet." She began to cry softly.

"Dorothy, hold on, I'll be there in a minute."

"You must help, oh, you must. Something's happened to him, I know it," she wailed. "Unless you do something, we'll never see him alive again."

Very slowly, he put the receiver back on its hook, her voice weeping inside it. The night crickets, quite suddenly, were very loud. He felt the hairs, one by one, go up on the back of his neck.

Hair can't do that, he thought. Silly, silly. It can't do that, not in *real* life, it can't!

But, one by slow pricking one, his hair did.

* * *

The wire hangers were indeed empty. With a clatter, Fortnum shoved them aside and down along the rod, then turned and looked out of the closet at Dorothy Willis and her son, Joe.

"I was just walking by," said Joe, "and saw the closet empty, all Dad's clothes gone!"

"Everything was fine," said Dorothy. "We've had a wonderful life. I don't understand it, I don't, I don't!" She began to cry again, putting her hands to her face.

Fortnum stepped out of the closet.

"You didn't hear him leave the house?"

"We were playing catch out front," said Joe. "Dad said he had to go in for a minute. I went around back. Then—he was gone!"

"He must have packed quickly and walked wherever he was going, so we wouldn't hear a cab pull up front of the house."

They were moving out through the hall now.

"I'll check the train depot and the airport." Fortnum hesitated. "Dorothy, is there anything in Roger's background—"

"It wasn't insanity took him." She hesitated. "I feel—somehow—he was kidnapped."

Fortnum shook his head. "It doesn't seem reasonable he would arrange to pack, walk out of the house, and go meet his abductors."

Dorothy opened the door as if to let the night or the night wind move down the hall as she turned to stare back through the rooms, her voice wandering.

"No. Somehow they came into the house. Right in front of us, they stole him away."

And then:

". . . a terrible thing has happened."

Fortnum stepped out into the night of crickets and rustling trees. The Doom Talkers, he thought, talking their Dooms. Mrs. Goodbody. Roger. And now Roger's wife. Something terrible *has* happened. But *what*, in God's name? And *how*?

He looked from Dorothy to her son. Joe, blinking the wetness from his eyes, took a long time to turn, walk along the hall, and stop, fingering the knob of the cellar door.

Fortnum felt his eyelids twitch, his iris flex, as if he were snapping a picture of something he wanted to remember.

Joe pulled the cellar door wide, stepped down out of sight, gone. The door tapped shut.

Fortnum opened his mouth to speak, but Dorothy's hand was taking his now, he had to look at her.

"Please," she said. "Find him for me."

He kissed her cheek. "If it's humanly possible . . ."

If it's humanly possible. Good Lord, why had he picked those words?

He walked off into the summer night.

A gasp, an exhalation, a gasp, an exhalation, an asthmatic insuck, a vaporing sneeze. Someone dying in the dark? No.

Just Mrs. Goodbody, unseen beyond the hedge, working late, her hand pump aimed, her bony elbow thrusting. The sick-sweet smell of bug spray enveloped Fortnum heavily as he reached his house.

"Mrs. Goodbody? Still at it?!"

From the black hedge, her voice leapt:

"Blast it, yes! Aphids, waterbugs, woodworms, and now the *marasmius oreades*. Lord, it grows fast!"

"What does?"

"The *marasmius oreades*, of course! It's me against them, and I intend to win. There! There! There!"

He left the hedge, the gasping pump, the wheezing voice, and found his wife waiting for him on the porch almost as if she were going to take up where Dorothy had left off at her door a few minutes ago.

Fortnum was about to speak, when a shadow moved inside. There was a creaking noise. A knob rattled.

Tom vanished into the basement.

Fortnum felt as if someone had set off an explosion in his face. He reeled. Everything had the numbed familiarity of those waking dreams where all motions are remembered before they occur, all dialogue known before it fell from the lips.

He found himself staring at the shut basement door. Cynthia took him inside, amused.

"What? Tom? Oh, I relented. The darn mushrooms meant so much to him. Besides, when he threw them into the cellar, they did nicely, just lying in the dirt."

"Did they?" Fortnum heard himself say.

Cynthia took his arm. "What about Roger?"

"He's gone, yes."

"Men, men, men," she said.

"No, you're wrong," he said. "I saw Roger every day for the last ten years. When you know a man that well, you can tell how things are at home, whether things are in the oven or the mixmaster. Death hadn't breathed down his neck yet. He wasn't running scared after his immortal youth, picking peaches in someone else's orchards. No, no, I swear, I'd bet my last dollar on it, Roger—"

The doorbell rang behind him. The delivery boy had come up quietly onto the porch and was standing there with a telegram in his hand.

"Fortnum?"

Cynthia snapped on the hall light as he ripped the envelope open and smoothed it out for reading.

"TRAVELING NEW ORLEANS. THIS TELE-GRAM POSSIBLE OFF-GUARD MOMENT. YOU MUST REFUSE, REPEAT REFUSE, ALL SPECIAL DELIVERY PACKAGES! ROGER."

Cynthia glanced up from the paper.

"I don't understand. What does he mean?"

But Fortnum was already at the telephone, dialing swiftly, once. "Operator? The police, and hurry!"

At ten-fifteen that night, the phone rang for the sixth time during the evening. Fortnum got it, and immediately gasped. "Roger! Where are you?"

"Where am I?" said Roger lightly, almost amused. "You know very well where I am. You're responsible for this. I should be angry!"

Cynthia, at his nod, had hurried to take the extension phone in the kitchen. When he heard the soft click, he went on.

"Roger, I swear I don't know. I got that telegram from you—"

"What telegram?" said Roger, jovially. "I sent no telegram. Now, of a sudden, the police come pouring onto the southbound train, pull me off in some jerkwater, and I'm calling you to get them off my neck. Hugh, if this is some joke—"

"But, Roger, you just vanished!"

"On a business trip. If you can call that vanishing. I told Dorothy about this, and Joe."

"This is all very confusing, Roger. You're in no danger? Nobody's blackmailing you, forcing you into this speech?"

"I'm fine, healthy, free, and unafraid."

"But, Roger, your premonitions . . . ?"

"Poppycock! Now, look, I'm being very good about this, aren't I?"

"Sure, Roger."

"Then play the good father and give me permission to go. Call Dorothy and tell her I'll be back in five days. How *could* she have forgotten?"

"She did, Roger. See you in five days, then?"

"Five days, I swear."

The voice was indeed winning and warm, the old Roger again. Fortnum shook his head, more bewildered than before.

"Roger," he said, "this is the craziest day I've ever spent. You're not running off from Dorothy? Good Lord, you can tell *me.*"

"I love her with all my heart. Now, here's Lieutenant Parker of the Ridgetown police. Good-by, Hugh."

"Good—"

But the lieutenant was on the line, talking angrily. What had Fortnum meant putting them to this trouble? What was going on? Who did he think he was? Did or didn't he want this so-called friend held or released?

"Released," Fortnum managed to say somewhere along the way, and hung up the phone and imagined he heard a voice call all aboard and the massive thunder of the train leaving the station two hundred miles south in the somehow increasingly dark night.

Cynthia walked very slowly into the parlor.

"I feel so foolish," she said.

"How do you think I feel?"

"Who could have sent that telegram? And why?"

He poured himself some Scotch and stood in the middle of the room looking at it.

"I'm glad Roger is all right," his wife said, at last.

"He isn't," said Fortnum.

"But you just said—"

"I said nothing. After all, we couldn't very well drag him off that train and truss him up and send him home, could we, if he insisted he was okay? No. He sent that telegram, but he changed his mind after sending it. Why, why, why?" Fortnum paced the room, sipping the drink. "Why warn us against special delivery packages? The only package we've got this *year* which fits that description is the one Tom got this morning—" His voice trailed off.

Before he could move, Cynthia was at the wastepaper basket taking out the crumpled wrapping paper with the special-delivery stamps on it.

The postmark read: NEW ORLEANS, LA.

Cynthia looked up from it. "New Orleans. Isn't that where Roger is heading right *now?*"

A doorknob rattled, a door opened and closed in Fortnum's mind. Another doorknob rattled, another door swung wide and then shut. There was a smell of damp earth.

He found his hand dialing the phone. After a long while, Dorothy Willis answered at the other end. He could imagine her sitting alone in a house with too many lights on. He talked quietly with her awhile, then cleared his throat and said, "Dorothy, look. I know it sounds silly. Did any special delivery air mail packages arrive at your house the last few days?"

Her voice was faint. "No." Then: "No, wait. Three days ago. But I thought you *knew!* All the boys on the block are going in for it."

Fortnum measured his words carefully.

"Going in for what?"

"But why ask?" she said. "There's nothing wrong with raising mushrooms, is there?"

Fortnum closed his eyes.

"Hugh? Are you still there?" asked Dorothy. "I said: there's nothing wrong with—"

"—raising mushrooms?" said Fortnum, at last. "No. Nothing wrong. Nothing wrong."

And slowly he put down the phone.

The curtains blew like veils of moonlight. The clock ticked. The after-midnight world flowed into and filled the bedroom. He heard Mrs. Goodbody's clear voice on this morning's air, a million years gone now. He heard Roger putting a cloud over the sun at noon. He heard the police cursing him by phone from downstate. Then Roger's voice again, with the locomotive thunder hurrying him away and away, fading. And finally, Mrs. Goodbody's voice behind the hedge:

"Lord, it grows fast!"

"What does?"

"Marasmius oreades!"

He snapped his eyes open. He sat up.

Downstairs, a moment later, he flicked through the unabridged dictionary.

His forefinger underlined the words:

"Marasmius oreades: a mushroom commonly found on lawns in summer and early autumn."

He let the book fall shut.

Outside, in the deep summer night, he lit a cigarette and smoked quietly.

A meteor fell across space, burning itself out quickly. The trees rustled softly.

The front door tapped shut.

Cynthia moved toward him in her robe.

"Can't sleep?"

"Too warm, I guess."

"It's not warm."

"No," he said, feeling his arms. "In fact, it's cold." He sucked on the cigarette twice, then, not looking at her, said, "Cynthia . . . What if . . . ?" He snorted and had to stop. "Well, what if Roger was right this morning? Mrs. Goodbody, what if she's right, too? Something ter-

rible *is* happening. Like—well—" he nodded at the sky
and the million stars— "Earth being invaded by things
from other worlds, maybe."

"Hugh!"

"No, let me run wild."

"It's quite obvious we're not being invaded or we'd
notice."

"Let's say we've only half-noticed, become uneasy
about something. What? How could we be invaded? By
what means would creatures invade?"

Cynthia looked at the sky and was about to try something when he interrupted.

"No, not meteors or flying saucers. Not things we can
see. What about bacteria? That comes from outer space,
too, doesn't it?"

"I read once, yes—"

"Spores, seeds, pollens, viruses probably bombard
our atmosphere by the billions every second and have
done so for millions of years. Right now we're sitting out
under an invisible rain. It falls all over the country, the
cities, the towns, and right now . . . our lawn."

"*Our* lawn?"

"*And* Mrs. Goodbody's But people like her are always pulling weeds, spraying poison, kicking toadstools
off their grass. It would be hard for any strange life form
to survive in cities. Weather's a problem, too. Best climate might be South: Alabama, Georgia, Louisiana.
Back in the damp bayous, they could grow to a fine
size."

But Cynthia was beginning to laugh now.

"Oh, really, you don't believe, do you, that this Great
Bayou or whatever Greenhouse Novelty Company that
sent Tom his package is owned and operated by six-foot-
tall mushrooms from another planet?"

"If you put it that way, it sounds funny," he admitted.

"Funny! It's hilarious!" She threw her head back deliciously.

"Good grief!" he cried, suddenly irritated. "*Something's* going on! Mrs. Goodbody is rooting out and killing *marasmius oreades.* What is *marasmius oreades?* A
certain kind of mushroom. Simultaneously, and I sup-

pose you'll call it coincidence, by special delivery, what arrives the same day? Mushrooms for Tom! What else happens? Roger fears he may soon cease to be! Within hours, he vanishes, then telegraphs us, warning us not to accept what? The special delivery mushrooms for Tom! Has Roger's son got a similar package in the last few days? He has! Where do the packages come from? New Orleans! And where is Roger going when he vanishes? New Orleans! Do you see, Cynthia, do you see? I wouldn't be upset if all these separate things didn't lock together! Roger, Tom, Joe, mushrooms, Mrs. Goodbody, packages, destinations, everything in one pattern!"

She was watching his face now, quieter, but still amused. "Don't get angry."

"I'm not!" Fortnum almost shouted. And then he simply could not go on. He was afraid that if he did, he would find himself shouting with laughter, too, and somehow he did not want that. He stared at the surrounding houses up and down the block and thought of the dark cellars and the neighbor boys who read *Popular Mechanics* and sent their money in by the millions to raise the mushrooms hidden away. Just as he, when a boy, had mailed off for chemicals, seeds, turtles, numberless salves and sickish ointments. In how many million American homes tonight were billions of mushrooms rousing up under the ministrations of the innocent?

"Hugh?" His wife was touching his arm now. "Mushrooms, even big ones, can't think. They can't move. They don't have arms and legs. How could they run a mail-order service and 'take over' the world? Come on, now. Let's look at your terrible fiends and monsters!"

She pulled him toward the door. Inside, she headed for the cellar, but he stopped, shaking his head, a foolish smile shaping itself somehow to his mouth. "No, no, I know what we'll find. You win. The whole thing's silly. Roger will be back next week and we'll all get drunk together. Go on up to bed now and I'll drink a glass of warm milk and be with you in a minute . . . well, a couple of minutes . . ."

"That's better!" She kissed him on both cheeks, squeezed him, and went away up the stairs.

In the kitchen, he took out a glass, opened the refrigerator, and was pouring the milk when he stopped suddenly.

Near the front of the top shelf was a small yellow dish. It was not the dish that held his attention, however. It was what lay in the dish.

The fresh-cut mushrooms.

He must have stood there for half a minute, his breath frosting the refrigerated air, before he reached out, took hold of the dish, sniffed it, felt the mushrooms, then at last, carrying the dish, went out into the hall. He looked up the stairs, hearing Cynthia moving about in the bedroom, and was about to call up to her, "Cynthia, did you put *these* in the refrigerator!?"

Then he stopped. He knew her answer. She had not.

He put the dish of mushrooms on the newel at the bottom of the stairs and stood looking at them. He imagined himself, in bed later, looking at the walls, the open windows, watching the moonlight sift patterns on the ceiling. He heard himself saying, Cynthia? And her answering, yes? And him saying, there *is* a way for mushrooms to grow arms and legs . . . What? she would say, silly, silly man, what? And he would gather courage against her hilarious reaction and go on, what if a man wandered through the swamp, picked the mushrooms, and *ate* them . . . ?

No response from Cynthia.

Once inside the man, would the mushrooms spread through his blood, take over every cell, and change the man from a man to a—Martian? Given this theory, would the mushroom *need* its own arms and legs? No, not when it could borrow people, live inside and become them. Roger ate mushrooms given him by his son. Roger became "something else." He kidnaped himself. And in one last flash of sanity, of being "himself," he telegraphed us, warning us not to accept the special delivery mushrooms. The "Roger" that telephoned later was no longer Roger but a captive of what he had eaten! Doesn't that figure, Cynthia? Doesn't it, doesn't it?

No, said the imagined Cynthia, no, it doesn't figure, no, no, no . . .

There was the faintest whisper, rustle, stir from the cellar. Taking his eyes from the bowl, Fortnum walked to the cellar door and put his ear to it.

"Tom?"

No answer.

"Tom, are you down there?"

No answer.

"Tom?"

After a long while, Tom's voice came up from below. "Yes, Dad?"

"It's after midnight," said Fortnum, fighting to keep his voice from going high. "What are you doing down there?"

No answer.

"I said—"

"Tending to my crop," said the boy at last, his voice cold and faint.

"Well, get up out of there! You hear me?!"

Silence.

"Tom? Listen! Did you put some mushrooms in the refrigerator tonight? If so, why?"

Ten seconds must have ticked by before the boy replied from below. "For you and Mom to eat, of course."

Fortnum heard his heart moving swiftly, and had to take three deep breaths before he could go on.

"Tom? You didn't . . . that is . . . you haven't by any chance eaten some of the mushrooms yourself, have you?"

"Funny you ask that," said Tom. "Yes. Tonight. On a sandwich after supper. Why?"

Fortnum held to the doorknob. Now it was his turn not to answer. He felt his knees beginning to melt and he fought the whole silly senseless fool thing. No reason, he tried to say, but his lips wouldn't move.

"Dad?" called Tom softly from the cellar. "Come on down." Another pause. "I want you to see the harvest."

Fortnum felt the knob slip in his sweaty hand. The knob rattled. He gasped.

"Dad?" called Tom softly.

Fortnum opened the door.

The cellar was completely black below.

He stretched his hand in toward the light switch. As if sensing this intrusion, from somewhere Tom said:

"Don't. Light's bad for the mushrooms."

Fortnum took his hand off the switch.

He swallowed. He looked back at the stair leading up to his wife. I suppose, he thought, I should go say good-by to Cynthia. But why should I think that! Why should I think that at *all?* No reason, is there?

None.

"Tom?" he said, affecting a jaunty air. "Ready or not, here I come!"

And stepping down in darkness, he shut the door.

THE MILLION-YEAR PICNIC

Somehow the idea was brought up by Mom that perhaps the whole family would enjoy a fishing trip. But they weren't Mom's words; Timothy knew that. They were Dad's words, and Mom used them for him somehow.

Dad shuffled his feet in a clutter of Martian pebbles and agreed. So immediately there was a tumult and a shouting, and very quickly the camp was tucked into capsules and containers, Mom slipped into traveling jumpers and blouse, Dad stuffed his pipe full with trembling hands, his eyes on the Martian sky, and the three boys piled yelling into the motorboat, none of them really keeping an eye on Mom and Dad, except Timothy.

Dad pushed a stud. The water boat sent a humming sound up into the sky. The water shook back and the boat nosed ahead, and the family cried, "Hurrah!"

Timothy sat in the back of the boat with Dad, his small fingers atop Dad's hairy ones, watching the canal twist, leaving the crumbled place behind where they had landed in their small family rocket all the way from Earth. He remembered the night before they left Earth, the hustling and hurrying, the rocket that Dad had found somewhere, somehow, and the talk of a vacation on Mars. A long way to go for a vacation, but Timothy said nothing because of his younger brothers. They came to Mars and now, first thing, or so they said, they were going fishing.

Dad had a funny look in his eyes as the boat went up-canal. A look that Timothy couldn't figure. It was made of strong light and maybe a sort of relief. It made the deep wrinkles laugh instead of worry or cry.

So there went the cooling rocket, around a bend, gone.

"How far are we going?" Robert splashed his hand. It looked like a small crab jumping in the violet water.

Dad exhaled. "A million years."

"Gee," said Robert.

"Look, kids." Mother pointed one soft long arm. "There's a dead city."

They looked with fervent anticipation, and the dead city lay dead for them alone, drowsing in a hot silence of summer made on Mars by a Martian weatherman.

And Dad looked as if he was pleased that it was dead.

It was a futile spread of pink rocks sleeping on a rise of sand, a few tumbled pillars, one lonely shrine, and then the sweep of sand again. Nothing else for miles. A white desert around the canal and a blue desert over it.

Just then a bird flew up. Like a stone thrown across a blue pond, hitting, falling deep, and vanishing.

Dad got a frightened look when he saw it. "I thought it was a rocket."

Timothy looked at the deep ocean sky, trying to see Earth and the war and the ruined cities and the men killing each other since the day he was born. But he saw nothing. The war was as removed and far off as two flies battling to the death in the arch of a great high and silent cathedral. And just as senseless.

William Thomas wiped his forehead and felt the touch of his son's hand on his arm, like a young tarantula, thrilled. He beamed at his son. "How goes it, Timmy?"

"Fine, Dad."

Timothy hadn't quite figured out what was ticking inside the vast adult mechanism beside him. The man with the immense hawk nose, sunburned, peeling—and the hot blue eyes like agate marbles you play with after school in summer back on Earth, and the long thick columnar legs in the loose riding breeches.

"What are you looking at so hard, Dad?"

"I was looking for Earthian logic, common sense, good government, peace, and responsibility."

"All that up there?"

"No. I didn't find it. It's not there any more. Maybe it'll never be there again. Maybe we fooled ourselves that it was ever there."

"Huh?"

"See the fish," said Dad, pointing.

There rose a soprano clamor from all three boys as they rocked the boat in arching their tender necks to see. They *oohed* and *aahed*. A silver ring fish floated by them, undulating, and closing like an iris, instantly, around food particles, to assimilate them.

Dad looked at it. His voice was deep and quiet.

"Just like war. War swims along, sees food, contracts. A moment later—Earth is gone."

"William," said Mom.

"Sorry," said Dad.

They sat still and felt the canal water rush, cool, swift, and glassy. The only sound was the motor hum, the glide of water, the sun expanding the air.

"When do we see the Martians?" cried Michael.

"Quite soon, perhaps," said Father. "Maybe to-night."

"Oh, but the Martians are a dead race now," said Mom.

"No, they're not. I'll show you some Martians, all right," Dad said presently.

Timothy scowled at that but said nothing. Everything was odd now. Vacations and fishing and looks between people.

The other boys were already engaged making shelves of their small hands and peering under them toward the seven-foot stone banks of the canal, watching for Martians.

"What do they look like?" demanded Michael.

"You'll know them when you see them." Dad sort of

laughed, and Timothy saw a pulse beating time in his cheek.

Mother was slender and soft, with a woven plait of spun-gold hair over her head in a tiara, and eyes the color of the deep cool canal water where it ran in shadow, almost purple, with flecks of amber caught in it. You could see her thoughts swimming around in her eyes, like fish—some bright, some dark, some fast, quick, some slow and easy, and sometimes, like when she looked up where Earth was, being nothing but color and nothing else. She sat in the boat's prow, one hand resting on the side lip, the other on the lap of her dark blue breeches, and a line of sun-burned soft neck showing where her blouse opened like a white flower.

She kept looking ahead to see what was there, and, not being able to see it clearly enough, she looked backward toward her husband, and through his eyes, reflected then, she saw what was ahead; and since he added part of himself to this reflection, a determined firmness, her face relaxed and she accepted it and she turned back, knowing suddenly what to look for.

Timothy looked too. But all he saw was a straight pencil line of canal going violet through a wide shallow valley penned by low, eroded hills, and on until it fell over the sky's edge. And this canal went on and on, through cities that would have rattled like beetles in a dry skull if you shook them. A hundred or two hundred cities dreaming hot summer-day dreams and cool summer-night dreams . . .

They had come millions of miles for this outing—to fish. But there had been a gun on the rocket. This was a vacation. But why all the food, more than enough to last them years and years, left hidden back there near the rocket? Vacation. Just behind the veil of the vacation was not a soft face of laughter, but something hard and bony and perhaps terrifying. Timothy could not lift the veil, and the two other boys were busy being ten and eight years old, respectively.

"No Martians yet. Nuts." Robert put his V-shaped chin on his hands and glared at the canal.

Dad had brought an atomic radio along, strapped to his wrist. It functioned on an old-fashioned principle:

you held it against the bones near your ear and it vibrated singing or talking to you. Dad listened to it now. His face looked like one of those fallen Martian cities, caved in, sucked dry, almost dead.

Then he gave it to Mom to listen. Her lips dropped open.

"What——" Timothy started to question, but never finished what he wished to say.

For at that moment there were two titanic, marrow-jolting explosions that grew upon themselves, followed by a half-dozen minor concussions.

Jerking his head up, Dad notched the boat speed higher immediately. The boat leaped and jounced and spanked. This shook Robert out of his funk and elicited yelps of frightened but ecstatic joy from Michael, who clung to Mom's legs and watched the water pour by his nose in a wet torrent.

Dad swerved the boat, cut speed, and ducked the craft into a little branch canal and under an ancient, crumbling stone wharf that smelled of crab flesh. The boat rammed the wharf hard enough to throw them all forward, but no one was hurt, and Dad was already twisted to see if the ripples on the canal were enough to map their route into hiding. Water lines went across, lapped the stones, and rippled back to meet each other, settling, to be dappled by the sun. It all went away.

Dad listened. So did everybody.

Dad's breathing echoed like fists beating against the cold wet wharf stones. In the shadow, Mom's cat eyes just watched Father for some clue to what next.

Dad relaxed and blew out a breath, laughing at himself.

"The rocket, of course. I'm getting jumpy. The rocket."

Michael said, "What happened, Dad, what happened?"

"Oh, we just blew up our rocket, is all," said Timothy, trying to sound matter-of-fact. "I've heard rockets blown up before. Ours just blew."

"Why did we blow up our rocket?" asked Michael. "Huh, Dad?"

"It's part of the game, silly!" said Timothy.

"A game!" Michael and Robert loved the word.

"Dad fixed it so it would blow up and no one'd know where we landed or went! In case they ever came looking, see?"

"Oh boy, a secret!"

"Scared by my own rocket," admitted Dad to Mom. "I *am* nervous. It's silly to think there'll ever be any more rockets. Except *one*, perhaps, if Edwards and his wife get through with *their* ship."

He put his tiny radio to his ear again. After two minutes he dropped his hand as you would drop a rag.

"It's over at last," he said to Mom. "The radio just went off the atomic beam. Every other world station's gone. They dwindled down to a couple in the last few years. Now the air's completely silent. It'll probably remain silent."

"For how long?" asked Robert.

"Maybe—your great-grandchildren will hear it again," said Dad. He just sat there, and the children were caught in the center of his awe and defeat and resignation and acceptance.

Finally he put the boat out into the canal again, and they continued in the direction in which they had originally started.

It was getting late. Already the sun was down the sky, and a series of dead cities lay ahead of them.

Dad talked very quietly and gently to his sons. Many times in the past he had been brisk, distant, removed from them, but now he patted them on the head with just a word and they felt it.

"Mike, pick a city."

"What, Dad?"

"Pick a city, Son. Any one of these cities we pass."

"All right," said Michael. "How do I pick?"

"Pick the one you like the most. You, too, Robert and Tim. Pick the city you like best."

"I want a city with Martians in it," said Michael.

"You'll have that," said Dad. "I promise." His lips were for the children, but his eyes were for Mom.

They passed six cities in twenty minutes. Dad didn't say anything more about the explosions; he seemed much more interested in having fun with his sons, keeping them happy, than anything else.

Michael liked the first city they passed, but this was vetoed because everyone doubted quick first judgments. The second city nobody liked. It was an Earth man's settlement, built of wood and already rotting into sawdust. Timothy liked the third city because it was large. The fourth and fifth were too small and the sixth brought acclaim from everyone, including Mother, who joined in the Gees, Goshes, and Look-at-thats!

There were fifty or sixty huge structures still standing, streets were dusty but paved, and you could see one or two old centrifugal fountains still pulsing wetly in the plazas. That was the only life—water leaping in the late sunlight.

"This is the city," said everybody.

Steering the boat to a wharf, Dad jumped out.

"Here we are. This is ours. This is where we live from now on!"

"From now on?" Michael was incredulous. He stood up, looking, and then turned to blink back at where the rocket used to be. "What about the rocket? What about Minnesota?"

"Here," said Dad.

He touched the small radio to Michael's blond head. "Listen."

Michael listened.

"Nothing," he said.

"That's right. Nothing. Nothing at all any more. No more Minneapolis, no more rockets, no more Earth."

Michael considered the lethal revelation and began to sob little dry sobs.

"Wait a moment," said Dad the next instant. "I'm giving you a lot more in exchange, Mike!"

"What?" Michael held off the tears, curious, but quite ready to continue in case Dad's further revelation was as disconcerting as the original.

"I'm giving you this city, Mike. It's yours."

"Mine?"

"For you and Robert and Timothy, all three of you, to own for yourselves."

Timothy bounded from the boat. "Look, guys, all for

us! All of *that!*" He was playing the game with Dad, playing it large and playing it well. Later, after it was all over and things had settled, he could go off by himself and cry for ten minutes. But now it was still a game, still a family outing, and the other kids must be kept playing.

Mike jumped out with Robert. They helped Mom.

"Be careful of your sister," said Dad, and nobody knew what he meant until later.

They hurried into the great pink-stoned city, whispering among themselves, because dead cities have a way of making you want to whisper, to watch the sun go down.

"In about five days," said Dad quietly, "I'll go back down to where our rocket was and collect the food hidden in the ruins there and bring it here; and I'll hunt for Bert Edwards and his wife and daughters there."

"Daughters?" asked Timothy. "How many?"

"Four."

"I can see that'll cause trouble later." Mom nodded slowly.

"Girls." Michael made a face like an ancient Martian stone image. "Girls."

"Are they coming in a rocket too?"

"Yes. If they make it. Family rockets are made for travel to the Moon, not Mars. We were lucky we got through."

"Where did you get the rocket?" whispered Timothy, for the other boys were running ahead.

"I saved it. I saved it for twenty years, Tim. I had it hidden away, hoping I'd never have to use it. I suppose I should have given it to the government for the war, but I kept thinking about Mars. . . ."

"And a picnic!"

"Right. This is between you and me. When I saw everything was finishing on Earth, after I'd waited until the last moment, I packed us up. Bert Edwards had a ship hidden, too, but we decided it would be safer to take off separately, in case anyone tried to shoot us down."

"Why'd you blow up the rocket, Dad?"

"So we can't go back, ever. And so if any of those evil men ever come to Mars they won't know we're here."

"Is that why you look up all the time?"

"Yes, it's silly. They won't follow us, ever. They haven't anything to follow with. I'm being too careful, is all."

Michael came running back. "Is this really *our* city, Dad?"

"The whole darn planet belongs to us, kids. The whole darn planet."

They stood there, King of the Hill, Top of the Heap, Ruler of All They Surveyed, Unimpeachable Monarchs and Presidents, trying to understand what it meant to own a world and how big a world really was.

Night came quickly in the thin atmosphere, and Dad left them in the square by the pulsing fountain, went down to the boat, and came walking back carrying a stack of paper in his big hands.

He laid the papers in a clutter in an old courtyard and set them afire. To keep warm, they crouched around the blaze and laughed, and Timothy saw the little letters leap like frightened animals when the flames touched and engulfed them. The papers crinkled like an old man's skin, and the cremation surrounded innumerable words:

"GOVERNMENT BONDS; Business Graph, 1999; Religious Prejudice: An Essay; The Science of Logistics; Problems of the Pan-American Unity; Stock Report for July 3, 1998; The War Digest . . ."

Dad had insisted on bringing these papers for this purpose. He sat there and fed them into the fire, one by one, with satisfaction, and told his children what it all meant.

"It's time I told you a few things. I don't suppose it was fair, keeping so much from you. I don't know if you'll understand, but I have to talk, even if only part of it gets over to you."

He dropped a leaf in the fire.

"I'm burning a way of life, just like that way of life is being burned clean of Earth right now. Forgive me if I talk like a politician. I am, after all, a former state governor, and I was honest and they hated me for it. Life on Earth never settled down to doing anything very good. Science ran too far ahead of us too quickly, and the people got lost in a mechanical wilderness, like children making over pretty things, gadgets, helicopters, rockets; emphasizing the wrong items, emphasizing machines instead of how to run the machines. Wars got bigger and bigger and finally killed Earth. That's what the silent radio means. That's what we ran away from.

"We were lucky. There aren't any more rockets left. It's time you knew this isn't a fishing trip at all. I put off telling you. Earth is gone. Interplanetary travel won't be back for centuries, maybe never. But that way of life proved itself wrong and strangled itself with its own hands. You're young. I'll tell you this again every day until it sinks in."

He paused to feed more papers to the fire.

"Now we're alone. We and a handful of others who'll land in a few days. Enough to start over. Enough to turn away from all that back on Earth and strike out on a new line——"

The fire leaped up to emphasize his talking. And then all the papers were gone except one. All the laws and beliefs of Earth were burnt into small hot ashes which soon would be carried off in a wind.

Timothy looked at the last thing that Dad tossed in the fire. It was a map of the World, and it wrinkled and distorted itself hotly and went—flimpf—and was gone like a warm, black butterfly. Timothy turned away.

Now I'm going to show you the Martians," said Dad. "Come on, all of you. Here, Alice." He took her hand.

Michael was crying loudly, and Dad picked him up and carried him, and they walked down through the ruins toward the canal.

The canal. Where tomorrow or the next day their future wives would come up in a boat, small laughing girls now, with their father and mother.

The night came down around them, and there were stars. But Timothy couldn't find Earth. It had already set. That was something to think about.

A night bird called among the ruins as they walked. Dad said, "Your mother and I will try to teach you. Perhaps we'll fail. I hope not. We've had a good lot to see and learn from. We planned this trip years ago, before you were born. Even if there hadn't been a war we would have come to Mars, I think, to live and form our own standard of living. It would have been another century before Mars would have been really poisoned by the Earth civilization. Now, of course—"

They reached the canal. It was long and straight and cool and wet and reflective in the night.

"I've always wanted to see a Martian," said Michael. "Where are they, Dad? You promised."

"There they are," said Dad, and he shifted Michael on his shoulder and pointed straight down.

The Martians were there. Timothy began to shiver.

The Martians were there—in the canal—reflected in the water. Timothy and Michael and Robert and Mom and Dad.

The Martians stared back up at them for a long, long silent time from the rippling water. . . .

THE SCREAMING WOMAN

My name is Margaret Leary and I'm ten years old and in the fifth grade at Central School. I haven't any brothers or sisters, but I've got a nice father and mother except they don't pay much attention to me. And anyway, we never thought we'd have anything to do with a murdered woman. Or almost, anyway.

When you're just living on a street like we live on, you don't think awful things are going to happen, like shooting or stabbing or burying people under the ground, practically in your back yard. And when it does happen you don't believe it. You just go on buttering your toast or baking a cake.

I got to tell you how it happened. It was a noon in the middle of July. It was hot and Mama said to me, "Margaret, you go to the store and buy some ice cream. It's Saturday, Dad's home for lunch, so we'll have a treat."

I ran out across the empty lot behind our house. It was a big lot, where kids had played baseball, and broken glass and stuff. And on my way back from the store with the ice cream I was just walking along, minding my own business, when all of a sudden it happened.

I heard the Screaming Woman.

I stopped and listened.

It was coming up out of the ground.

A woman was buried under the rocks and dirt and

glass, and she was screaming, all wild and horrible, for someone to dig her out.

I just stood there, afraid. She kept screaming, muffled.

Then I started to run. I fell down, got up, and ran some more. I got in the screen door of my house and there was Mama, calm as you please, not knowing what I knew, that there was a real live woman buried out in back of our house, just a hundred yards away, screaming bloody murder.

"Mama," I said.

"Don't stand there with the ice cream," said Mama.

"But, Mama," I said.

"Put it in the icebox," she said.

"Listen, Mama, there's a Screaming Woman in the empty lot."

"And wash your hands," said Mama.

"She was screamin' and screamin' . . ."

"Let's see now, salt and pepper," said Mama, far away.

"Listen to me," I said, loud. "We got to dig her out. She's buried under tons and tons of dirt and if we don't dig her out, she'll choke up and die."

"I'm certain she can wait until after lunch," said Mama.

"Mama, don't you believe me?"

"Of course, dear. Now wash your hands and take this plate of meat in to your father."

"I don't even know who she is or how she got there," I said. "But we got to help her before it's too late."

"Good gosh," said Mama. "Look at this ice cream. What did you do, just stand in the sun and let it melt?"

"Well, the empty lot . . ."

"Go on, now, scoot."

I went into the dining room.

"Hi, Dad, there's a Screaming Woman in the empty lot."

"I never knew a woman who didn't," said Dad.

"I'm serious," I said.

"You look very grave," said Father.

"We've got to get picks and shovels and excavate, like for an Egyptian mummy," I said.

"I don't feel like an archaeologist, Margaret," said Father. "Now, some nice cool October day, I'll take you up on that."

"But we can't wait that long," I almost screamed. My heart was bursting in me. I was excited and scared and afraid and here was Dad, putting meat on his plate, cutting and chewing and paying me no attention.

"Dad?" I said.

"Mmmm?" he said, chewing.

"Dad, you just gotta come out after lunch and help me," I said. "Dad, Dad, I'll give you all the money in my piggy bank!"

"Well," said Dad, "So it's a business proposition, is it? It must be important for you to offer your perfectly good money. How much money will you pay, by the hour?"

"I got five whole dollars it took me a year to save, and it's all yours."

Dad touched my arm. "I'm touched. I'm really touched. You want me to play with you and you're willing to pay for my time. Honest, Margaret, you make your old Dad feel like a piker. I don't give you enough time. Tell you what, after lunch, I'll come out and listen to your screaming woman, free of charge."

"Will you, oh, will you, really?"

"Yes, ma'am, that's what I'll do," said Dad. "But you must promise me one thing?"

"What?"

"If I come out, you must eat all of your lunch first."

"I promise," I said.

"Okay."

Mother came in and sat down and we started to eat. "Not so fast," said Mama.

I slowed down. Then I started eating fast again.

"You heard your mother," said Dad.

"The Screaming Woman," I said. "We got to hurry."

"I," said Father, "intend sitting here quietly and judiciously giving my attention first to my steak, then to my potatoes, and my salad, of course, and then to my ice cream, and after that to a long drink of iced coffee, if you don't mind. I may be a good hour at it. And another thing, young lady, if you mention her name, this Screaming What-sis, once more at this table during lunch, I won't go out with you to hear her recital."

"Yes, sir."

"Is that understood?"

"Yes, sir," I said.

Lunch was a million years long. Everybody moved in slow motion, like those films you see at the movies. Mama got up slow and got down slow and forks and knives and spoons moved slow. Even the flies in the room were slow. And Dad's cheek muscles moved slow. It was so slow. I wanted to scream, "Hurry! Oh, please, rush, get up, run around, come on out, run!"

But no, I had to sit, and all the while we sat there slowly, slowly eating our lunch, out there in the empty lot (I could hear her screaming in my mind. *Scream!*) was the Screaming Woman, all alone, while the world ate its lunch and the sun was hot and the lot was empty as the sky.

"There we are," said Dad, finished at last.

"Now will you come out to see the Screaming Woman?" I said.

"First a little more iced coffee," said Dad.

"Speaking of Screaming Women," said Mother. "Charlie Nesbitt and his wife, Helen, had another fight last night."

"That's nothing new," said Father. "They're always fighting."

"If you ask me, Charlie's no good," said Mother. "Or her, either."

"Oh, I don't know," said Dad. "I think she's pretty nice."

"You're prejudiced. After all, you almost married her."

"You going to bring that up again?" he said. "After all, I was only engaged to her six weeks."

"You showed some sense when you broke it off."

"Oh, you know Helen. Always stagestruck. Wanted to travel in a trunk. I just couldn't see it. That broke it up. She was sweet, though. Sweet and kind."

"What did it get her? A terrible brute of a husband like Charlie."

"Dad," I said.

"I'll give you that. Charlie has got a terrible temper," said Dad. "Remember when Helen had the lead in our high school graduation play? Pretty as a picture. She wrote some songs for it herself. That was the summer she wrote that song for me."

"Ha," said Mother.

"Don't laugh. It was a good song."

"You never told me about that song."

"It was between Helen and me. Let's see, how *did* it go?"

"Dad," I said.

"You'd better take your daughter out in the back lot," said Mother, "before she collapses. You can sing me that wonderful song later."

"Okay, come on you," said Dad, and I ran him out of the house.

The empty lot was still empty and hot and the glass sparkled green and white and brown all around where the bottles lay.

"Now, where's this Screaming Woman?" laughed Dad.

"We forgot the shovels," I cried.

"We'll get them later, after we hear the soloist," said Dad.

I took him over to the spot. "Listen," I said.

We listened.

"I don't hear anything," said Dad, at last.

"Shh," I said. "Wait."

We listened some more. "Hey, there, Screaming Woman!" I cried.

We heard the sun in the sky. We heard the wind in the trees, real quiet. We heard a bus, far away, running along. We heard a car pass.

That was all.

"Margaret," said Father. "I suggest you go lie down and put a damp cloth on your forehead."

"But she was here," I shouted. "I heard her, screaming and screaming and screaming. See, here's where the ground's been dug up." I called frantically at the earth. "Hey there, you down there!"

"Margaret," said Father. "This is the place where

Mr. Kelly dug yesterday, a big hole, to bury his trash and garbage in."

"But during the night," I said, "someone else used Mr. Kelly's burying place to bury a woman. And covered it all over again."

"Well, I'm going back in and take a cool shower," said Dad.

"You won't help me dig?"

"Better not stay out here too long," said Dad. "It's hot."

Dad walked off. I heard the back door slam.

I stamped on the ground. "Darn," I said.

The screaming started again.

She screamed and screamed. Maybe she had been tired and was resting and now she began it all over, just for me.

I stood in the empty lot in the hot sun and I felt like crying. I ran back to the house and banged the door.

"Dad, she's screaming again!"

"Sure, sure," said Dad. "Come on." And he led me to my upstairs bedroom. "Here," he said. He made me lie down and put a cold rag on my head. "Just take it easy."

I began to cry. "Oh, Dad, we can't let her die. She's all buried, like that person in that story by Edgar Allan Poe, and think how awful it is to be screaming and no one paying any attention."

"I forbid you to leave the house," said Dad, worried. "You just lie there the rest of the afternoon." He went out and locked the door. I heard him and Mother talking in the front room. After a while I stopped crying. I got up and tiptoed to the window. My room was upstairs. It seemed high.

I took a sheet off the bed and tied it to the bedpost and let it out the window. Then I climbed out the window and shinnied down until I touched the ground. Then I ran to the garage, quiet, and I got a couple of shovels and I ran to the empty lot. It was hotter than ever. And I started to dig, and all the while I dug, the Screaming Woman screamed . . .

It was hard work. Shoving in the shovel and lifting the rocks and glass. And I knew I'd be doing it all afternoon and maybe I wouldn't finish in time. What could I do? Run tell other people? But they'd be like Mom and Dad, pay no attention. I just kept digging, all by myself.

About ten minutes later, Dippy Smith came along the path through the empty lot. He's my age and goes to my school.

"Hi, Margaret," he said.

"Hi, Dippy," I gasped.

"What you doing?" he asked.

"Digging."

"For what?"

"I got a Screaming Lady in the ground and I'm digging for her," I said.

"I don't hear no screaming," said Dippy.

"You sit down and wait a while and you'll hear her scream yet. Or better still, help me dig."

"I don't dig unless I hear a scream," he said.

We waited.

"Listen!" I cried. "Did you *hear* it?"

"Hey," said Dippy, with slow appreciation, his eyes gleaming. "That's okay. Do it again."

"Do what again?"

"The scream."

"We got to wait," I said, puzzled.

"Do it again," he insisted, shaking my arm. "Go on." He dug in his pocket for a brown aggie. "Here." He shoved it at me. "I'll give you this marble if you do it again."

A scream came out of the ground.

"Hot dog!" said Dippy. "Teach *me* to do it!" He danced around as if I was a miracle.

"I don't . . ." I started to say.

"Did you get the *Throw-Your-Voice* book for a dime from that Magic Company in Dallas, Texas?" cried Dippy. "You got one of those tin ventriloquist contraptions in your mouth?"

"Y-yes," I lied, for I wanted him to help. "If you'll help dig, I'll tell you about it later."

"Swell," he said. "Give me a shovel."

We both dug together, and from time to time the Woman screamed.

"Boy," said Dippy. "You'd think she was right under

foot. You're wonderful, Maggie." Then he said, "What's her name?"

"Who?"

"The Screaming Woman. You must have a name for her."

"Oh, sure." I thought a moment. "Her name's Wilma Schweiger and she's a rich old woman, ninety-six years old, and she was buried by a man named Spike, who counterfeited ten-dollar bills."

"Yes, *sir,*" said Dippy.

"And there's hidden treasure buried with her, and I, I'm a grave robber come to dig her out and get it," I gasped, digging excitedly.

Dippy made his eyes Oriental and mysterious. "Can I be a grave robber, too?" He had a better idea. "Let's pretend it's the Princess Ommanatra, an Egyptian queen, covered with diamonds!"

We kept digging and I thought, oh, we will rescue her, we *will.* If only we keep on!

"Hey, I just got an idea," said Dippy. And he ran off and got a piece of cardboard. He scribbled on it with crayon.

"Keep digging!" I said. "We can't stop!"

"I'm making a sign. See? SLUMBERLAND CEMETERY! We can bury some birds and beetles here, in matchboxes and stuff. I'll go find some butterflies."

"No, Dippy!"

"It's more fun that way. I'll get me a dead cat, too, maybe . . ."

"Dippy, use your shovel! Please!"

"Aw," said Dippy. "I'm tired. I think I'll go home and take a nap."

"You can't do that."

"Who says so?"

"Dippy, there's something I want to tell you."

"What?"

He gave the shovel a kick.

I whispered in his ear. "There's really a woman buried here."

"Why sure there is," he said. "You said it, Maggie."

"You don't believe me, either."

"Tell me how you throw your voice and I'll keep on digging."

"But I can't tell you, because I'm not doing it," I said. "Look, Dippy. I'll stand way over here and you listen there."

The Screaming Woman screamed again.

"Hey!" said Dippy. "There really *is* a woman here!"

"That's what I tried to say."

"Let's dig!" said Dippy.

We dug for twenty minutes.

"I wonder who she is?"

"I don't know."

"I wonder if it's Mrs. Nelson or Mrs. Turner or Mrs. Bradley. I wonder if she's pretty. Wonder what color her hair is? Wonder if she's thirty or ninety or sixty?"

"Dig!" I said.

The mound grew high.

"Wonder if she'll reward us for digging her up."

"Sure."

"A quarter, do you think?"

"More than that. I bet it's a dollar."

Dippy remembered as he dug. "I read a book once of magic. There was a Hindu with no clothes on who crept down in a grave and slept there sixty days, not eating anything, no malts, no chewing gum or candy, no air, for sixty days." His face fell. "Say, wouldn't it be awful if it was only a radio buried here and us working so hard?"

"A radio's nice, it'd be all ours."

Just then a shadow fell across us.

"Hey, you kids, what you think you're doing?"

We turned. It was Mr. Kelly, the man who owned the empty lot. "Oh, hello, Mr. Kelly," we said.

"Tell you what I want you to do," said Mr. Kelly. "I want you to take those shovels and take that soil and shovel it right back in that hole you been digging. That's what I want you to do."

My heart started beating fast again. I wanted to scream myself.

"But Mr. Kelly, there's a Screaming Woman and . . ."

"I'm not interested. I don't hear a thing."

"Listen!" I cried.

The scream.

Mr. Kelly listened and shook his head. "Don't hear nothing. Go on now, fill it up and get home with you before I give you my foot!"

We filled the hole all back in again. And all the while we filled it in, Mr. Kelly stood there, arms folded, and the woman screamed, but Mr. Kelly pretended not to hear it.

When we were finished, Mr. Kelly stomped off, saying, "Go on home now. And if I catch you here again . . ."

I turned to Dippy. "He's the one," I whispered.

"Huh?" said Dippy.

"He *murdered* Mrs. Kelly. He buried her here, after he strangled her, in a box, but she came to. Why, he stood right here and she screamed and he wouldn't pay any attention."

"Hey," said Dippy. "That's right. He stood right here and lied to us."

"There's only one thing to do," I said. "Call the police and have them come arrest Mr. Kelly."

We ran for the corner store telephone.

The police knocked on Mr. Kelly's door five minutes later. Dippy and I were hiding in the bushes, listening.

"Mr. Kelly?" said the police officer.

"Yes, sir, what can I do for you?"

"Is Mrs. Kelly at home?"

"Yes, sir."

"May we see her, sir?"

"Of course. Hey, Anna!"

Mrs. Kelly came to the door and looked out. "Yes, sir?"

"I beg your pardon," apologized the officer. "We had a report that you were buried out in an empty lot, Mrs. Kelly. It sounded like a child made the call, but we had to be certain. Sorry to have troubled you."

"It's those blasted kids," cried Mr. Kelly, angrily. "If I ever catch them, I'll rip 'em limb from limb!"

"Cheezit!" said Dippy, and we both ran.

"What'll we do now?" I said.

"I got to go home," said Dippy. "Boy, we're really in trouble. We'll get a licking for this."

"But what about the Screaming Woman?"

"To heck with her," said Dippy. "We don't dare go near that empty lot again. Old man Kelly'll be waitin' around with his razor strap and lambast heck out'n us. An' I just happened to remember, Maggie. Ain't old man Kelly sort of deaf, hard-of-hearing?"

"Oh, my gosh," I said. "No *wonder* he didn't hear the screams."

"So long," said Dippy. "We sure got in trouble over your darn old ventriloquist voice. I'll be seeing you."

I was left all alone in the world, no one to help me, no one to believe me at all. I just wanted to crawl down in that box with the Screaming Woman and die. The police were after me now, for lying to them, only I didn't know it was a lie, and my father was probably looking for me, too, or would be once he found my bed empty. There was only one last thing to do, and I did it.

I went from house to house, all down the street, near the empty lot. And I rang every bell and when the door opened I said: "I beg your pardon, Mrs. Griswold, but is anyone missing from your house?" or "Hello, Mrs. Pikes, you're looking fine today. Glad to see you *home.*" And once I saw that the lady of the house was home I just chatted a while to be polite, and went on down the street.

The hours were rolling along. It was getting late. I kept thinking, oh, there's only so much air in that box with that woman under the earth, and if I don't hurry, she'll suffocate, and I got to rush! So I rang bells and knocked on doors, and it got later, and I was just about to give up and go home, when I knocked on the *last* door, which was the door of Mr. Charlie Nesbitt, who lives next to us. I kept knocking and knocking.

Instead of Mrs. Nesbitt, or Helen as my father calls her, coming to the door, why it was Mr. Nesbitt, Charlie, *himself.*

"Oh," he said. "It's you, Margaret."

"Yes," I said. "Good afternoon."

"What can I do for you, kid?" he said.

"Well, I thought I'd like to see your wife, Mrs. Nesbitt," I said.

"Oh," he said.

"May I?"

"Well, she's gone out to the store," he said.

"I'll wait," I said, and slipped in past him.

"Hey," he said.

I sat down in a chair. "My, it's a hot day," I said, trying to be calm, thinking about the empty lot and air going out of the box, and the screams getting weaker and weaker.

"Say, listen, kid," said Charlie, coming over to me, "I don't think you better wait."

"Oh, sure," I said. "Why not?"

"Well, my wife won't be back," he said.

"Oh?"

"Not today, that is. She's gone to the store, like I said, but, but, she's going on from there to visit her mother. Yeah. She's going to visit her mother, in Schenectady. She'll be back, two or three days, maybe a week."

"That's a shame," I said.

"Why?"

"I wanted to tell her something."

"What?"

"I just wanted to tell her there's a woman buried over in the empty lot, screaming under tons and tons of dirt."

Mr. Nesbitt dropped his cigarette.

"You dropped your cigarette, Mr. Nesbitt," I pointed out, with my shoe.

"Oh, did I? Sure. So I did," he mumbled. "Well, I'll tell Helen when she comes home, your story. She'll be glad to hear it."

"Thanks. It's a real woman."

"How do you know it is?"

"I heard her."

"How, how you know it isn't, well, a *mandrake* root."

"What's that?"

"You know. A mandrake. It's a kind of a plant, kid. They scream. I know, I read it once. How you know it ain't a mandrake?"

"I never thought of that."

"You better start thinking," he said, lighting another cigarette. He tried to be casual. "Say, kid, you, eh, you *say* anything about this to anyone?"

"Sure, I told lots of people."

Mr. Nesbitt burned his hand on his match.

"Anybody doing anything about it?" he asked.

"No," I said. "They won't believe me."

He smiled. "Of course. Naturally. You're nothing but a kid. Why should they listen to you?"

"I'm going back now and dig her out with a spade," I said.

"Wait."

"I got to go," I said.

"Stick around," he insisted.

"Thanks, but no," I said, frantically.

He took my arm. "Know how to play cards, kid? Black jack?"

"Yes, sir."

He took out a deck of cards from a desk. "We'll have a game."

"I got to go dig."

"Plenty of time for that," he said, quiet. "Anyway, maybe my wife'll be home. Sure. That's it. You wait for her. Wait a while."

"You think she will be?"

"Sure, kid. Say, about that voice; is it very strong?"

"It gets weaker all the time."

Mr. Nesbitt sighed and smiled. "You and your kid games. Here now, let's play that game of black jack, it's more fun than Screaming Women."

"I got to go. It's late."

"Stick around, you got nothing to do."

I knew what he was trying to do. He was trying to keep me in his house until the screaming died down and was gone. He was trying to keep me from helping her. "My wife'll be home in ten minutes," he said. "Sure. Ten minutes. You wait. You sit right there."

We played cards. The clock ticked. The sun went down the sky. It was getting late. The screaming got fainter and fainter in my mind. "I got to go," I said.

"Another game," said Mr. Nesbitt. "Wait another hour, kid. My wife'll come yet. Wait."

In another hour he looked at his watch. "Well, kid, I guess you can go now." And I know what his plan was. He'd sneak down in the middle of the night and dig up his wife, still alive, and take her somewhere else and bury her, good. "So long, kid. So long." He let me go, because he thought that by now the air must all be gone from the box.

The door shut in my face.

I went back near the empty lot and hid in some bushes. What could I do? Tell my folks? But they hadn't believed me. Call the police on Mr. Charlie Nesbitt? But he said his wife was away visiting. Nobody would believe me!

I watched Mr. Kelly's house. He wasn't in sight. I ran over to the place where the screaming had been and just stood there.

The screaming had stopped. It was so quiet I thought I would never hear a scream again. It was all over. I was too late I thought.

I bent down and put my ear against the ground.

And then I heard it, way down, way deep, and so faint I could hardly hear it.

The woman wasn't screaming any more. She was singing.

Something about, "I loved you fair, I loved you well."

It was sort of a sad song. Very faint. And sort of broken. All of those hours down under the ground in that box must have sort of made her crazy. All she needed was some air and food and she'd be all right. But she just kept singing, not wanting to scream any more, not caring, just singing.

I listened to the song.

And then I turned and walked straight across the lot and up the steps to my house and I opened the front door.

"Father," I said.

"So there you are!" he cried.

"Father," I said.

"You're going to get a licking," he said.

"She's not screaming any more."

"Don't talk about her!"

"She's singing now," I cried.

"You're not telling the truth!"

"Dad," I said. "She's out there and she'll be dead soon if you don't listen to me. She's out there, singing, and this is what she's singing." I hummed the tune. I sang a few of the words. "I loved you fair, I loved you well . . ."

Dad's face grew pale. He came and took my arm.

"What did you say?" he said.

I sang it again, "I loved you fair, I loved you well."

"Where did you *hear* that song?" he shouted.

"Out in the empty lot, just now."

"But that's *Helen's* song, the one she wrote, years ago, for *me!*" cried Father. "You *can't* know it. *Nobody* knew it, except Helen and me. I never sang it to anyone, not you or anyone."

"Sure," I said.

"Oh, my God!" cried Father and ran out the door to get a shovel. The last I saw of him he was in the empty lot, digging, and lots of other people with him, digging.

I felt so happy I wanted to cry.

I dialed a number on the phone and when Dippy answered I said, "Hi, Dippy. Everything's fine. Everything's worked out keen. The Screaming Woman isn't screaming any more."

"Swell," said Dippy.

"I'll meet you in the empty lot with a shovel in two minutes," I said.

"Last one there's a monkey! So long!" cried Dippy.

"So long, Dippy!" I said, and ran.

THE SMILE

In the town square the queue had formed at five in the morning while cocks were crowing far out in the rimed country and there were no fires. All about, among the ruined buildings, bits of mist had clung at first, but now with the new light of seven o'clock it was beginning to disperse. Down the road, in twos and threes, more people were gathering in for the day of marketing, the day of festival.

The small boy stood immediately behind two men who had been talking loudly in the clear air, and all of the sounds they made seemed twice as loud because of the cold. The small boy stomped his feet and blew on his red, chapped hands, and looked up at the soiled gunny sack clothing of the men and down the long line of men and women ahead.

"Here, boy, what're you doing out so early?" said the man behind him.

"Got my place in line, I have," said the boy.

"Whyn't you run off, give your place to someone who appreciates?"

"Leave the boy alone," said the man ahead, suddenly turning.

"I was joking." The man behind put his hand on the boy's head. The boy shook it away coldly. "I just thought it strange, a boy out of bed so early."

"This boy's an appreciator of arts, I'll have you know," said the boy's defender, a man named Grigsby. "What's your name, lad?"

"Tom."

"Tom here is going to spit clean and true, right, Tom?"

"I sure am!"

Laughter passed down the line.

A man was selling cracked cups of hot coffee up ahead. Tom looked and saw the little hot fire and the brew bubbling in a rusty pan. It wasn't really coffee. It was made from some berry that grew on the meadowlands beyond town, and it sold a penny a cup to warm their stomachs; but not many were buying, not many had the wealth.

Tom stared ahead to the place where the line ended, beyond a bombed-out stone wall.

"They say she *smiles*," said the boy.

"Aye, she does," said Grigsby.

"They say she's made of oil and canvas."

"True. And that's what makes me think she's not the original one. The original, now, I've heard, was painted on wood a long time ago."

"They say she's four centuries old."

"Maybe more. No one knows what year this is, to be sure."

"It's 2061!"

"That's what they say, boy, yes. Liars. Could be 3000 or 5000, for all we know. Things were in a fearful mess there for a while. All we got now is bits and pieces."

They shuffled along the cold stones of the street.

"How much longer before we see her?" asked Tom uneasily.

"Just a few more minutes. They got her set up with four brass poles and velvet rope, all fancy, to keep folks back. Now mind, no rocks, Tom; they don't allow rocks thrown at her."

"Yes, sir."

The sun rose higher in the heavens, bringing heat which made the men shed their grimy coats and greasy hats.

"Why're we all here in line?" asked Tom at last. "Why're we all here to spit?"

Grigsby did not glance down at him, but judged the sun. "Well, Tom, there's lots of reasons." He reached absently for a pocket that was long gone, for a cigarette that wasn't there. Tom had seen the gesture a million times. "Tom, it has to do with hate. Hate for everything in the past. I ask you, Tom, how did we get in such a state, cities all junk, roads like jigsaws from bombs, and half the cornfields glowing with radioactivity at night? Ain't that a lousy stew, I ask you?"

"Yes, sir, I guess so."

"It's this way, Tom. You hate whatever it was that got you all knocked down and ruined. That's human nature. Unthinking, maybe, but human nature anyway."

"There's hardly nobody or nothing we don't hate," said Tom.

"Right! The whole blooming kaboodle of them people in the past who run the world. So here we are on a Thursday morning with our guts plastered to our spines, cold, live in caves and such, don't smoke, don't drink, don't nothing except have our festivals, Tom, our festivals."

And Tom thought of the festivals in the past few years. The year they tore up all the books in the square and burned them and everyone was drunk and laughing. And the festival of science a month ago when they dragged in the last motorcar and picked lots and each lucky man who won was allowed one smash of a sledgehammer at the car.

"Do I remember *that*, Tom? Do I *remember?* Why, I got to smash the front window, the window, you hear? My Lord, it made a lovely sound! *Crash!*"

Tom could hear the glass fall in glittering heaps.

"And Bill Henderson, he got to bash the engine. Oh, he did a smart job of it, with great efficiency. Wham!

"But best of all," recalled Grigsby, "there was the time they smashed a factory that was still trying to turn out airplanes.

"Lord, did we feel good blowing it up!" said Grigsby. "And then we found that newspaper plant and the munitions depot and exploded them together. Do you understand, Tom?"

Tom puzzled over it. "I guess."

It was high noon. Now the odors of the ruined city stank on the hot air and things crawled among the tumbled buildings.

"Won't it ever come back, mister?"

"What, civilization? Nobody wants it. Not me!"

"I could stand a bit of it," said the man behind another man. "There were a few spots of beauty in it."

"Don't worry your heads," shouted Grigsby. "There's no room for that, either."

"Ah," said the man behind the man. "Someone'll come along someday with imagination and patch it up. Mark my words. Someone with a heart."

"No," said Grigsby.

"I say yes. Someone with a soul for pretty things. Might give us back a kind of *limited* sort of civilization, the kind we could live in in peace."

"First thing you know there's war!"

"But maybe next time it'd be different."

At last they stood in the main square. A man on horseback was riding from the distance into the town. He had a piece of paper in his hand. In the center of the square was the roped-off area. Tom, Grigsby, and the others were collecting their spittle and moving forward —moving forward prepared and ready, eyes wide. Tom felt his heart beating very strongly and excitedly, and the earth was hot under his bare feet.

"Here we go, Tom, let fly!"

Four policemen stood at the corners of the roped area, four men with bits of yellow twine on their wrists to show their authority over other men. They were there to prevent rocks being hurled.

"This way," said Grigsby at the last moment, "everyone feels he's had his chance at her, you see, Tom? Go on, now!"

Tom stood before the painting and looked at it for a long time.

"Tom, spit!"

His mouth was dry.

"Get on, Tom! Move!"

"But," said Tom, slowly, "she's *beautiful!*"

"Here, I'll spit for you!" Grigsby spat and the missile flew in the sunlight. The woman in the portrait smiled serenely, secretly, at Tom, and he looked back at her, his heart beating, a kind of music in his ears.

"She's beautiful," he said.

"Now get on, before the police——"

"Attention!"

The line fell silent. One moment they were berating Tom for not moving forward, now they were turning to the man on horseback.

"What do they call it, sir?" asked Tom, quietly.

"The picture? *Mona Lisa*, Tom, I think. Yes, the *Mona Lisa.*"

"I have an announcement," said the man on horseback. "The authorities have decreed that as of high noon today the portrait in the square is to be given over into the hands of the populace there, so they may participate in the destruction of——"

Tom hadn't even time to scream before the crowd bore him, shouting and pummeling about, stampeding toward the portrait. There was a sharp ripping sound. The police ran to escape. The crowd was in full cry, their hands like so many hungry birds pecking away at the portrait. Tom felt himself thrust almost through the broken thing. Reaching out in blind imitation of the others, he snatched a scrap of oily canvas, yanked, felt the canvas give, then fell, was kicked, sent rolling to the outer rim of the mob. Bloody, his clothing torn, he watched old women chew pieces of canvas, men break the frame, kick the ragged cloth, and rip it into confetti.

Only Tom stood apart, silent in the moving square. He looked down at his hand. It clutched the piece of canvas close to his chest, hidden.

"Hey there, Tom!" cried Grigsby.

Without a word, sobbing, Tom ran. He ran out and down the bomb-pitted road, into a field, across a shallow stream, not looking back, his hand clenched tightly, tucked under his coat.

At sunset he reached the small village and passed on through. By nine o'clock he came to the ruined farm dwelling. Around back, in the half silo, in the part that still remained upright, tented over, he heard the sounds of sleeping, the family—his mother, father, and brother. He slipped quickly, silently, through the small door and lay down, panting.

"Tom?" called his mother in the dark.

"Yes."

"Where've you been?" snapped his father. "I'll beat you in the morning."

Someone kicked him. His brother, who had been left behind to work their little patch of ground.

"Go to sleep," cried his mother, faintly.

Another kick.

Tom lay getting his breath. All was quiet. His hand was pushed to his chest, tight, tight. He lay for half an hour this way, eyes closed.

Then he felt something, and it was a cold white light. The moon rose very high and the little square of light moved in the silo and crept slowly over Tom's body. Then, and only then, did his hand relax. Slowly, carefully, listening to those who slept about him, Tom drew his hand forth. He hesitated, sucked in his breath, and then, waiting, opened his hand and uncrumpled the tiny fragment of painted canvas.

All the world was asleep in the moonlight.

And there on his hand was the Smile.

He looked at it in the white illumination from the midnight sky. And he thought, over and over to himself, quietly, *the Smile, the lovely Smile*.

An hour later he could still see it, even after he had folded it carefully and hidden it. He shut his eyes and the Smile was there in the darkness. And it was still there, warm and gentle, when he went to sleep and the world was silent and the moon sailed up and then down the cold sky toward morning.

DARK THEY WERE, AND
GOLDEN-EYED

The rocket metal cooled in the meadow winds. Its lid gave a bulging *pop*. From its clock interior stepped a man, a woman, and three children. The other passengers whispered away across the Martian meadow, leaving the man alone among his family.

The man felt his hair flutter and the tissues of his body draw tight as if he were standing at the center of a vacuum. His wife, before him, seemed almost to whirl away in smoke. The children, small seeds, might at any instant be sown to all the Martian climes.

The children looked up at him, as people look to the sun to tell what time of their life it is. His face was cold.

"What's wrong?" asked his wife.

"Let's get back on the rocket."

"Go back to Earth?"

"Yes! Listen!"

The wind blew as if to flake away their identities. At any moment the Martian air might draw his soul from him, as marrow comes from a white bone. He felt submerged in a chemical that could dissolve his intellect and burn away his past.

They looked at Martian hills that time had worn with a crushing pressure of years. They saw the old cities, lost in their meadows, lying like children's delicate bones among the blowing lakes of grass.

"Chin up, Harry," said his wife. "It's too late. We've come over sixty million miles."

The children with their yellow hair hollered at the deep dome of Martian sky. There was no answer but the racing hiss of wind through the stiff grass.

He picked up the luggage in his cold hands. "Here we go," he said—a man standing on the edge of a sea, ready to wade in and be drowned.

They walked into town.

Their name was Bittering. Harry and his wife Cora; Dan, Laura, and David. They built a small white cottage and ate good breakfasts there, but the fear was never gone. It lay with Mr. Bittering and Mrs. Bittering, a third unbidden partner at every midnight talk, at every dawn awakening.

"I feel like a salt crystal," he said, "in a mountain stream, being washed away. We don't belong here. We're Earth people. This is Mars. It was meant for Martians. For heaven's sake, Cora, let's buy tickets for home!"

But she only shook her head. "One day the atom bomb will fix Earth. Then we'll be safe here."

"Safe and insane!"

Tick-tock, seven o'clock sang the voice-clock; *time to get up.* And they did.

Something made him check everything each morning—warm hearth, potted blood-geraniums—precisely as if he expected something to be amiss. The morning paper was toast-warm from the 6 A.M. Earth rocket. He broke its seal and tilted it at his breakfast place. He forced himself to be convivial.

"Colonial days all over again," he declared. "Why, in ten years there'll be a million Earthmen on Mars. Big cities, everything! They said we'd fail. Said the Martians would resent our invasion. But did we find any Martians? Not a living soul! Oh, we found their empty cities, but no one in them. Right?"

A river of wind submerged the house. When the windows ceased rattling Mr. Bittering swallowed and looked at the children.

"I don't know," said David. "Maybe there're Martians around we don't see. Sometimes nights I think I hear 'em. I hear the wind. The sand hits my window. I get scared. And I see those towns way up in the mountains where the Martians lived a long time ago. And I think I see things moving around those towns, Papa. And I wonder if those Martians *mind* us living here. I wonder if they won't do something to us for coming here."

"Nonsense!" Mr. Bittering looked out the windows. "We're clean, decent people." He looked at his children. "All dead cities have some kind of ghosts in them. Memories, I mean." He stared at the hills. "You see a staircase and you wonder what Martians looked like climbing it. You see Martian paintings and you wonder what the painter was like. You make a little ghost in your mind, a memory. It's quite natural. Imagination." He stopped. "You haven't been prowling up in those ruins, have you?"

"No, Papa." David looked at his shoes.

"See that you stay away from them. Pass the jam."

"Just the same," said little David, "I bet something happens."

Something happened that afternoon.

Laura stumbled through the settlement, crying. She dashed blindly onto the porch.

"Mother, Father—the war, Earth!" she sobbed. "A radio flash just came. Atom bombs hit New York! All the space rockets blown up. No more rockets to Mars, ever!"

"Oh, Harry!" The mother held onto her husband and daughter.

"Are you sure, Laura?" asked the father quietly.

Laura wept. "We're stranded on Mars, forever and ever!"

For a long time there was only the sound of the wind in the late afternoon.

Alone, thought Bittering. Only a thousand of us here. No way back. No way. No way. Sweat poured from his face and his hands and his body; he was drenched in the hotness of his fear. He wanted to strike Laura, cry, "No, you're lying! The rockets will come back!" Instead, he stroked Laura's head against him and said, "The rockets will get through someday."

"Father, what will we do?"

"Go about our business, of course. Raise crops and children. Wait. Keep things going until the war ends and the rockets come again."

The two boys stepped out onto the porch.

"Children," he said, sitting there, looking beyond them, "I've something to tell you."

"We know," they said.

In the following days, Bittering wandered often through the garden to stand alone in his fear. As long as the rockets had spun a silver web across space, he had been able to accept Mars. For he had always told himself: Tomorrow, if I want, I can buy a ticket and go back to Earth.

But now: The web gone, the rockets lying in jigsaw heaps of molten girder and unsnaked wire. Earth people left to the strangeness of Mars, the cinnamon dusts and wine airs, to be baked like gingerbread shapes in Martian summers, put into harvested storage by Martian winters. What would happen to him, the others? This was the moment Mars had waited for. Now it would eat them.

He got down on his knees in the flower bed, a spade in his nervous hands. Work, he thought, work and forget.

He glanced up from the garden to the Martian mountains. He thought of the proud old Martian names that had once been on those peaks. Earthmen, dropping from the sky, had gazed upon hills, rivers, Martian seats left nameless in spite of names. Once Martians had built cities, named cities; climbed mountains, named mountains; sailed seas, named seas. Mountains melted, seas drained, cities tumbled. In spite of this, the Earthmen had felt a silent guilt at putting new names to these ancient hills and valleys.

Nevertheless, man lives by symbol and label. The names were given.

Mr. Bittering felt very alone in his garden under the

Martian sun, anachronism bent here, planting Earth flowers in a wild soil.

Think. Keep thinking. Different things. Keep your mind free of Earth, the atom war, the lost rockets.

He perspired. He glanced about. No one watching. He removed his tie. Pretty bold, he thought. First your coat off, now your tie. He hung it neatly on a peach tree he had imported as a sapling from Massachusetts.

He returned to his philosophy of names and mountains. The Earthmen had changed names. Now there were Hormel Valleys, Roosevelt Seas, Ford Hills, Vanderbilt Plateaus, Rockefeller Rivers, on Mars. It wasn't right. The American settlers had shown wisdom, using old Indian prairie names: Wisconsin, Minnesota, Idaho, Ohio, Utah, Milwaukee, Waukegan, Osseo. The old names, the old meanings.

Staring at the mountains wildly, he thought: Are you up there? All the dead ones, you Martians? Well, here we are, alone, cut off! Come down, move us out! We're helpless!

The wind blew a shower of peach blossoms.

He put out his sun-browned hand and gave a small cry. He touched the blossoms and picked them up. He turned them, he touched them again and again. Then he shouted for his wife.

"Cora!"

She appeared at a window. He ran to her.

"Cora, these blossoms!"

She handled them.

"Do you see? They're different. They've changed! They're not peach blossoms any more!"

"Look all right to me," she said.

"They're not. They're wrong! I can't tell how. An extra petal, a leaf, something, the color, the smell!"

The children ran out in time to see their father hurrying about the garden, pulling up radishes, onions, and carrots from their beds.

"Cora, come look!"

They handled the onions, the radishes, the carrots among them.

"Do they look like carrots?"

"Yes . . . no." She hesitated. "I don't know."

"They're changed."

"Perhaps."

"You know they have! Onions but not onions, carrots but not carrots. Taste: the same but different. Smell: not like it used to be." He felt his heart pounding, and he was afraid. He dug his fingers into the earth. "Cora, what's happening? What is it? We've got to get away from this." He ran across the garden. Each tree felt his touch. "The roses. The roses. They're turning green!"

And they stood looking at the green roses.

And two days later Dan came running. "Come see the cow. I was milking her and I saw it. Come on!"

They stood in the shed and looked at their one cow.

It was growing a third horn.

And the lawn in front of their house very quietly and slowly was coloring itself like spring violets. Seed from Earth but growing up a soft purple.

"We must get away," said Bittering. "We'll eat this stuff and then we'll change—who knows to what? I can't let it happen. There's only one thing to do. Burn this food!"

"It's not poisoned."

"But it is. Subtly, very subtly. A little bit. A very little bit. We mustn't touch it."

He looked with dismay at their house. "Even the house. The wind's done something to it. The air's burned it. The fog at night. The boards, all warped out of shape. It's not an Earthman's house any more."

"Oh, your imagination!"

He put on his coat and tie. "I'm going into town. We've got to do something now. I'll be back."

"Wait, Harry!" his wife cried.

But he was gone.

In town, on the shadowy step of the grocery store, the men sat with their hands on their knees, conversing with great leisure and ease.

Mr. Bittering wanted to fire a pistol in the air.

What are you doing, you fools! he thought. Sitting here! You've heard the news—we're stranded on this planet. Well, move! Aren't you frightened? Aren't you afraid? What are you going to do?

"Hello, Harry," said everyone.

"Look," he said to them. "You did hear the news, the other day, didn't you?"

They nodded and laughed. "Sure. Sure, Harry."

"What are you going to do about it?"

"Do, Harry, do? What *can* we do?"

"Build a rocket, that's what!"

"A rocket, Harry? To go back to all that trouble? Oh, Harry!"

"But you *must* want to go back. Have you noticed the peach blossoms, the onions, the grass?"

"Why, yes, Harry, seems we did," said one of the men.

"Doesn't it scare you?"

"Can't recall that it did much, Harry."

"Idiots!"

"Now, Harry."

Bittering wanted to cry. "You've got to work with me. If we stay here, we'll all change. The air. Don't you smell it? Something in the air. A Martian virus, maybe; some seed, or a pollen. Listen to me!"

They stared at him.

"Sam," he said to one of them.

"Yes, Harry?"

"Will you help me build a rocket?"

"Harry, I got a whole load of metal and some blueprints. You want to work in my metal shop on a rocket, you're welcome. I'll sell you that metal for five hundred dollars. You should be able to construct a right pretty rocket, if you work alone, in about thirty years."

Everyone laughed.

"Don't laugh."

Sam looked at him with quiet good humor.

"Sam," Bittering said. "Your eyes——"

"What about them, Harry?"

"Didn't they used to be gray?"

"Well now, I don't remember."

"They were, weren't they?"

"Why do you ask, Harry?"

"Because now they're kind of yellow-colored."

"Is that so, Harry?" Sam said, casually.

"And you're taller and thinner——"

"You might be right, Harry."

"Sam, you shouldn't have yellow eyes."

"Harry, what color eyes have *you* got?" Sam said.

"My eyes? They're blue, of course."

"Here you are, Harry." Sam handed him a pocket mirror. "Take a look at yourself."

Mr. Bittering hesitated, and then raised the mirror to his face.

There were little, very dim flecks of new gold captured in the blue of his eyes.

"Now look what you've done," said Sam a moment later. "You've broken my mirror."

Harry Bittering moved into the metal shop and began to build the rocket. Men stood in the open door and talked and joked without raising their voices. Once in a while they gave him a hand on lifting something. But mostly they just idled and watched him with their yellowing eyes.

"It's suppertime, Harry," they said.

His wife appeared with his supper in a wicker basket.

"I won't touch it," he said. "I'll eat only food from our Deepfreeze. Food that came from Earth. Nothing from our garden."

His wife stood watching him. "You can't build a rocket."

"I worked in a shop once, when I was twenty. I know metal. Once I get it started, the others will help," he said, not looking at her, laying out the blueprints.

"Harry, Harry," she said, helplessly.

"We've got to get away, Cora. We've *got* to!"

The nights were full of wind that blew down the empty moonlit sea meadows past the little white chess cities lying for their twelve-thousandth year in the shallows. In the Earthmen's settlement, the Bittering house shook with a feeling of change.

Lying abed, Mr. Bittering felt his bones shifted, shaped, melted like gold. His wife, lying beside him, was dark from many sunny afternoons. Dark she was, and golden-eyed, burnt almost black by the sun, sleeping, and the children metallic in their beds, and the wind roaring forlorn and changing through the old peach trees, the violet grass, shaking out green rose petals.

The fear would not be stopped. It had his throat and heart. It dripped in a wetness of the arm and the temple and the trembling palm.

A green star rose in the east.

A strange word emerged from Mr. Bittering's lips.

"Iorrt. Iorrt." He repeated it.

It was a Martian word. He knew no Martian.

In the middle of the night he arose and dialed a call through to Simpson, the archaeologist.

"Simpson, what does the word *Iorrt* mean?"

"Why that's the old Martian word for our planet Earth. Why?"

"No special reason."

The telephone slipped from his hand.

"Hello, hello, hello, hello," it kept saying while he sat gazing out at the green star. "Bittering? Harry, are you there?"

The days were full of metal sound. He laid the frame of the rocket with the reluctant help of three indifferent men. He grew very tired in an hour or so and had to sit down.

"The altitude," laughed a man.

"Are you *eating*, Harry?" asked another.

"I'm eating," he said, angrily.

"From your Deepfreeze?"

"Yes!"

"You're getting thinner, Harry."

"I'm not!"

"And taller."

"Liar!"

His wife took him aside a few days later. "Harry, I've used up all the food in the Deepfreeze. There's nothing left. I'll have to make sandwiches using food grown on Mars."

He sat down heavily.

"You must eat," she said. "You're weak."

"Yes," he said.

He took a sandwich, opened it, looked at it, and began to nibble at it.

"And take the rest of the day off," she said. "It's hot. The children want to swim in the canals and hike. Please come along."

"I can't waste time. This is a crisis!"

"Just for an hour," she urged. "A swim'll do you good."

He rose, sweating. "All right, all right. Leave me alone. I'll come."

"Good for you, Harry."

The sun was hot, the day quiet. There was only an immense staring burn upon the land. They moved along the canal, the father, the mother, the racing children in their swimsuits. They stopped and ate meat sandwiches. He saw their skin baking brown. And he saw the yellow eyes of his wife and his children, their eyes that were never yellow before. A few tremblings shook him, but were carried off in waves of pleasant heat as he lay in the sun. He was too tired to be afraid.

"Cora, how long have your eyes been yellow?"

She was bewildered. "Always, I guess."

"They didn't change from brown in the last three months?"

She bit her lips. "No. Why do you ask?"

"Never mind."

They sat there.

"The children's eyes," he said. "They're yellow, too."

"Sometimes growing children's eyes change color."

"Maybe *we're* children, too. At least to Mars. That's a thought." He laughed. "Think I'll swim."

They leaped into the canal water, and he let himself sink down and down to the bottom like a golden statue and lie there in green silence. All was water-quiet and deep, all was peace. He felt the steady, slow current drift him easily.

If I lie here long enough, he thought, the water will work and eat away my flesh until the bones show like coral. Just my skeleton left. And then the water can build on that skeleton—green things, deep water things, red things, yellow things. Change. Change.

Slow, deep, silent change. And isn't that what it is up
there?

He saw the sky submerged above him, the sun made
Martian by atmosphere and time and space.

Up there, a big river, he thought, a Martian river, all
of us lying deep in it, in our pebble houses, in our
sunken boulder houses, like crayfish hidden, and the
water washing away our old bodies and lengthening the
bones and——

He let himself drift up through the soft light.

Dan sat on the edge of the canal, regarding his father
seriously.

"Utha," he said.

"What?" asked his father.

The boy smiled. "You know. *Utha*'s the Martian
word for 'father.' "

"Where did you learn it?"

"I don't know. Around. *Utha!*"

"What do you want?"

The boy hesitated. "I—I want to change my name."

"Change it?"

"Yes."

His mother swam over. "What's wrong with Dan for
a name?"

Dan fidgeted. "The other day you called Dan, Dan,
Dan. I didn't even hear. I said to myself, That's not my
name. I've a new name I want to use."

Mr. Bittering held to the side of the canal, his body
cold and his heart pounding slowly. "What is this new
name?"

"Linnl. Isn't that a good name? Can I use it? Can't I,
please?"

Mr. Bittering put his hand to his head. He thought of
the silly rocket, himself working alone, himself alone
even among his family, so alone.

He heard his wife say, "Why not?"

He heard himself say, "Yes, you can use it."

"Yaaa!" screamed the boy. "I'm Linnl, Linnl!"

Racing down the meadowlands, he danced and
shouted.

Mr. Bittering looked at his wife. "Why did we do
that?"

"I don't know," she said. "It just seemed like a good idea."

They walked into the hills. They strolled on old mosaic paths, beside still pumping fountains. The paths were covered with a thin film of cool water all summer long. You kept your bare feet cool all the day, splashing as in a creek, wading.

They came to a small deserted Martian villa with a good view of the valley. It was on top of a hill. Blue marble halls, large murals, a swimming pool. It was refreshing in this hot summertime. The Martians hadn't believed in large cities.

"How nice," said Mrs. Bittering, "if we could move up here to this villa for the summer."

"Come on," he said. "We're going back to town. There's work to be done on the rocket."

But as he worked that night, the thought of the cool blue marble villa entered his mind. As the hours passed, the rocket seemed less important.

In the flow of days and weeks, the rocket receded and dwindled. The old fever was gone. It frightened him to think he had let it slip this way. But somehow the heat, the air, the working conditions—

He heard the men murmuring on the porch of his metal shop.

"Everyone's going. You heard?"

"All going. That's right."

Bittering came out. "Going where?" He saw a couple of trucks, loaded with children and furniture, drive down the dusty street.

"Up to the villas," said the man.

"Yeah, Harry. I'm going. So is Sam. Aren't you Sam?"

"That's right, Harry. What about you?"

"I've got work to do here."

"Work! You can finish that rocket in the autumn, when it's cooler."

He took a breath. "I got the frame all set up."

"In the autumn is better." Their voices were la the heat.

"Got to work," he said.

"Autumn," they reasoned. And they sounded sible, so right.

"Autumn would be best," he thought. "Plenty of time, then."

No! cried part of himself, deep down, put away, locked tight, suffocating. No! No!

"In the autumn," he said.

"Come on, Harry," they all said.

"Yes," he said, feeling his flesh melt in the hot liquid air. "Yes, in the autumn. I'll begin work again then."

"I got a villa near the Tirra Canal," said someone.

"You mean the Roosevelt Canal, don't you?"

"Tirra. The old Martian name."

"But on the map—"

"Forget the map. It's Tirra now. Now I found a place in the Pillan Mountains—"

"You mean the Rockefeller Range," said Bittering.

"I mean the Pillan Mountains," said Sam.

"Yes," said Bittering, buried in the hot, swarming air. "The Pillan Mountains."

Everyone worked at loading the truck in the hot, still afternoon of the next day.

Laura, Dan, and David carried packages. Or, as they preferred to be known, Ttil, Linnl, and Werr carried packages.

The furniture was abandoned in the little white cottage.

"It looked just fine in Boston," said the mother. "And here in the cottage. But up at the villa? No. We'll get it when we come back in the autumn."

Bittering himself was quiet.

"I've some ideas on furniture for the villa," he said after a time. "Big, lazy furniture."

"What about your encyclopedia? You're taking it along, surely?"

Mr. Bittering glanced away. "I'll come and get it next week."

They turned to their daughter. "What about your New York dresses?"

The bewildered girl stared. "Why, I don't want them any more."

They shut off the gas, the water, they locked the s and walked away. Father peered into the truck.

"Gosh, we're not taking much," he said. "Considering all we brought to Mars, this is only a handful!"

He started the truck.

Looking at the small white cottage for a long moment, he was filled with a desire to rush to it, touch it, say good-bye to it, for he felt as if he were going away on a long journey, leaving something to which he could never quite return, never understand again.

Just then Sam and his family drove by in another truck.

"Hi, Bittering! Here we go!"

The truck swung down the ancient highway out of town. There were sixty others traveling in the same direction. The town filled with a silent, heavy dust from their passage. The canal waters lay blue in the sun, and a quiet wind moved in the strange trees.

"Good-bye, town!" said Mr. Bittering.

"Good-bye, good-bye," said the family, waving to it.

They did not look back again.

Summer burned the canals dry. Summer moved like flame upon the meadows. In the empty Earth settlement, the painted houses flaked and peeled. Rubber tires upon which children had swung in back yards hung suspended like stopped clock pendulums in the blazing air.

At the metal shop, the rocket frame began to rust.

In the quiet autumn Mr. Bittering stood, very dark now, very golden-eyed, upon the slope above his villa, looking at the valley.

"It's time to go back," said Cora.

"Yes, but we're not going," he said quietly. "There's nothing there any more."

"Your books," she said. "Your fine clothes."

"Your *Illes* and your fine *ior uele rre,*" she said.

"The town's empty. No one's going back," he said. "There's no reason to, none at all."

The daughter wove tapestries and the sons played songs on ancient flutes and pipes, their laughter echoing in the marble villa.

Mr. Bittering gazed at the Earth settlement far away

in the low valley. "Such odd, such ridiculous houses the Earth people built."

"They didn't know any better," his wife mused. "Such ugly people. I'm glad they've gone."

They both looked at each other, startled by all they had just finished saying. They laughed.

"Where did they go?" he wondered. He glanced at his wife. She was golden and slender as his daughter. She looked at him, and he seemed almost as young as their eldest son.

"I don't know," she said.

"We'll go back to town maybe next year, or the year after, or the year after that," he said, calmly. "Now—I'm warm. How about taking a swim?"

They turned their backs to the valley. Arm in arm they walked silently down a path of clear-running spring water.

Five years later a rocket fell out of the sky. It lay steaming in the valley. Men leaped out of it, shouting.

"We won the war on Earth! We're here to rescue you! Hey!"

But the American-built town of cottages, peach trees, and theaters was silent. They found a flimsy rocket frame rusting in an empty shop.

The rocket men searched the hills. The captain established headquarters in an abandoned bar. His lieutenant came back to report.

"The town's empty, but we found native life in the hills, sir. Dark people. Yellow eyes. Martians. Very friendly. We talked a bit, not much. They learn English fast. I'm sure our relations will be most friendly with them, sir."

"Dark, eh?" mused the captain. "How many?"

"Six, eight hundred, I'd say, living in those marble ruins in the hills, sir. Tall, healthy. Beautiful women."

"Did they tell you what became of the men and women who built this Earth settlement, Lieutenant?"

"They hadn't the foggiest notion of what happened to this town or its people."

"Strange. You think those Martians killed them?"

"They look surprisingly peaceful. Chances are a plague did this town in, sir."

"Perhaps. I suppose this is one of those mysteries we'll never solve. One of those mysteries you read about."

The captain looked at the room, the dusty windows, the blue mountains rising beyond, the canals moving in the light, and he heard the soft wind in the air. He shivered. Then, recovering, he tapped a large fresh map he had thumbtacked to the top of an empty table.

"Lots to be done, Lieutenant." His voice droned on and quietly on as the sun sank behind the blue hills. "New settlements. Mining sites, minerals to be looked for. Bacteriological specimens taken. The work, all the work. And the old records were lost. We'll have a job of remapping to do, renaming the mountains and rivers and such. Calls for a little imagination.

"What do you think of naming those mountains the Lincoln Mountains, this canal the Washington Canal, those hills—we can name those hills for you, Lieutenant. Diplomacy. And you, for a favor, might name a town for me. Polishing the apple. And why not make this the Einstein Valley, and farther over . . . are you *listening*, Lieutenant?"

The lieutenant snapped his gaze from the blue color and the quiet mist of the hills far beyond the town.

"What? Oh, *yes*, sir!"

THE TROLLEY

The first light on the roof outside; very early morning. The leaves on all the trees tremble with a soft awakening to any breeze the dawn may offer. And then, far off, around a curve of silver track, comes the trolley, balanced on four small steel-blue wheels, and it is painted the color of tangerines. Epaulets of shimmery brass cover it, and pipings of gold; and its chrome bell bings if the ancient motorman taps it with a wrinkled shoe. The numerals on the trolley's front and sides are bright as lemons. Within, its seats prickle with cool green moss. Something like a buggy whip flings up from its roof to brush the spider thread high in the passing trees from which it takes its juice. From every window blows an incense, the all-pervasive blue and secret smell of summer storms and lightning.

Down the long, elm-shadowed streets the trolley moves, alone, the motorman's gray gloves touched gently, timelessly, to the controls.

At noon the motorman stopped his car in the middle of the block and leaned out. "Hey!"

And Douglas and Charlie and Tom and all the boys and girls on the block saw the gray glove waving, and dropped from trees and left skip ropes in white snakes on lawns, to run and sit in the green plush seats, and there was no charge. Mr. Tridden, the conductor, kept his glove over the mouth of the money box as he moved the trolley on down the shady block. "Hey," said Charlie. "Where are we going?"

"Last ride," said Mr. Tridden, eyes on the high electric wire ahead. "No more trolley. Bus starts tomorrow. Going to retire me with a pension, they are. So—a free ride for everyone! Watch out!"

He moved the brass handle, the trolley groaned and swung round an endless green curve, and all the time in the world held still, as if only the children and Mr. Tridden and his miraculous machine were riding an endless river, away.

"Last day?" asked Douglas, stunned. "They can't *do* that! They can't take off the trolley! Why," said Douglas, "no matter how you look at it, a bus ain't a trolley. Don't make the same kind of noise. Don't have tracks or wires, don't throw sparks, don't pour sand on the tracks, don't have the same colors, don't have a bell, don't let down a step like a trolley does!"

"Hey, that's right," said Charlie. "I always get a kick watching a trolley let down the step, like an accordion."

"Sure," said Douglas.

And then they were at the end of the line; the tracks, abandoned for thirty years, ran on into rolling country. In 1910 people took the trolley out to Chessman's Park with vast picnic hampers. The track still lay rusting among the hills.

"Here's where we turn around," said Charlie.

"Here's where you're wrong!" Mr. Tridden snapped the emergency generator switch. "Now!"

The trolley, with a bump and a sailing glide, swept past the city limits, turned off the street, and swooped downhill through intervals of odorous sunlight and vast acreages of shadow that smelled of toadstools. Here and there creek waters flushed the tracks and sun filtered through trees like green glass. They slid whispering on meadows washed with wild sunflowers, past abandoned way stations empty of all save transfer-punched confetti, to follow a forest stream into a summer country, while Douglas talked. "Why, just the *smell* of a trolley, *that's* different. I been on Chicago buses; they smell funny."

"Trolleys are too slow," said Mr. Tridden. "Going to put buses on. Buses for people and buses for school."

The trolley whined to a stop. From overhead Mr. Tridden reached down huge picnic hampers. Yelling, the children helped him carry the baskets out by a creek that emptied into a silent lake, where an ancient bandstand stood crumbling into termite dust.

They sat eating ham sandwiches and fresh strawberries and waxy oranges, and Mr. Tridden told them how it had been forty years ago: the band playing on that ornate stand at night, the men pumping air into their brass horns, the plump conductor flinging perspiration from his baton, the children and fireflies running in the deep grass, the ladies with long dresses and high pompadours treading the wooden xylophone walks with men in choking collars. There was the walk now, all softened into a fiber mush through the years. The lake was silent and blue and serene, and fish peacefully threaded the bright reeds, and the motorman murmured on and on, and the children felt it was some other year, with Mr. Tridden looking wonderfully young, his eyes lighted like small bulbs, blue and electric. It was a drifting, easy day, nobody rushing, and the forest all about, the sun held in one position, as Mr. Tridden's voice rose and fell, and a darning needle sewed along the air, stitching, restitching, designs both golden and invisible. A bee settled into a flower, humming and humming. The trolley stood like an enchanted calliope, simmering where the sun fell upon it. The trolley was on their hands, a brass smell, as they ate ripe cherries. The bright odor of the trolley blew from their clothes on the summer wind.

A loon flew over the sky, crying.

Somebody shivered.

Mr. Tridden worked on his gloves. "Well, time to go. Parents'll think I stole you all for good."

The trolley was silent and cool-dark, like the inside of an ice-cream drugstore. With a soft green rustling of velvet buff, the seats were turned by the quiet children so they sat with their backs to the silent lake, the deserted bandstand, and the wooden planks that made a kind of music if you walked down the shore on them into other lands.

Bing! went the soft bell under Mr. Tridden's foot, and they soared back over sun-abandoned, withered flower meadows, through woods, toward a town that seemed to crush the sides of the trolley with bricks and asphalt and wood when Mr. Tridden stopped to let the children out.

Charlie and Douglas were the last to stand near the opened tongue of the trolley, the folding step, breathing electricity, watching Mr. Tridden's gloves on the brass controls.

Douglas ran his fingers over the green creek moss, looked at the silver, the brass, the wine color of the ceiling.

"Well . . . So long again, Mr. Tridden."

"Good-bye, boys."

"See you around, Mr. Tridden."

"See you around."

There was a soft sigh of air; the door collapsed gently shut, tucking up its corrugated tongue. The trolley sailed slowly down the late afternoon, brighter than the sun, all tangerine, all flashing gold and lemon, turned a far corner, wheeling, and vanished, gone away.

"School buses." Charlie walked to the curb. "Won't even give us a chance to be late for school. Come get you at your front door. Never be late again in all our lives. Think of that nightmare, Doug, just think it all over."

But Douglas, standing on the lawn, was seeing how it would be tomorrow, when the men would pour hot tar over the silver tracks so you would never know a trolley had ever run this way. He knew it would take as many years as he could think of now to forget the tracks, no matter how deeply buried. Some morning in autumn, spring, or winter, he knew he'd wake, and if he didn't go near the window, if he just lay deep and snug and warm in his bed, he would hear it, faint and faraway.

And around the bend of the morning street, up the avenue, between the even rows of sycamore, elm, and maple, in the quietness before the start of living, past his house, he would hear the familiar sounds. Like the ticking of a clock, the rumble of a dozen metal barrels rolling, the hum of a single immense dragonfly at dawn. Like a merry-go-round, like a small electrical storm, the color of blue lightning, coming, here, and gone. The trolley's chime. The hiss like a soda-fountain spigot as it let down and took up its step, and the starting of the dream again, as on it sailed along its way, traveling a hidden and buried track to some hidden and buried destination. . . .

"Kick-the-can after supper?" asked Charlie.

"Sure," said Douglas. "Kick-the-can."

ICARUS MONTGOLFIER WRIGHT

He lay on his bed and the wind blew through the window over his ears and over his half-opened mouth so it whispered to him in his dream. It was like the wind of time hollowing the Delphic caves to say what must be said of yesterday, today, tomorrow. Sometimes one voice gave a shout far off away, sometimes two, a dozen, an entire race of men cried out through his mouth, but their words were always the same:

"Look, look, we've done it!"

For suddenly he, they, one or many, were flung in the dream, and flew. The air spread in a soft warm sea where he swam, disbelieving.

"Look, look! It's done!"

But he didn't ask the world to watch, he was only shocking his senses wide to see, taste, smell, touch the air, the wind, the rising moon. He swam along in the sky. The heavy earth was gone.

But wait, he thought, wait now!

Tonight—what night is this?

The night before, of course. The night before the first flight of a rocket to the Moon. Beyond this room on the baked desert floor one hundred yards away the rocket waits for me.

Well, does it now? Is there *really* a rocket?

Hold on! he thought, and twisted, turned, sweating,

eyes tight, to the wall, the fierce whisper in his teeth. Be certain-sure! You, now, who *are* you?

Me? he thought. *My* name?

Jedediah Prentiss, born 1938, college graduate 1959, licensed rocket pilot, 1971. Jedediah Prentiss . . . Jedediah Prentiss. . . .

The wind whistled his name away! He grabbed for it, yelling.

Then, gone quiet, he waited for the wind to bring his name back. He waited a long while, and there was only silence, and then after a thousand heartbeats he felt motion.

The sky opened out like a soft blue flower. The Aegean Sea stirred soft white fans through a distant wine-colored surf.

In the wash of the waves on the shore, he heard his name.

Icarus.

And again in a breathing whisper.

Icarus.

Someone shook his arm and it was his father saying his name and shaking away the night. And he himself lay small, half-turned to the window and the shore below and the deep sky, feeling the first wind of morning ruffle the golden feathers bedded in amber wax lying by the side of his cot. Golden wings stirred half-alive in his father's arms, and the faint down on his own shoulders quilled trembling as he looked at these wings and beyond them to the cliff.

"Father, how's the wind?"

"Enough for me, but never enough for you. . . ."

"Father, don't worry. The wings seem clumsy now, but my bones in the feathers will make them strong, my blood in the wax will make it live!"

"My blood, my bones too, remember; each man lends his flesh to his children, asking that they tend it well. Promise you'll not go high, Icarus. *The* sun or *my* son, the heat of one, the fever of the other, could melt these wings. Take care!"

And they carried the splendid golden wings into the morning and heard them whisper in their arms, whisper his name or a name or some name that blew, spun, and settled like a feather on the soft air.

Montgolfier.

His hands touched fiery rope, bright linen, stitched thread gone hot as summer. His hands fed wool and straw to a breathing flame.

Montgolfier.

And his eye soared up along the swell and sway, the oceanic tug and pull, the immensely wafted silver pear still filling with the shimmering tidal airs channeled up from the blaze. Silent as a god tilted slumbering above French countryside, this delicate linen envelope, this swelling sack of oven-baked air would soon pluck itself free. Draughting upward to blue worlds of silence, his mind and his brother's mind would sail with it, muted, serene among island clouds where uncivilized lightnings slept. Into that uncharted gulf and abyss where no bird-song or shout of man could follow, the balloon would hush itself. So cast adrift, he, Montgolfier, and all men, might hear the unmeasured breathing of God and the cathedral tread of eternity.

"Ah . . ." He moved, the crowd moved, shadowed by the warm balloon. "Everything's ready, everything's right. . . ."

Right. His lips twitched in his dream. Right. Hiss, whisper, flutter, rush. Right.

From his father's hands a toy jumped to the ceiling, whirled in its own wind, suspended, while he and his brother stared to see it flicker, rustle, whistle, heard it murmuring their names.

Wright.

Whispering: wind, sky, cloud, space, wing, fly . . .

"Wilbur, Orville? Look, how's *that?*"

Ah. In his sleep, his mouth sighed.

The toy helicopter hummed, bumped the ceiling, murmured eagle, raven, sparrow, robin, hawk; murmured eagle, raven, sparrow, robin, hawk. Whispered eagle, whispered raven, and at last, fluttering to their hands with a susurration, a wash of blowing weather from summers yet to come, with a last whir and exhalation, whispered hawk.

Dreaming, he smiled.

He saw the clouds rush down the Aegean sky.

He felt the balloon sway drunkenly, its great bulk ready for the clear running wind.

He felt the sand hiss up the Atlantic shelves from the soft dunes that might save him if he, a fledgling bird, should fall. The framework struts hummed and chorded like a harp, and himself caught up in its music.

Beyond this room he felt the primed rocket glide on the desert field, its fire wings folded, its fire breath kept, held ready to speak for three billion men. In a moment he would wake and walk slowly out to that rocket.

And stand on the rim of the cliff.

Stand cool in the shadow of the warm balloon.

Stand whipped by tidal sands drummed over Kitty Hawk.

And sheathe his boy's wrists, arms, hands, fingers with golden wings in golden wax.

And touch for a final time the captured breath of man, the warm gasp of awe and wonder siphoned and sewn to lift their dreams.

And spark the gasoline engine.

And take his father's hand and wish him well with his own wings, flexed and ready, here on the precipice.

Then whirl and jump.

Then cut the cords to free the great balloon.

Then rev the motor, prop the plane on air.

And crack the switch, to fire the rocket fuse.

And together in a single leap, swim, rush, flail, jump, sail, and glide, upturned to sun, moon, stars, they would go above Atlantic, Mediterranean; over country, wilderness, city, town; in gaseous silence, riffling feather, rattle-drum frame, in volcanic eruption, in timid, sputtering roar; in start, jar, hesitation, then steady ascension, beautifully held, wondrously transported, they would laugh and cry each his own name to himself. Or shout the names of others unborn or others long dead and blown away by the wine wind or the salt wind or the silent hush of balloon wind or the wind of chemical fire. Each feeling the bright feathers stir and bud deep-buried and thrusting to burst from their riven shoulder blades! Each leaving behind the echo of their flying, a sound to encircle, recircle the earth in the winds and speak again in other years to the sons of the sons of their sons, asleep but hearing the restless midnight sky.

Up, yet farther up, higher, higher! A spring tide, a summer flood, an unending river of wings!

A bell rang softly.

No, he whispered, I'll wake in a moment. Wait . . .

The Aegean slid away below the window, gone; the Atlantic dunes, the French countryside, dissolved down to New Mexico desert. In his room near his cot stirred no plumes in golden wax. Outside, no wind-sculpted pear, no trapdrum butterfly machine. Outside only a rocket, a combustible dream, waiting for the friction of his hand to set it off.

In the last moment of sleep someone asked his name.

Quietly, he gave the answer as he had heard it during the hours from midnight on.

"Icarus Montgolfier Wright."

He repeated it slowly so the questioner might remember the order and spelling down to the last incredible letter.

"Icarus Montgolfier Wright.

"Born: nine hundred years before Christ. Grammar school: Paris, 1783, High school, college: Kitty Hawk, 1903. Graduation from Earth to Moon: this day, God willing, August 1, 1971. Death and burial, with luck, on Mars, summer 1999 in the Year of Our Lord."

Then he let himself drift awake.

Moments later, crossing the desert Tarmac, he heard someone shouting again and again and again.

And if no one was there or if someone was there behind him, he could not tell. And whether it was one voice or many, young or old, near or very far away, rising or falling, whispering or shouting to him all three of his brave new names, he could not tell, either. He did not turn to see.

For the wind was slowly rising and he let it take hold and blow him all the rest of the way across the desert to the rocket which stood waiting there.

ABOUT THE AUTHOR

RAY BRADBURY was born in Waukegan, Illinois, in 1920. He graduated from a Los Angeles high school in 1938. His formal education ended there, but he furthered it by himself—at night in the library and by day at his typewriter. He sold newspapers on Los Angeles street corners from 1938 to 1942, a modest beginning for a man whose name would one day be synonymous with the best in science fiction. Ray Bradbury sold his first science fiction short story in 1941, and his early reputation is based on stories published in the budding science fiction magazines of that time. His work was chosen for best American short story collections in 1946, 1948 and 1952. His awards include The O. Henry Memorial Award, the Benjamin Franklin Award in 1954 and The Aviation-Space Writer's Association Award for best space article in an American magazine in 1967. Mr. Bradbury has written for television, radio, the theater and film, and he has been published in every major American magazine. Editions of his novels and shorter fiction span several continents and languages, and he has gained worldwide acceptance for his work. His titles include *The Martian Chronicles, Fahrenheit 451, Dandelion Wine, Something Wicked This Way Comes, I Sing the Body Electric, The Golden Apples of the Sun, A Medicine for Melancholy, The Illustrated Man, Long After Midnight, The Toynbee Convector, Death Is a Lonely Business, A Graveyard for Lunatics* and *Green Shadows, White Whale.*